BOOKE OF THE HIDDEN

JERI WESTERSON

DIVERSIONBOOKS

Diversion Books
A Division of Diversion Publishing Corp.
443 Park Avenue South, Suite 1008
New York, New York 10016
www.DiversionBooks.com

For more information, email info@diversionbooks.com

First Diversion Books edition October 2017.
Paperback ISBN: 978-1-63576-050-7
eBook ISBN: 978-1-63576-049-1

LSIDB/1709

To my husband Craig,
whose love and support is *never* hidden.

CHAPTER ONE

I didn't believe in ghosts or the supernatural...but that weird noise in the wall was testing my convictions.

The unpleasant scratching sound that made the hairs on the back of my neck stand at attention had been going on for days. Look, I'm not some scaredy-cat to jump at every sound. But this? Ever since I moved into my shop-slash-house two weeks ago, this noise had been coming from *inside* the walls.

"Probably rats," I muttered for the umpteenth time. I hated stuff like that; rats, spiders, and snakes—the litany of creepy crawly things. I made a mental note to buy rattraps at the local hardware store.

Pouring myself another glass of Chardonnay, I sipped and wandered around my soon-to-be-opened tea shop, fluffing a pillow here, adjusting a lamp there. I still had a long way to go, but I would be ready by Friday for my grand opening.

Then my eye went toward an awkwardly smiling shelf. Warped and too unwieldy for my wares, it had to come down. I grabbed a crowbar from my toolbox, and with the crowbar in one hand and my wine glass in the other, I crossed to the shelf and took another hearty swig before setting the glass aside. Buoyed by the courage of several glasses of wine, I took up the crowbar again, and wedged the straight edge behind the warped wood. I yanked. Nothing. I yanked again, bracing my foot against the toe kick at the floor. Still nothing.

"Stubborn son of a—" I jammed it in hard, braced not only my leg, but my hip against the counter, and pulled, making a lot of obscene sounds as I did so…and *wham!* Tumbled ass over tea kettle to the floor. Luckily, the crowbar was still in my hand and not embedded in my forehead. I looked up. The dust settled. Not only had I finally dislodged the misshapen shelf, but I had also yanked out a poster-sized portion of the wall as well.

"Ah, crap! How am I going to fix this?"

I dusted myself off and rose, rubbing my bruised behind, and stared forlornly at all the ancient plaster strewn about the floor and the gaping maw that was once my wall. The lathe behind the plaster had even torn free, and a few choice words I had never spoken aloud rampaged through my head.

Maybe I could hang a picture over it. But no. Who knew what sort of varmints could crawl out of there? Hadn't I heard them? You couldn't just slap some drywall in there. It had to be fixed with plaster by someone who knew what they were doing, and *that* meant big bucks.

I checked the ruined wall. "That's funny." This was an outside wall, and there were no buildings abutting it. And since the whole structure itself was wooden with clapboard sides, I wondered why there was brick in there at all. I turned around. The fireplace was on the other side of the room, and the one upstairs in my apartment followed suit, sharing a flue. So why was there brick inside *this* wall?

"The Cask of Amontillado!" I said aloud in a scary voice. But even as I looked, maybe that wasn't so funny. Curiosity was getting the better of me. I'd heard about treasure being bricked up in walls, and this was a genuine eighteenth-century building. It could play host to all manner of treasures. I'd already found some great antiques in the back room. There could be spectacular finds in a bricked-up wall. Pirate booty?

Or…it could just be plumbing.

Grabbing the wine glass, I took another drink. But instead of fortifying me, a spike of uncertainty intruded instead. What was I doing? I hadn't even the vaguest idea of where to find a local plumber, let alone run this business. I had moved across the whole country, escaping. I had sunk every penny my mother had left me into this herb and tea shop, without a business plan and without really a clue. Sure, I'd learned a lot about tea and herbs in the last few years at Jeff's shop, and a little about business, but that wasn't the same thing as running your own store alone. And I had no friends here to commiserate about it. I didn't really have them back home, either, because they were *his* friends. But at least I was familiar with Southern California. I didn't know anything about Moody Bog, Maine.

When I saw the ad on Craigslist, I had become intrigued. A rugged coast, a vast sweep of forest, and a quaint little New England town. I was captivated by the romance of it. And by the distance it was from California. But perhaps it was more than that, especially after I'd Skyped with the realtor, pored over the pictures she'd sent me of the shop with its living quarters above, the picturesque village—it seemed familiar, even though I'd never ventured out of southern California before. I felt I knew those clapboard houses, those rustic porches, and the town square. Felt like…maybe I could make a new start there.

And the price was right.

But had I made too hasty a decision, giving myself only days to decide? My heart began to pound. Had I made the biggest mistake of my life?

I took another drink—definitely feeling it now—and leaned into the hole, cautiously turning my head to look up into the wall's dark interior and assess the damage.

My phone rang in my pocket and I slammed the back of my head against the joist.

"Ow!" I rubbed the bump I was sure was forming, took out my phone, and looked at the number. Crap. Jeff.

Should I answer? My first instinct was to hurl the phone across the room, but I needed my phone. I blew out a breath. Figures that at my lowest ebb, *he'd* call.

I hit the button and put it to my ear. I took another swig of wine. "Jeff."

"Kylie, baby. It's so good to hear your voice."

I said nothing. Just stood there, phone at my ear, leg jiggling. His beach-boy twang always melted my resolve. Blond hair, blue eyes, sultry smile. He got away with a lot with his good looks and honeyed words. It took me a long time—too long—to see past it.

He began again. "I was hoping you were around so we could talk. You know. Just talk."

I sighed. "Jeff…"

"A month is enough cooling-off time, don't you think? Come on, baby."

"It's been *two* months, Jeff. And I'm in Maine now. I *told* you."

"Whoa. No shit? I thought that was just talk."

"No! I left three weeks ago, and I'm making a go of it with my own shop."

There was a pause. "Your own shop?"

"Yes. I'm opening my own herb and tea shop."

Silence again. "So let me get this straight." His laid-back voice suddenly changed, flattened. "You're taking all of *my* expertise, all that *I* taught you, and you're opening your own place?"

I changed the phone to my other ear and twirled the wine glass stem in my fingers. "You didn't teach me that stuff."

"I've had this place for years and you just up and steal all my ideas?"

"It's an herb and tea shop, Jeff. This isn't rocket science."

"I can't believe this. This is such an act of betrayal."

"Oh my God, you have such nerve saying that to me! All you ever did was betray me. You forged checks on *my* personal checking account—"

"Only a couple of times!"

"Not to mention the women." I huffed a breath, took another swig of wine, and emptied the glass.

"What women?"

I stomped to the kitchen, grabbed the bottle from the fridge, and splashed more wine into the glass, cradling the phone with my shoulder. "Really, Jeff?"

There was a pause. "Okay, okay. Just chill. We…we need to talk this out. You need to come home."

"This *is* my home now, get it? Not Huntington Beach."

"Kylie, sweetheart—"

"Don't. Just don't. I'm…I'm hanging up now."

"Babe, wait!" He laughed a little. "What makes you think you have the chops to do this on your own? Let me in. I can help."

I gripped the phone, my patience running out. "I *can* do it, Jeff. I don't need you. Hanging up."

"Wait—"

Click. And I turned the phone off for good measure.

My arms were shaking. I brought the glass to my lips and drank until I emptied it again. Bastard. *Don't have the chops.* "Well you know what?" I was slurring, but so what? "It's *my* freakin' place. Mine! And I can do whatever I want."

I glanced at the hole in my wall. "And you know what, Jeff? If I want to look at what's in this wall, I'm gonna do it. Because I *can*!" I swung around unsteadily, squinted toward the back room, and headed there.

"Sledgehammer, sledgehammer," I chanted. I knew I saw one in the back room where I stored my tools. Found it! It was heavier than I remembered, and when I lugged it back to the wall within a wall, I stared at the old brick. This was from the seventeen-bleeding-hundreds. Was I going to ruin another perfectly good wall, which might, after all things considered, be a sewer line, just because of my burning curiosity, anger, and a whole lot of wine?

Raising the sledgehammer, I decided that yes. Yes, I was. "Here comes treasure!"

With both hands, I cocked the thing back and slammed it against the bricks. "Ow! Son of a bitch!" The sledgehammer dropped to the floor, missing my foot by inches, and I did a little pain dance. Shaking out my fingers, I glared at the bricks. Definitely a crack. I was encouraged, and I forgot the discomfort long enough to retrieve the sledge again.

Another whack, bracing for the shock this time, and a wider crack formed.

I decided one more should do it, and then gave it my all. The sledge's head hit. I *heard* a crack that time, and a loud hiss as gases expelled. Oh, shit! I knew it. I destroyed the sewer line!

And did those gases stink! Like, three-hundred-year-old stink.

I took several steps back, dropping the hammer as I did so, and covered my mouth. Oh, God, what had I done? The dollar signs were quickly accumulating in my mind. A little voice in my head started to say that Jeff was right, but I punched it down with my mental sledgehammer.

As both the smell and gases cleared, I got a view of the crumbled brickwork. No, not a sewer line. But something was definitely in there. Now those dollar signs were dancing in my favor. New England treasure! It looked like a box. No, wait. Not a box, but a...

"A book?"

I shivered and drew closer. When I was right up against the calamity of broken plaster and scattered brick, I could now plainly see, as the dust settled, that inside the strange bricked-up space was a book. A big book. And an old one.

"Damn!" Not treasure exactly, but a quick post on eBay and this just might pay for the damage. And more.

I looked in before I reached for it—didn't want any spiders dropping down on me—and lifted it out. Heavy. I laid it down on the nearby counter. It was at least twelve inches wide by eighteen inches tall. They made 'em big in the olden days. The cover was of ancient leather, worn at the edges, and even my unpracticed eye could tell that it was hand-bound. An ornate metal latch sealed the book. But the title in gold leaf took me aback a little.

Booke of the Hidden. What did *that* mean?

Finding the thing bricked up in a wall—a very old wall—and now this title, sent a chill rippling over my skin. Of course, I was alone, and of course it was dark outside. The wind was actually picking up, and the rattle of dried leaves stirring outside and clattering against my windows didn't help.

Licking my lips, I lifted the latch and cracked open the cover.

A whoosh of cold air blasted me in the face and ruffled my hair. I screamed at the suddenness of it and dropped the book. I turned a glare back at the open hole in the brickwork and blamed it for the unexpected wind…but with another chill in my bones, I had to admit, that the wind hadn't come from that direction.

My gaze fell to the book once more. *Booke,* I corrected in my head.

That wind had not come from the wall, but from the open Booke itself. But that was impossible. That couldn't have happened. So it must have come from that suddenly opened passage in the wall. The wind that was blustering outside came down this new makeshift flue and whooshed around the strange configuration of the room…

I was running out of excuses.

Whoa. Just slow down there, Kylie. I was sobering fast. I didn't believe in this kind of stuff, and windy holes and "olde bookes" notwithstanding, I wasn't about to start.

"It's just a drafty old place, that's all." My voice seemed loud in the quiet, creaking building. "The important thing is this Booke." It could be valuable. Had to be, especially with the story of being holed up in the wall. Who would have put this in a wall, and why?

I knew I could get some extra cash on eBay just for its strange story alone. Where was my phone? I grabbed it from my pocket and shot some pictures of the hole in the bricks and then the Booke on the counter. That would certainly add some veracity to my seller's points.

But first, the Booke. It was about three inches thick with either parchment or handmade paper making up the pages. I didn't believe in spooks, but I did hesitate when I touched it. "Come on, Kylie. You are not afraid of this."

My fingers reached for the cover again, and I jumped out of my skin as a knock sounded on the door.

"Holy cats, what now?" I twisted around. The shape through the wavy glass door stood out against the moonlight. Distinctly male…and tall, with what looked like a black duster coat whipping in the wind around his calves.

I tossed my discarded sweater over the Booke—no need to let the cat out of the bag before I could get it appraised—and cautiously approached the door. With my hand on the knob, I said, "We're closed, sorry."

He didn't seem to have heard and knocked again, harder this time, rattling the glass in the frame.

Muttering under my breath about pushy villagers, I unlocked the door. "I'm sorry, but I'm not opened yet—"

Suddenly shouldered aside, I stumbled back as he strode in, looked around as if he owned the place, and then turned his gaze on me. I sucked in my breath, not only from being so manhandled, but also by the man's face. On a scale of one to gorgeous, he surpassed the scale. His hair was black and long, ruffling around his face like a model on a romance novel. His eyes were dark, too, and fastened on me with steely concentration. And when he opened his mouth—Double tap! English accent!

"*Who* are *you*?" he said.

"Uh…wha…I…"

He took a step closer to me and furrowed his brows. "*Who*… are…*you*?" he enunciated, as if I were an idiot.

Okay, so he was rude. But the package was still worth staring at. He *was* wearing a duster, one of those long coats that cowboys wore in movies. It was black leather and furled around him like a cape. In fact, except for a pendant around his neck, all of his clothes were black. The pendant hung to his chest and gleamed silver, and the beastly face on the pendant seemed to be made of dark gunmetal, with rubies for eyes. The whole thing was quite a look. And on him—the dark, broody type—it worked. At least to my wine-soaked mind it did.

I squared my shoulders. I worked hard to avoid a slurred enunciation. "I happen to be the proprietress of this new establishment, Strange Herbs & Teas." *Take* that, *Jeff!* "I'm Kylie Strange. And *you* are…?"

He swept past me, turning his glare around the room. "Where is it?"

"Excuse me?" I sidestepped in front of him. "I don't know who you are—"

"That's not important."

"Okay, but don't you think it's a little forward barging into a place of business—that clearly isn't open yet—and starting to make demands?"

He stopped his perusal of the shop and fastened his glare on me again. "Miss Strange, did you say?"

"Kylie." I was *not* giggling coyly. "Uh…Kylie. I don't believe in formalities—"

But he interrupted me again. "*Miss* Strange, I know it's here. And I—" His gaze caught the gaping hole in the wall. "Aha! I'm not wrong."

What the hell? How could he possibly know about that?

He whirled on me. "I demand to know where—" But his focused pronouncement was interrupted by a prolonged and trumpeting sneeze. He looked up, somewhat abashed. "I beg your pardon." He licked his lips…and the sight caught me. "What I meant to say—" Another volley of sneezes followed and he stumbled back. When he'd controlled himself he looked up at me accusingly. "Did you say…*tea*?"

"Yes, it's an herb and tea shop."

"Beelze's tail!" he swore. He put his hand over his face. "I'm *allergic* to tea!"

"You're an Englishman and you're allergic to tea? Isn't that against the law or something?"

He sneered and raised his arm, aiming his finger at me. "Mark my words: If you have it, you are doomed."

With that, a swirl of his duster, and another few sneezes that completely ruined his exit, he stumbled out the door.

I walked toward it and slammed it shut, the bell above it tinkling merrily. "Freakin' villagers!" What was *with* this place?

And then I spun back around, staring at the sweater-covered

Booke. I glanced back over my shoulder toward the door, half-expecting Mr. Englishman to be skulking there. But he seemed to have disappeared. "I'm 'doomed,' am I? My life savings might be doomed for sinking it into this insane town..." I approached the door and locked it. Then on second thought, I threw the deadbolt *and* the chain.

The book-shape under my sweater beckoned, but this time, I scooped it up, sweater, Booke, and all, and hurried to the windowless back room where no prying eyes were likely to watch me.

So, Mr. Englishman back there obviously knew about a book walled up in this shop, but finders, keepers, buddy. I'd haggle over it at Sotheby's. I whipped off the sweater and ran my hands over the warm leather cover and binding. "Okay, let's see what's in a *Booke of the Hidden*." I lifted the cover and opened the Booke again. Tawny sheets of parchment crackled under my fingertips. It smelled musty, of old attics and forgotten memories. Eagerly, I turned the first few pages to discover its buried secrets and my easy fortune.

But no matter what page I turned to in this gigantic, ancient tome, I couldn't find a single word written in it...anywhere.

CHAPTER TWO

Disappointment. And pique. Disappointment that the Booke seemed, well, less than complete, which probably meant it really wasn't worth anything. And pique because that guy really got under my skin. It was bad enough that Jeff was harassing me with calls, but how dare *this* guy barge into *my* shop, make demands, and then drop the curse of doom on me? Did people do that nowadays? Maybe they did in Moody Bog, but I also had the feeling that he wasn't from around here. And neither was I. And then I realized with a lonely pang that I really didn't know any locals to confer with, to ask about this stuff: Who was that guy, and why was there this big blank Booke in my wall?

I shook my head. No more feeling sorry for myself. Despite Jeff's gloomy forecast I wasn't about to succumb to mawkishness and doubt. I couldn't afford to.

And as far as Mr. Englishman, I didn't trust that guy. He might try to break in and steal the Booke, since he seemed so bent on it. Call the sheriff? I didn't want to become "that person" who always panics, bothering the police.

Funny about the allergy to tea, though. I'd never heard of that one.

I clutched the Booke to my chest and turned off the lights. Slipping through the door to the back stairs, I locked it behind me and trudged up the stairwell.

I locked my bedroom door, too, and stuffed the Booke, still wrapped in my sweater, under the creaky old bed. I slept on and off, disturbed by odd dreams of running through the woods with a dark shadow pursuing me.

Once the morning dawned crisp and bright through my bedroom window, I was on the Internet with a slight wine headache and a huge mug of coffee at my elbow. Every which way I Googled it, I couldn't find anything having to do with this particular "Booke of the Hidden," although there were certainly many variations.

I was about to give up, when my random search turned up something that gave me pause.

"Magical Books and Their Provenances," said an encouraging page. I scrolled. And there, drawn in what looked like an old engraving, was my Booke, being held to the chest of a wild-eyed woman running from…I looked closer. A handsome man all in black. The date at the bottom of the drawing said 1720.

I blinked.

The strangely familiar picture was accompanied by only a small paragraph:

> *The eighteenth-century Booke of the Hidden is said to have unusual properties in that the person who opens it is compelled to fill its pages, or dread consequences await. Tales of this particular book have turned up in New Hampshire, Massachusetts, and Maine. The last person who purportedly owned it was sentenced to be burned as a witch, but was said to have gone mad, escaped her captors, and threw herself from a cliff.*

"Oh, nice." I scanned the rest of the site for more information, but that single paragraph in its unhelpful brevity seemed to be it. Again, I Googled "Booke of the Hidden, Maine," but nothing else turned up. I returned to the last page and clicked on the photo of the engraving. It gave the name of a museum in the next town over. "No freakin' way," I muttered, my coffee long forgotten.

I clicked on the museum page and looked it over. Hitting the "contact" button, I sent off a quick email, asking for more information.

"Now I really *am* insane. *And* I'm talking to myself." Shaking out the mental cobwebs, I took my now cold coffee and headed downstairs. I still had a lot to do, not the least of which was scouring the yellow pages for a bricklayer *and* a plasterer.

After a long bout of unsuccessful phoning, I decided to take a break and head to the local market. I suspected I could ask around there and get a recommendation. I kept picturing some local yokel stalling their way through long, costly hours of fixing my wall.

I threw on my L.L. Bean jacket and closed the shop door behind me. The cold air gave me a shock, even though I was expecting it. *Not* like a Southern California autumn, that was for sure. I took a moment to appreciate the confetti of fall colors along the hills behind my shop and the dusting of leaves dancing and crackling in swirls at my feet. I inhaled the fresh air full of promise and savory soups soon to be on the stove. My shop stood by itself on the corner of Lyndon Road and Main Street, and there was a wood just across the way. I'd seen foxes and deer come out of its shadows from my window and loved the idea of wilderness all around. About thirty yards away the first houses sprouted up. Even though it was still September, there were several porches with bright orange pumpkins sitting proudly on their steps or railings. It looked like a holiday card to me, and I smiled.

I turned at Main Street and walked briskly down the leaf-littered sidewalk toward the one and only market in town. Their prices were a little higher than I had expected, but they did corner the market, as it were.

Crossing the street—without a car in sight—I stepped onto the curb, and before I entered the market's mudroom, I thought I caught something out of the corner of my eye. I turned my head sharply to capture it. There, among the trees, I thought I had seen a lone figure…with a billowing duster coat.

I stared, frozen on the spot, but no one was there. It had, no doubt, been the dapple of the dense canopy of leaves, the dark shadows, the straight trunks of textured bark that fooled the eye. Had to be.

And then I heard whimpering. Maybe a dog? I looked around. Didn't see anything. Then I heard it again, coming from the woods and dense underbrush. It sounded so pathetic I backed off the porch and took a few steps toward the sound. Maybe it was some creature caught in an animal trap. I hated those things. Cruel and barbaric. I walked faster. "Hello?" I called out stupidly, as if the animal could answer. But then I heard the whimpering again, only louder. The sharp ends of twigs caught on my coat, dragging on it as I pushed my way through the waist-high foliage. It was darker here, dense with shadows. I thought I saw something moving just beyond the grille of slender tree trunks, something pale and crouched over.

"Hey, pup. Hey, boy. It's okay."

The whimpering stopped. A low growl sounded from the shadows.

"It's okay, boy. I'll get you some help. Let me just…"

I parted the branches of a particularly thorny brake. The growl was loud, turning to a keening howl the likes of which I had never heard. The sound pierced my bones with its unnatural tenor. The pale form in the shadow looked something like a white and boney greyhound, and it suddenly lifted its head. Bright red eyes flashed, and then, in a heartbeat, the creature charged. I screamed, fell back, and something whooshed over me, knocking me down the rest of the way. It all happened so fast I wasn't certain what I saw. I squirmed onto my stomach, looking back toward wherever it had gone…

Nothing.

I scrambled to my feet, mouth wide open. "What…?" I panted, barely able to stand up. That was…weird. It was a weird thing. It had been pale and thin, with red eyes. I could have sworn it had a sort of human face, but it couldn't have. Maybe it was a dog or a mangy coyote. But I'd never seen a white one before.

I stood a moment longer before I decided I probably shouldn't stay there. I rubbed my arms and ran for the market, casting open the mudroom door and feeling the warmth melt my chilled cheeks almost instantly. Someone was baking a pie, or maybe cinnamon buns. The air smelled deliciously buttery and spicy.

The shadows of my encounter were fading, but I still felt I had to warn the hefty middle-aged woman behind the register. I knew from previous trips to the market and from her nametag that she was Marge.

"Th-there's something out there!" I cried.

She cocked her head at me. "What's wrong, hon? You look like you've seen a ghost."

"I...I think it was a dog. It tried to attack me."

"Oh, you poor dear." She rushed from behind the counter and grabbed me, feeling my arms and searching over my face and body. "Are you all right? Did it bite you?"

"No. No, I'm fine as far as that goes. But it was...weird. Whitish. It seemed to have red eyes."

"Red eyes? I'll let the sheriff know. Could have been a dog gone rabid." She shook her head. "That's a shame. But a lot of folks up in the hills let their dogs loose, and next thing you know they get bit by a raccoon or squirrel and then they get rabies. Doesn't matter how many times you tell them."

"Yeah. I guess."

"Why don't you sit down here and just calm yourself. Do you want some water? Coffee?"

"No, thanks. I'll be fine in a minute. It was just a surprise, that's all."

"I'll bet. Charged right for you, huh?"

"Yes. But it didn't touch me, except to knock me down. Wow. That was weird."

"Sometimes you see a lot of weird things in these woods. It's the shadows. There are some places in the woods that never do get any sun."

The more I breathed, the sillier I felt. It was just a dog after all. Of course it was. I felt foolish with Marge hovering over me, a concerned look on her face.

"Say, listen." I straightened my coat and brushed off the leaves.

"I'm, uh, having a sort of wall issue. Do you know of anyone in town who does plastering? And maybe some brickwork?"

She shook her head and her short gray perm never moved an inch. "I knew that place was falling apart. I hope you got a good deal. Those people have been trying to unload it for years."

"Really?" Not news I wanted to hear.

"Oh, yes, it was one thing after another with that place. First the chimneys, then the drains, then the roof."

My heart began to jolt. "And...were those things fixed?" Maybe I should have had a lawyer look at that title.

"Every repair man in the village has been there one time or another."

Everything *appeared* to be working now. I'd even checked the fireplace flue ahead of time.

"So how about a plasterer? I don't want their union feeling left out."

She chuckled, looking more at ease the calmer I was. "Well, that would be Doc Boone."

"Plaster doctor?"

She chuckled again. "No, folks around here have to do more than one thing to make a village work. He's a retired doctor, but he also does plastering. As a hobby. Here, I'll give you his number." She jotted it down on a piece of blank receipt paper.

"What else do *you* do around here, then?" I was only half-joking, but she answered me seriously.

"I work at the beauty parlor. Come on in and we'll dye your tips. How about something fun like purple or green?"

"No thanks. I feel with a name like 'Strange' I'm already asking for it."

"Ay-yuh," she said with a smile.

"Well. Thanks. I think I'll be okay now."

"You sure? Do you want to wait for the sheriff?"

"No, I'm only down the street." I turned away, though I really didn't want to leave the warmth and safety of the market. But I slowed as I thought of my recent visitor. "By the way, have you seen a man around here dressed all in black with an English accent?"

"Is he good-looking?" she asked eagerly.

"Yeah, he is."

"Nope. Haven't seen anyone like that. But if I do…I'm going after him myself!"

She laughed and I joined her warily, trying to find it amusing.

"It's Kylie, isn't it?"

I extended my hand. "Kylie Strange. I suppose we should officially meet."

"And I'm Marge Todd, assistant manager here, as well as beautician extraordinaire." She chuckled again. "Nice to meet you. Sorry about that encounter. That's a terrible way to welcome you to town. I can assure you, it doesn't happen every day." I nodded, trying to reassure *her* that I held the town in no ill will. "I just wanted to mention that we're having a Chamber of Commerce Get-Together on Tuesday, over at the church," she went on. "You should come."

"Oh. I should! I should join the chamber."

"Well, that was a tough sell." She smiled. "Come to the church—it's at the center of town with the white steeple—around five. Get to know the movers and shakers."

"That sounds perfect, thanks."

"Don't mention it. See you there."

I decided I needed that apple pecan loaf that smelled so good baking. It gave me an idea, about getting some scones and a few other things to sell in my shop. She gave me the name of Bob Hitchins, the market's owner. With his card in my hand, I thanked her and told her I'd call.

Flush with my purchases and feeling better about things, I walked back to my shop, only looking over my shoulder about a dozen times. Standing in the middle of the street, I turned around, glancing back to the trees where I thought I saw someone before.

Off in the distance, I heard a howl.

I double-timed it back to the shop unharmed, hurriedly

unlocked the door, and slipped inside. I was struck again at how cozy the place looked, and my fears and doubts seemed to melt away. Forget Jeff. Forget weird animals. This was going to be a great place and I'd make a good go of it.

I set the bag down and pulled the phone number out of my pocket. As I tucked the eggs into the fridge and the pecan loaf on the counter, the hole in the wall seemed to gape at me. I trudged up the stairs to my bedroom.

When I called the number, someone answered with an, "Ay-yuh?"

"I'm looking for a Doc Boone."

"That'd be me."

"Oh! Hi, I'm Kylie Strange. Marge down at the Moody Bog Market told me you do plaster work?"

"Ay-yuh."

I told him about my wall problem and he said he'd be right over.

I hung up, energized. I decided to put on a big kettle of water and make a generous pot of tea for my visitor.

Almost ten minutes on the dot, a knock came at the door. I opened it to a gray-haired man who could have been the Maine twin of Kris Kringle from *Miracle on 34th Street*. He was nothing but smiles as he shuffled in, wearing overalls and carrying a toolbox like it was a doctor's bag.

"Miss Strange, I presume?"

"And do I call you 'Doc'?"

"Why not? Everyone else does." He looked around. "This is a mighty pretty place you've got here. Mighty pretty. Oh! Except for that." He headed for the hole immediately. "What happened here?"

I pushed my bangs off my forehead and sighed. "Well, there was this shelf and I tried to pull it out and half the wall came with it."

"These old buildings. Tricky, sometimes." He leaned in and stuck his head in the gap. "And this brick wall. That broken, too?"

"I sort of made that hole on purpose. Wondered why the bricks were there."

He pulled his head out and looked at me. "I know it's your place and all, but you make it a habit of just bustin' through walls 'cause you're curious?"

"Not usually, no." It had seemed perfectly logical at the time, especially with a little wine in me.

"Want me to brick this up, too?"

"Could you? But…uh…how much do you think this will run?"

"Well now." He set down his toolbox and leaned against the counter. From his pocket he pulled out a small notebook. He licked the end of a pencil and began scratching on the pages. "Gotta supply replacement bricks. Won't be antiques like these, but they'll work just fine. Mortar. Hour's work. Then plaster, another hour. Paint?"

"I can take care of that," I said eagerly.

"Right. Okay. Comes to this." He showed me the number and I wilted with relief. I expected the village to gouge the newcomer, but that price was right neighborly.

"That looks fine. Can you get started on it right away?"

"Ay-yuh."

"Would you like some tea? I have a pot steeping."

"I'd be much obliged. Let me bring in my supplies from my car." As he shuffled away, I felt a giddy sense of homecoming. He was right out of Central Casting; the kind, old country doctor, mending my wall like he'd mend a broken bone. My sense of unease at Mr. Doom from the other night and the rabid dog was dissipating.

I busied myself with painting and cleaning up the place while Doc Boone shuffled to and from his Rambler, the bell dinging over the door and wind gusting each time he came and went. I listened to the soft slap of mortar and the tap, tap of his trowel on brick as he did the masonry while I hung the curtain rods over the windows, and then I listened to the scrape of plaster as he mixed it up in a tub on the newspaper-covered floor, and then as he smoothed that over the wire mesh he'd earlier hammered in place.

I had refilled his tea mug several times, and he thanked me each time before turning quickly back to his work.

My phone buzzed with a text, and when I saw it was from Jeff, I clicked the phone off and stuffed it back in my pocket. When would that guy take a hint? Time to change my number.

I hadn't realized how many hours had passed before Doc came up to me with his bill in hand.

"Oh!" I glanced over to the wall that was darker in color, but smooth as silk and looked like nothing had ever happened to it. "Wow! Good work there."

"Thank you, young lady. And here's the bad news. I had to charge you a bit extra. The plasterin' took a bit longer than I anticipated. But I wanted to make sure it blended with the old."

"And it looks perfect." I checked the bill, but I really couldn't tell that he'd added much to it. "Let me get my checkbook." As I went into the back room, I could hear him talking.

"Ay-yuh. This is a mighty pretty shop you got here."

"Thank you. I hope to be open by Friday." Tearing off the check, I came back out and handed it to him. He didn't even look at it before stuffing it into the front pocket of his overalls.

"Now don't touch that wall for at least a few days. Needs to cure. Then you can paint it."

"Sure thing. And thanks again."

He shoved his arms into the sleeves of his jacket. "Looks like she's breezed up out there. Storm on the horizon, I'm thinkin'."

"Good day for a fire in the fireplace."

"Ay-yuh. Oh, by the way. I hear tell Seraphina will be paying you a call."

"Seraphina?"

"I just wanted to let you know not to worry too much over her. I know she can be a bit overwhelming at times. She's part of our local coven."

"Coven? As in witches?" This had to be a joke. Maybe a bit of hazing for the new guy?

"The coven is harmless. And 'Wiccan' is the preferred term."

"Ah, I see." Okay, definitely a joke then. I put a smile on my face. "Is there a difference?"

"I don't think Seraphina would like you to picture her as an old crone leaning over a cauldron." We shared a laugh. "And I'll be damned if anyone starts calling *me* a warlock. No, Wiccan's fine by me."

"Uh…warlock?" My smile faded.

"Oh, didn't I mention? I'm part of the coven, too." He winked before he turned toward the door, grasped the knob, and pushed through it.

CHAPTER THREE

I knew I stood staring at the door for a long time once Doc Boone had made his pronouncement. It started me wondering a bit about Moody Bog. When I called that number on Craigslist and found the town just off the main highway, I had thought, why not? And then I drove across country and through the little berg of woods, old church, village green, and quaint houses—the newest ones from the 1930s, the oldest from the 1700s—and it all looked so perfect. Serene. Just like the pictures. A place one could settle down in.

But what did I really know about this village or its villagers?

And this Booke. It occurred to me that I might have asked Doc about it, but was glad I hadn't. How involved did I want to get with this *coven* anyway?

But he was right about one thing: There was a storm brewing, and the afternoon sky had darkened considerably. The wind picked up and the trees on the opposite side of the street were whipping around, their limbs looking like a stormy sea and doing their best to shake off the last of their colorful leaves.

It must have been the moving tree limbs, then, because I could have sworn I heard that same scratching I heard yesterday before I broke through my wall. I stopped moving and listened. Scratching, all right. Was I going to have to call an exterminator too? I approached the wall, sure the sound came from there…but was surprised when it didn't. *Great, it's moving.* But even as I listened, it didn't seem to be coming from the wall at all.

I looked up at my ceiling, at the rafters and the plaster centuries old.

Grabbing a fireplace poker, I headed up the stairwell. Cautiously, I pushed open the door to my bedroom, poker at the ready. I was hoping for a squirrel rather than a raccoon, or worse, a rat. The scratching was getting louder. I threw open the door…

Silence. No scratching and no varmint. I looked under the bed anyway and tore open the wardrobe. Nothing.

As I lowered the poker, my eyes immediately went to the Booke on my corner desk, and I shook my head. Odd men with their doom-sayings were getting to me. But I did notice a flashing on my laptop that told me I had mail. I set down the poker and leaned over the computer, pressing a button to bring it up. It was from that museum about the Booke.

Sliding into the chair, I opened the email.

> *Dear Ms. Strange,*
>
> *Thank you for your recent email. The little information I have on the Booke of the Hidden can be found at my museum. I'd be glad to talk with you about it.*
>
> *Best,*
>
> *Karl Waters*

Making sure I had plenty of business cards in my purse, I shrugged into my jacket, and stood at the bottom of my stairs, looking for the shop key in the cavern of my bag. The scratching started again upstairs, and I froze. I hadn't seen anything, though I hadn't looked very hard either, picturing giant Sumatran rats. *Must be a tree.* All the same, I didn't trust the presence of Mr. Gloom-and-Doom somewhere outside, so I scuttled upstairs and grabbed the Booke before returning downstairs and locking the shop.

I backed my Jeep out of the parking area. There was a little bit of rain with the wind, and I switched on the windshield wipers as I headed up the lonely highway. The asphalt wound through the dense walls of trees shouldering both sides of the road. I could just see the stormy gray ocean in the distance through the "V" in the hills. Maine was very different from California. The few times I'd ventured into the mountains in my Southern California home, I had found the forests sparse, with their live oaks, sycamores, and telephone-pole-like pines. I wasn't prepared for the incredible concentration of growth that meandered over the surrounding Maine hills, nor the deep shadows they cast that crept onto the road as the sun followed its arc across the sky. It was as if no sun ever penetrated the canopy at all. But I never expected quite such a spectacular vista as I experienced here in my first of hopefully many autumns. How the dense canopy morphed from one remarkable array of color to the next. My eyes flicked involuntarily from road to scenery. I couldn't seem to stop staring at it. And especially into the dark shadows rimming the road.

As I rounded a curve, four motorcycles riding abreast took over the highway coming toward me, including my side of it. I kept expecting them to move over, but they didn't. They were playing a dangerous game of chicken. My elbows locked and my hands gripped the steering wheel. Heart pumping, I swerved at the last minute, slamming the brakes and skidding hard, nearly ramming into the mountain. Shaking, I pulled over and looked back.

Nope. Not one of them stopped. I could have been killed! Just a smear on the hillside. I watched them ride away. Each wore a leather jacket with a lame club logo on their backs: an upside-down pentagram with some goat head in the middle. My car and I were fine, so after a few moments to catch my breath, I shook off my shock and indignation and pulled carefully back onto the road. Idiots.

The sign for the village of Gifford Corner was just up ahead, and I quickly forgot about rogue biker gangs. When I made the turn, I saw why there were names such as so-and-so's "Corner" or "Hill" or "Bog," because there were so many little villages in Maine, a place founded by a single farmer centuries ago, that had, over the years, only extended itself by adding a market or gas station but little else. Countless little bergs sprouted up all along the roads, and Gifford Corner didn't disappoint.

The "museum" was hard to miss, because it was really only one of two structures on the highway. Weathered mailboxes leaned into the road at the end of the curving asphalt. Those must be the other inhabitants of Gifford Corner. I made the turn into the museum parking lot, just a gravel expanse in front of what looked like an old clapboard market. I shut off the engine and got out, grabbing the sweater-clad Booke in both hands.

The bell above the door tinkled as I entered. Inside was an open room with bookshelves and glass display cases. Pictures on the walls depicted local history in engravings and watercolors, obviously from an older period, based on the yellowed images and the dust on the frames.

"I'll be out in a minute!" came a voice from somewhere behind a counter among archive shelves. A man's head popped up, startling me. He smiled. He wore glasses, and the laugh-lines behind the wire frames gave him a friendly appearancc.

"Hi. I just emailed you. Kylie Strange?" I extended a hand. "Nice to meet you."

"Karl Waters." He took it and gave it a few shakes before releasing. He leaned on the counter and looked me over. "So, not from around here?"

"What gave me away?"

"Your tan, for one."

I laughed. "Yes, I just made the big move from Southern California."

"Aha! Welcome to the neighborhood."

I gave the space another look. "This is great. And you run this yourself?"

"It's not much. But I do like to dabble in the past. It's my little way of giving back. I archive most of the local history." He glanced pointedly at the package in my hands. I set the Booke on the counter.

"I'm opening an herb and tea shop in Moody Bog. And while I was getting the place in shape, I came across this."

I pulled off the sweater to reveal the old Booke in all its dusty glory.

Karl gasped. "Wow. She's a honey. May I?" His hands were poised to touch it.

"Go right ahead."

He carefully turned it so the cover was facing him. "'Booke of the Hidden,'" he read. "Wow. I've heard about this for a long time, read about it in some of the more obscure texts, but I never expected to see this in the flesh."

"Kind of creeps me out a bit, to tell the truth, but I figured it might be valuable. I actually found it bricked up in the wall."

His mouth fell open. "*In* the wall?"

"Um…yeah. I made quite a mess getting it out. What can you tell me about it? I saw the picture on your website."

He fiddled with the metal clasp that kept the Booke shut. "You wouldn't have the key for this, would you?"

"It's not locked," I told him.

He toyed with it a moment more. "It seems locked now."

"What?" Another thing I ruined somehow? I spun it on the counter, grabbed the clasp, and it practically jumped open. "Oh!"

Karl made a pleased sound, but when he grabbed the Booke to turn it toward him again, the cover slammed shut, the lock closing with a click. "So it's just a bit tricky."

"Seems so," I said, feeling uneasy.

He tried to compress the locking mechanism, but it was stuck again. "It doesn't seem to like me," he quipped, struggling.

I reached over when he pulled his hands away, and at my touch, the Booke sprang open once more. We both stared at each other.

Karl huffed a breath. "Well that's certainly…different."

"Did you *see* that?"

He said nothing. But when he tried to turn a page, the parchment was stuck together.

"This is completely nuts," I muttered and reached over to turn the perfectly unsticky page.

Karl shook his head, looking over the blank sheet. "It *does* seem to like you."

"This is crazy."

"Maybe not," he murmured. He didn't try to touch the Booke again but instead laid his arms on the counter and simply leaned into it. "Are all the pages blank?" he asked as I turned over each leaf for him.

"Yes. That's odd, isn't it? It seems old. It shouldn't be blank, right?"

"It is old, I can assure you. I've seen many similar books in the archives here."

"Books like this?"

"Well, nothing quite like this. Or this big. Or this…stubborn."

"Look." I edged away from the Booke without realizing it. "I came here because I went online and found only one reference to this, and there was this kind of scary engraving and not much else. It led me to you. I *had* hoped you could help with more information."

He nodded. "I know the engraving you mean." He gave the Booke one more wistful glance before he made another attempt to touch it. The cover slammed shut.

"What the…?" I said, stunned.

But Karl was looking at me as if he'd expected that to happen. "Come back here with me."

I gave the Booke a reproachful glare and slid behind the counter to follow him. He went to the far end of a row and removed an archive box and pulled it from the shelf. Laying it on the table behind him, he lifted off the lid, pulled on cotton gloves from his jeans pocket, and shuffled carefully through the papers. They were all old foxed papers and some parchment with faded ink scrawled in a tiny old-fashioned hand. He took out an engraving on yellowed paper and laid it in front of me. "Is this the one you're talking about?"

I leaned over to look. Sure enough, it was the same disturbing drawing of the wild-eyed woman, clutching a large book to her chest and fleeing a dark man. "Yeah," I said breathlessly. "That's the one."

"I thought so." He picked it up with his gloved hands, running a finger along the printed caption. "The Booke of the Hidden." He turned it over, and there was a hand-written paragraph in the center of the page. "This was the last owner, according to the text. That was in 1720."

I tried to read it over his shoulder, but I wasn't exactly versed in chicken scratch. "What does it say?"

He cleared his throat and read:

> *Mistress Constance Howland opened the Booke of the Hidden and was cursed with containing the demons she released therein. For her sins, she was hounded by the booke's Demon until she ended her damned life by hurling herself from the cliffs. Before her much deserved death, she is said to have contained sixteen evil spirits, but the Dark, the wickedest of devils, finally consumed her soul.*

"What's all that supposed to mean?" I asked, voice rough.

He slowly shook his head. "Damned if I know. But when I discovered this engraving some years ago, I wondered about it and did a little digging." He riffled carefully through the papers and pulled out a small book. It was also of great age, hand-bound with uneven paper within its covers. He opened it, turning the pages. It was a printed book, with each letter just a little askew, and all the s's looking like swashy f's.

"This is also from around this same time period," Karl explained. "You have no idea how much trouble this was to acquire. It's something like an almanac, talking about the weather, the crops of this area, the general terrain. But it's also full of little histories as well. It offers great insight about where some of the early homesteads came from around here and the families who owned them, almost better than local family bibles. Now, there's a lot of water damage and some of the pages aren't legible, but it also had this weird little bit about your book. See here." His finger found the paragraph and I followed along where he read aloud:

> *The local parſon, Parſon Simmons, warned of the ſtrange happenſtance in Moody Bog. Mistress Howland lay down with the devil and began to write in a booke the horrors from hell. She had always decried that ſhe had not called them forth, that ſhe was instead in the business of slaying them.*

He shook his head and tapped the page. "Water damage obscures the rest until we get to this passage: *...Mistress Howland deſired the return of the booke*—something, something—and then*: ſhe took the booke to the next village of Moody Bog and there it diſappeared. Mistress Howland, having diſpatched her duties, declared that the village was safe. But soon thereafter, purſued by the aldermen of the village, ran to the edge of the Falcon's Point and threw herſelf into the pit. The Dark Man was ſeen at the edge of the cliff, curſed the town, and was seen no more.*"

His voice stilled and I realized I had been holding my breath. "Um...what about this...Dark Man? Who is he?"

"I haven't been able to determine that. But in other writings of the day, I've seen it used interchangeably with 'Mr. Scratch,' 'Old Scratch,' 'Beelzebub,' and the like. It's another local term for the Devil."

"Oh." It made sense, of course. The early New Englanders were obsessed with the Devil. But if I remembered my history correctly, this was at the *end* of the witch trial frenzy, when more secular heads prevailed. Yet it seemed that any strange event involving a woman had villagers up in arms, attributing odd happenings to her being a witch and consorting with the Devil. "What do you make of that whole story?"

"Well, besides pure fabrication to somehow do away with poor misunderstood Constance Howland, it's quite a tale. I mean, it's really something out of fiction. She's like some pseudo-Van Helsing."

"What? I'm not going to find a coffin walled up in my shop, too, am I?"

He chuckled half-heartedly. "I don't think so, but though there are scant details it certainly reads like that sort of thing. Here, look at this. This is a copy of the court records of her trial, and it wasn't much of one. Basically, they accused her with this long list of all sorts of things she was supposed to have done, from souring the local cows' milk to some really outlandish stuff, like flying over rooftops. Whatever was going on, she sure scared the hell out of the locals."

"Yeah," I said, my voice quavering. "But what about that part about demons?"

Karl thumbed through the loose pages. "It's one of the more interesting parts. Let me read you her speech from the trial. She was only allowed to speak once and no one wanted her to do that much. It's actually quite amazing that it was even taken down at all. Listen:

> *I swear by almighty God that my testimony is true and honest. For I never wished this upon me, and as all the angels can attest, I am a godly Christian woman, without a husband, and doing honest labour. But this thing was thrust upon me, not by the Devil, but by God to do His work. I opened the Booke and did not mean for the evil to escape into the world, but now that I know my mission I shall fulfill it, heartily so. I am to capture and subdue all that I released, and after so doing, write it in the Booke so to keep them captured for all eternity. And because the cursed Booke cannot be destroyed, to keep it locked up safe ne'er to be opened more. Even should I have to subdue myself I shall do it. I mean no harm and only grace to my village. I so swear my oath."*

"Wow," I said. Though none of it was any clearer. "What do you think it means?"

Karl shrugged. "Looks to me as if the book acts like a Pandora's

Box, letting evil into the world, and then she was stuck jamming it all in again. It's what I get out of it."

"That's...scary." I couldn't help but recall how Karl hadn't been able to open the Booke, but *I* could. Because I had already opened it first? Shit.

"Sooo..." I gestured toward the Booke on the counter.

He looked back at it. "Ah-yuh, that's weird, isn't it? Pretty interesting if that's the same book. You said you found it *in* the wall?"

"Yeah. Bricked up." I had joked to myself at the time about the Cask of Amontillado, but now I didn't think it was funny at all.

But wait a minute! This was insane. This was fiction! Salem witch trial craziness. Some tale from long ago. It had *nothing* to do with me now... Right?

Karl had been talking and I suddenly tuned back in.

"...all just a story," he said. "Besides, I don't suppose you've seen this Dark Man lurking about, have you?"

I must have paled because he was suddenly right beside me, grabbing my arm. "Are you okay? Sit down." I was shoved into a chair. "You're not buying all this, are you? I mean it's only a story. An interesting one, but just a story nonetheless. And all the pages are blank, anyway. They'd be full of Mistress Howland's ramblings, wouldn't they?" I nodded. "If you don't mind," he went on, "I'd love for you to leave the book so that I can study it. It's a fine example of eighteenth-century binding, at any rate. Might even be older than that."

"I'd like nothing better than to leave it with you...but..." The oddest sensation flared through me. And as much as I wanted to leave the Booke with him, I knew I couldn't.

"Can I get you a glass of water?"

I shooed him away and stood—albeit a little unsteadily. "I'm fine. Just...a little overwhelmed. Look, I have to get back. Got a lot to do to get the shop open. I don't think I should leave it here just yet. Should get pictures. Document it. You know."

His shoulders slumped in disappointment. "Of course. No

problem. Maybe I could come by your shop and take a look at it again."

"Oh, sure, that would be fine." I dug into the purse over my shoulder and grabbed a handful of business cards. "Here. Maybe you could leave a few of these around?"

He read the card and smiled. "This looks great. I can see a lot of interest in this around here. Maybe you didn't know this, but there's a coven of local Wiccans in the area."

"I met one of them."

"Really? That was fast. They're all nice people. It's not like you see on TV. They're all normal."

"I'm glad you think so. One of them fixed the hole in my wall."

"Doc Boone? Oh, he's a sweetheart."

"But now all I can think of is him dancing naked in the moonlight."

He chuckled. "I can assure you, none of them do that."

"You aren't...one of them, are you?"

"Oh no! I don't go in for that stuff. Plus I don't think my pastor would like me to." He grinned. "But it would make for interesting conversation at bingo."

"I don't suppose that biker gang is part of the coven."

His face drooped. "What do you know about them?"

"Nothing, except they tried to run me off the road without so much as a wave. They had a pentagram on their jackets."

He shuffled some papers, not looking at me. "Best to stay away from those guys."

"I have little interest in biker clubs. And I'm pretty sure they won't be buying any tea cozies from me."

"Just the same. The ODD isn't anything to mess with."

"ODD?"

"Doesn't matter," he said curtly. His smile perked again. "I tell you what. You should try to get a hold of Ruth Russell. She's one of the descendants of the founders of Moody Bog. She's got quite an archive of family history and local genealogy. Been trying for years to get her to share it with me. She's not quite the sharing type, though. She's related to the Howlands."

"As in 'Constance Howland'? The one with the Booke?"

"The very same. As I said, she isn't too keen on this part of her family history. But I bet she's got more information. If she warms to you, you could find out a lot."

"I'll try that, certainly. Hopefully I'll meet her soon."

He watched me clutch the Booke tightly to my chest. "It was sure nice meeting you, Miss Strange. Funny…that name sounds familiar to me, too."

"I don't see how. My family is from the West Coast."

"Always? Never came out east? I'll have a look in the archives and see what I can dig up. I love a challenge."

I shrugged. "If you like. And thanks, Karl. I'll be talking to you soon. When you can, let me know about the Booke and…" I shook my head. "Is it weird that in my head I keep thinking of it as the capital 'B-o-o-k-*e*'?"

His eyebrows rose and he seemed to be considering.

"Never mind. Don't answer that. I'll be going. You can find my number on the card. Call me if you find out anything interesting. Like how much it might be worth. I'm definitely interested in selling it."

I wrapped the Booke—*book, dammit!*—back in its sweater and clasped it to my chest. The cold hit me again as I got out the door and I quickly climbed into the Jeep, setting the Booke beside me on the passenger seat.

I drove back to Moody Bog, feeling a sense of homecoming now as I navigated her familiar streets. I turned off the highway onto Lyndon Road and pulled onto my gravel driveway. I had left a few lights on in the shop and I was pleased at how welcoming the place looked.

After I had secured the Booke behind the counter, I worked for several more hours hanging curtains on the front windows and putting up more shelves. All the while, in the back of my mind, was a niggling feeling, like I'd forgotten something important.

It was an odd sensation. I stopped my work and looked around. I glanced at the Booke and a shiver ran up my spine. I trotted upstairs to get a sweater. It wasn't *just* a feeling. There was a draft in here, somewhere. I was sure of it.

An hour or two later, I was at the point where I could unpack some of my boxes. A siren startled me from my happy musing.

A black and white Ford Interceptor SUV rushed by the window with a flashing light-bar on the roof, heading out of town. Its wail pierced the peace of the countryside, even from a long way off, as it climbed the roads of the wilderness. A lonely sound. Maybe there was an accident on the highway. I hoped it wasn't anything too bad. I sent up a good thought for whatever it was.

Out the window the forest across the way was dark and getting darker with the falling light. For an instant, the good, warm feelings I had about my new life seemed to shift away from me like a blinking beacon. It was the oddest sensation, as if melancholy was a living thing and had come to perch on my roof.

A streetlight was trying to come on, winking like small flashes of lightning. It lit a figure of a man in a long coat just standing at the edge of the wood.

I gasped and drew back, startled. But then I heaved down the package of mugwort I had in my hand and it hit the floor with a splat. *That's it!* Whoever this stalker was, it had to stop.

I pulled out my phone and dialed 9-1-1. It was ringing. I went to the door and yanked it open. "See this!" I yelled so he could hear me. "I'm calling the cops."

In the blink of an eye—I hadn't even seen him move!—Mr. Doom of the English accent stood right in front of me, glowering. "Now see what you have done," he said. "You *opened* the *book*!"

I didn't even realize I was lowering the phone. Distantly I heard it pick up and a male voice say, "9-1-1. What is your emergency?"

"What?" I gasped, barely registering that the person on the phone had repeated himself and was now asking, "Hello? Hello?"

"Who *are* you?" I demanded.

The man in the duster looked behind him into the woods. "It's too late. Too late for him. Too late for you."

A scream, deep in the forest. We both turned toward it. I'd heard that sound before. That same half-howl, half-scream from the dog that attacked me. But I knew—from the squirming pit of my stomach—that it wasn't a dog at all.

CHAPTER FOUR

I pushed him into the shop and slammed the door. "Just who the hell do you think you are?"

"Who the *hell* do I think I am? You have no idea." He arched a cultivated brow.

The guy on the phone kept saying, "Hello? This is 9-1-1 emergency." I clicked the phone off. "I'm a little tired of your stalking me and I'd like you to stop with the gloom and doom crap. So say what you need to say—no matter how insane—and hit the road."

He started toward me. "'Hit the road'? I have absolutely no intention of *hitting the road*, as you so quaintly put it."

I looked around for a possible weapon and ended up grabbing a bag of tea. "Allergic, right? Just *how* allergic?"

He pulled up short with a look of horror on his face. Aha! His kryptonite!

"Don't come any closer," I warned, brandishing the tea covered with cellophane. "I've got Earl Grey and I know how to use it."

He frowned and pulled grumpily at his coat. "Fine. What do you want to know?"

I held the bag of fragrant tea above my head. "First, I want to know who you are."

"Very well. I am Dark. Erasmus Dark."

I lowered the tea to my thigh and barked a laugh. "A likely story. You can do better than that."

He sneered. "I *beg* your pardon! Look who's talking...Miss *Strange*?"

He had a point.

His eyes flicked to the bag of tea in my hand. "Do you have to keep holding that?"

"Yes." I stepped forward and was satisfied when he took a step back. "Now what's your *real* name?"

"I told you. It is E-ras-mus Dark. *Mister* Dark, to you."

"Oh, really? Okay. Let's suppose for just a minute that this *is* your name. Just what is it you want? Why are you skulking around outside and why did you say all those things about the... the Booke?"

"You opened it, didn't you?"

"How do you even know about it?"

His eyes took in the room, the rafters, and the shelves. "I remember this place. From a long time ago."

"That doesn't explain how you knew the Booke was in the wall."

He turned back toward me. "Was it?"

"You damn well know it was...and I want to know how!"

Carefully, he folded his arms over his chest. "I'll make a bargain with you." The aristocratic way about him was a bit annoying. On the one hand, he seemed dangerous, as if something were seething just below the surface. But on the other, I was drawn to him for the sheer animal magnetism he exuded seemingly without effort. "You put aside that...that *package*," he continued with smooth, dark tones, "and I'll explain."

I looked down at the forgotten bag of tea in my hand. I clutched it tighter. "No way. Nothing doing." I did a little posturing myself. "I tell you what *I'll* do. I won't break open this package and heave it at you—" He cringed back. "—and instead, I'll hold it right here and you tell me what crazy tale you have to tell. And if I like it, well, we'll sit down and talk. And if I don't like it, you'll get a face full of this. Deal?"

He sputtered his indignation. "That's no kind of *deal* at all!"

"It's the only one you're getting. It's that or you can leave now. Either way I'm probably calling the cops."

"They'll do you little good," he sneered. "Besides, I have a feeling they'll soon be contacting *you*."

The phone in my hand rang and I jumped about three feet. Heart racing, I looked down at the unfamiliar number. Putting the phone to my ear, I held the tea out to Mr. Dark to prevent him from rushing me, which it looked like he wanted to do.

"Is this Kylie Strange?" said the male voice.

"Yes?"

"This is Sheriff Bradbury. Do you know Karl Waters?"

"Um…yes. I just met him today." I turned away from Mr. Dark's piercing gaze and concentrated on the call.

"Do you live at 331 Lyndon Road, Moody Bog?"

"Yes. What's wrong? Is everything all right?"

"Are you at your home now, Ms. Strange?"

"Well…yes. Sheriff, what's wrong?"

"I'll be there in five minutes. Please remain where you are, Ms. Strange."

"What is this about?" But he'd already hung up. I spun toward Mr. Dark, who was looking at me warily. "The sheriff is on his way."

"I know," he said, looking a bit pained. "He's about to tell you that Karl Waters has been murdered and that you are a suspect."

"*What?* And how do *you* know that?" I brandished the tea again and he took a step back.

"Really, Miss Strange. Is that strictly necessary?"

"It damn well is! Now talk or eat Earl Grey."

He took a deep breath and let it out slowly. "You really have no idea what you've unleashed. No idea. You opened the book. And you *saw* that it was walled up. Why couldn't you just leave well enough alone?"

"When I meant 'talk' I also meant to make sense."

Suddenly he was in my face. He had rushed me within a split second. He could have killed me, could have slammed me against the wall, but he hadn't. He was mere inches from me, dark eyes glaring menacingly into mine. "You opened the book!" he said, as if that should have explained it all.

"Okay! All right! I opened the stupid *Booke*! Are you saying it's like…Constance Howland all those years ago? Did I open a Pandora's Box?"

His eyes narrowed. "You've heard of Mistress Howland?" His voice was low and silky. "Then this will be easier. Yes," he said. "A Pandora's Box. Just like that."

"I don't get what you mean. The Booke was empty. The pages are blank."

"Of course they are blank. Each comes to the book as if it were a new thing, a blank slate. *Tabula Rasa*."

I shook my head, still mystified.

He scoffed. "The point is, the cycle has started again, because you have opened. The. Book!"

"That's what Karl Waters said. He said…" I stared at him, into his shadowy eyes. "Did *you* kill him?" I whispered, taking a step back.

He sneered at me again. "No, I did *not* kill him! Something far worse has done so. And time is running out!"

The sound of a car pulling up broke our conversation, and he stalked to the window and looked out. "The police are here," he said unnecessarily.

I stood where I was, stunned by everything that was happening, but relieved that the sheriff had arrived.

Dark spun toward me. "You must not tell them about the book. They will not believe you in any case."

"Believe what? I don't know anything!"

He gave me a crooked smile. "Don't you?"

Car doors slammed and my front door burst open. I stepped back, my mouth parting in surprise as two police officers barged in.

"Kylie Strange?" asked the sheriff. He was wearing a heavy jacket with fake fur at the collar, and a Smokey Bear hat on his dark-haired head. He had a handsome face, rugged from the weather, and was, I guessed, about five or so years older than me.

"Yes?"

The sheriff looked me over, seeming surprised by what he saw, and hid it by glancing around quickly. His deputy stood by the door, a dour expression on his face. He was about my age, and wore a clipped mustache.

The sheriff came closer. "I'm Sheriff Bradbury. And this is Deputy Miller." He thumbed over his shoulder toward the mustached officer. "I talked to you on the phone. I'd like to ask a few questions."

"Can you tell me what this is about?"

"Karl Waters was found dead this afternoon at his museum," he said. But since I already knew that, my little breath of surprise was all for show. My eyes darted, looking for our friendly neighborhood Mr. Dark, but he had simply vanished.

"When? I mean I left him no more than a few hours ago."

"About that, Ms. Strange. We wanted to know why you went to see Mr. Waters. Did you know him?"

"No. I had a question about a book I saw online. A historical question. And…wait. How did you know to contact me?"

"He was clutching your business card in his hand."

"He…*died* holding my card?"

"That's right. And so we need to ask you—"

"What did he die of?"

"That…has yet to be determined."

"Look," I said, "there's someone you need to talk to. This mysterious Englishman who keeps coming around with messages of gloom and doom. He said his name is Erasmus Dark, but I don't think that can be real."

He tipped his hat back on his head and scratched his brow. "I'm sorry. Who?"

"He's about your height, slim figure, maybe late thirties, dark longish hair, dark eyes, English accent, snooty attitude. Oh, and he wears a black duster coat. He knew about the murder before you told me."

"Is that right? And where did you meet him?"

"He just keeps showing up. I saw him outside. He was here before you came in."

"And where is he now?"

I faltered. "He was here...a minute ago."

He straightened his hat again. "What sort of vehicle does he drive?"

"I never saw a car. He just shows up. Uninvited."

"How long have you known him?"

"Just since yesterday. I mean, I don't know him. Never saw him before in my life."

"Uh-huh." He glanced back at his deputy, who was taking notes. "And so this—this Mr. Dark—he told you about the death?"

"Yes. He said I would be blamed for it, which is just ridiculous. I don't know anything. I just met him today."

"And you met this alleged Erasmus Dark yesterday."

"He's not alleged. He's a real guy."

He merely looked at me.

"Look, I'm not crazy. I saw him lurking around here yesterday and I took this Booke over to Karl Waters today to see if he knew anything about it."

"What book?"

I just opened my mouth to tell him about the Booke when I remembered Mr. Dark's words: "They will not believe you." How could I mention the Booke without going into Constance Howland and...everything? That would make me look like more of a suspect...and a lunatic. Instead, I asked, "Look, can you tell me what happened? This is terrible. Was it a heart attack?"

"No. Not a heart attack. He was somehow..."

My neck hairs stood up. "Somehow?"

The sheriff clearly struggled to explain, using his arms. "Sort of...crushed. From the inside. Like...something sucked everything out of him."

My eyes must have widened to saucers. "Whoa." I had to sit. I stumbled backwards into the nearest chair and flopped down on it. "Wh-who could have done that?" I croaked.

"That's what we're investigating." He glanced around again. "Mind if we just take a look?"

Stunned, I nodded.

He nodded to his deputy, and he began nosing about in my backroom. I felt fairly confident that they wouldn't find anything incriminating, though I still wondered about the mysterious appearance and even more mysterious *disappearance* of Erasmus Dark.

The sheriff was peering at something. "Booke of the Hidden," he read. "This the book you meant?"

I jolted up from my chair and staggered toward him. I all but pushed him out of the way to stand in front of the Booke. A surge of overwhelming protectiveness swept over me. "Yeah. It's pretty old. Might be valuable."

"You said *you* brought it to him?"

"I did. I found it in my house. In the wall. I thought that was unusual and so I wanted him to appraise it."

"Do you have any proof of ownership?"

"Of the Booke? I found it in my wall. And I do own the shop and house. I have a picture." I fumbled for the phone in my pocket, called up the pictures, and showed him. "See, it left a hole."

He looked around. "Where's the hole now?"

"Doc Boone was here and fixed it."

"Hmm..."

"You don't honestly think I had anything to do with Karl's death, do you?"

Sheriff Bradbury gave me a sharp look. "Miss, I just don't know what to think."

"There was a dog," I blurted.

"A dog?"

"Um...I'm not sure. Marge Todd at Moody Bog Market said it might be rabid. It was whitish with red eyes. It knocked me down. I heard it howl earlier."

"A whitish dog with red eyes?"

"It...knocked me down..." I said feebly.

"When did this happen?"

"Yesterday. Before I saw Karl. Could he have been...I don't know...bitten?"

He frowned thoughtfully. "I guess that's all for now. We'll

be on the lookout for this Erasmus Dark…and this…dog. But at the moment we consider you a person of interest. Please don't leave town."

I wrung my hands. "Person of—Sure. No problem. I mean…" I gestured around the shop. "This is my new business. Where would I go?"

He conferred with his deputy quietly for a few moments. The deputy looked back at me once before they broke apart and headed for the door. He went out first, and the sheriff held the door open, letting the cold in. He turned and looked around the shop, then at me again. "Nice little place you have here."

"Thanks," I said dully.

He nodded to me and seemed slightly embarrassed by something. Touching the brim of his hat, he said, "Miss," and out the door he went.

I stepped forward and closed it with a shuddering sigh. This was ridiculous. Crazy. I turned around and stifled a scream.

"Do you see now?" said Erasmus Dark, who was suddenly standing behind me. He quirked that half-smile again before he pushed forward, blocking the door. I opened my mouth to scream for the sheriff, but Dark was on me in an instant, hand over my mouth. My spirits fell as I heard the sheriff's car drive away.

He hissed into my ear, "You must stop being an hysterical woman and listen to me." I glared at him. "It will do you no good to scream. No one can hear you."

A spike of dark fear jabbed my chest and I stared straight ahead, waiting. Waiting for him to make a move to stop me. But nothing happened. Being that close to a person, you feel a sense of warmth, of presence. But it was the opposite with Mr. Dark. There was a distinct coldness surrounding him, like a draft had suddenly appeared. And no matter how close he was, it felt like the *absence* of something rather than its presence.

He merely looked at me, eyes scanning over my face as if examining me, until he slowly drew his hand away from my mouth and stepped back.

I scrambled away from him and breathed hard. "Who's a hysterical woman? I think I've earned the right to be a little...*high strung* at the moment."

"But it won't help."

I grabbed my phone from my pocket and punched in 9-1-1 again.

"That will do you no good."

I put the phone to my ear and heard a busy signal. What the—? I stared at the phone and then up at him. "What...?"

"You have work to do now."

"Just who the hell are you?"

"What did Karl Waters tell you?"

My eyes found the Booke again and I couldn't help that creeping feeling heading up my neck. "We...looked at the court documents of Constance Howland."

"And?"

"And she claimed that she let out demons or spirits and had to send them all back or something. She was chased to her death by a dark man. So the accounts say."

"Did they?"

"Yes. And there's this engraving of her clutching a book and heading for a cliff...with a rather intimidating fellow on her heels."

The corners of his mouth edged upward. "You can't believe everything you read."

"What *am* I supposed to believe?"

His eyes tracked over my face. I took an awkward step back. "Who are you really?" I whispered.

He did smile then, but there was no warmth in that either. "One concerned about the book. About containing it. About ...you."

"What about me?" When had I become so breathless?

He shifted closer still. His heavy brows drew down, shadowing his eyes. "You and Mistress Howland would seem to have a great deal in common."

"What do you mean?"

His smile was reptilian. "You, too, have a task now. You, too, must now contain that which you have let escape. The book is a gateway. It unleashes unholy forces, forces that kill and strike fear in the hearts of you mortals."

"'*You* mortals'? What about you? Don't you belong in that category?"

He chuckled. "I think you know that there is something… different…about me, Miss Strange."

I stared at him, running my gaze over his features, perfectly *human* features. Except I had the feeling that if I didn't look directly at him, if I saw him peripherally, he wouldn't quite look the same. And that feeling, that deep subconscious prehistoric *knowing* froze me to the spot.

"Karl Waters said Constance Howland had to write in the Booke. Had to write about those…spirits or whatever they were… to trap them."

He studied me. And now that I knew something about his true nature—and I was certain of it now—I could see something other than causal interest in his eyes. He was interested in me, yes, but more like he was looking at a menu than at a woman. "That's one way," he said.

"What's another?"

He smiled again. It looked like too many teeth. But when I looked a second time it was the normal amount, after all… wasn't it?

"We don't need to discuss that…for the moment."

"Okay." I sat on a nearby stool. "Then tell me, since you seem to know everything. What happened to Karl Waters?"

Erasmus Dark sighed. "I'm not allowed to say."

I shot to my feet, hands clenched. "Who is not allowing you to say?"

"My superiors." He inclined his head toward the Booke. "Keep it close, Miss Strange. You have a job to do now." With that, he spun on his heel and grasped the doorknob.

"Wait!" He paused, but he didn't turn around. "That's it? Just 'keep the book close'?" I said in the best imitation of his posh accent. He turned at that with an insulted sneer. "Is that *your* job? To make these outrageous pronouncements and then sweep away? No help? No suggestions? What sort of oracle are you?"

"I'm not an oracle."

"Then what the hell are you, Mister Dark?"

He leaned in and for just a moment, I thought I caught the strong whiff of sulfur. "There are some things in life worse than nightmares," he rasped.

I shoved him. He hadn't expected it and landed inelegantly against the door. His eyes shot to mine in surprise.

"But there's nothing worse than a pissed-off woman, and you have crossed over the line," I said shakily. "If you're not going to be helpful, then get out!"

He straightened his jacket and with a huff, he yanked open the door and stepped outside. "I…I was planning on it."

I tried to watch him go, to see in which direction he traveled, but a gust of wind swept up, bringing with it a shower of dried leaves and dust, and once I opened my eyes again he was gone. "This is so not good."

CHAPTER FIVE

I slammed the door and locked it. Then I stalked over to the Booke—*book, dammit!*—and glared at the thing. "This is your fault!" I shook a finger at it. It seemed to vibrate and I took a cautious step back, which stopped it. This was blatantly insane, as if I had stepped into one of those paranormal shows on TV.

Peering out the window, I tried to catch of glimpse of Mr. Dark, but there was no sign of him.

Now what was I going to do? That good-looking sheriff—Sheriff Bradbury, was it?—suspected me of foul play. But Mr. Dark knew a little too much about it for my liking. My only other ally was dead, the life sucked out of him. I needed help.

I ran to my purse and rummaged around before digging out Doc Boone's card. I punched in his phone number and waited impatiently for it to pick up.

"Doc Boone!" I yelled.

"Ay-yuh? This Ms. Strange?"

"Yes. I've changed my mind. I do want to meet your Wiccans. How soon can we get together?"

• • •

That evening I drove the few blocks into Moody Bog's pleasant tree-lined neighborhood and pulled my car up to a small cottage covered in shingles, with a wide porch all around it. Several wooden whirligigs out front twirled overtime with the wind that was swaying the trees. I slammed my car door and quickly hustled up the flagstone walkway.

My first knock brought footsteps to the door and Doc Boone opened it. I was relieved to see him wearing an ordinary flannel shirt and dark slacks. I guess I was expecting robes and flowers braided into his hair.

"Come in, Kylie, come in." I stepped through to a warm interior. There were lit candles in sconces above a fireplace. The hearth crackled with a log fire, and more lit votives on the coffee table gave it a cozy feel. When I faced the room to peel off my coat, I saw the rest of the coven. My heart sank just a little.

A striking older woman was there, with lots of eye make-up and wearing large earrings and gobs of necklaces over a flowing blouse covered with a chiffon shawl. She sat next to a young man wearing a loose-fitting dark sweater. When he saw me, he jumped to his feet. He was slim, with a pronounced Adam's apple on his skinny neck and floppy dyed black hair hanging over his eyes, which he swatted away with a giant paw of a hand. He wore spike earrings, but his Goth vibe was cut by his extreme politeness.

He reached across the coffee table to offer his hand. "Hi. I'm Nick Riley."

The woman wiggled her fingers and scrunched her nose at me in greeting.

In a wooden rocker sat a girl, sixteen or so, with her feet tucked under her. She was wearing dark leggings under a short dark skirt and a heather gray sweatshirt with sleeves that covered most of her hands. A wool hat with knitted animal ears was pulled down over her brown, shoulder-length hair. She waved distractedly.

"This is Seraphina," said Doc Boone, gesturing toward the fine-boned woman. "And Nick works at the Coffee Shack over on Main. And this is Jolene Ayrs, the junior member of our coven." He leaned into me, and in a stage whisper added, "Her parents say it's okay."

I waved vaguely to Jolene who seemed to sink behind her clear plastic-framed glasses. She dropped her nose back into the book on her lap.

"You're a little young to be a Wiccan," I said, hoping it sounded friendly.

She squinted up at me through her thick lenses. "There's no age requirement," she said with a hint of teen irritation.

"No politeness requirement either, apparently," I muttered.

There was incense burning and something that smelled cinnamony coming from the kitchen. It was all so normal. Just coffee with the neighbors…except when I looked down and noticed I was surrounded by a chalked pentagram on the floor. I jumped out of it and scrambled toward the rug, ending up perched on the hearth.

"Oh, don't pay that any mind," said Doc. "It's there to bring us more in tune with the forces of Nature."

"Okaaay," I muttered. He motioned for me to sit on the couch next to Nick, who seemed overly exuberant about the prospect. I opted instead to sit in a wooden ladder-back chair on the other side of the coffee table.

"It's funny you should call," said Doc. "Seraphina here is a bit of a psychic—"

"She's as psychic as this plate of Chex Mix," said Nick, frowning at Seraphina, who was looking daggers back at him. "She just thinks she is."

"I am so psychic!"

"If you're so psychic then why don't you pick the lottery numbers?"

"I'm not that kind of psychic!" she cried, snapping her shawl across her chest.

"What does that even mean?"

Doc gestured calming motions. "Now, you two. As I was saying, Seraphina is our little psychic. She picks up feelings about Nature and what's going on. Isn't that right, Seraphina?"

Seraphina's eye shadow was a deep teal and painted to a point out to the edges of her eye, making her look like an Egyptian queen. The silver bangles on both her wrists clanked as she moved her arms. "Oh yes," she purred, closing her eyes. "I felt something odd the other day. Like a door in the cosmic plane opening. It was very strange."

A chill ran down my back. "Really?"

"Yes." She leaned forward. Her giant hoop earrings tangled in her blazing red hair. "Did you feel it, too?" She looked at the others. "I think Kylie is a 'sensitive.'"

I looked around at the four of them looking back at me curiously: a bejeweled middle-aged cougar, an old country doctor, a gangly barista, and a kid. How in the world were they supposed to help me in this supposed mission?

I rose. "Look, maybe I'm wasting your time."

"Now, now." Doc Boone took my shoulders gently. "You sounded a mite upset to me on the phone and you seemed to think we could help."

Slowly I sat again. What did I have to lose? The coven couldn't very well look down their noses at me for *my* Booke-of-the-Hidden problem. I centered myself. "Okay. What do you know of the local history? Like eighteenth-century history?"

They exchanged glances until they all turned as one toward Jolene. She heaved a world-weary sigh. Snapping her book closed she gave me an impatient look. "I guess I'm your girl."

"Right. So in Moody Bog there was this Constance Howland in 1720, and she was charged with witchcraft. She had this Booke..."

Jolene peered at me with narrowed eyes. "This sort of sounds familiar. Is this the one who threw herself from Falcon's Point?"

"Yeah, Falcon's Point. I think that was the name of the place."

"Okay." She seemed to be accessing her memory banks by staring up into Doc Boone's ceiling rafters. "I remember that. They accused her of being a witch and she was chased or something over the cliff before they could hang her. Witch burning had been outlawed by then. But they were allowed to burn the remains. She jumped off of Falcon's Point. They never recovered her body, or never bothered trying to find it."

"Nice," I muttered. "Well, there was slightly more to it than that. There was this Booke she found, the Booke of the Hidden, and when she opened it, it released all these evil spirits and stuff into the world and it became her responsibility to put them all back. I think she was able to accomplish it by writing about them in the Booke."

Jolene frowned. "Interesting." She put down her book and picked up her tablet, and began typing into the keyboard and swiping pictures past her screen with a swoosh of her finger. "This sounds like something I read over at the Gifford Corner Museum once."

"Oh. Yeah. About that." I swallowed hard. "Well, it seems I found something…um…in my shop. And it looked like an old book. Holed up in my wall." I flicked a glance at Doc Boone and he put his fingers up to his lips. "Yeah," I said to him. "*That* hole. I got the information I just told you from Karl Waters at the Gifford Corner Museum but…he was murdered today."

Everyone gasped. I took in each wide-eyed face in turn. "It was after he told me about the Booke. I brought it over there for him to look at…but after a few hours…something had killed him. Sucked the life out of him."

No one spoke. Only the crackle of the fire broke the numb silence. Doc moved on his chair, causing it to creak. "How do you mean, Kylie?" he asked.

"Well…that's what the sheriff said. I don't exactly understand what that means." They hadn't moved, hadn't stopped staring at me. "And then there's this guy. Actually, I'm not so sure about him. But he calls himself Erasmus Dark—"

"The dark figure in the engraving!" said Jolene. "Look." She passed her tablet to Nick, who looked at it with raised brows before he passed it to Seraphina. She scanned it a moment before handing it to me. It was the same drawing that Karl Waters had. I showed it to Doc. "Yeah. A dark figure, all right. He knew all about the Booke, knew it was in the wall, and that I'd opened it. And he also knew about the murder before I did, before the sheriffs came calling."

"That's not good," said Miss Teen Understatement of the Year, taking her tablet back.

I looked desperately from one to the other. "What does it mean?"

Doc slapped his hands on his thighs before he rose. "It means…it's time for a great big pot of tea."

• • •

We sat around the dining room table, sipping dark, strong tea from colorful mugs and stealing surreptitious glances at one another.

Jolene stirred her tea thoughtfully. "So are you saying that you think this Mr. Dark killed Karl Waters?"

"He knew about it. That makes it pretty suspicious in my book."

"And you think he's also trying to insinuate that he's that same 'dark figure' in this 1720 engraving?"

I nodded. "I know it's crazy, but there *is* something odd about him. I mean…" I shook my head. "I don't know."

"Have you told the sheriff?" asked Doc.

"A little. But I think he thought I was crazy, too." Their silence was unnerving. "Look, I'm not into the occult or anything like that. I'm sorry, guys, but I didn't know who else there was to turn to. Maybe you're not that kind of Wiccan, but…" I shrugged. "Any Wiccan in a storm."

Jolene stopped stirring and just stared into her cup. "It's the real deal," she whispered. Then she looked up. "You're all thinking it. We meet once a week and talk about nature gods and the supernatural and we have our rituals, but we've never really felt anything…"

"*I* have," said Seraphina primly.

"You have *not*," said Nick. "She thinks this is *Bell, Book, and Candle*, and she's Kim Novak. You just like to dress up and play Wiccan, *Esther*!"

I looked from one to another. "Esther?"

"Her real name is—"

"Don't!" cried Seraphina.

"Esther Williams. That's why she calls herself 'Seraphina.'"

She raised her chin. The blush to her cheeks had nothing to do with make-up. "And who wouldn't?"

"Guys!" said Jolene. "The point is…this is the real deal. Real spirits. Real…demons."

"Demons?" I squeaked.

"Yeah." She turned to me with a concentrated stare. "Just who do you think this Mr. Dark is? My bet is that he's a demon. You said he knew all about the book."

"Now wait a minute. He's just trying to make himself seem all woo-woo. The guy might be a murderer. And just because he knew about the Booke doesn't mean he's the same guy in the engraving. That's impossible."

Jolene placed her tablet on the table. "He knows a lot. And you said he just disappeared and reappeared."

"Anyone can pull a trick like that. Any street magician can do the same thing."

"Then why do you want our help?" asked Doc.

"This Booke. There is something weird about it. Karl couldn't open it. Only I could. Something strange *is* going on. Have any of you ever heard of anything like this before?"

Doc rubbed the back of his neck. "Can't say I have. But I suppose there's a first time for everything." His normal jovial expression was absent. He seemed to be thinking deeply. "Let me make a call to the coroner. He's an old friend of mine. Maybe he can throw some light on this."

He rose and I got up with him. "I'll make more tea," I said. "It's what I'm good at." I turned toward the kitchen. "Whoa!" I yelled, and flung myself back, stumbling over Doc's toes.

On the sideboard sat the Booke of the Hidden. The Booke I had deliberately left at home. I pointed. "Holy cats!"

Chairs squealed back as everyone jolted to their feet.

Nick's voice was shaky. "Is that…?"

"Yeah," I said breathlessly. *Keep the book close.* That's what Mr. Dark had said. What he hadn't said was that the Booke seemed to decide what "close" was all on its own.

CHAPTER SIX

Cautiously, we all approached the Booke. Everyone looked afraid, except, strangely, Seraphina. She just seemed genuinely interested.

Doc reached out a tentative hand until Nick cried out, "Don't!"

He snatched his hand back on instinct, but then frowned back at Nick. "Just stay back," he told everyone. But as his hand approached I felt jittery and an overwhelming sense of protectiveness. Not for him...but for the damned Booke! "Um..." I began.

He glanced at me, hand still outstretched.

"I don't think it wants you to touch it," said Seraphina and I at the same time. I whipped my head toward her. She wasn't looking at me, but at the Booke. "I felt that," she said simply. "It doesn't want anyone touching it...but Kylie."

"You really felt that?" asked Nick, softly.

"Yes, I really did." She looked at him smugly.

Licking my lips, I pushed forward and grasped the Booke. I felt somewhat better that it was back in my hands, and at the same time it creeped me out.

"This is weird," I said aloud. "It feels like...like it's supposed to be with me. In my hands. But it also feels...annoyed."

"That you left it at home," finished Seraphina.

"This is getting freaky," said Jolene with a wide grin.

I blew out a breath. "Glad you're enjoying it." I held the Booke to my chest for a moment and then slowly set it down on the table. I opened the metal clasp and carefully peeled the cover back. The pages were still blank. Everyone leaned in, looking. "What do I do? Just start writing stuff?"

"I think a quill and ink," said Doc Boone.

"Where am I going to get—?"

But Seraphina was already running to his roll top desk. She grabbed something and held them up in her hands triumphantly.

"Of course," I said. Quill and ink.

• • •

I settled in front of the buff pages of the Booke, dipped quill in hand. It wasn't a fancy quill like an ostrich feather with a metal tip, but an honest-to-goodness goose quill with most of the barbs removed up the shaft, leaving only a white tuft at the top. The coven assured me they used it for only good rituals. Poised over the parchment, I looked around. "What do I say?"

"Maybe you just write your experiences," offered Nick.

"Your feelings," said Seraphina.

Jolene shook her head. "I think it has to be substantial. Something about the thing that killed Mr. Waters."

"But I don't know anything about that."

Doc Boone came into the room again. He put his wireless phone back in its cradle. "Well, I just talked to Gunther Wilson, the coroner. He said it was the damnedest thing he ever saw. Karl looked almost as if he was mummified. Not a bit of moisture left in him. Blood turned to dust."

"But that's impossible!" I dropped the quill and kicked my chair back. "I saw him just this morning. I talked to him."

"Gunther was trying to pin it down to some kind of freak accident. But neither of us could think of anything that could have done that. Not that quickly. He can't find any cause of death… except for extreme and sudden dehydration. He was found back in his archives, clutching your business card."

"That's what the sheriff said." I sat again. Leaning my elbow on the table I gnawed on a fingernail, something I hadn't done since childhood.

Nick sat beside me. "A flash fire, maybe?"

But Doc shook his head. "There were no burns anywhere."

"Maybe he wasn't killed there," said Jolene. "Maybe he was kidnapped, shoved in an oven, and then dumped there."

I was a bit uncomfortable with the brightness in her eyes when she said it, but I owed it more to teenaged gruesome exuberance than any malice.

Erasmus the Devil Wannabe could be just playing me. "So maybe Dark didn't do it," I muttered. "I mean, how could he? How could he do *that*?" He was just a regular guy, after all. An annoying guy with a great accent, but just a guy. "Maybe it *was* some *thing* that got him, like Erasmus said. That whitish animal."

"What animal?" said Doc.

I explained how it came at me, and my impression of what it looked like. But it defied description, especially as shadowed as it was. "I just assumed it was a dog. It was, wasn't it?"

Seraphina put forth a bangled arm. "It's possible that *was* Mister Dark. As Jolene said, he might be a demon."

"I'm sorry, I just don't believe that. There's got to be a logical explanation for all of this." And I gave a nod toward the Booke. "I wonder if all those papers are still there. At the museum. His murder might have been a cover-up to hide stolen papers."

"I'm sure the sheriff is investigating that," said Doc. "And Karl was pretty meticulous about his archives. It would be noticed if something went missing."

"And it wouldn't matter anyway," said Jolene. "He put it all online. Wanna see?" She didn't wait for my response. Her fingers flew silently over her touchscreen and the images of the Gifford Corner Museum flew by. She dug deep, tapping on link after link and finally called up all the Constance Howland archives in layer on layer of opened windows. The engraving was there in all its parchmenty glory. And the inked testimony, the printed works, fancy s's and all.

One particular paragraph of Howland's testimony caught my interest and held it.

> *I opened the Booke and did not mean for the evil to escape into the world, but now that I know my mission I shall fulfill it, heartily so. I am to capture and subdue all that I released, and after so doing, write it in the Booke so to keep them captured for all eternity.*

There *must* be a logical explanation. I wracked my brain, thinking. "But what if what they wanted wasn't in his archive? What if he had information that wasn't yet archived and someone wanted it badly enough?"

Doc took a sip of his tea. "You're still suggesting that Karl was murdered by a human."

"And you're not?"

"What Gunther described was not anything from my medical experience."

"Are you really saying—from your position as a doctor—that you think Karl Waters was killed by…supernatural means?"

Doc hesitated. His Wiccan nature clearly warred with his physician's nature. "Well…I haven't actually *seen* the body."

"This *is* the twenty-first century, after all," I chided. But then I thought about the Booke…

Seraphina laid a manicured hand on my own. Her nails were a cobalt blue. "My dear. There is far more to life than anyone can ever imagine. There are strata upon strata of planes. This is only one of them. The spirits can cross over, move from one to the other to the other. Good spirits as well as evil. It's up to us to make sure the good outweigh the bad."

"Us?"

She blinked at me. "Why of course! You don't think you're alone in this? You came for our help and we'll give it. Won't we?"

Nick nodded guardedly, thin-lipped. Jolene smiled. Doc Boone looked thoughtful, but he, too, nodded.

Relief flooded through me and I felt lighter suddenly. I hadn't realized how much the weight of it all had borne down on me.

"Thanks. I appreciate it. I don't know how dangerous it is. I mean, it didn't turn out so well for Constance Howland."

"That's because she didn't have any friends. *You* do." Seraphina patted my hand and stood up and cast a glance down at the Booke. "I think the first thing we need to do is establish what she wrote in the book in the first place."

Jolene bit her lip as she scrolled through the archive. She shook her head. "No one seems to know. But I stand by what I said before. I think Kylie has to write about whatever killed Mr. Waters in the book. Creature or demon. And she also has to kill the monster with a crossbow."

I snapped to attention. "A what?"

"A crossbow. Says so here." She began typing something. "I looked it up on Wiccanpedia—"

I shot a sidelong glance at her. "Seriously?"

She shrugged and concentrated on her screen. Nick leaned in to look over her arm.

"Yeah. Here it is. It's cross-referenced. Something called the chthonic crossbow. Kills supernatural creatures."

"K-thonic?"

Jolene pointed it out to me on the page. "As pertains to the underworld," she went on. "Spirits and demons. It's Greek."

"Wait a minute. We're still assuming that there are creatures escaping from this empty Booke."

Jolene nodded. "That's what it says here."

"And the internet doesn't lie?"

She folded her arms over her tablet and sighed, looking up at me with an annoyed tilt to her head. "I *do* cross-reference, you know. *And* check to see that there are adequate citations. It's not like I'm getting it from Reddit."

"All right. Suppose...just *suppose* this Booke is a supernatural whatsit. And suppose there *are* creatures getting out of it. I'm not saying I believe they killed Karl. I still have my suspicions of this Mr. Dark. But now I'm supposed to...to *kill* them with a chthonic crossbow? Where am I supposed to get that? Chthonic Crossbows R Us?"

"No, it says you need to get it from a demon. From a black demon, or more accurately described in the Greek translation as…" She looked up at me. "Dark."

"Oh fine! That's just great. What am I supposed to do? Summon him? 'Oh, Erasmus, mind handing over your chthonic crossbow? I'm hunting creatures.'"

"All you need do is ask," a voice said from behind me.

Everyone screamed, including me. I jumped back a foot, a hand on my heart. Doc Boone had the presence of mind to drag everyone back to the living room to stand in the middle of the pentagram. I didn't think this was a good idea, but they seemed to find a measure of comfort in it.

Okay, this was not some David Blaine trick. Erasmus Dark really had appeared out of nowhere between locked windows and doors. He couldn't possibly have known I was headed here. No cars had followed me. No people had been along the road.

Erasmus strode through the dining room archway and observed us huddled together on the carpet. He looked down at the pentagram with disdain.

"Do you really think that will stop me?"

His overbearing tone suddenly pushed away my fear and pissed me off instead. I wrestled my arm away from Doc and stepped from the pentagram, ready to confront him. Too late, I realized that this was exactly what he wanted. Faster than a blink he was at my side, gripping my arm. "I don't have to play this game, you know. I could make this easy. So easy. But I find your kind…fascinating. Stupid, but fascinating."

I tried to throw off his grip, but he never even broke a sweat. Maybe he couldn't. I faced him, even as my chin trembled. "I want that crossbow."

He chuckled. "Do you? How very amusing. Just how do you propose to get it?"

I looked him right in the eye…and stomped hard on his foot.

His eyes opened wide and he let out a yell, releasing me. I scrambled back into the pentagram. "Some demon you are." I was feeling braver surrounded by my Wiccans, but when he turned his face toward me, my newfound confidence faltered. His eyes turned red, glowing. That was no trick.

"Do you think you can toy with me, *human*?"

Where was an exorcist when you needed one?

His face froze in that scary expression for a few more seconds, but when he noticed it didn't intimidate like it ought, he frowned. His eyes went back to their normal dark color and he straightened his coat.

"You still can't toy with me," he muttered, more like a mulish schoolboy than the wrath of Hell.

I jumped out of the circle and grabbed the nearest teacup. He was immediately on alert and took a step back. It wasn't holy water. It was better.

"Look," I said, "are you going to cooperate? I've got the message that I have a job to do, okay? So just calm the heck down and let's discuss this like civilized…uh…beings."

He eyed the cup in my hand and the liquid threatening to splash out of it. Would he melt like the Wicked Witch of the West? No, I needed him. I needed him to explain.

My Wiccans were perplexed that I managed to hold off a demon with a teacup and I shrugged. "I'll tell you later. Let's just all sit down, shall we?" They didn't want to leave the safety of their pentagram, but I pulled out a dining room chair and sat. Gesturing to Erasmus to sit, he kept looking sourly at the Wiccans before he grabbed the chair and gingerly lowered onto it.

The Wiccans exchanged glances, but it wasn't until Doc edged from the carpet that the others seemed to have no choice but to join us around the table. Everyone sat at the far end of the dining room, giving Erasmus a wide berth.

"So," I said, still holding the teacup, ready to heave it at the demon if I needed to. "As incredible as it seems, we've all got a job to do. Well, at least I do, right, Erasmus?"

"I beg your pardon?" he said in his most disdainful tone. "Are you by any chance addressing me?"

"Yes. *Erasmus*. Can you please tell us—?"

"It's *Mister* Dark—"

"Tough. I'm using your first name."

"No one in two thousand years has dared to call me anything but *Mister* Dark. No one has had the gall!"

Doc leaned over to me and whispered in my ear. "I think you've made an excellent move, Kylie. Calling a demon by his name confers certain powers over him. And this familiarity is even better."

"What are you jabbering about over there?" Demons might not be able to sweat, but Erasmus was doing a fair imitation.

"Don't worry your pretty little horned head over it," I said. He scowled.

"I don't have horns," he muttered. He reached up to his head as if to check, and snatched his hand away when I raised my brows at the gesture.

"Can you focus? I've got a problem here. Someone killed an innocent man."

He leaned back and folded his arms over his chest. "Not someone. Some*thing*. And it will kill again."

My gaze flicked toward the Wiccans. I still wasn't convinced he hadn't done it, but I decided, at least for now, to play along. "Then for God's sake, what do I do about it?"

A small smile cracked the corner of his mouth. "You *do* want to stop it, don't you?"

"Of course I do!"

"Humans. I shall never understand you lot." He leaned forward, one hand cupping his square chin. He stroked it, running a finger across the beard-stubbled contour. I wondered if this was what he really looked like. Or was his real appearance too horrible to contemplate?

"So what is it?" I pleaded.

He lowered his hand. "I can't tell you."

"Why not?"

"It isn't permitted."

"Who makes these screwed-up rules?"

"The Powers That Be."

"What kind of answer is that?"

"Kylie," Nick whispered. "Maybe you shouldn't make him angry?"

I followed Nick's gaze. The table smoldered where Erasmus touched it.

"Uh…" I made a vague gesture toward the table. "You want to tone it down? You're scorching the furniture."

He looked down and the smoke dissipated. "My apologies." He nodded at Doc Boone, who made a dignified nod back.

"How did he even get in here?" rasped Nick. "No one invited him in."

"He's not a vampire," I hissed back. Turning to Erasmus, I asked, "Are you?"

He smiled and shook his head. "Nothing so pedestrian."

"I didn't think so. So you show up with fire and brimstone, and you can't tell me anything helpful."

His smile broadened and he leaned back, crossing his arms comfortably over his chest. "No. I'm afraid it's rather your problem…not mine."

"So I'm supposed to believe that some creature murdered Karl and it wasn't you?"

He frowned. "Why would *I* kill the man?"

"For something he had. Some knowledge he was privy to."

"You make a very poor inquisitor."

"I just don't want to be helping you if you're the culprit."

"This has nothing to do with me. I had no interest whatsoever in that man. What is he to me? He was a mortal, nothing more. My concern, my *only* concern, is the book. It must be closed. And the only way to close it is to capture the creatures *you* released."

"Okay. So let's just suppose for now that some creature escaped from the Booke. And I need this crossbow that you have, but you won't give to me."

Thank goodness Jolene had had the presence of mind to snatch her tablet before the Wiccans ushered themselves into the pentagram, because she was furiously typing into it the whole time. "That's not entirely true," she said.

Erasmus sat up straight. "Don't listen to that little girl. She's lying."

Jolene made a face at him, leaned in to me, and said quietly, "You can make him give it to you. You only have to steal something of his and call out his name."

"What's that? What are you two whispering about over there?"

My eye instantly fell on the pendant hanging around his neck. That would do. I got up and marched over to him. He tried to scramble to his feet but got caught up in the tablecloth.

I pointed toward the kitchen behind him. "Look! A werewolf!"

"Where?" he cried, jerking his head where I pointed.

I reached for the pendant, and with all my might, yanked it from his neck. The chain broke and the strangely hot metal was in my hand.

He lurched to his feet, eyes wide, hand clamped to his empty throat.

I winced as the amulet burned my palm, but I held it up by its broken chain and declared in the most melodramatic way possible, "*Erasmus Dark, give me the chthonic crossbow!*"

He stumbled back. "What have you done?"

A clap of thunder roared over the house and the lights went out. Thank goodness for the lit candles or we would have been in complete darkness.

"Beelze's tail!" he swore. "Damn you! Give me back my amulet and I'll…I'll fetch it for you."

"Fetch it for me and I'll give you back your amulet."

He struggled not to say the things he clearly wanted to.

"I'm waiting, Erasmus."

"Stop calling me that. No one calls me that."

I crossed my arms. The amulet dangled from my fingers. He

looked like he wanted to snatch it back, but perhaps he wasn't allowed to by the nebulous rules of the "Powers That Be."

"All right, all *right!*" He pointed a finger at me. "Don't move."

"Wouldn't dream of it."

We blinked and he disappeared. No cloud of smoke, no thunderclap. Just there one minute, gone the next. It was sort of anticlimactic, given the circumstances.

CHAPTER SEVEN

I think we just assumed he'd be back instantly, but time ticked away. Maybe he forgot where he put it.

"Maybe he pawned it," said Nick. The power had returned and we made ourselves at home in the living room with the comfort of electricity humming around us. Jolene returned to the rocking chair and I joined Nick and Seraphina on the couch. Doc stood by the fireplace, a finger on his lip, thinking.

"Pawn shops aren't open at this hour," I said.

"They might be open all night…down there," he said significantly. We all looked down toward the floor, as if expecting it to open up into a fiery pit.

Jolene grinned and typed away on her tablet. "This is the best meeting *ever*!"

I rolled the still-warm amulet absently in my hand. The chain had repaired itself as soon as Erasmus had gone, and it gleamed as if mocking these whole proceedings. It was the face of a horned demon, sticking its long tongue out, with eyes made of red gemstones. I was quickly losing my skepticism. "Assuming he brings this crossbow," I said, and I couldn't believe the word "crossbow" was even passing my lips, "I still don't know what I'm supposed to do with it. And forgive me for stating the obvious, but I've never done anything like this before."

"Few have," said Seraphina, eyes closed, concentrating, I assumed, on the different planes of existence.

"So what is this thing I'm supposed to stop? Kill. Stop." I didn't like the idea at all of killing something, even if it was a monster.

"Aha!" cried Jolene, startling us all. Would this night never end? It was just one startle after another. I glanced toward the roll top desk where the Booke waited for me. I could actually *feel* it waiting. *This is crazy*, I told myself for the umpteenth time.

Jolene laid the tablet flat on the coffee table. "Check this out. A succubus."

No one moved or spoke. Finally, I couldn't stand it. "Okay, what's a succubus?"

"A succubus is probably the culprit. The thing that killed Karl Waters." She sighed. "I know you want to believe it was Mr. Dark, but just take a look at this." She turned the tablet toward me. I read the entry beside a rendering of a ghostly figure of a woman with glowing red eyes.

> *A succubus is a female sexual predator demon who attacks men in their sleep. Legends of Incubi and Succubae can be found as far back as ancient Sumer in 3000 BCE. They are said to visit their victims in the night and have intercourse with them. Sometimes the encounter can lead to death by the Succubus sucking the life force from their victims, leaving an empty husk.*

Crap.

I turned toward Doc. "But Karl Waters wasn't asleep. At least I'm guessing he wasn't. He was in his archives. Can we assume he wasn't making nookie back there?"

Jolene seemed adamant. "There isn't anything else mentioned that could have done this."

"Maybe nothing we know of. Also, if Erasmus *is* a demon, then couldn't he fake the symptoms of a succubus?"

It was Jolene's turn to roll her eyes at me. "You sure are trying to make a case for Mr. Dark."

"Well, I don't like him! He's an arrogant bastard. And I don't like him just sweeping in here, telling me what to do."

"We're just trying to get at the facts," Doc said. "And after some consideration, I'm inclined to believe that Karl's death was due to supernatural means. Now as far as I'm concerned, it puts Mr. Dark front and center. But we cannot discount this information on a succubus from Jolene. Mr. Dark's presence may simply mean that he is somehow tied to the book."

"Well...okay. That makes sense." As much as any of it could. I wanted to blame Erasmus, I guess. Someone tangible. But Doc was probably right. He was tied to the Booke. The demon of the Booke. Swell. But Karl had died clutching *my* business card. Could it be that he had found out something about the Booke and was about to call me?

My restless fingers caught on the amulet. I stared at it and held it up toward Doc Boone. "Doc, what do you make of this?"

I was reluctant to let it go and just allowed him to hold the charm while I kept the chain. "Looks like some sort of talisman. The face of the Beast."

"When you say 'beast' do you mean...?"

"*The* Beast. The Devil."

"Great."

I took it back and paced, opening and closing my fist over the amulet. Talisman. Whatever. "What if he never comes back?"

"He'll be back," said Jolene over her tablet.

"How do you know?"

She shrugged.

"This is ridiculous!"

"Now, Kylie," Doc said as he stood in front of me again. "I think it best to try to calm down. None of us have ever encountered anything like this before."

I couldn't help but stare at the beast face on the amulet. "Should I give this back to him?"

"You made a bargain," said Jolene, not looking up. "I think you have to."

"But what if this has some sort of power over him?"

Doc nodded. "I think it likely does."

"Then maybe I should keep it. At least for a while."

I looked down at it again, running my finger over the protruding silver tongue.

An odd tingle in my senses that had nothing to do with the amulet sparked in me and I jerked toward the Booke. Nick was leaning over it with a magnifying glass. "What are you doing?" My voice was a little more strident than I intended.

He looked up guiltily. "I just wanted to take a closer look."

"It doesn't like you doing that." I pulled up short. "God, that's weird."

"Wow," he whispered. "It's sentient."

I rubbed my arm uncomfortably. "Not really. Not in the strictest sense of the word. But it does give off these…vibes. And they seem to be getting stronger."

Seraphina nodded from across the room, eyes still closed. Was she in communion with it? I found myself feeling jealous, and then disgusted with myself for feeling that at all.

"So…demons and stuff. What do you guys know about them?"

They exchanged glances. Nick looked at me sheepishly. "Well…not much. To tell you the truth…" He fumbled with his fingers, chipped black nail polish and all. "We've only just…you know…chanted and dabbled with a few potions. I never even…" He winced, looking at Doc. "Sorry, but I really didn't half believe in it. I just thought it would be something cool to do on a weeknight. Gets pretty boring around here."

"I see." I looked at the rest of them. "And *you* guys? Just a fun thing to do between reruns of your favorite shows?"

Seraphina touched my arm. "That's not true for all of us, Kylie." She gave Nick the stink eye. "I've been a practitioner of Wicca for most of my adult life. I've seen it work. I have faith in the gods and spirits. I helped Doc find his way to it."

"That's true," said Doc. "It's also true that our rituals have been simple, more for calming and energy. We've never delved deeper, though I have witnessed more meaty rituals in Africa and the Amazon some years ago when I was on sabbatical."

Jolene raised her head but kept her eyes on her tablet. "I've never done anything more than a potion and a charm, but the results were ambiguous, far from actual empirical evidence. Didn't make it any less cool, though. And I like the company. Seraphina knows a lot. So does Doc, and Nick—he tries really hard to understand it all. I can respect that."

"Then this is all just theoretical to you guys?"

"Until tonight!" said Jolene brightly. "Mr. Dark is the genuine article. A real demon."

"What makes you so sure?"

"That was no magic trick. And look at that amulet. *You* didn't fix the chain."

I squeezed it in my palm. The Beast face warmed my skin. "Well, I guess I really don't have any other choice, do I?"

Doc took up my hand and gave it gentle pressure. "We won't desert you, Kylie. We aren't entirely helpless. We have the advantage of intellect and gumption. We *will* help you."

I nodded. "Okay, then. Answer this, Jolene. What do we know about this 'dark demon'? Doc said I had some measure of control over him by the use of his name. How can we protect ourselves? Crucifixes? Holy water?" I wasn't exactly excited about the possibility of donning religious symbols, since I didn't have any religion myself. *Maybe I should reconsider that one.*

"There's a lot of collective wisdom about demons," she said, still poring over her tablet screen. "Lots of different perspectives from every culture. I did a paper on it for my social studies class. Should have been an 'A.' Who knew my teacher was such a religious crank?" she muttered. "The one universal about demons, though, is that they like to deceive."

"Naturally. Do you think he's playing with us?"

"Wouldn't put it past him."

I stomped my foot. This was bad enough, but this waiting was killing me. "Erasmus! Where the hell are you!" I bellowed. "Get your scaly demon ass back here!"

"I do *not* have a scaly—never mind."

I turned. There he was. Again. I looked at the thing he was carrying. Holy cats! He actually brought it.

It was a crossbow, all right, but not like any I'd ever seen before. Not that I'd ever seen one in person. At least three feet long, with a silver handle and trigger, all carved into organic shapes that seemed familiar and sensuous and entirely inappropriate for a crossbow. The wood was a deep black and polished to a high gloss.

He held it up. "I have brought the chthonic crossbow. Now give me my amulet."

"Give me the crossbow," I said, holding out my hand.

He growled and narrowed his eyes, but handed it over. When I took it I nearly dropped it; it was just as heavy as it looked. I used both hands to heft it.

"Now my amulet." He held his hand out expectantly. It was trembling. Either he was angry or…frightened?

I rested the crossbow on the ground against my leg, and held up the amulet. Then, on instinct, I dropped the chain over my own head and let the thing hang over my chest. "I don't think so. I think I'll just keep this safe for the time being."

"*What?*" he bellowed. He tried to lunge for me but at the last moment held himself in check. "Give it back to me!"

"No!"

"You don't have any idea what you are doing."

"I'm pissing *you* off, so that's a plus."

He started to literally smolder again and I shook my finger at him. "Stop it. Or else."

The smoke dispersed and he rolled his shoulders. "You leave me very little choice," he rasped.

"That's the idea." The amulet was heavy on my chest. I resisted the urge to look at it. "So. This thing." I hefted up the crossbow again, resting the butt on my hip. The arrow-whatsits were cleverly incorporated into the silver butt's intricate vines and twisting tendrils. At least I thought they were vines. "How do you use this thing?"

Erasmus folded his arms over his chest in defiance, but I had already turned toward Nick. "Don't look at me," said Nick, eyeing Erasmus suspiciously. "*I've* never used a crossbow. But I know in theory, anyway. From video games." He wiggled a finger at one of the arrow thingies. "These are called bolts or quarrels. You take one of those, fit it there"—he pointed toward the groove in the stock—"aim it, and pull the trigger. Oh, you have to pull back the bow string so the quarrel can fire."

"It's more complicated than I thought," I muttered.

"You have no idea," said Erasmus.

"I know I need to use this to kill whatever it is that's out there. But you have to tell me about the Booke. What do I have to do?"

Erasmus flitted his gaze from me to each of the Wiccans in turn. "I don't have to tell you. Not really."

My hand closed over the amulet. It felt almost hot to the touch. "Don't you?"

His gaze tried to pierce my closed hand but couldn't. He growled again and bared his teeth. "You are a most annoying woman."

"Thanks. So tell me. Is this a succubus we're after?"

He threw back his head and laughed. We all watched him as the laughter rolled around the room, until he came back to himself and stared anew at me. "Oh. You were serious." He shrugged. "Possibly."

I shook the crossbow at him. "Do you know where it is?"

He took an index finger and carefully redirected the bow away from himself. "Do be careful with that. No, I don't know where it is. If it *is* a succubus."

"Right. Well, let's go then."

"Go? Go where?"

"Back to my place."

"Whoa," said Nick, holding up his hands. "You're leaving?"

"Just as it was getting good?" said Jolene, face finally out of her computer.

"Erasmus and I—"

"Stop calling me that!"

"—have business to attend to. I'll call you guys later. Let me know if you find out anything."

I went to the roll top desk and picked up the Booke, holding it to my chest with one arm while toting the crossbow with the other. Doc stopped me at the door. "Kylie, are you certain you want to be going anywhere with…*him*?"

Erasmus's sneer was world class, but he suddenly didn't look particularly scary. "I have to talk to him. I get the feeling he doesn't want to talk in front of you guys. I'll be fine," I added when Doc seemed reluctant to let me go.

"Call me when he's gone," said Doc. "No matter how late."

"Okay, will do. Jolene?" She looked up. "Keep digging. If we've got to find this thing that killed Karl, I want to know all I'm up against."

She saluted and sank down in front of her tablet again. Doc still held my arm but gave it a squeeze before finally releasing me. Nick was frowning from across the room when I closed the door on their warm camaraderie. Was I making a mistake? Should I have stayed there safe in their little chalked pentagram?

I cast a glance at Erasmus. He was scowling but didn't seem dangerous. I unlocked the Jeep, opened the trunk, and shoved in the Booke and the crossbow. I looked at both of them sitting on a blanket in the back of my car when a sense of the surreal washed over me. Without overthinking it, I quickly pulled down the trunk door.

I moved to the driver's side while Erasmus remained motionless on the driveway. "Well, don't just stand there," I told him. "Get in."

His dark brows shot upward. "What do you mean?"

"I mean get in the car. What do you think I mean?"

"You want me…in your conveyance?"

"Why not? Are you going to smolder again? Set yourself on fire? If not, get in."

I got into the car, and the headlights sprang to life and covered the front of Doc's house. I could see them all standing in the window, looking back at us through the curtains. Erasmus stood tentatively on the driveway, swaying a little. I rolled down my window. "Are you getting in or not?"

He moved sluggishly to the other side of the car and cautiously took hold of the door handle. He fumbled with it a bit before he got it open and peered inside the cab.

"We don't have all night, you know."

Awkwardly he swung inside and settled into the seat.

"Seatbelt," I sighed.

He looked at me inquiringly and I motioned to it, miming at my own. He still didn't seem to understand, and I had to unbuckle mine to reach across and grab his. He startled back into his seat and I looked up at him. He was still looking at me curiously, but this time his face wasn't scrunched in disdain but full of genuine interest. It was an awfully handsome face, with a nose worthy of a Greek statue, and sculpted lips that would be perfect if they smiled without that smug snarkiness, and a square chin with a bit of scruff. His eyes, dark and intense, scrutinized my face, and seemed surprised to be pleased by what they saw. Okay, that last bit could have been my overactive imagination. I had to remind myself that he really wasn't a *he* at all, but more likely an *it*. Boy, it really had been a while since I'd left Jeff.

I drew away hastily and cleared my throat. "All buckled in?"

I threw the car into gear and slid it backwards out of the driveway. We bumped jerkily over the verge and settled onto the main road.

As we drove through the darkened woods back to my place, I kept snatching glances at him out of the corner of my eye. He grabbed the door and the center console for dear life. His fingers whitened.

In silence, we drove over the curving road to my brightly lit shop, where I got out and went to the trunk. After a few moments, Erasmus opened his door and stumbled free.

Slamming the trunk down, I carried the Booke and crossbow to the pool of light over the front porch. I handed him the key under my bundle. "Open that, would you? My hands are full."

By the astonished look on his face, I realized he might not have been offered the niceties before, but he took the keys with two fingers and did as bid. He opened the door for me and stood aside as I entered, flipped on a light, and set down the Booke and the crossbow beside it. Turning toward Erasmus, I noticed he seemed to be a little cowed.

"Why did you drive me here? I could have just appeared."

"I know. But this is more civilized, don't you think?"

"No."

"Are you contrary on purpose?" I asked, peeling off my coat. "Or is that just your way?"

"I—" After a pause he shrugged. He wouldn't stop his concentrated stare at me even as I motioned for him to take a seat. He didn't take off his jacket. Reluctantly, he sat in one of the wing chairs by the fireplace. I knelt beside it, getting kindling together and crumpling up wads of newspapers.

He reached over and lightly touched my shoulder. "No, no. Allow me." He pointed a finger at the fireplace and the logs instantly ignited.

I fell back onto my backside. With a calming breath I got to my feet. "Oh. That's…handy." Even after his disappearing and reappearing trick I still had a hard time thinking of him as anything but human. I knew it was dangerous to make that mistake. I vowed to be more vigilant.

I sat in the chair opposite him and we simply stared for a while.

"So," I finally said. "Demon, huh?"

The sneer was back. He settled into the chair, hands curled around the arms. "So…*human*, eh?"

I chuckled. "Okay. Maybe that was rude, but I've never met a demon before. Didn't know they really existed."

"I am afraid what you know about the world around you can fill one of your little tea cups."

"Granted. But I'm learning. And I'm curious. Just what *is* a demon? I thought they were all red with horns, a tail, and a pitchfork."

He studied me. With his elbow resting on the chair arm, he ran his finger lightly over his lips. I couldn't help but follow the movement with my eyes. "Do you *really* want to know?"

I nodded. "I mean, this is all pretty new to me. It would be helpful."

He sat back, still studying me.

I looked over to where the Booke sat. I felt it in waves, this understanding I had with it. The Booke had its own instinct. And it seemed to be telling me that *my* instincts were correct. Erasmus might try to lie to me, but the Booke would assure that I always knew the truth. I didn't know how I knew that, but it was as solid an answer as I had ever gotten anywhere. Maybe he *was* tied to the Booke.

Erasmus saw me looking and frowned.

"The Booke," I said. "The Booke knows."

He steadfastly refused to glance back at the Booke. I thrummed with satisfaction. I hadn't known I was engaged in a contest, but now I knew I'd won. At least the first round.

"So." I settled in. The fire was cozy. A handsome man was sitting beside me. Under other circumstances this would have been an ideal situation. "Where do demons come from? Where did *you* come from?"

"You wouldn't—it's too difficult to explain."

"Look, I'm buying all this, all right? I don't understand any of it but I'm coming to believe it. I have to, don't I? I think I can take in a little demon history."

He'd halfway risen from his seat. "No, you can't!"

"Sorry. I just thought…" I sighed. "Well, what can you tell me about the Booke?"

He settled down again. "You've already sussed what you need to do."

"But not enough. I want to know where it came from and why it turns up when it does. It's not just from 1720. I feel…I feel like it's older than that. Much older." I squinted at the Booke over my shoulder, annoyed that I *knew* things about it against my will.

"There you have it. You already know much. I suspect the book is telling you."

"Yes, but why?" He remained tight-lipped. I blew out an exasperated breath. "If you won't tell me about the Booke, why do you bother making an appearance at all? What is it you're not telling me?"

"I don't know what you mean."

I rolled my eyes. "Look, I'm not stupid. You appeared the same time the Booke did. So I'm thinking you're somehow connected. Come on, throw me a bone here. It seems like we both want the Booke closed again."

Erasmus stared into the fire. The firelight flickered deep in his eyes, eyes that seemed to reach back for fathoms. "I am not permitted—"

"Oh come *on*!" I leaned closer. "Surely you can give me a hint. Me and my chthonic crossbow."

"Which you stole."

"I only asked for it."

"By *stealing* my amulet."

My hand went to the dangling necklace and closed over the warm metal. Strangely, it made me think of him, Erasmus, not the beast-face on the thing. "Well, I'm sorry. I'm playing by your rules. Ordinarily I wouldn't do something like that. But these circumstances seem far from ordinary." I looked down at it again, unable to resist this time. The jeweled eyes seemed to glow at me, and I closed my fingers over it just to stop it from staring back. "Have you had this a long time?" I asked quietly.

"Yes. A very long time. Centuries."

"Sorry. You'll get it back. Promise. But you *have* to help me."

One brow raised and he angled his face toward mine. "I suppose," he said grudgingly.

I slapped my thighs. "There! Now you see? We *can* work together. So. First. Who are these Powers That Be?"

He sighed and glared into the fire again. "They are the *Powers* That *Be*. All-powerful. Hence the name."

"What do you mean? Like...gods?"

"Yes, like gods! Of course. Why would I be concerned with anything less?"

"I don't know. I don't know anything about gods or demons."

We both sat staring into the fireplace, both with arms crossed with pouts on our faces. I decided to be the bigger man first. "Look, Erasmus, if we're to work together, then it only makes sense to start by my telling you a little about me."

"I have no desire to know anything about you. You're mortal; you live, you die. End of story."

"Well, there's a little more to it than that."

"No, there isn't. I've lived hundreds of years. Hundreds. I've seen your lot pass through this place like dried leaves. Your life means nothing to me."

"Fine!" One thing I knew for certain about demons; they were rude! "Then what's so important about this Booke? Why should you care if it kills more of us mere mortals? What's it to you?"

"The book should not be opened!"

"Why? Because the Powers That Be declare it so?"

"Yes! Yes, that's part of it."

"What's the rest?"

He shot to his feet. "It doesn't matter. None of it matters."

I scrambled from my seat and stood in front of him. "It matters to me! I'm stuck with this thing now. I'm the one who's got to kill *something* and write it down in that damned Booke. I didn't ask for this! I want nothing to do with it."

He got up right in my face, those dark eyes glaring into mine. "Neither did I! I'm just as cursed as you are! As soon as you opened that book, I—"

He stopped, freezing in place.

I was about to ask, but then I stopped, too. I heard it a split second after him.

That strange inhuman scream, deep in the woods.

He looked off in that direction, head cocked. "I hope you're satisfied," he whispered. "It's killed again."

CHAPTER EIGHT

I slapped his shoulder. "How come you didn't tell me about that ahead of time!"

"Ow!" He rubbed his shoulder indignantly. "What! I'm not omnipotent. You don't know *anything* about the world's religions, do you?"

"I think the world's religions would be failing me miserably at this point. So, whom did it kill? And is it a succubus?"

"I don't know—to both questions." He moved toward the window and looked out, squinting into the moonlight. "It's close, though. Very close. It…is aware of you."

A chill shivered over my skin. Okay, so maybe that meant Erasmus was in the clear. Maybe. "Can it…can it hurt me?"

He looked me over. "If it is a succubus, it can't kill you but it can harm you. It would take an incubus to kill you. But it is dangerous nonetheless."

"What's the difference?"

"Good grief. Look it up!"

"You're the most unhelpful demon I've ever met."

"Met many, have you?"

"You'd be surprised."

He snorted and headed toward the door.

"Where do you think you're going?"

"I'm not your personal pet. I have places to go, people to see."

"But—" I swept my hands around the empty room. "What am I supposed to do?" I didn't mean for my voice to get so small, but despite my earlier bravado, I was concerned about all this dropped in my lap.

He flicked his head toward the crossbow. "Get to know that." He pointed a finger at me. "And keep my amulet safe!"

My hand flew to it again. He gave me a parting sneer, before he threw open the door and disappeared into the night.

• • •

Dutifully, I called Doc Boone once Erasmus didn't look as if he would be coming back. I told him my suspicions, that the demon was not only tied to the amulet but perhaps the Booke as well. "You'd better keep in touch with your coroner friend," I sighed into the receiver. I couldn't help but stare out the window, searching the darkness for that which I knew I couldn't see and certainly had no desire to. "That thing killed again. And yes, I'm pretty sure it wasn't Erasmus because he was right beside me when I heard the…howl. It was a pretty horrible sound."

Doc was silent on the line for a moment. "I can't exactly call him and ask the coroner if he's heard about another body."

"I know. But just…keep in touch, you know?"

"I will. Kylie, I'm concerned with you being alone with this… this Mr. Dark."

"I'm fine. As long as I have this amulet, I don't think he can hurt me. And for some reason, he needs this Booke closed again as much as I do. I think he'll be forced to work with me. Or at least not work against me."

"Hmm. Well, Jolene has been working nonstop to find out about the book and that amulet."

"I appreciate it." I looked at my watch. Wow. It was late. "I hope you took her home by now."

"Yes, she's home. But I have a feeling the Wiccans will be more than a once a week society from now on."

I smiled. "You don't know what a relief that is to me."

He laughed. "Well, I must admit, this puts a whole new spin on it for me, too."

"I meant to ask you but didn't quite know how to put it."

"What's a man of science like me doing with hocus pocus like this?"

"Well, to put it bluntly, yeah. Of course, I guess *I* don't look at it as hocus pocus anymore."

"The physical world, biology, has always been a mainstay of mine, of course. I couldn't be a doctor without full knowledge. But several years' back, I took a sabbatical to Africa and I learned a thing or two about herbal remedies. I began doing my own research on it and also the spiritual nature of native medicine. It was more than the placebo effect. I began to think there could be more than we in the West understood. I devoted more time to this study after I retired. And when Seraphina brought her Wiccan beliefs to town, well, it looked mighty interesting to me. She brought the spiritual and I brought the practical. That's when Nick and Jolene came into the picture. We're a small group but dedicated. And frankly, young lady, your being here, well, it's brought a whole other level to it that has forever changed us. We're meeting again tomorrow night. You're welcome to come."

"Thanks, Doc. I appreciate it. I'll be there. Tell the others to be careful. They'll need protection from whatever's out there."

"Maybe it would be best to meet up at your place. We might need the use of some of your more unusual herbs."

"Of course! I'd be happy to host. Oh." I glanced at the wall calendar. "There's a Chamber of Commerce thing at five. Let's meet after. And I'll put you all to work, too. I've got to open these doors by the end of this week or I'll be out of business before I've begun."

"Ay-yuh, we'll be there."

The silence that followed the phone call enveloped me. I knew it was best to get upstairs to see if I could get some sleep, though I didn't hold much hope for it. I glanced at my copper kettle on its hob behind the counter. A little chamomile would do the trick, with maybe a pinch of lavender.

• • •

By the next morning I was busily trying to get my shop ready. There were still boxes and boxes of herbs to open and sort through. I knew that once my inventory was all in the right places it wouldn't seem so daunting, but those endless boxes and those empty cubbyholes seemed a bit overwhelming.

And I kept passing both the Booke and the crossbow. I started taking them into various rooms I was working in. Last night they had both been in my bedroom. I had to throw an afghan over both of them, getting the feeling that they were *looking* at me. Once I was showered and dressed, I carried them down to the kitchen, and now the shop, like two lethargic pets.

More than once I slowed as I passed the crossbow, and ran my fingers over the smooth organic silver shapes embedded in it. Finally, I gave in and picked it up. I looked around the empty shop. Surely it couldn't hurt to fire it at least once. After all, Erasmus had told me to get to know it.

I pulled out one of the quarrels, as Nick had called them. I examined it and noticed that each one of the ten quarrels looked slightly different. All of them had metal tips except two, which were just sharpened wood. One had a crystal of some kind embedded in the shaft, and each one had a different set of fletching, the feathered part.

The thing had to be cocked. A quick look online told me that I had to pull the string back until it held into place. Once it was pulled back all the way, I placed a bolt chosen at random into a groove right in front of the taut string. Slowly, I lifted it up and pressed the stock into my shoulder like a rifle. With one eye closed, I swung it toward the back door and aimed. Slowly, I squeezed the trigger.

All at once, the crossbow was slammed upward and my trigger hand fell away to nothing. I snapped my head up and found myself staring into dark, dark eyes.

"This is not a toy!" Erasmus shouted in my face.

"I know that! I'm practicing."

"You cannot *practice*. You either accomplish or you don't."

"What kind of asinine thing is that to say?"

"Oh, of course. Anything *you* don't understand is plainly asinine."

"It just makes no sense. How am I ever going to hit some creature with this if I've never used it before?"

"Has it never occurred to you that these things have been created with a purpose? Things that have been created with a purpose simply *work*."

I snatched the crossbow back and clutched the quarrel in my other hand. "Well…nobody told me," I grumbled. "You could have told me last night. *When I asked*. I do recall asking stuff."

"You don't ask the right questions."

"What *are* the right questions?"

He smiled. "You're getting warmer."

"You know what? This is bullshit. I'm tired of your Yoda answers. Why don't you just cut the crap and tell me?"

"Where would be the fun in that?"

I slapped the bolt in place and swung the crossbow toward him, aiming for his heart. "I'm not messing around. Either you start talking or so help me God…"

Genuine fear crossed over his face and he froze. "Don't."

I couldn't help it. I dropped it to my thigh. He looked so lost, so forlorn. So human. "I won't be able to do this. If it looks human like you do, I won't be able to do this."

"Humans," he said quietly. "You have too much compassion. It is one of your great faults."

"Yeah, well. You should be lucky I have that 'great fault' or you'd be wearing a hole about now."

He looked down at his decidedly untouched chest. "Quite." He waited for me to remove the bolt completely and stick it back in its place on the shaft. I aimed the crossbow toward the floor and pulled the trigger, releasing the taut bowstring. It twanged harmlessly, but it had shaken my arm when it fired.

"I don't think I can do this."

He sighed and touched my shoulder gently. He swept the crossbow up, plucking it from my hand, and laid it down on the counter. His other hand had not stopped touching my shoulder and now closed over it warmly. I glanced at the Booke for something like confirmation that the contact was safe.

He turned me toward him and for once, his eyes seemed full of concern. "You *can* do this. The book…chose you. You can."

"What do you mean, it chose me?"

"It…sleeps. For centuries, sometimes. And then…when the right one comes along…it awakens."

I blinked. "But that makes no sense. It seems that it wants to contain these things that get loose. So why would it 'awaken' just so some poor schmuck like me or Constance Howland is duped into opening it again?"

His eyes searched mine. "Even inanimate objects get bored."

I pushed him away but he still held me tight. "Is everything a joke to you?"

"I like that! I finally tell you something about the book and you refuse to believe it."

"But it doesn't make sense!"

"What about any of this makes sense to you?"

That stopped me. It took only a moment for me to burst out laughing. He was still holding my shoulders as I laughed into his face. I thought by his expression that he would yell at me. Maybe I hurt his demon sensibilities, but he surprised me instead by laughing with me.

Deep dimples scored his cheeks and his eyes grew soft with his laughter.

I eased out of his grip and stepped back. He stopped laughing and straightened. His hair fell to either side again, shadowing his face. "And so," he muttered. "So you see that logic does not necessarily dictate the demon realm."

"So I do see."

He looked around the back room as if searching for a distraction. He wrinkled his nose. "Tea!" he said with disdain.

"Yes, well it is a tea shop. Bound to have tea in it."

"No doubt this is the Powers That Be's sense of humor at play."

"No doubt." I shuffled. "Well…do you like coffee? I can make some coffee for you. If you'd like."

I didn't think I could ever get used to his undisguised astonishment at my very human pleasantries.

"I…yes. I will drink your coffee."

"Wow. Okay. Didn't expect that." Off I went to the kitchen to make coffee for my friendly neighborhood demon. And to think I had to move all the way from California to Maine for this.

I had just poured him a cup (black, of course) when I heard a knock. I poked my head out of the kitchen to stare at the front door. Through the wavy glass, I recognized the tall figure of the sheriff. I trotted to the door, took a deep breath, and opened it. "Sheriff," I greeted. "What can I do for you?"

"Ms. Strange. May I come in?"

I opened the door wider and let him enter. He took off his hat and moved the brim around in his hands. "Ms. Strange, can you tell me where you were last night between the hours of seven and midnight?"

At least this time I had a decent alibi. "I was with Doc Boone. Why?"

"Wiccan night," he muttered. "So the Doc can vouch for you?"

"Why would he need to vouch for me?" I braced for the news.

"There was another one. Someone else died last night. Just like the last one."

"So am I in the clear, then?"

"Yeah." He lowered his hat to his thigh. "Heck, you were just a person of interest. We sure didn't suspect you of…well. It's all mighty strange."

"That's the name of the game," I said, smiling. I rocked on my heels. Sheriff Bradbury's *aw shucks* manner was appealing. Especially when he wasn't accusing me of murder.

He caught the joke. "Ah, sure. 'Strange.' Must have been a fun name to have in school. Unless…" He raised his dark brows. "Unless that's a married name." His eyes dropped to my empty left hand.

Subtle. I couldn't help but smile, though. "Uh…no. Maiden name. Never married."

"Well that's…that's just fine." He swept his hat up onto his head. He was making ready to leave when he glanced over my shoulder toward the backroom and a frown suddenly creased his pleasant face. "Who's that?"

Crikey. I forgot about Erasmus.

He stood in the doorway, duster sweeping around him, face dark and unreadable under the shade of his long black hair. Sheriff Bradbury was immediately on alert. His hand lingered by his pistol in its holster as he edged me out of the way.

"Sir, may I speak to you?"

Erasmus hadn't moved from his place in the doorway. "About what, Sheriff?"

Sheriff Ed tensed. I did, too. I didn't know what the hell Erasmus was doing. Why couldn't he just disappear like he did the other day?

Ed moved slightly closer to Erasmus, who barely blinked. "I just have a few questions for you, sir."

"Ask your questions," he said through gritted teeth.

"Are you Erasmus Dark?"

Erasmus nodded.

"This young lady says that you knew about the murder of Karl Waters before we contacted her. Would you mind explaining that?"

Erasmus narrowed his eyes. I knew he was about to say something strangely enigmatic which was sure to get us both in trouble. So I piped up with, "He has a police scanner."

Sheriff Ed looked at me. "I thought you said you didn't know this man."

"He's an old friend…from California. From a long time ago.

He arrived just yesterday. An old friend. He…uh…changed his name and I didn't recognize him at first…"

He turned back to Erasmus, who was now looking at me curiously. "That true?" Ed asked.

"Whatever she says," he drawled.

I had never lied to the law before, but here I was looking him right in the eye. "The truth of the matter is…we used to punk each other. All the time. And I'm afraid I might have gone a little overboard yesterday. Punking. Sorry."

I tried not to wince. Sheriff Ed blinked at me. "That's some serious punking. That kind of thing can get you both thrown in jail."

"I'm so sorry, Sheriff. Really. It was incredibly stupid. We just fell into old habits."

I hated that he was angry with me now. He turned to Erasmus. "You wouldn't mind showing me some ID, would you?"

"And what, pray, is that?"

"He means your identification, Erasmus," I said more calmly than I felt.

He pointed at me—at the amulet on my chest. "But *you* have it."

I laughed, a little hysterically. "Yeah, I do. I…uh. Well, I washed his trousers with the ID in it and it's now drying. Because I spilled coffee on him. Accidentally."

Sheriff Ed was noncommittal. He took a deep breath and his tense shoulders seemed to relax somewhat. "I see. Is he staying here? With you?" He didn't seem happy about that prospect, which gave my stomach a little flutter.

"No," I said at the same time Erasmus stepped forward out of the doorway and said, "Yes."

I glared at Erasmus. What the hell did he think he was doing?

He raised his chin defiantly toward the sheriff.

Ed stood his ground. "Okay. I'll let the two of you work this out."

He turned to leave and I stopped him. "But you never told me. What happened? Who…died?"

"Bob Hitchins, from the grocery store."

My hand flew to my mouth. "Oh no!"

"Same thing as Karl Waters. All the moisture was drained out of him. Damnedest thing you ever saw."

"Are there any leads?"

He straightened his hat and adjusted his jacket. "No, miss. Nothing I can share with the public."

I had to think fast. I knew the sheriff could really help us here. But there was no way he would believe the things I needed to tell him. Especially with the suspicious glares he was throwing toward Erasmus, and Erasmus, the idiot, was throwing equally suspicious glares back at Ed. What was he up to?

"I'm glad you stopped by, Sheriff," I said, steering him toward the door. "Please drop by anytime. You know, when you're off duty. Maybe get a cup of my specialty tea and a scone or two."

He seemed to snap out of it, looking down at me with genuine interest again. "That would be very nice."

Yes, it would, I thought, feeling his taut bicep through his heavy jacket. No ring on *his* left hand either.

"Thanks for stopping by."

"Yes, well, we don't know what we're up against, Ms. Strange."

"Call me Kylie."

"Kylie." He smiled. "We…we don't know who's out there doing this. Best to keep your door locked, and don't fraternize with strangers." His eyes drifted toward Erasmus again.

"She won't," he said, striding into the room. "I'll make certain of that."

"Kind of hard to do that when I have a shop to run," I said, stepping in front of Erasmus. "I mean, it's all about keeping the doors open and welcoming strangers."

Ed conceded with a courteous nod. "You know what I mean. Be careful." And he was out the door.

I wheeled on Erasmus. "What the hell was that? Why didn't you just bug out of here like you did last time?"

"I wanted to see this sheriff. Law enforcement intrigues me. Has done since the Inquisition."

"We're a little more civilized now."

"I've seen no evidence to support that."

"Just…stay out of sight next time, okay? And what do you mean, you're staying here?"

"In a sense. I can't very well go very far now, can I? Not when you retain that which is not yours to keep."

My fingers twitched over the amulet again. "It's by necessity. You know I wouldn't keep it otherwise."

His anger seemed to melt away. "I know," he said softly.

"Right." I looked around at the opened boxes and the boxes yet to be opened. "I have work to do. It would go faster if you helped, made yourself useful."

He suddenly looked appalled. "I think not."

"Come on. You said you're staying here. Why don't you earn your keep?"

"I'm earning it by helping you contain the creature from the book. I should think that was adequate enough."

"And yet, we still don't know what it is or how to find it."

"Your little witches were working that out, weren't they?"

"But *you* know for certain."

"That's where you are wrong. I *don't* know for certain. I only know with *un*certainty."

"That's better than nothing."

"Uncertainty is *not* better than nothing. Where in Beelze's name did you learn your appalling logic?"

"Uh…I don't…"

"Clearly. I'll be back when your witches arrive."

"But…" No use. He'd disappeared again.

• • •

I knew I had a lot to do at the shop, but after an hour of unpacking and sorting, I just couldn't stand it there any longer. I had to get out. After a moment of consideration, I wrapped the crossbow in a coat and took it with me. One couldn't be too careful, after all. I placed it in the passenger side of the Jeep and started up the car.

Driving aimlessly up the highway, I didn't have anywhere in particular in mind. I just needed to clear my head and see if I couldn't get any ideas on hunting a succubus, whatever that was.

I found myself driving slowly in front of the Gifford Corner Museum. Yellow police tape surrounded the building. I didn't know what I expected to see. There was no one there. All the techs had gone, but the warning tape remained. And the lights were dark inside. I took a moment to mourn poor Karl Waters. I couldn't help but feel that it was my fault he was killed. It wasn't fair that these innocent people got in the way. It raised my concern for the Wiccans exponentially. But if anyone could work on a safeguard, it was Doc Boone. I was sure of it.

I pulled into the parking lot. Stepping out of the Jeep, I stood at the edge of the police tape for a moment before I ducked under it and walked slowly toward the museum entrance across the gravel.

Peering into the dark window of the door, I shielded my eyes with my cupped hands. Looked like there had been a fight. Whatever happened, Karl had not gone quietly. Or perhaps the destruction had happened afterward. Maybe the creature *had* been looking for information. I'd have to ask Doc Boone if he could get more out of his coroner friend without arousing suspicion.

I touched the doorknob and was surprised when it turned in my hand. Looking hastily behind me, I pushed open the door and went inside. Almost immediately I felt something odd, cold. Different. Like the absence of something. Like a hole in space.

I knew I shouldn't be going *toward* this strangeness, but approaching it made some kind of sense, at least the new wacky reality of sense that seemed to characterize my life in Moody Bog. I needed to know. I needed to see that it was all real. And despite the pulsating feelings I was getting from the Booke—even as far away as it was from me right now—I had to confirm whatever happened here for myself.

I walked to the front counter. There were notes and tape and bits of papers everywhere. Some looked like they might be from Karl's files and some were obviously from the police techs.

I walked past the counter to the stacks behind it. A smell. Not of death, not like I had feared. But something else. Metallic. Sharp. Like a match was struck. And it got colder the deeper inside I ventured. Colder and darker. Yet even though my heart was pounding, I couldn't stop. I drew closer to...whatever it was.

The place Karl died.

Tape outlined on the floor. And also faint chalk lines, but nothing to do with the shape of a body. And stubs of black candles. What the...?

There was also a hole here. Not a physical one, or at least one that could be seen by ordinary means, but a hole nonetheless. Whatever it was that the Booke did—open a door or a gateway—it had opened here. And it was still open. How the hell was I supposed to fight a hole?

Suddenly I could see my breath. It fogged around my mouth and nose as if I were in an icy place, even though the thermostat on the nearby wall showed it was 62 degrees.

I looked deep into the dark ahead of me, the dark between the shelves. "H-hello?"

I didn't expect an answer. Didn't really want one.

And then I realized I'd left my crossbow in the car.

Now *there's* a sentence I never thought I'd say.

I backed away from the "nothing" and stopped when the sound of voices—many voices all chorusing together but making no sense—issued from it.

"Okaaay. Not good."

I backed away quicker. But not quick enough. Something closed over my wrist...and yanked. I screamed. Resisting the tug with all my might, I pulled hard, even though there was nothing to see. I turned toward the sound of something whistling behind me and instinctively opened my hand. I stared when the crossbow smacked into it.

No time to be amazed. It was already cocked with a bolt in place. I swung it up to my shoulder with my free hand and aimed it toward the hole, which had begun to glow a dull green. A shriek pierced the air and my wrist was released. I felt the hole recede and get smaller. It didn't close completely, but it certainly seemed less dangerous.

I swung the crossbow this way and that. There was nothing to fire at, so I didn't pull the trigger. Backing away toward the door, I never lowered it until I was outside.

My heart pounded. An unseen hand grabbing my wrist, the crossbow coming automatically to my aid out of nowhere, and a hole of evil? It was shaping up to be quite a week.

When I turned, I found myself facing a group of leather-clad bikers. And they were smiling.

CHAPTER NINE

There were four of them, and one was a woman. She was about my age, thin but with a big bust that made me think, "boob job." Her stringy red hair hung down her back in a long braid, and on her neck was a serpent tattoo that scrolled down into her t-shirt and disappeared to god-knew-where. She also had a nasty scar on her cheek that looked like it might have been from a knife.

One of the men stood slightly in front of the others, and I wondered if he was the leader. He was tall and broad-shouldered. Under different circumstances, I might have called him good-looking. His face, under its dark hair and beard, reminded me a bit of the sheriff's, but that was where the resemblance ended. He, too, had tats on the parts of his arms I could see, and a silver skull earring hung from his left lobe.

The man to his right was tall and wiry, with dirty blond hair. He reminded me of a farm boy, and he looked like he'd be right at home in overalls.

The other to his left was a husky skinhead with an upside-down pentagram tattooed on the side of his head. Ouch.

"Uh…hi there," I said, sort of saluting with the crossbow.

The leader edged forward. "Nice weapon. Can I see?"

"Oh…" I backed toward the Jeep, though I noticed the bikes were parked in a line right behind it. "You know I just got it and I'm a little reluctant to pass it around just yet."

"I just want to look," he said, taking another step closer.

"She said no, Doug," said the woman. "And no means no. Right?" She smiled, indicating she meant the opposite.

I'd had biker acquaintances back at the beach, so I generally wasn't afraid of them. I knew a lot of the posturing was just for show. At least with the guys I knew. But these guys were an unknown quantity. They shifted closer, and the more they did, the more hemmed in I felt.

"Kind of weird, you stopping here with this police tape on the building," I said, giving it my best dumb brunette.

"As weird as your stopping here?" said Doug, edging closer.

Touché. And my explanation was probably as lame as his would be. I tried another tack. "Well," I squeaked. "I've got to be getting along now."

"What's your hurry?"

"I have work to do. Lots of stuff. You know."

"But you have time for one beer, don't you?"

"Doug," warned the woman.

"Shut up, Charise," he said out of the side of his mouth. "How about it, pretty lady? Have a beer with us."

"It's a little early for me…"

They closed ranks and I was effectively trapped. Even if I could make it to the Jeep, there was no guarantee of locking them out and bashing through those bikes. And then they'd *really* be mad.

"Just one," said Doug. "We can talk about this crazy crossbow of yours." The others exchanged glances. Not Doug. He was still looking steadily at me, rocking slightly on his boot heels, and smiling. "There's a place up the road."

Gifford Corner was one lonely place, and now it was down by one resident. There was only sporadic traffic along the highway, and I couldn't see anyone in the one-pump gas station across the street. For all I knew, these guys owned that. Heart racing, I didn't see any alternative. "Okay," I said breathlessly. "I'll follow you there."

"How about you ride along with me? It's just up the road."

My heart had been thundering already from my encounter with the vortex of evil and hadn't had a chance to settle down yet. All of my instincts were telling me to get the hell out of there, but I didn't see that I could just make a break for the car. Besides, the crossbow was thrumming in my hand. Could I really use it on a person? I started to raise it when something caught my eye.

Doug moved, exposing his throat. And there, shining from beneath the leather jacket on his chest was a necklace with a pendant; a pendant with the face of a demon, just like mine.

My hand automatically went to my throat to touch the amulet hiding under my shirt. It was an impossible coincidence if he just happened to get one from the local Hot Topic, with green jewels for eyes instead of red.

I guess that decided it for me. "Sure," I said warily.

Doug smiled, revealing a gold eyetooth. He gestured me toward the bikes.

Oh shit, oh shit, oh shit! I clenched the crossbow for dear life and walked to the back of my Jeep, wondering if I'd ever see it again.

They looked like newer bikes. I knew a little about motorcycles, but not a lot. Though they all had the classic peanut fuel tanks, they also had fat front wheels, slammed handlebars, and blockhead engines. They were clean with shiny chrome and smooth leather. Not bad rides. It was just the company I didn't like.

Doug got on the black bike on the far right. Then he looked at me over his shoulder. I gave one more look around to see if there wasn't any help and blew out a breath. *It's you and me, chthonic crossbow.* I mounted behind him, getting a good look at the emblem of their club on the back of his leather jacket. An upside-down pentagram with a goat-faced dude with bat wings. It was surrounded by the words *Ordo Dexterae Diaboli*, whatever that meant. I had no choice but to slide one arm around him and tuck the crossbow into my side to keep it safe and out of the wind. He kick-started and the engine roared to life.

The others quickly mounted their own Harleys and dual engines deafened me. He peeled out and I held on tight. Cold wind slapped my face and my breath whooshed out of me. My heart still hammered, because who knew what I was getting into now. Was it better than that evil vortex?

I kept my eye on the road and glanced at our companions flanking their leader. I wondered about my chances if I just jumped off, but we were going a bit too fast to even consider it. I just hoped we really were going to a bar and not some deserted cabin in the woods.

I tightened my hold on the crossbow.

We seemed to be driving forever. My hand around his waist was freezing to numbness and my face was definitely feeling the burn.

Finally, we slowed as we got to a bend in the road, and I saw a structure that looked like a wooden stable with a corrugated metal roof. It had a long porch following its face, with lots of bikes parked in rows in front. "Mike's," said the sign.

We pulled in, the others coasting in right next to Doug into their spaces. He killed the engine and everything suddenly quieted, though my ears rang. I got off quickly and stood back, checking out every possible escape. Just this bar surrounded by forest. The others dismounted and headed in. Doug gestured me forward. I clutched the crossbow to my chest, followed the others up to the wooden porch, and went inside. I was instantly hit with warmth and smells of sweat, stale beer, and oily fries. The jukebox played grinding rock music.

Some of the pool players greeted the gang with calls and arms waving. The place was fairly crowded for a Tuesday afternoon and most of the tables were occupied. But as my group made their way through, there was an empty booth, which seemed to be reserved for them. I was aware of people's gazes. I didn't know if they were staring at me—a decidedly un-biker chick with no tats—or the crossbow I was holding.

They made me slide in first so I was hemmed in. Beers were ordered and I tried not to look like I was scared out of my wits. Although I felt just the tiniest bit hopeful that we were in a public setting and maybe they couldn't try anything here.

"Okay, pretty thing," said Doug, swiveling toward me. "Why don't you tell us about this crossbow?"

I swallowed a hot lump in my throat. "Hey, how about some names? I mean I'm new around here. It's, uh, nice to meet new people."

He grinned and turned toward his friends. They didn't seem to share in his merriment and looked on with stoic faces. "She's right. I'm Doug. This here's Charise," and he gestured toward the woman. She had a ring in one of her nostrils, now that I had a better look. "That's Bob Willis," he said, pointing to the man who looked like a farm boy, "and this is Dean Fitch." The skinhead only raised a brow when Doug said his name. "The whole family. And, uh, *you* are?"

"Oh. Kylie. Kylie Strange." Charise chuckled at my name. "I'm…I'm over in Moody Bog."

"Kylie," said Doug, scooting closer. "And what's a nice girl like you doing with a crossbow like this?"

"Well, it was a gift."

"A gift." He shared a glance with the others but didn't move away, even when the waitress—a woman with more rings and pins in her face than I was comfortable looking at—brought the beers and set them down in front of all of us. He waited for her to leave before he slid his arm over the seat back, edging closer to me. "And what were *you* doing behind that police tape at Waters's place?"

"Oh, you know. Just…looking around. Could never resist police tape." I tried to stare him down, but I was no good at it. I could stare down a demon, but not these guys. They somehow scared me more. I dropped my gaze to my lap and shook my head. "Karl Waters was helping me with something and the next thing I know he was killed. I just wanted to know if he left something for me."

"This crossbow, maybe?" He reached for it but I twisted away.

"No! This was mine. I brought it for protection."

He leaned in so far I could smell his beer breath, and that was before he'd taken a drink. "Protection from what?" he rasped.

Charise reached over the table and snatched the crossbow out of my hand before I could squeak a protest. "Just take the fucking thing," she said, shaking her head in exasperation.

I sat stunned. I had somehow thought she wouldn't be able to take it. She was studying it and the others were gawking, trying to reach over her to touch it, but she shied away. "Hands off!" she cried. "I'm lookin' at it."

"You want that, baby?" said Doug. "Maybe Kylie will give it to you as a present."

"I think she already did." She smirked and rested the crossbow on her raised knee.

Maybe it was the Booke, maybe the crossbow, but I suddenly got my wind up. "No, I didn't. I'd like that back, please."

They all laughed, Charise the loudest. "Oh, you would, would you?" Her face suddenly changed to a grimace. "Try and take it, bitch."

Something was compelling me not to back down. "I don't want any trouble, but I really think you need to return that." My voice was a little shaky, but my expression was determined.

Charise stroked the weapon and looked at me through her long, fake lashes. "Why should I?"

"'Cause it doesn't belong to you."

She snorted a laugh and rocked her head back.

Doug glanced at Charise and her uncomfortable stroking of the crossbow. "Just where did you come from?"

At first I thought he was talking to the crossbow, but when his gaze shifted to mine again, I straightened.

"California."

He laughed. "Oh really. With *that*?"

"I don't see how it's any of your business. I'd like to go now. *With* my crossbow, if you don't mind."

He leaned in, a little too close into my personal space. "Well, I'll tell you, little lady. The thing of it is, we need that. It's a very special crossbow. We're on a sort of…mission."

"Oh yeah? So am I. And I need it, too. And…and I had it first." He was scary, all right, but strangely appealing at the same time. And then a little itch in the back of my head chased some of the fear away and gave me pause. "Why were *you* at the museum… and why do you know about this crossbow?"

He smiled. "We were sent there. By a…friend."

The amulet.

My skin broke out in gooseflesh. I had unwittingly moved from California to Demon Central. Crap.

His eyes narrowed, gaze tracing over my amulet. It had slipped from my shirt and I had unconsciously covered it with my hand. He didn't touch it but he nodded. "Are you a mage?"

"A what?"

"Kylie, Kylie." He shook his head. "It's not nice to ignore other practitioners in the area. At the very least, you should have introduced yourself. That smacks as…unfriendly."

"I'm not a mage," I stammered. "Or a practitioner of whatever. I just sell tea and herbs. That's it."

He gestured to the amulet. "This says otherwise."

"I don't care what you think it says."

He glanced around at his companions before he turned back to me. "Okay. You want to play it this way? That's fine. But know this. We don't play nice. We don't share. This is our territory. I've got plans. And I don't intend to be just a slacker in this shit-kicking berg much longer. Always in the shadow of others. Me and my… my posse, here…have plans, see? We've got that promise straight from a…greater authority…that we'll earn our reward. And that little item there—" He pointed to the crossbow. "—is our ticket."

My heart had been pounding before, but now it was doing double time. If he had a demon amulet, then it meant he, too, had a demon on the hook. Maybe one that wasn't as friendly as Erasmus Dark.

"Who *are* you guys?" I rasped.

Doug smiled but it never reached his eyes. "People you don't want to cross."

"If you know about the crossbow," I said quietly, gaining courage from the thrumming weapon, "and this," and I raised my amulet, "then you know...*I* shouldn't be messed with either." Shakily, I raised my chin. I tried to rise but Doug pushed me back.

"I'll ask you again. Where'd you get it?"

I blinked but said nothing. No way was I going to rat out Erasmus. And I definitely wasn't going to mention the Booke.

Doug bit his lip then pulled a hand over his beard. "You could...you could join us."

"Doug," warned Charise.

"Be *part* of our plan."

"Doug!" Charise was more insistent.

He turned to her. "*What?*"

She fiddled with the crossbow. Her red lips twisted. "We don't know anything about her. Just because she has *this*...and that amulet..."

"Yeah," said Dean, the skinhead. He turned his suspicious gaze on me. "We don't know her."

"I don't like it," said Farm Boy Bob. "Let's just take the crossbow and go. That's what Shabiri told us to do—"

Doug slammed his hand on the table. "Shut *up*!"

His gang quieted. Charise smoothed her hand over my crossbow, and I didn't like the feeling I got from her hands all over it, as if she were touching something precious to me. I was really getting pissed off at these weird feelings of possessiveness, and I entirely blamed Erasmus for them.

Doug turned back to me then, his gaze steady.

"You say you're up in Moody Bog?"

"Yeah." My eyes darted around the noisy bar.

Charise was yanking on one of the bolts but it wouldn't budge from its slot. "Piece of shit," she muttered. But in a whiney voice and with a coquettish tilt of her head that didn't match the outward package, she said, "*Doug*. This doesn't work."

"What's that, baby?"

She showed him by yanking harder on the bolt. I bit my lip, worried she would break it. "It doesn't come out. None of them come out."

Bob leaned over her, reaching for a quarrel. "Maybe you're not doing it right."

She slapped his hand and he drew back. The look on his face was pathetic, like a little boy getting slapped by his mother. "Don't touch it! It's mine."

She fiddled with it some more, and sighed dramatically. "*Doug*," she whined again. "Make her show us."

Like an electric jolt running through me, I felt the need to *move*. Not just because of how hemmed in I was or because of the greater circumstances of my being forced to be here, but because I was being compelled. There was no other word for it. My limbs buzzed uncomfortably as much as they had on the back of the bike. I didn't think. I just reacted.

I was suddenly up on the seat back, and I sprang over it, landing feet-first on the floor. I didn't know *how* I did it, but I had clearly somersaulted over the bench and made as perfect a landing as a superhero. Before I could be further shocked by my out-of-character actions, the crossbow suddenly slapped into my hands. It was armed. I swung it up, aiming the business end at a shocked Doug, who only had time to swivel in his seat.

Charise screamed. "Did you see that? Did you *see* that?"

"Shut up, Charise," said Doug, eyes glued to the crossbow.

They were all staring at me. And if the drop in noise of the place was any indication, everyone else was staring at me, too.

The pool players froze, cues in hand, mouths agape. The bartender stopped in mid-pour. Patrons at tables suddenly fell silent. Only the jukebox continued to churn its music into the bar.

I licked my lips. "So…I'd like to go back to my car now." The thrumming from the crossbow was so intense that I felt slightly light-headed, but also empowered in an electric sort of way, with energy pulsing through my veins and pinging off my joints. I felt I could take on anyone in the place.

Chthonic crossbow: my new best friend!

Doug slowly pushed his way from the seat, dislodging the gangly Bob. Bob stumbled up, and allowed Doug to stand in front of him. I kept my aim on Doug. "If you aren't going to join us," he growled, "then you're against us."

"I'm not *anything*," I insisted. "I just want to be left alone."

"Then I recommend you and your crossbow stay out of Hansen Mills."

"Jesus Christ!" huffed Bob. "Just take the thing back, Doug!"

Doug glared at him. "You want to get shot with that? Be my guest." Bob hesitated. "And that's why I'm the leader, ass-wipe."

"She can't touch us," said Bob, still hesitant, body tense and coiled. "We've got the talisman, too. We have *Shabiri*—"

"Shut the hell up, Willis!" His wild eyes took in the shocked patrons. He cocked his head at them and Bob finally slumped back.

Everyone was still in standoff mode, and I wondered how long I could maintain it. Bob Willis still seemed itching to take me on, crossbow or no. Dean, with his skinhead tattoo, had pushed his way out of the bench along with Charise, and kept his steady gaze on me, as if looking for holes in my defenses. And Charise had her sharp-nailed hands curled into claws, anxious to scratch my eyes out.

Finally, after too long a pause, Doug said, "Dean, take her back."

The skinhead choked. "Me? Why me? I haven't finished my beer."

Doug swung toward him and bared his teeth. His amulet dangled free, its dark green-jeweled eyes seemed to glow for a moment. "Because I told you to."

"Jesus Christ," muttered Dean. He slowly grabbed for his keys from his back pocket, which were hanging from a long, braided thong of leather that looked like a sawed-off bullwhip.

I backed toward the door, never lowering the crossbow. "Uh… thanks for the beer."

"Don't mention it," Charise bit out. She eyed my crossbow with an envious glare.

"We're just going to let her go?" said Bob.

Doug stepped aside for Dean. "Yeah. For now. Take her back to her car."

"Why don't we ask her—"

"Willis," he growled. "Learn when to shut the fuck up."

I moved past the jukebox, pleased, until Doug jerked forward, making me startle against the doorjamb. "Just the one warning, Kylie Strange." His brown eyes bored into mine. "Keep to your side of the hill. It'll be safer that way. There isn't enough room from more than one practitioner around here."

I nodded. "Okaaay." I slid through the doorway, backing toward the bikes in the parking lot, waiting for a reluctant Dean Fitch to join me.

• • •

The ride back was just as cold. And the engine even louder, if that were possible, and full of vibrations that tingled my legs unpleasantly. I got a good look at that tattoo on the side of his shiny head: an upside-down pentagram. Just like the one on the backs of their matching leather jackets.

He pulled up behind my car and skidded to a stop, throwing up a spray of gravel right against my Jeep's paint job. He grinned when I gave him a sour look. I hopped off.

I was just able to bite out, "What was all that about?" before he turned away from me, and with a roar of the throttle, he sped back up the road toward Hansen Mills.

I stood for a long time just staring up the road until I shook myself loose. I had dodged a bullet, that was for sure. I was lucky to have escaped unscathed.

But when I thought about my exchange with Doug, my stomach did a butterfly jamboree. He had said he was sent by a "friend" to get the crossbow. And he had an amulet, too. That meant only one thing in my mind. Doug's posse had a demon helper as well. And that could not be good.

I looked down at the crossbow, which had disarmed itself again. "Nice crossbow," I cooed, petting it. "Thanks for getting me out of a jam."

Now what?

I opened the car door, set the crossbow reverently on the passenger's seat, and sat for a long moment. My legs had suddenly turned to jelly and I was hyperventilating. I leaned forward and rested my forehead on the steering wheel, getting my breathing under control before I looked up.

The crossroad was still deserted. I zoomed down the highway back to my shop, parked a little lopsidedly, and hurried back inside, locking the door behind me. I tossed the crossbow to a chair and whipped off my coat, hurling it at the hall tree. I glared at the Booke. "This is all your fault!"

I stomped over to the desk where it sat, threw it open, and grabbed a pen. On the first blank page I started to write through the sudden tears in my eyes:

This insane Booke has come into my life and given me a huge headache.

The blue ink stayed visible for only a moment before it disappeared, sinking into the parchment as if it never was.

Oh, no you don't! I penned.

It disappeared smoothly.

I threw the pen down. "Dammit!"

I screamed when hands warmed my shoulders.

"There is no use," Erasmus said softly, holding me in place. "It will only take in the words it needs to see."

"I was almost eaten by a vortex," I said shakily.

"I shouldn't be surprised." He released me and stepped away.

"And attacked by a biker gang."

"That…I did not know about."

"You know, it would really help if you warned me about this stuff before I get sucked into some vortex."

"I wouldn't have allowed that."

"Nice to know. But you weren't exactly there. That crossbow, however, did seem to come to the rescue."

"Yes, it's good at that."

"And there's something else. Those bikers. One of them had an amulet just like yours."

His hands squeezed my shoulders just a little too tightly. "Listen very carefully. What color were the eyes?"

I swallowed. "G-green."

He released me at once. "Beelze's tail," he muttered.

"They've got a demon helping them, haven't they?"

Erasmus wouldn't look at me, but he nodded curtly.

"And…you know who it is."

He nodded again. And then he turned. "It doesn't matter. You still have a job to do."

"But what about this other demon? Doesn't that complicate things? What's going on?"

"Nothing to concern yourself over. I'll see to it that you do not get abducted again."

"But those bikers were there, where Karl—" Forget the succubus. I was beginning to think that those bikers killed Karl in some sort of ritual. With a little demon help.

My adrenaline was seeping away. It had kept me going the whole time but now it was leaving me and I felt weak-kneed. I dropped into the chair and put my head in my hands. Anything could have happened to me. Anything! That vortex, those bikers. I couldn't help it. I burst into tears.

I hugged myself and wiped at my face. I hadn't even done this when I finally broke up with my ass-hat of a boyfriend. I sobbed uncontrollably, just letting it all out.

"Beelze's tail," Erasmus muttered. "Don't do that."

I think I tried to tell him that it was my party and I'd cry if I wanted to, but it just came out as more sobs.

He shuffled uncertainly before me. "Why are you crying? Damn mortal women and their tears! It's useless, I tell you. Stop it at once."

I took a deep breath and wiped my face sloppily with my hand. "You're so comforting." Jumping up, I searched for a tissue from the kitchen. There were none to be had so I grabbed a paper towel from the roll and wiped my face and blew my nose. Erasmus followed me. "Okay. I'm better now. Your pep talk did me wonders," I added sourly.

I walked back into the desk alcove and stood over the Booke. The parchment under my fingertips felt dry and brittle and I turned pages, just to look at them, all those blank pages. "Do you know what that evil hole, that vortex was? Is?"

"It is…disconcerting."

"Yeah. An understatement."

"You're not hurt?"

It was only then I noticed his hand encircling my wrist. Its warm presence soothed but at the same time spiked something that had lain dormant within me.

His face had lost its sneer, its predatory sharpness. It smoothed to something like concern and that unsettled me. It seemed so human. The notion unfurled a knot of anger in my gut. How dare he look human when he wasn't? What did his concern even mean?

I slipped my hand free of him and leaned back against the desk, crossing my arms. "Those biker guys. They wanted the crossbow. They know what it is. They were told."

Erasmus grew thoughtful. "Yes. Who are they exactly?"

I shrugged. "Just some biker guys with an upside-down pentagram as a logo. Along with a goat guy."

"'Goat guy'?"

"You know. A guy with a goat head and bat wings."

Erasmus cursed under his breath.

"What? What is it?"

"It is nothing. Merely a complication."

"A complication that doesn't sound good for me. One of them wanted me to join them, and the others thought it wasn't a good idea. They seemed scared of me."

"I don't blame them."

I gave him a withering look. Then I thought about Karl again. "Are we sure it was a succubus that killed Karl? Could it have been a demon?"

He rolled the thought over in his mind. "It *could* have been. But we know the book was opened and we know that two men died in the same way. It is likely that the culprit is our creature."

"It's likely, but not certain."

"Nothing is certain."

My gaze was dragged back toward the Booke again. What was it about this thing? All sorts of nastiness seemed to stem from it. No wonder Howland walled it up. She thought she was doing the future a solid. Until I stumbled along.

It made me think of the terrified look on her face as she ran for the edge of the cliff. "So. Care to tell me what happened to the last volunteer?"

"Howland?" He moved into the kitchen area, turned toward the old maple table, and pulled out a chair. He sat, and his long pale fingers drew patterns on the wood. For all I knew, he was cursing the place. "She got careless. Got herself caught by the authorities. She thought the book was best walled up and hidden. That's not how it works."

I glared at the Booke. "So how *does* it work? You say it will only take the writing it wants to see. Which is…?"

"About the creature you must capture and subdue. You subdue it, the book captures it when you write it down."

"That's so weird. Why does it wait for a victim like me to open again? And don't give me that crap about 'even inanimate objects get bored,'" I said in my best imitation of his posh accent.

The old sneer was back along with a deep sigh. "The book lies in wait. It was…created by Others long ago, those that oppose the Powers That Be. The Powers do not condone the release of the creatures into this realm, and so they must be retrieved and subdued. It was they who…attached a demon to it…"

"You?"

"Yes. The book, however, is very old and comes with its own set of rules. It's been waiting."

"If the Powers That Be don't like all these creatures getting out, then why don't they just destroy the Booke?"

He rolled his eyes and glanced toward the kitchen. "Do you have any more of that coffee?"

"Wait a second." I leaned in. "Answer the question. Why don't they just destroy it?"

He shrugged. "Because they clearly do not wish to."

I just breathed. He regarded me with dark eyes. They looked like they were trying to figure me out, genuinely curious. And then they'd flick down to that amulet again with a hungry expression.

I covered it with my hand.

"So what happened to Constance Howland?"

"It all depends on whom you ask. Coffee?"

"Jeez, all right!" I stomped toward the kitchen. He remained at the table, hands still on the wood as he watched me prepare the beans, empty the grounds into the basket of a French press, and turn on the fire under the kettle.

"What about her being chased by some dark figure and jumping over the cliff?" I asked as I worked. "Or was she pushed?" He continued to draw his patterns, not looking at me. "Was it you? Were you chasing her to her doom?" I stepped away from the counter and stood over him, gripping my elbows. "Are you going to do that to me, too?"

Deliberately, he lifted his head until he was looking me in the eye. Those eyes of his. Dark and roiling with unidentifiable power and emotion. He kicked the chair back and stood. He was nearly a foot taller than me.

"That was a long time ago," he whispered.

"That's not answering the question."

He spun away, black duster swirling around his legs. "There are things I must not discuss with you."

"Like what really happened?" I shook my head and backed away. "I don't like this. I don't like any of this. I think, maybe, you should leave."

Hurt flickered over his eyes before it disappeared quickly. "I still have much to impart to you."

"I'll get what I need from my Wiccans."

He snorted. "Those? They are not mages. They can only offer minimal help and protection. And believe me, you'll need far more than that."

That word again, "mages." And "practitioners." What was the point in asking him about it? He'd only give me more circular answers. "I've gotten along fine so far." I swallowed. "But I can't trust you. You're a demon, after all."

"You don't know what you're talking about."

"Maybe so. But I need real help. And I just can't trust you to give it."

Anger and hurt flared in his eyes.

"You never answer my questions," I whispered.

Shoving the chair harshly against the table, he stomped through the kitchen doorway. I followed and leaned against the jamb, watching him grab the front door handle.

"I've done what I could," he ranted. "No one can say I didn't."

"Better check that with your Powers That Be."

He looked momentarily horrified before he masked it again with a sneer. He yanked open the door without another word and stalked outside. The wind took him and suddenly he was gone.

"And he doesn't even bother to shut the door," I muttered, moving forward to do it. Until it slammed shut on its own. I sighed. "Must be the demon time of the month."

CHAPTER TEN

I wondered if I should have called the sheriff about those bikers. Why were they at the museum? Clearly they were sent, but I couldn't tell the sheriff that. But maybe they had something to do with Karl's death. Maybe they didn't do it themselves, but their demon buddy did it. Erasmus all but said that was likely the truth.

Good God, another Erasmus Dark! On the face of it, no harm was actually done, I guess, because my best bud Chthonic Crossbow knew what to do. But who knows what might have occurred if that weapon hadn't kicked in with the super powers?

I grabbed the phone several times before I put it back. Something about the whole situation freaked me out, and I supposed that was saying a lot these days. I looked over my shoulder at the crossbow standing up in the corner and felt again its wash of protection. I wondered why Charise couldn't get the quarrels out. Was it only attuned to me?

And Erasmus was no better. Teasing me with little bits of information that might or might not help. It was all a game to him. He could be a murderer for all I knew. I hadn't entirely discounted him. After all, Constance Howland didn't come out of it so good.

But I did have to call someone. I picked up the phone. "Ayyuh," came that friendly and reassuring voice on the line.

"Hi, Doc. I'm sorry to keep bothering you, but there's been a new development." I told him about the museum, the bikers, and then the amulet. "So Biker Doug's got one, too, and I'm pretty sure it means they have another demon in their gang…coven…

whatever. And Erasmus seemed to think so, too, though he didn't come out and say it."

Silence.

"Doc?"

"That's…not good news, is it?"

"No. It sure doesn't sound like it. And here's something you can share with Jolene. They kept saying the word 'Shabiri.' It might be a name, the name of this demon. It might be something else, but it did seem pretty important. Maybe she can look that up. I don't know whether any of it has any connection with the Booke or not, but they definitely knew about the crossbow, and they wanted it. For what? What else can it be used for? I didn't get the impression that it was to do anything good."

He hmmed on the line for a bit. "It's all something to think about, isn't it? Jolene's in school right now, but I'll text her with this new information. I think we should definitely meet tonight."

"I agree." I told him the best time and felt better when I hung up, knowing the Wiccans would be on it.

Still, an uneasy feeling followed me all day. And with it, the unnerving sensation of being watched. It was that Booke. I took detours for the rest of the day to stalk by the Booke and glare at it. I tried once more to pen something in it, once with a Sharpie and another with a quill, but nothing stayed. Stupid picky Booke.

I chewed on my thumbnail. If Erasmus wasn't going to help me then I had to find out what I needed to know on my own. The Wiccans could only do so much, and I hated to wait. After all, the Booke wasn't going to write itself.

I ran upstairs to grab my laptop. Googling a bit didn't give me what I wanted. Instead, I searched for the nearest library on my phone, called up the map, and rushed downstairs. It wouldn't hurt to spend an hour getting a few books.

When I grabbed my coat off the hall tree, I looked back at the crossbow. Better safe than sorry. I snatched it up, and then wrapped it in an afghan from the window bench. I snuck out of my own shop, locked the door, and quickly clambered into the Jeep. Off I went, shooting glances at the map on my phone. It wasn't far, just up the highway. At least it wasn't near Hansen Mills. And what was so special about that? Another question for Doc. Unless Doc had already done it, I had decided I'd tell the Wiccans about the bikers and let them choose whether I called the sheriff or not.

I nearly passed it. The library sign was situated behind a large sweeping pine, but I made a U-turn and pulled into the parking lot.

It was a little stone building from an earlier century with a wide expanse of stairs in the front, and concrete lions lying at either side of the steps. The library was surrounded by maples and birches littering leaves all across the parking lot. When I walked through the door I fell instantly in love with the marble floors and high vaulted ceiling, the rococo of the pillars, and the dark stacks marching away like an army of shelves. The place smelled like books, and I smiled when I walked up to the computer to call up a few titles.

With my scrap of paper full of Dewey Decimal numbers, I strolled the stacks and found one book, then another, and finally the last on the list.

I settled into a carrel, opened the first book to the end, and ran a finger down the index. "Succubus, succubus," I muttered. Finding it, I turned to the pages and began to read. Okay, so it looked like they preyed on men, usually in their sleep. But maybe this one—the real one—worked a little differently. It wouldn't be after me, but then again, if it knew about me as Erasmus said, it still might try something.

I closed the book and gathered all of them in my arms.

I had to fill out some forms to get my library card, and the librarian did a double take at my last name—as everyone always did—before entering it into her system. "Strange, eh?" she said.

"Yup. You haven't lived till you've sat in your brand-new third grade class and had the teacher call out that name."

"I can imagine," she said, continuing to type. "You a flatlander?"

"A what?"

She chuckled. "That's our affectionate term for someone not born in Maine."

"Yeah. I'm from California. How long does it take for someone to be considered a Mainer? Or is it Mainiac?"

"It's both. But if you aren't born here, I'm afraid it never happens. You'll always be thought of as 'from away.'"

I took out a business card. "Here. I'm opening a tea and herb shop in Moody Bog. Maybe you'd like to stop in some time."

"Oh!" She read the card and smiled. "That sounds lovely. Leave a few."

As I walked down the leaf-strewn steps, it occurred to me. I would have to make some other arrangements with the Moody Bog market about baked goods in my shop. Now that Bob Hitchins was…well, no more. And wasn't that my fault, too, for opening the Booke…

No! I refused to be blamed for something I couldn't possibly have known about. Yet the guilt lingered, and the urgency to *do* something intensified. Was it my own hubris, or was it coming from the Booke? "Oh that's just great. I can't even tell if it's my own feelings or from some supernatural object!" But when I swiped at my face I felt my own very real tears on my cheek.

Once I was back in my shop with my library finds on the desk next to the Booke, I was about to fire up my kettle when I noticed the time. Holy cats! I'd be late for the Chamber of Commerce Get-Together. And despite biker gangs and succubi, I *did* have a business to run.

It was weird worrying about mundane matters when my life was in danger. But like my herbs and tea, everything had a cubbyhole to be sorted into, prioritized. And though each minute felt a little like the Sword of Damocles had one last thread left, I still had to get on with it.

Once I checked myself in the mirror, I was back in the Jeep, wending my way over the shadowed street, heading toward the white steeple.

Cars filled the parking lot. The church looked like one of

those old New England jobs—white clapboard sides, tall windows, and distinctive pointed steeple, but the one-story building nestled beside it was from the forties, a typical church hall.

I found a spot and pulled in. And then I rushed into the hall and peeled off my coat in the warmth.

The noise of the crowd echoed throughout the building, and it looked like half the population of Moody Bog was there. The smell of countless church pancake breakfasts and Sunday night stews permeated the very walls, and I couldn't help but feel a certain camaraderie with the folks milling and drinking coffee, even though they were all strangers to me.

Marge spotted me the same time I caught sight of her, and she waved and scuttled over.

"Glad you made it," she said, slightly less cheerily than usual. She gestured toward a framed picture of someone flanked by flowers. "We just did a tribute to Bob Hitchins."

I told her I was sorry to hear about Bob and she gave a little sniff.

"Yeah, he was pretty beloved. Sheriff Ed is being tight-lipped about what happened, though everyone suspects it was probably a heart attack. Bob did like his pastries."

"I'm so sorry. I never had a chance to meet him."

"Bob was quite a fixture around here, that's for sure." She made a swiping gesture with her hand and put on a brave smile. "Come on. Let me introduce you around."

She led me first to a tight klatch. A thin woman in her fifties wearing a plaid skirt with a sweater draped over her shoulders was talking earnestly to a group of business movers and shakers. Beside her, listening with barely the patience to do so, was a man, blond, overweight, with a red nose, blotchy red cheeks, and a bristly mustache. He fingered his plastic cup full of what looked like pink punch, probably wishing it were spiked, by the look on his face. Another man, with dark, longish hair tucked behind his ears stood listening. He wore a sweater vest unbuttoned that hung over the baggy waist of his corduroys. His eyes were wandering, as if he'd heard it all before. A middle-aged man in a clerical collar and cardigan listened attentively to the woman.

"Sorry to interrupt, Ruth," Marge said, imposing us into their little circle.

The woman, Ruth, looked startled. If the look on her face was any indication, interrupting her simply was not done.

But the men seemed relieved, and then they perked up when they looked me over. My twenty-six years decidedly brought down the average age of the room.

"I just wanted to introduce our newest entrepreneur," said Marge. "She's young but I have a feeling she's pretty savvy. Everyone, this is Kylie Strange. She's opening that cute Strange Herbs & Teas on Lyndon Road."

"I did wonder about that sign," said Ruth, mouth pinched slightly.

"And this is Ruth Russell," Marge went on. Ruth didn't offer her hand so my arm stalled in mid-flight. But I changed direction and held it out to the clergyman. "And this is Reverend Howard Cleveland."

He shook my hand with a firm, curt shake, likely borne of many Sundays and many hands. "A pleasure to meet you, Ms. Strange."

"Kylie, please."

Marge grinned and clutched my shoulders for a moment. "I'll leave you to it. Must see how the punch is doing."

She whisked away and the red-nosed man held out a beefy hand. "John Fairgood, of Fairgood Gun Shop. Are you a gun owner, young lady?" His grip squeezed my hand hard. I resisted shaking it out when he finally released me.

Does a crossbow count? I wondered.

"No, but I'm not opposed to it on principle."

He frowned slightly, trying to ferret out my meaning.

The last man in the circle with the longish hair offered a weak handshake. "Sy Alexander. I own the Coffee Shack. I hope we won't be competitors."

"I don't really plan to sell prepared brews. Just the makings."

I was suddenly bombarded by waves of silk, perfume, and clicking bracelets. Seraphina swept in and gave me an encompassing hug. "Kylie, I completely forgot to mention this to you. I'm glad you found us anyway." She glanced around our little circle, and a small line creased the center of her brow. "Well…I'll let you meet our chamber. I'll see you later this evening. Bye!" She waved her fingers at the others and glided quickly to the next group.

Ruth tsked. "Of course, *she'd* have met you already. I'm sure all these herbs come in handy for her notions or potions or whatevers. Is that what your shop is for? All that witchcraft nonsense?"

Reverend Howard shook his head. "Now Ruth, the Wiccans have every right to—"

"It's *not* right, Reverend! And I'm surprised at you for condoning such devil worship in your parish. Someone should put a stop to it."

"It's not illegal," said Sy, brushing a lock of hair out of his face. "And it isn't devil worship. I know the kids involved. The Wiccan tradition is—"

"That's baloney and you know it, Sy," she said, pulling her sweater taut over her chest. "It's disgraceful. To allow children access to that. Isn't the Ayrs girl far too young? I'm surprised at her parents for allowing it. But just you wait. She's a high school drop-out in the making."

"Jolene?" I said incredulously. "She's whip-smart. I wouldn't be surprised if she graduated early. And Wicca is just as much a cultural tradition as any religion, really." I turned to Reverend Howard. "No offense."

"None taken, Kylie. Wicca has combined some very old traditions into a fairly new nature faith. The ritual practices of Wicca today, as I understand it, stem from around the forties."

"Oh?" I said. "I didn't know that."

"Some think the traditions are older. What's the harm?"

"Worshipping the moon, for heaven's sake," spat Ruth.

"You can't trust people like that," said John. "Too flighty. Seraphina. She doesn't even have a shop in town. Uses the *Internet*."

He said the last as if it left a bad taste in his mouth. "Tax dodger, if you ask me."

Reverend Howard breathed an irritated sigh. "Now John, that's not very charitable talk."

John glared at me. "Just what *kind* of herbs are you selling in that shop of yours?"

Reverend Howard took me by the arm and steered me away before I could open my mouth to reply as sharply as I had wanted to.

"Let's meet some others," he said in my ear. He led me across the linoleum floor and said confidentially, "They're mostly harmless, believe it or not. Just a little set in their ways. A closed mind is an unhappy mind, I'm afraid. Even though many of them have known Doc Boone for ages—have you met Doc?"

"Oh yes. He's great."

"Isn't he? But when he stopped coming to church and took up with the Wicca way, lots of folks in the village were…well, less than Christian about it. They broke ties they had had with him for decades. A shame, really."

"That's a kind of funny thing for you to say, Reverend. I mean, Wicca is pagan, right?"

We reached the table with the pink punch in a pressed glass bowl. Small piles of cookies set on individual napkins surrounded it. "Well, Kylie, I'll tell you." His accent was vaguely Midwestern. I guessed Reverend Howard, like me, was "from away." "I think that God has left room on this good earth for all sorts of beliefs. And as long as their main tenet is love, I don't see a conflict of interest, do you?"

I smiled. I liked Reverend Howard's face—the crinkles at the corners of his eyes, his gray pelt of hair. "Neither do I."

He chuckled and ferried me around the room, introducing me to more business owners. I passed out my cards and let them know that I'd be opening by Friday.

I even saw Deputy Miller wandering about, and I strained above the crowd, looking for the handsome sheriff. He didn't appear to be there. The deputy caught sight of me and scowled, making his way to Ruth and John, who were still talking. I sized up the room. One might divide it into Pro-Wiccan and Anti-Wiccan. Unfortunately, it looked as if Deputy Miller was definitely in the Anti-Wiccan camp.

I got myself a glass of punch and after a careful sip, felt my teeth squeak in pain at all the sugar. I glanced back at Ruth Russell, still pontificating to her audience, thinking that *she* probably made the punch. Anyone that sour needed all this sugar. *And here's a nice ripe, red apple for you, deary.* Anti-Wiccan my ass. She could be the head witch, with her perfect pinched face and dark frown that would look just fine under a tall pointy hat.

I pulled myself back. What was it that Reverend Howard said about charity? I needed to practice a little myself, I guessed.

Ruth caught me looking at her and furrowed her already wrinkled brow.

"How's it going?" asked Marge, startling me.

"Oh, fine. Some interesting folks here."

"That's one way to put it." She smiled, crossing her arms over her ample chest. "Don't let Ruth bother you. She's the local president of the Knitting Society, the DAR, and Mayflower Descendants. I daresay if she could trace her family back to Eden she'd be president of that, too. But she would more than likely end up being related to the snake!" She made a honk of a laugh and clapped her hand over her mouth. "I shouldn't have said that. It wasn't nice. But Ruth does have ancestors that go all the way back to the founding of Moody Bog, at least."

Wait a sec. Didn't Karl Waters say…? "Isn't she supposed to be related to the Howlands?"

"*You've* heard of them? Well, stay in this town long enough and you're bound to."

"I, uh, only heard about them peripherally. What's so special about them?"

"They're just one of the founders. Although to hear Ruth tell it, they're John Alden and George Washington all rolled into one."

"Isn't there a Howland who was, um, on trial for witchcraft?"

She laid a hand on my shoulder. "Oh my dear. If you want to get in good with Ruth, *never* mention Constance Howland. She's the black sheep of the family. No one talks about *her* around Ruth."

I turned to look at Ruth Russell holding court with her cronies.

Marge excused herself to do more mingling while I surveyed the village chamber. Mostly men, as I expected, but there were a few women here and there, like Marge. But I was definitely the youngest by far.

I would have to find a way to talk to Ruth Russell. As a descendant of Constance Howland, she might have information I could use.

I brought the cup to my lips again and then thought better of it. What I needed was water to wash the sugar away. Behind me was a doorway to a narrow corridor. I passed through onto shiny floors that smelled of pine-scented cleaner. The overhead fluorescents were turned off, but I could plainly see that one side of the corridor was the kitchen, with its swinging door and roll-down metal gate over a wide cafeteria-style window. On the other was what appeared to be a storeroom with its door ajar.

As I passed it on my way to the kitchen, I glanced inside.

Mop, bucket, long rolls of colored paper leaning upright in a corner, plastic flowers arranged in centerpieces, shelves of cleaning supplies…and something drawn on the floor, partially hidden by a rubber mat.

I stepped in without thinking, fumbling for the light switch on the wall but not quite finding it.

"What are you doing there?"

I whipped around and came face to face with an old man in overalls, who I guessed was the janitor.

"Sorry. I was just looking for some water." I held up my glass.

"Kitchen's over there," he said, thumbing over his shoulder. He stood in the doorway as I slid past him and then he pulled the storeroom door shut, locking it.

"Sorry," I said again, and hurried to the kitchen. He was still standing in the shadowed corridor, watching me as I dumped the punch in the sink and filled my little plastic cup with tap water. I drank, glancing over the rim at the man *still* watching, before I scuttled past him again, head down, and rejoined the Get-Together.

After a few more minutes, my watch told me that it was, thankfully, time to go. I said my good-byes. Before I left, I made a beeline toward Ruth Russell, who, by the look on her face, was fairly surprised to see me again. I grabbed her hand and shook it. "It was so nice meeting you," I said with a smile, as sincerely as I could make it. "I'd love to chat sometime. About knitting!"

Startlement still on her face, she forced a smile. "Of course. Our Knitting Society meets Wednesday afternoons. You wouldn't want to come to that, would you?"

And as nice an invitation as I had never heard.

"Why, I'd *love* to." I gave her my card. "Why don't you email me with the address and time. Should I bring my knitting?"

She looked like she'd swallowed that poison apple prepared for Snow White. "That would be a wonderful idea. Well. Then I suppose we'll see you tomorrow."

I gave her hand one more shake before I let it go. "Awesome! I'll see you there." *You old crone.*

As I was leaving, I made sure I spoke to Reverend Howard once more, thanking him for being so nice to me, before I darted for the door.

But as I drove back to my shop, leaves falling around my car in a colorful rain, my thoughts didn't fall on Ruth Russell and her Howland ancestry, but instead on what I saw in that storeroom. The room had been dark, but surely I hadn't seen the edge of a pentagram etched on the floor under that mat?

• • •

When I got back to my shop, I put the kettle on, collected some Formosa oolong from my private stash, stuffed it in an infuser, and got down my favorite cup and saucer. Some people go for a mug for their tea, and that's all right for coffee. But for me, tea deserved more respect. I believed it always tasted better in a proper cup and saucer.

I tapped my fingernail on the counter, waiting for the water to boil. Now that it was quiet again, my mind drifted. Thoughts of succubi, vortexes, bikers, Anti-Wiccans, and pentagrams swirled in my head like so many tea leaves in a pot of boiling water. Was this whole village a hotbed of the paranormal? I made a note to myself to find out about that janitor.

And tomorrow I had committed myself to go to the Knitting Society. If Ruth would even deign to email me. There was a problem, though. I didn't know how to knit. Surely there was a shop here with knitting supplies. I'd just...get some things and, well. Fake it.

And then there was Erasmus Dark. I kept thinking of the hurt look in his eyes. Can you even hurt a demon's feelings? I wandered into the main room, looking at all the work yet to be done, trying *not* to think of Erasmus. But each little annoyance made me think of him again, and his posh accent and high-toned attitude...and unarguably handsome features.

Why did he have to get all snooty about it anyway? He didn't deny chasing Howland off that cliff. "He never just comes out and says what he means!"

"Who doesn't?"

Startled again, I spun. Seraphina stood in my doorway, a strange little smile on her face.

"Oh. Hi, Seraphina. I didn't expect you so early."

"Thought I'd pop by to help you. How did you like our little villagers?"

"I think, everything aside, I like them."

She gave me a knowing smile. "But?"

I shook my head. "There's always a few who are 'better than thou.' I've seen the like before."

She nodded sagely. I suppose she had, too.

"So Seraphina, I'm ashamed to say that I never asked what it is *you* did for a living. I just assumed…"

"You assumed I'm retired? Independently wealthy? Hardly. I have my own internet business. I make jewelry." She wiggled her fingers and the light twinkled off her bat- and cat-faced rings and bangles. "And essential oils. That's another reason why I'm so happy you happened to come to town. I've been dying to experiment with some of your herbs. And despite what my esteemed colleagues say, I do pay taxes. I've heard it all before." She blinked languidly. "Looks like you've gotten a lot done."

I looked around with her. Almost all the cubbies were full of herbs and marked accordingly. I had filled apothecary jars with tea, and they marched across the back of the buffet with its shelves now displaying teapots and mugs of various colors and designs. All were priced with stickers, and I had kept careful tabs of the entire inventory with the latest software.

And it smelled heavenly, too. Like all the different wild, rich, and flowery forms of tea, and every woodsy, earthy herb. It smelled like where I was supposed to be.

"Yes, it's finally whipping into shape. Should be ready by the end of the week." *If I'm not attacked by a succubus, or a biker gang, or a stray demon before then.* This was all more complicated than I had bargained for.

"It's just darling," she said, removing her cape. I took it from her and hung it on the hall tree. "So cozy." She headed toward the facing wingback chairs positioned in front of the fireplace. Her manicured fingers smoothed over the chintz upholstery of one chair. "You've done so much work."

"More to go, I'm afraid."

She faced me. She was wearing more practical clothes since the chamber get-together. Tight jeans and a sweater with a neckline that kept sliding off one shoulder. Sort of practical. "Put me to work."

I did. We had our tea in cups and saucers, which we moved with us as we worked. I had her pricing the little knick-knacks of cherry bark tea scoops, infusers, and agave sticks. She sat on the floor, shoes kicked off, with merchandise all around her. I thought she'd be chattier as she worked, but instead she proceeded silently, only occasionally making a comment. I still couldn't make out how old she was. Wicca was good to her, I guessed.

I told her about the vortex and the bikers and she only looked at me thoughtfully. "I already told Doc about all this," I said when she continued on in her strange silence. "And also…that those bikers seemed to have the help of their own demon."

"Oh!" She put her fingers to her blood-red lips. "That's…a complication."

"That's what Erasmus said."

"But you're safe here now."

I looked around. I did feel safe. Was that a false sense of security? The crossbow and the Booke were right there, but was all that enough?

"How long have you lived here, Seraphina?"

"Oh, for about ten years. I was born and raised in New Hampshire."

"Why did you come here?"

"That's a good question. I…just had a feeling about it."

I didn't roll my eyes. After all, I'd seen stranger things lately. "So, do you know any of the local history? You know the kind of stuff. About the founders?"

"Can't say I do. That's never been my interest."

I decided not to mention the Howlands—if Seraphina didn't know more details, there wasn't much use discussing it.

We continued to work quietly, our heads in their own places. Maybe it was when she saw me glance out the window for the umpteenth time that she finally asked, "Who are you looking for?"

"Oh. No one. I mean…" I sighed. I cradled a rounded orange ceramic teapot in my hand. "I got so frustrated. With Erasmus Dark. I told him to leave."

She shook her head as she stuck out her tongue, writing a

price and description on a tag with her tiny careful lettering. "He was here?"

"Yes. Just breezes in whenever he feels like it. All these cryptic sentences that don't actually answer any questions. He lies, you know. So I kicked him out." I barked a harsh laugh. "Seems I've been doing that a lot with men lately. They all seem to lie."

She bent her head and continued to write on the tag. "Want to talk about it?"

I must have said that with a little too much vehemence. "Well…" I set down the pot, picked up a rag, and began polishing the wood of the apothecary shelves. "I had a boyfriend back in California. Jeff. I was with him for two whole years and I still can't believe it. He was sort of my first serious relationship. Maybe I didn't know how they're supposed to be. I don't remember much of my father and my mother never re-married, never dated, so I just had the example of her being alone. I was alone pretty much all through college except for the occasional dalliance."

Seraphina grinned. "Ooh la la," she purred.

I smiled back and felt my cheeks heat with a blush. "Yes, well. So it wasn't like I'd had *no* relationships, but nothing…you know…serious. Until Jeff."

"What attracted you to him?"

"Oh he was the consummate beach boy. Blond, good-looking, everyone's pal. Funny, great personality."

"So what went wrong?"

"It was all a lie. Yes, he had the kind of personality that drew people to him, but it was only skin deep. I'm painting a pretty dark picture. It wasn't all bad. And it wasn't that he was that terrible a person, but he could be a prick on occasion, pardon the expression."

"Oh, no. Don't mind me. I've met quite a few pricks in my day."

"Yeah, so." I polished the wood with vigor; once one spot shined, I moved on to the next. "Jeff and I hit it off right away. Mutual interests. He had this small herb shop and after we became boyfriend and girlfriend we became business partners. I added the tea and a few knick-knacks and the place seemed to take off after that. What I didn't know is that he was spending all the profits, getting us into debt. He handled the books, but when our venders began cutting us off I took a look and was, well, appalled. How had I let him do that? I trusted him. And then there were the women…"

"Oh Kylie."

"It took me too long to realize what exactly was going on. By the time my mom got sick I had almost been wiped out. We broke up and got together a bunch of times. But when Mom died…"

Seraphina made a small sound of empathy. I glanced at her soft expression. "She left me some money along with the life insurance and I made the decision to just leave. Pack up and go and end up at god-knows-where. Which turned out to be here."

"And aren't we lucky it was."

I turned back to my polishing, scrubbing the beeswax deep into the old wood. "You may not think so after all this crazy stuff blows up in our faces."

"I suppose that all remains to be seen." She unfolded her legs and stretched them out before picking up the next tiny tag and tying it around a package of sugar swizzle sticks. "This Mr. Dark," she began. I set my rag down and looked up. "I don't really think you can put him in the same class as the erstwhile and soon-to-be-forgotten Jeff. Maybe he was trying to help you…in his way."

"I don't know."

"But I think you're right to be cautious. We don't know his nature. He could be here to trick you."

"I think he chased Constance Howland to her death. You saw that engraving."

"Did you ask him about that?"

"Of course! Still, no straight answer. I can't trust him, Seraphina. What happens if he comes back?"

"When the coven gets here tonight, we'll work on some protection spells for you. I don't think you should entirely trust him, but I don't think you can afford to send him away permanently either. He has much to tell you."

"That's what he said." I set the rag aside and screwed the lid back on the wax. "I don't know who to believe. And there is still something out there. And then there was this evil hole or vortex or something." I suddenly felt weary. I slid into a chair, sitting across the wingback with my legs draped over the arm. "I don't think I'm cut out for this."

"He told you the book chose you, right?"

"And can I believe that?"

"What do *you* think? What do you *feel*?"

She was big on feelings. Me, not so much. But I couldn't help but glance over at the Booke. I *did* feel something. I knew in my heart of hearts that the Booke *had* chosen me. Okay, so he hadn't lied about that. That look of injury in his eyes. Demon or not, I'd hurt his feelings, and now I felt guilty.

"It's true," I said softly. "Seraphina, there's just so much we don't know. There's something out there and it's killed twice. I can't let it kill again, but I have no idea how to find it."

She reached over and patted my hand. "We'll figure something out. Tonight, when the coven meets."

CHAPTER ELEVEN

With Seraphina's help, I got a lot done. I'd also put on a pot of chili, baked fresh corn bread, and waited for my guests to arrive. Doc arrived first and gushed about how the place looked. Then Nick arrived with Jolene. They all found places to settle and we ended up with our bowls in front of the fire, Doc and Jolene on the wingbacks, Seraphina on a ladder-back chair, and Nick and me on the floor rug.

I filled them in on what had transpired today, scooping up spoonfuls of chili in between my sentences. "And then there was this biker gang in front of the museum. They took me on a little unscheduled ride to a bar. Wanted my crossbow but after I performed some acrobatic feat that I still don't understand and got the drop on them, they let me go. They had some pentagram logo on their jackets with some goat guy. When I told that to Erasmus he kind of got all quiet."

Nick looked on, mouth agape, spoon frozen halfway to his lips.

"They also had a motto of some kind. Ordo Dextra something or other."

"*Ordo Dexterae Diaboli*," said Nick. "The ODD."

"They certainly were," I said gesturing with my beer bottle. "Odd, I mean. Hey, wait a minute. I think Karl Waters said something about them—about the ODD."

Jolene squinted at me through her glasses. I could see her tablet peeking out from a canvas tote at her feet, a bag plastered with a pink Hello Kitty skull sporting a witch's hat.

Nick took a drag on his beer and set it down. His hands shook.

"But that's not all," I said, scanning all of them. "The reason the biker guys were there in the first place was that they were *told* to be there."

"Told?" said Nick, looking paler than usual. "By who?"

"Well, looks like by their own demon." Everyone gasped. It was beginning to feel like old hat to me but not so much for the Wiccans. They'd had just as much time to get used to it, but I supposed they didn't have a weird Booke whispering to their subconscious. "They said as much," I clarified. "He sent them to get the crossbow. Doug, their leader, had an amulet just like this one." I raised mine.

"Then they'll try again," said Doc.

I took a swig of beer. "I guess so."

Everyone drank or stirred their spoons in their bowls.

Nick remained quiet as we all ate. But it wasn't until we both met in the kitchen for second helpings that he touched my arm, checked that his companions were still in the main shop, and pulled me aside.

"Kylie, that was a lot of crazy stuff today. But I gotta tell you. You don't want to mess with those biker guys."

"Believe me, I had no intention."

"No, seriously. They are really bad news. Their logo isn't just for show. They're followers of Baphomet."

"Baphomet?"

"The goat guy. They're demon worshippers. They're the anti-us."

I leaned back against the counter. "So you mean, they go for the dark stuff."

"Yeah. Really dark stuff. Black masses and all that. *Ordo Dexterae Diaboli* means the 'Order of the Right Hand of the Devil.'"

"Crap. I thought that was all made-up stuff, black masses." I glanced back at my Wiccans in the next room. "Right. Don't take anything for granted anymore. Plus they have their own demon in their pocket. Wait. You don't suppose it's Baphomet?"

"No. Baphomet is like a god. Almost. No amulet is going to control him."

"And you know all this because…?"

"I used to sort of hang with them. Well…not 'hang.' I was a wannabe. But then I found out the sort of stuff they *really* did. I mean, I was ready to be badass and all, roll with the bikers, but…" His black dyed hair and spike earrings did give him a Goth vibe, but I never got the feeling that he took it to the nth degree. More like Goth-Lite. He certainly didn't seem the biker type.

"I don't see you hanging out with guys like that."

"Yeah, neither did they. They weren't so keen on me being gay either. I got into a *lot* trouble from my folks when they found out I was ditching school and hanging around Mike's Roadhouse. I wasn't twenty-one yet and they blew their tops when they thought I might want to be with those guys, get tattooed and stuff. I was so grounded."

"They sound like good, responsible parents," I said, reminding myself disturbingly of my mother.

He smiled briefly and blushed. "Yeah, they're okay. Anyway, I met Jolene at the Coffee Shack where I work. She'd come in all the time and be on her computer. She seemed pretty mature for a high school junior and we'd get to talk sometimes. She's the one who told me about the Wiccans. After the Ordo, that sounded more like my speed. The Ordo used to talk about doing rituals. I didn't want to go into that dark stuff after all, with animal sacrifices and whatever. They said the rituals had to be dangerous and kind of gross in order to yield power and money. But even though a lot of it seemed like talk—you know, trying to look more dangerous than you really are—they looked like they were getting deeper into it. They did get into some trouble—vandalism and a few fights at Mike's. But they never, you know, *killed* anyone, or did anything really badass. It was just talk. But with all this Baphomet stuff and the rituals… It sounded like maybe they were going more hardcore. Maybe that was just more talk, but who knows?" He took another swallow of beer. "When I got in with the Wiccans,

I learned all kinds of stuff about nature and nature spirits. Doc's really good with that. And the occult is interesting. But it can be dangerous if you don't do it right."

"Except I guess *we're* getting into some dangerous stuff."

"Yeah, but this is the *Light*!" He smiled, but it took no time for his mood to darken again. "The fact that the Ordo were outside the vortex *and* they wanted your crossbow…that is not a good combination."

"Are you saying you think *they* conjured that vortex? I thought it was part of the Booke."

He shrugged, picked at the corn bread he nabbed from the dish, and nibbled on it. "I don't know. I don't know the extent of their power."

"Have you told this to Doc? About the Ordo?"

"I've told him before, but he didn't believe they were a threat."

"Well I think this changes things, don't you?"

I marched back into the shop and Nick followed close behind. "Nick has something to tell you," I announced, and all eyes turned toward us.

Nick stumbled through his explanation. After he'd stopped talking and sipped at his chilled beer, Doc looked thoughtfully at each of us.

"And Karl Waters said something about the Ordo, too," I said. "But it was just in passing, and I didn't understand it at the time."

Doc nodded. "Gifford Corner is just a hop and a skip from Hansen Mills. But this news of another demon in town. That concerns me."

"What's a mage?" I asked suddenly. Jolene was startled and tried to hide it by fixing her glasses. "Or a practitioner. The Ordo said something about that. They asked if I was a mage or practitioner. Erasmus mentioned mages, too."

Doc set his bowl down on the coffee table. "A mage is a powerful witch or warlock capable of doing some off-the-cuff magic. That is, they don't require preparation or ritual to perform Craft.

A practitioner is someone who can do the same to a lesser extent. The apprentice of a mage, if you will."

"Why did they think I was one of those?"

"Could be their demon thought so. Maybe it sensed something powerful in the neighborhood."

"Do you think it knows about the Booke?"

"Hard to say. But it knows about the crossbow at any rate. I suppose it would have thought only a powerful mage could obtain it."

Seraphina nodded sagely. "I told you I sensed something about Kylie. That she was sensitive."

"I'm not sensitive!"

"Or," said Doc thoughtfully. He stroked his chin and stared into the middle distance. "Now that I think about it, it *could* be that there's power in the book that extends to you in a sort of surrounding aura."

"That reminds me!" piped up Jolene. She rummaged in her bag and drew out a long clear crystal tied to a stick.

"What's that?"

The crystal was carefully wrapped to the stick with a leather thong, wrapped many times and knotted intricately, even beautifully, with two dangling leather pieces with a feather tied to the end of one, and a polished pebble to the other. "It's a scrying stick. I worked on this for two whole days. I'm hoping it works."

Everyone nodded, and there I was again, the outsider. "I don't know what a scrying stick is."

"That's okay," she said brightly. "I didn't expect you to. It's a way to be able to find the paranormal. Like a metal detector. Only I'm not looking for metal, but for…you know, magic stuff."

"Oh." Sounded reasonable. As reasonable as any of it did.

"So…you don't mind, do you?"

It took me a moment to understand that she wanted to wave her stick at me. I blew out a breath. "No, go right ahead. It won't hurt, will it?"

"Oh no. At least…I don't think so." She held the stick in both her hands and seemed to center herself. She aimed the crystal at me and slowly waved it in a figure eight pattern, over and over again.

I felt a bit foolish. And a little embarrassed for her. I peeked at the others but they were solemnly watching her stick.

A spark.

I snapped my head, staring at the crystal. It sparked again and then suddenly the thing started to glow. *No way!*

She stopped swishing it around and just stared at it. She carefully rose and walked around me, and as she moved the crystal farther away, the glow dimmed. It brightened when she got closer again. I began to see that she was measuring the extent of my, well, aura, I guessed.

She lowered it with one hand and the glow disappeared. "That was...interesting," she said breathlessly.

Seraphina nodded. "Yes, yes. I sensed her aura, too."

Nick rolled his eyes.

Doc took the scrying stick from Jolene's hand and examined it, taking it to the lamp to look it over under the light. "That's some fine work you did there, Jolene. Seemed to work like a charm... so to speak."

"I soaked the stick in charmed oil for two days, and then I wiped it with pure linen. And I polished the crystal and the stone myself."

"And the feather?"

"Got it from inside a nest, so it wasn't taken in violence."

I was sure all that meant something to the two of them. They conferred quietly about it for some time before I rose and stood behind them. "All that's well and good, but what did that prove?"

"Well now." Doc held the scrying stick across both his hands. "This indicates that there is some kind of magical aura around you."

"Wait. So you mean if you did the same thing to all of you, it wouldn't glow?"

"That's about the size of it."

"Prove it." I raised my chin. If we were going about this scientifically, then I wanted some empirical evidence.

"Ay-yuh. I agree." He handed it back to Jolene and she held it in both hands again, taking a moment before holding it up to Doc. At first nothing happened, but then the merest of glimmers started in the depths of the crystal. No matter how close Jolene aimed the stick at him, though, the glow wouldn't get any brighter.

She turned to Seraphina and an even softer glow came from the crystal. And when she aimed it at Nick, the same tentative glow. She handed the stick to Nick, and when he dutifully turned it toward Jolene, it also glowed dimly. When he lowered it the light winked out.

Everyone looked at the other. "That's weird," said Jolene.

"You mean you didn't expect that?" I said.

"No, not really. I didn't expect it to glow for any of us." She turned to Doc. "What does it mean?"

Doc looked at me, then at the Booke, then at me again, all the while pinching his lip with his fingers. "I don't quite know. Here, Nick. Give that over." Nick seemed a little too anxious to be rid of the crystal and Doc examined it. He took a breath, and held it toward me again. The thing glowed as bright as a floodlight. When he lowered it the light went out.

"Damnedest thing," he said.

"Okay," I admitted. "So we're all a little glowy."

"But you the most," said Nick, staring at me slack-jawed. "And Doc next."

"Well that's 'cause…" I looked at Jolene. "Why is that?"

"Because…of the book?" She turned to Doc for confirmation.

"Ay-yuh. Unless…you *are* a mage."

I felt their eyes on me and I raised my hands. "Nope. Not a mage. Never maged in my life." But my gaze traveled toward the Booke. I felt as if it were staring at me, too. "It's that," I said, and I pointed. "I know it's that."

They all turned and looked at it.

Doc nodded. "Makes sense. And it justifies what I've been contemplating. I think we need to perform some protective

Craft. You are too vulnerable, especially with that other demon lurking about."

"I agree," said Seraphina. She set her empty bowl aside and folded her fingers together. Her bright purple fingernails gleamed in the firelight.

"What about that evil vortex?" I asked. "We can't leave it open. For all we know, it killed Karl Waters."

"I'm still pretty sure that was a succubus," said Jolene.

"But maybe that's where the succubus comes from," I told her. "Maybe this vortex opens and then bang! That's how you get your victim."

Jolene shook her head. "I don't think that's how it works."

"Why not? Who here is an expert?"

"Well, I've been doing a lot of reading..." Jolene said.

"As have I," said Doc.

"But I went there *with* the Booke..."

"This vortex is a problem," he went on, "regardless of what it means. What did Mr. Dark have to say about it?"

"Not much," I said into my beer bottle. "But don't you think we should go over there? Check it out?"

Nick sputtered his beer. "To where the vortex is?"

"Well, yeah. You should all get a closer look at it. Assess the situation. Aim your stick at it."

No one seemed overly enthusiastic about that prospect. "Guys, come on! This doesn't happen every day, right?"

Nick put his beer down on a coaster. "Kylie, it might have escaped your notice, but we"—and he encompassed the Wiccans with a gesture—"don't really know what we're doing."

There was a general sound of disagreement but Nick put his hands in the air. "Come on, guys. We meet once a week and talk about the spirits of nature, we do a chant or two, and break for snacks. We're not exactly *Bewitched*, here. I mean, Jolene's scrying stick was cool, but..."

They fell silent. All my fears were closing in. I had asked for their help, but what could they really do? I was definitely in it over my head.

Doc nodded. "Well, I don't know about the rest of you, but I think we have started taking this a bit more seriously."

"I've got the research," said Jolene. "And I worked on the scryer. And it works."

Seraphina giggled. "I'm raring to go!"

Doc turned at last to Nick. "Nick? What about you?"

"The scryer glowed for you, too, Nick," said Jolene in a pleading voice.

Nick seemed to gather himself and jumped to his feet. "Yeah. Yeah, okay. If everyone else is in, then so am I. I'm ready. Ready to be the warlock I was meant to be."

Doc's cheeks pinked with his smile. "All right then. Kylie. I think you're right. We have to at least take a look at this vortex and then…well, we'll go from there."

• • •

Everyone trundled into my car. I pulled onto Lyndon Road and headed toward the highway. They all fell silent as the night drew around us, and all we could see of our little hamlet was what the headlights revealed in the dark. As we approached Gifford Corner, I worried that the bikers would be there. Right hand of the Devil, eh? Maybe that was just bravado, like Nick said, though these days, I couldn't afford to doubt.

The headlights illuminated the museum and its yellow tape. But no motorcycles. I was relieved until I remembered what we were doing there. We all got out of the car as quietly as we had ridden there. I approached the front door first and was still surprised to find it open. I couldn't think of a way to tell the sheriff about that without justifying myself. Why had I gone back to the scene of the crime?

My Wiccans followed me in. The place was cold but the temperature had dropped with the sunset. Did it seem *unusually* cold? My breath fogged around my face and I turned to the stacks, toward the place Karl had died. A faint glow lit the shelves.

I pointed. "See that?" I whispered. They gathered near me. Doc nodded to me and ventured forward. "Don't get too close," I told him.

I stuck to his back and went with him. Seraphina was behind me, followed by Nick, with Jolene in the rear.

We edged around the counter and moved down the aisle. But once we turned the corner of the shelves, we saw it. Like a crack in midair that was fully three-dimensional. It shone a bright green. It wasn't the wide-open maw I'd seen before, but instead a glowing crack in…what? The space-time continuum?

"Awesome," breathed Jolene.

"No one get any closer," I warned. "It might open. It grabbed me before."

"What's this?" said Seraphina. She knelt and scraped something off the floor with her fingernail. "Looks like wax. Black wax."

"I saw black candle stubs here earlier. Thought it was strange that the police would need that."

"Ritual," said Nick. He pointed to the floor. There were faint chalk lines and more dribbled wax. I thought the chalk was something the cops did but maybe not. Surely this hadn't been here when the police investigated or they would have taken it as evidence.

Nick gave me a significant look.

"What should we do?" I asked Doc.

He looked as scared as anyone. "I don't know. Jolene, why don't you scry it. See what it might turn up."

Jolene reached into her bag with a trembling hand and brought out her scryer. She barely lifted it when it started to glow. Not the clean white light that it had emitted for me and the Wiccans, but a blood red light that broke into beams and lit up the whole museum. Deep rumbling voices emerged from the vortex crack, that sound I'd heard before just as it grabbed me.

We all took a step back. All except Jolene, who seemed rooted to the spot.

"Jolene!" I hissed. "Put that thing away and let's go."

But she was frozen in place, too scared to move. I grabbed her shoulders and whirled her around. The scryer fell to the floor and the beams of light shut off, but when I looked at her face her eyes were glowing with that same red light, almost the way Erasmus's eyes did when he was angry.

"Whoa, Jolene!" I turned desperately to Doc. "What's happening?"

"You fools," said Jolene, but definitely not with her voice. It was a basso profondo, the same voice that had come from the vortex. Her face was left strangely blank. "You have no idea, no idea at all."

"Then why don't you tell us," I said, unable to entertain where I got the courage.

"*Tell* you? Oh no, dear Kylie. The game must be played. All of it. To the last man. Or woman." And then it laughed, a bone-chilling deep laughter.

"Who *are* you? What are you doing here? What do you want?"

But the voice only laughed again. "Go now. Stay out of the shadows. For the game is not for the weak of heart. What has begun cannot now be stopped."

And as quickly as it had seized her, the red light left her eyes and she collapsed. I was close enough to catch her before she hit the floor, but Nick was right beside me, cradling her, too.

Jolene blinked and looked up at us. "That was seriously weird." She leaned into Nick.

Doc was at her side. "Jolene, were you aware during the…the possession?"

"Yeah. It was like I was pushed aside and this other guy moved into my place, using my mouth. I couldn't stop him."

"Who was it?" I asked.

She shook her head. "I don't know. I feel like I should, but he was also sort of blocking me, so I wouldn't be able to say. But I could tell something, too." She pushed away from Nick and retrieved the scryer. "He was controlling me, but I heard some of his thoughts."

"What?" said Doc. "What did you hear?"

"This," she said, showing the scryer. "This is more than a detector. It's a way *in*."

Chills were now running up my back. "Into…what?"

She stared at me. "It's like trying to retrieve an elusive dream. It's all slipping away. So I'm not sure. But…dammit! It's important. But I can't…I can't remember…"

"I've seen enough," said Doc urgently. "This is way beyond my experience. I suggest we leave. Now. Before we disturb anything else."

We backed away, giving the glowing crack a wide berth. I felt we should lock the place down but didn't know how. And I thought maybe we should call in the sheriff. Perhaps an anonymous call. Though what the cops could do about a vortex to the Netherworld I didn't know. On second thought, maybe it was best *not* to call them. No need to get anyone else killed.

Just as silently as we arrived, we drove back to my place. Solemnly, we marched inside and stood around the fireplace.

"What do we do now?" I asked. Jolene hadn't stopped looking at the scryer in her hand, turning it over and over, as if trying to discern what went wrong with it. I couldn't help the disturbing thought that it had worked exactly right. I wondered if it wouldn't be safer just storing that thing away because whatever it did, we didn't seem capable of controlling it. It might take a mage to do that. And then I remembered how much the thing glowed when aimed at me.

But that was all the Booke, right? There was nothing mage about me.

I just knew those bikers, the Ordo, were doing something over there, making rituals where poor Karl died. Probably *because* Karl died there. Even if they didn't have anything to do with his death, it seemed a cold-blooded thing to do.

I looked toward my Wiccans. "So did the Ordo conjure that vortex, or did the vortex just show up there?"

"That's not something I'm equipped to say," said Doc as Nick helped him off with his coat. "But I think it's more important than ever for us to perform our Craft to protect you, either from the creature from the book or these Ordo members and their demon." He turned to Jolene. "Did you bring…?"

"Got it all here, Doc." She had recovered, looking like her old determined self again, and stuffed the scryer into her Hello Kitty bag before taking out various items and placing them on the small table beside her: chalk, a rather sharp-looking knife, a golden goblet, a stick, and a fat beeswax candle.

I was getting nervous. That scryer scared the heck out of me, and now Doc was talking about performing witchcraft, and I didn't know if I was okay with that. Then I mentally slapped myself. What was a little witchcraft to all that I'd seen so far?

Both Doc and Jolene rose from their chairs and began moving them out of the way. I rose, too. "So…what's involved here? No animal sacrifices, I hope." I was only half-kidding, because I really did hope that wouldn't be happening on my floor.

Doc helped Jolene move the small table out of the way, leaving a cleared spot on my braided rug. He chuckled. "Oh, no. Though I saw my share of that when I did my research in Africa. It's more the Satanists' thing than Wicca. Voodoo, Santeria…they all rely on ritual sacrifice. Personally, I don't think it's worth the mess."

"Neither do I," said Seraphina. "And the forest spirits don't like it. No need to hurt their creatures."

"And if the Ordo do it," said Nick, "then I'm definitely not into it."

Jolene handed the chalk to Nick, who rolled up the rug and pushed it aside, leaving a blank spot on my wood floor. He looked up at me. "I hope you don't mind," he said, pausing with the chalk. "It's just chalk. It'll wash right off."

"No, no. Go ahead. Don't let me stop you."

Nick etched a careful pentagram on my plank floor. *That had* better *come out*, I thought. At least I could put the rug over it if it didn't. Last thing I needed in my shop with the name "Strange" on the shingle was a pentagram in the middle of my floor.

"It's all quite necessary," Doc went on. "It makes a lot of sense when you stop to think about it." I just nodded. I couldn't imagine any of it making any sense, no matter how long I thought about it.

As Nick drew, I remembered the pentagram in the church hall storeroom. Should I say something about that? But after all, I wasn't actually certain of what I saw. And it didn't do to start making accusations against people I really didn't know. I vowed to check it out at some later point, though.

Nick finished his pentagram and began drawing strange symbols at each of the points. He looked back over his shoulder. "I know pentagrams scare people. But there's really nothing wrong with them. Just because it's upside down doesn't mean it's bad. It can mean whatever you want it to mean, like the Ordo guys," he went on. "This is a benign one. These symbols are the Guardians of the cardinal points. It starts up here at the top with 'Aether' or 'Spirit' symbolized by this circle." He drew it and moved on to the point on the right, where he drew an upside-down triangle. "For 'Water,'" he said. The bottom right leg got a right-side-up triangle. "'Fire,'" he said. The other leg got another inverted triangle with a horizontal line drawn across its center. "'Earth.'" And at the last point another right-side-up triangle also with a horizontal line through it. "And 'Air.' These are important symbols when practicing Craft. They unite all the elements under the Aether and reintegrate them within the magic circle, creating harmony and safety. It's to help protect you and this house."

"Right," I mumbled. Meanwhile, Doc was leaning into the fireplace and lighting a sage bundle on the glowing embers. After he got it smoking, he set it on a dish by the "Air" point of the pentagram. Jolene was pouring some bottled water into the cup. Seraphina had grabbed the stick.

"What's with the stick?" I asked.

She cocked her head at me and smiled with her over-rouged

lips. "It's not a stick, silly. It's a willow wand. Very powerful for protection." She waved it through the sage smoke and placed it at the "Earth" corner. Jolene set the goblet at the "Water" corner.

Nick lit the candle that had seen its share of burning before, judging by its drips, and set it in the "Fire" corner.

Doc took up the knife and held his hand out to me. I cringed back. "Kylie, please take your place within the pentagram." I took his hand and he helped me navigate the smoking, sloshing objects until I stood awkwardly in the center. He still held my hand and the knife in the other. "Now, I hope you'll forgive me, but I just have to prick you finger a little. Won't sting but a second."

I yanked my hand back. "Why?" My heart was thundering. The amulet felt strangely heavy against my chest.

"We need just a drop of your blood for the Aether, to unite the elements. It's really the best protection for you. Trust me."

"I don't know." The Wiccans had all taken up kneeling positions around me. They had started to hum.

"I know it looks odd, but we have done this kind of ritual before. A protection spell is one of the first any Wiccan learns. We all saw that vortex, and, frankly, if what we suspect about those Baphomet worshippers is true, you are going to need the most powerful magic we can craft. And it always involves blood, I'm sorry to say. I've sterilized the knife. I'm a doctor, after all."

He still held out his hand, with the knife gleaming in the other. I swallowed hard, looking around at the others. The humming was getting louder and they were beginning to sway. The smell of the sage was getting to me. There was something else infused with it, but I couldn't tell what it was. It was making me light-headed.

Scared but hopeful, I cautiously offered my hand.

He took it and gave it a squeeze of reassurance, along with a fatherly smile. Suddenly, I began to panic. What did I really know about these people? They all seemed innocent enough, but here I was standing in a chalked pentagram with a knife-wielding plaster doctor, entrusting my flesh to him, and the rest of them were humming. I almost longed for the reassuring sneer of Erasmus Dark.

Doc's fingers flipped my hand up, palm facing him. He lowered the sharp tip of his knife to the pad of my finger and flicked the blade. The momentary sting seemed to awaken me and I tried to pull my hand back, but he kept a tight grip and moved it over the "Aether" symbol, squeezing my finger so the blood dripped onto the chalked surface.

I saw my blood, dark red, blotch the wood and felt a wave of nausea. He kept hold of my hand and murmured, "You're doing fine, Kylie." He seemed to direct me over the tendrils of smoke rising from the sage bundle. Involuntarily, I inhaled it, and strangely, it calmed me, at least enough that I wasn't struggling in his grip anymore. Vaguely I wondered if there was some sort of hallucinogen in it. Doc wouldn't do that, would he? Again, the sense that I really didn't know these people made my stomach queasy.

Doc cleared his throat, and spoke loudly and clearly. "Spirit of Good Omen who will come to aid me, believe I have great need of thee. I beg of thee now to enter this circle, that in this house offer thy protection when anything is needed by your daughter Kylie, that she can call unto thee: be what it may, do not abandon her by night or day!"

I didn't know what I expected. Another thunderclap, maybe. A puff of smoke? But when all eyes darted toward the Booke, so did mine. It shuddered, flopping on the desk. My look of fear at Doc Boone made him shake his head. Great. He wasn't sure if it was helping or harming either.

The Booke trembled violently and then stilled.

The room felt unnaturally quiet. Even the crackling of the fireplace seemed muffled.

Jolene's strained voice rang out and she pointed at the floor. "Look at the chalk line!"

It was glowing. Doc kept a steady pressure on my hand. "Don't move, Kylie!" he rasped.

The urge to flee was strong, but I stood where I was. No one moved. Everyone just stared at the pentagram, which glowed a bright bluish light. The light seemed to rise, washing over us and disappearing right up into the ceiling with a splash of brightness. Then all appeared normal again.

"Was that it?" asked Nick breathlessly.

"I suppose so," said Doc. "To tell you the truth, that's the first time that happened." He made an uncomfortable chuckle and released my hand at last. I shook it out. I didn't think he realized just how tightly he had held on.

I sucked on my sore finger and stepped gratefully from the pentagram. "So…does that mean we're protected now?"

Seraphina, eyes closed, nodded. "Yes. Yes it does. I feel it."

"Oh, God," sighed Nick. "There she goes again."

She snapped open her eyes and glared at him. "Well I *do*!"

"Guys," I said, sinking into a chair. "I can honestly say I think she's right. Something here changed. Didn't you all feel it?"

Slowly they nodded, exchanging cautious glances.

Jolene settled her hands on her thighs and beamed. "This is way better than any club at school." She shook her head in disbelief and nudged Nick, urging him to help her clean up the smoking sage and other items, carefully stuffing them back into her Hello Kitty bag.

Doc walked slowly around the room, running his hands over my walls and shelves. With wonderment in his voice, he said, "I really do think it's safe now, Kylie."

I flopped back in my chair. "Oh, good."

"That vortex does worry me, though. Jolene, have you done any research—"

She gave him a withering look that sharply cut off his sentence. She flipped the tablet from her bag and laid it on her lap as she settled into a chair. "Right here."

Everyone gathered around, and I couldn't help but steal glances at my new companions. Mere minutes ago I doubted their sanity and their intentions. But I suddenly felt an overwhelming sense of camaraderie pouring off of them in waves. I did feel safe. Maybe it was the "spell." Maybe it was something else.

"It's a gateway," she said. I looked down at her tablet, where she was reading from some handwritten notes she had made with a stylus. "At least it sounds like one. It only opens at certain unknown times."

Nick pointed down to her handwritten notes. "What does that say, Jolene?"

"The 'Chosen Host.' That's what I keep finding in conjunction with vague references to a book. The Chosen Host is the one who can close the book. That's you," she said, pointing to me.

I cringed.

"So where does Mr. Dark come into it?" asked Nick. "Is he from the vortex?"

"No," I said, staring at Jolene's scrawl written in digital magic across her tablet. "I think he's from the Booke. He's like the guardian of the Booke or something. And he wants the Booke closed. He said the Powers That Be want it closed. But they don't want to destroy it. Where does it even come from?"

"He's a demon," said Seraphina. "He lies."

"I know. But not about this. The Booke..." I glanced back at it. "It gives me little clues. Though I'm still scared of him," I admitted quietly. Still, that wasn't quite the whole truth. I was scared of his power, of what it could do, of his intentions that I couldn't quite fathom. But I was also scared of my attraction to him, and the flicker of reciprocated attraction I saw in his eyes. I had been angry with him today, but I had fantasized just a bit, too. The intensity of his glare, his long-fingered hands, well-formed lips, that rumbling voice and even his ridiculously posh accent. If he had been a human stranger, he'd definitely be fair game to dream about. But as a demon? I had no business thinking the things I'd been thinking. Why couldn't I daydream about that sheriff instead? He was drool-worthy. And I *did* want to see him again in a non-murder-accusation scenario. But there was something about Erasmus. That bad boy thing, maybe? Just like my last boyfriend. *Jeez, Kylie, what's with this self-destructive behavior?*

Seraphina sidled up to me, bracelets clanking. "You don't need to be frightened of him. You're protected now. And we're here."

"But you're not here all the time. And he comes and goes when he pleases. Though I made him pretty mad today. He might not be back."

"He'll be back," said Doc. "He needs the book."

"There's no escaping him, then," I said wearily. Part of me was annoyed. But another was unreasonably excited. The guy was bad news…but when had that ever stopped me? "Just to be on the safe side," I said, going to the buffet. "I made these for you guys."

I pulled out the little pouches on silk strings. I handed one to each of them.

"What's this?" asked Nick as I draped it over his head. The string was long enough that the little pouch hung to his chest. "Is it a charm to ward off evil?" He lifted it and scrutinized it. "Cool. You did this yourself?"

"It's not magic," I said. "It's tea." I handed the next one to Doc and then another to Jolene. "Erasmus is allergic to tea. It'll keep him away from you guys."

"What about you?" Seraphina asked, putting the string over her head and fixing the little cotton bag in place among her other necklaces.

I shrugged. "I have his amulet. I don't think he can hurt me while I'm wearing it."

"Yes!" said Jolene. "It's a pretty powerful piece." She got her fingers close to it but wouldn't touch it. "And the way that you got it means it's a powerful deterrent. He really *can't* hurt you while you've got it. But…" She chewed on her lip.

"But?"

"You will eventually have to give it back. And then…"

"Oh." I couldn't help but touch it. It felt warm in my hand as always, like it was infused from the inside with a hot coal. *Well, think about where it came from, Kylie!* "Maybe I don't have to give it back…"

But she was shaking her head. "You do. There will come a time when you have to. I guess you'll know that time. And that's when you'll be your most vulnerable."

"That doesn't sound very promising."

"I tried to find out more." Her fingers squeezed the edges of her tablet so tightly they whitened. "But there just isn't any information. There's a scroll in Sumerian, but my ancient Mesopotamian languages are a bit rusty."

"You're kidding, right?"

She quirked a smile. "I'm looking into it."

I had a hunch that she wouldn't let it go, like a dog with a bone. I felt better about that.

I kept looking at Jolene.

"I'm fine!" she said in an irritated voice. "No aftereffects."

"Well excuse me for my concern, but maybe you don't know, since you were the one possessed."

"How about it, Doc?" asked Nick. "Is she going to be okay?"

"I'm afraid medical science doesn't cover this. But I'd be happier if you were no longer holding on to the scryer. Sorry, my dear."

Jolene made a face but reached into her bag and handed it over. He tucked it into his coat hanging on the hall tree.

We all fell silent, until I said, "Thanks everyone. For everything."

Nick gave me a sheepish smile. "No problem. It was wicked interesting. And don't worry about your floor. I can clean it later."

"Best leave it here for now," said Doc, shrugging into his coat.

"You'll want the Craft to settle," said Jolene. She grabbed her bag and slung the straps over her shoulder. "As for the succubus…"

Oh, God, I'd almost forgotten about that.

"I've been thinking." She looked around at our anxious faces. "Let me do a little more digging and I'll talk to you tomorrow."

"You're welcome to come here again tomorrow evening. Or, you know. After school," I told her. I felt obliged to keep an eye on her. It was my fault that something had been allowed to possess her.

She brightened. "Cool. I can help you around here, if you want. You don't need any hired help, by any chance, do you? My Dad said I'm going to have to earn my pocket money soon."

"Well, now that you mention it, I might be able to use some part-time help, I think."

Doc paused at the door. "Good. I'd feel better if one of us was here."

"I was here today," said Seraphina.

He nodded. "And a good thing, too. Well, good night, Kylie. That was some mighty fine chili you cooked up."

"My pleasure."

"I'll bring Chinese tomorrow night," said Nick.

"Okay," I said and smiled.

He grinned back and stomped toward the door, following Doc into the night. Seraphina took my hand and squeezed it. "You're doing fine, Kylie. I'll stop by tomorrow afternoon, too."

"Great. The more the merrier."

Jolene was hard on her heels. "And I'll be here right after school, around four."

"Awesome. Four is fine."

She nodded and took her knit cap with the animal ears from her coat pocket and slipped it over her head. "Bye!"

The bell over the door tinkled as they all left. I locked the door behind them. I waved from the window and watched as their cars backed out and drove away.

Quiet again. My hand was on the light switch but my gaze traveled over to the fireplace, whose crackling fire had dwindled down to glowing embers and ash. There was a chalked pentagram on my plank floor. And a splotch of my own blood. That was all that stood between me and a scary, evil vortex that did not want me to fulfill my obligations to some arcane Booke. Whatever I'd expected when I moved across the country to Maine, it sure wasn't this.

When I switched off the light, the glow from the fireplace cast reddish light over the pentagram. I knew it was protecting me but the sight of it still creeped me out, especially when I thought of the humming and the blood. I looked at my finger, trying to see the little slice in the darkness. It still stung and throbbed a little, but it was better than being scared. I crossed the shop and cautiously walked over to the rolled-up rug to close the metal screen over the dying embers. The clock on the mantel told me it was almost eleven and suddenly I felt exhausted. I picked up the rug and flopped it over the pentagram. I'd leave it alone, but I didn't have to look at it.

I flipped off lights as I went, finally putting a foot on the bottom step of the staircase. Above me, a rafter creaked. I froze. The house could have been settling. Or…someone was upstairs.

I looked up the stairwell lit by a single bulb. I waited. Was it my imagination?

It creaked again. Definitely someone…or some*thing*…moving up there.

CHAPTER TWELVE

But the house is safe, my mind complained to me.

I looked over my shoulder toward the crossbow. Taking my foot gently off the step, I crept across the shop and carefully picked up the weapon. I noticed it was cocked again with a bolt sitting in place. A different bolt from before. Like the thing knew which particular bolt I needed. I'd have to have a closer look at the crossbow later. If I had a later.

Another board upstairs creaked. Noisy bugger, whatever it was.

Placing the butt of the crossbow onto my shoulder, I started up the stairs, trying not to let the steps creak under me. I attempted to calm my breath, but I could feel my heart pounding in my chest and throat. I had seen pictures of the succubi in those books. Some just looked like women while other depictions resembled vampires with red eyes and sharp teeth. It made me wonder if the writers of these books had ever really seen one or were just going by old wives' tales.

I made it to the landing and looked up at my open bedroom doorway. The room was dark. Why hadn't I left a light on?

I stood on the landing, thinking. What was better: the element of surprise or giving the thing a chance to get out? I took a deep breath. "I know you're there!" My voice sounded surprisingly strong. "You've got three seconds to get out before I start firing."

A shape appeared at the top of the stairs. My breath caught. Was that a succubus? My hand tightened over the crossbow. My finger twitched on the trigger.

"That damned crossbow," came a wholly familiar posh voice.

My relief made me giddy and I lowered the weapon. "You're such an idiot!"

"Apparently." Erasmus took a step down and his face became clearer though still shadowed.

"What are you doing there? I could have killed you."

"Doubtful."

I climbed the steps two at a time, pointing the crossbow downward so it wouldn't go off accidentally. When I got to the top of the stairs we stared at each other.

"I thought you weren't coming back," I said quietly.

He dropped his gaze to the floor. "So did I. But I...thought better of it. You need my help. Despite the best efforts of your amateur Wiccans."

"They said the house was safe."

"From some things, yes." His eyes focused on mine again. "Not from me."

"I'm glad you're here. I'm sorry about earlier. I...I do trust you."

Brows rising, he looked at me sidelong. "Humans are very odd."

I barked a laugh from sheer relief. "Yes, we can be."

He was looking at me steadily when he raised a hand and, with a delicate finger, brushed a strand of my hair out of my eyes. I stilled while he carefully moved it and then lowered his hand. All at once he had a "why did I do that?" look on his face. His cheeks burnished to a dark blush and there was a soft intake of breath. He whirled away, stalking back up into my room, into the darkness. I followed him and switched on a lamp.

He squinted at it. "I hate electric light."

"Do you prefer candlelight?" I tossed the crossbow on the bed. I noticed that—now that the danger was gone—the string had released itself and the bolt was back in its niche on the handle.

"Candlelight, firelight. Much easier on the senses," he was saying.

"I never took you for a romantic, Erasmus."

"Miss Strange, it is not wise to taunt me."

"I don't know about that. It's my favorite hobby these days." I leaned back against a post, resisting the urge to toy with the amulet. "And it's Kylie."

"*Miss* Strange—"

"My friends call me Kylie."

He stopped, barely breathing. His brow furrowed and his eyes, so shadowed now, looked deep black. "You...consider me...a friend?"

I shrugged. "Might as well. You *are* going to help me, aren't you? That's why you came back, isn't it?"

He swallowed. Discomfort looked good on him. Too good. I forced myself to look away. It occurred to me that we were standing in my bedroom. I was wondering when it would occur to him.

No! It was time to get something straight in my head. There was far too much here that I shouldn't be messing with. A demon was just not suitable for me by any stretch of the imagination. No matter how overworked my imagination was. Even though that treacherous crossbow seemed to like him.

"Are you really a demon?" I blurted, breathless.

He was facing away from me, and his shoulders stiffened. Without turning he said, "Yes."

"But you're going to help me?"

"Yes."

"Is it because of the Booke?"

"Ye—"

"Is it *just* because of the Booke?"

Still he wouldn't face me, and he hadn't answered.

"Erasmus..."

Faster than I could blink he was right in front of me, closer than he'd ever been. His arms trapped me as he clutched the post above my head. I felt his breath on my face. I expected brimstone or something equally unpleasant, but it was soft and warm and slightly sweet. And much too close.

He leaned in. "No," he breathed. And before I could take another breath, his mouth was on mine.

His lips explored timidly at first, then they became bolder and he leaned in further, opening, easing his tongue against my mouth. I took him in with a gasp. I didn't know when my arms came up and encircled his neck, but I had pulled myself against him. He kissed like a man. He felt like a man from chest to knee, those parts that I was shamelessly pressed against. My fingers glided up into his thick hair and held on, even as his mouth released my lips and dragged down my chin, down my neck, and he flicked his tongue over the hollow of my throat.

With my fingers still in his hair, I pulled his head up again and fastened my mouth to his, feeling his lips pull at mine with growing intensity. I didn't even want to stop and think about what I was doing. I just wanted to feel him, whatever he was. He didn't feel evil. He felt like…

"Kylie," he murmured against my throat, his voice dark and rumbling. His hands eased over my shoulders and traveled to my back, pulling me tight against him again. His hot breath scorched the tender skin of my neck, up behind my ear as he nuzzled my hair. The painful hammering in my chest was matched by the drumbeat in his own. His skin smelled like hot sand and his breath, gusting over my chin and cheeks as his mouth traveled, was almost like darkly steeped tea, slightly sweetened.

His hands had moved downward to the hem of my sweater, and were slowly pushing it up, fingers tracing over my skin.

Then he stopped abruptly and jerked away, staring at me. He took a step back and all the warmth fell away as his hands left me. His eyes were rounded, horrified. "What am I doing?" he whispered. "I swore I'd never…"

"You…you…"

He took another step back. "No." He was panting, he couldn't deny it. All my excitement turned to a panicked ache.

"What…?"

"Kylie…Miss Strange, I…"

I slumped back against the post. "You're about to say this was a bad idea."

He nodded, eyes darting, his face awash with confusion.

I tilted my chin upward, staring at the ceiling. I let my heartbeat slow, but I couldn't stop the simmering anger beneath. I made *such* bad choices when it came to men. "Is this your idea of a joke? Toy with the human?"

He snapped his head toward me. "No. No…believe me, I…" He wrung his hands before curling them into fists. He stomped across the room, his duster swirling around his legs. From as far away as he could get, he stared back at me over his shoulder. He pushed his fingers through his hair. I had never seen him so discomfited, but I got no pleasure from it.

"This…cannot be allowed to happen."

"Funny. I knew you'd say something like that."

"Kylie…Miss Strange…" There was pleading in his voice. It tore at my heart.

"Okay. Message received."

I'd never seen him so forlorn. It couldn't be an act. Pretending with that face would surely send him straight to Hell. Oh, wait…

"We…we need to discuss this succubus," he said finally.

I waved noncommittally at the desk. "I have books."

"Which you have not looked at." His old grouchy self was back. *You don't fool me. Not anymore.*

"So…let's look at them now." If he could affect indifference, then so could I. I walked to the desk and spread them out. I sat in the desk chair, forcing him to pull another chair closer.

"These are less than informative," he said.

"You haven't even looked at them," I said with a scowl.

He reached for one and so did I. Our hands touched for only a moment before I darted mine forward and clutched a book as if my life depended on it. And in all likelihood it did. Opening it, I scanned down the table of contents and found the chapter. "Okay," I said. Erasmus was near. I could feel him, feel his breathing. I could also tell that he was looking at me, but when I raised my face, his eyes flicked down to the book. Was this normal demon behavior? "All I found in this book was this." I began to read the passage aloud:

> *The succubus and likewise the incubus are ancient creatures, cited in clay tablets from the Sumerian empire. The succubus preys on men while the incubus preys on women. Because the succubus was blamed for male nocturnal emissions, modern scholars believe that a misunderstanding of biology and normal bodily functions created the notion of succubi, particularly in the Christian era when such emissions were considered sinful. To blame them on a mythical creature took the culpability away from the hapless victim. Likewise, the female version of nightly events or sexual dreams could be attributed to a beast visiting the woman in the night. But there were other instances where the creature is blamed for violence and even death. Deaths from dehydration have been reported in ancient Egypt, the early Roman Empire, medieval France, and Renaissance Italy. Even in the Americas there have been reports very like a succubus attack, which are cited from the Mayan and Aztec empires, up to the Jamestown settlement in the early seventeenth century, and various accounts in New England throughout the eighteenth century.*

I sat back. "That's uninformative. It just reports attacks, not if anyone did anything about them."

"I doubt you will find that information in these texts. Nothing useful, at any rate."

"Then what can I do?"

He bolted out of his chair and swept up the crossbow from the bed. He looked at it a moment and then sat down on my comforter. "Come here."

I rose and walked toward him. He was examining the crossbow. Well, more like stroking it. I sat gingerly beside him, not too closely.

"Do you see these quarrels?" he said, fingering the bolts in their cavities.

"Yes. I was wondering why they all look so different."

"For different prey, of course. You can't expect to take down a succubus with the same quarrel as you would for a red cap."

"A what?"

He pulled a quarrel free and turned it in his hand, holding it up to the light. The wood of its shaft was highly polished, more like an ornament than a dart for taking down a creature. The tip looked like silver and as I examined it more closely, I could see scrollwork designs on the small sharp point. The feathers were black and gleamed with iridescence. Raven feathers? I was about to touch the tip when Erasmus snatched it away from me.

"Beelze's tail, woman! Don't you know better than to touch things?"

"What *now*?"

He huffed. "The point is poisoned."

"Oh." I shrank back. I had planned on looking at the bolts on my own. What if I had and Erasmus hadn't been there? "I'll be more careful. Is that for a succubus?"

"Yes. See the carvings. Look, don't touch!" He showed me the carvings on the metal tip, which looked like phases of the moon. "This is also appropriate for werewolves."

"Werewolves? You don't mean to tell me those are real, too?"

He looked at me askance. "Of course they are. Thank your gods we won't have to deal with that." He placed the quarrel in the firing groove and I watched as the string pulled back on its own.

"Wow. I thought I had to—"

"No, you don't. It's already become attuned to you."

"It did load itself. Even the bolt was in place. I was wondering how it did that."

"Really? It is *quite* attuned to you, then."

I smiled. "It likes me."

"You could say that."

"It likes you, too, since once I knew who you were it disarmed itself."

"And a good thing. I didn't fancy getting shot with this."

I took the crossbow from his hands and ran my fingers over the surfaces again. I didn't look up when I asked, "Could it kill you?"

"Hmm. A good question. I'm not quite certain of the answer." He smirked. "I do hope you don't intend to find out."

"No, of course not!"

His smirk turned to a tender smile. But even as I watched, the smile, too, faded. "Don't be so sure," he muttered.

I didn't like what he implied and so to change the subject, I pulled another quarrel from its slot. "So what about this one?"

The shaft looked to be made of ebony, black and polished smooth. The tip looked more like pewter, and the feathers were a dark red and clipped to razor sleekness.

Erasmus frowned. "You don't want to encounter the beast that can be felled with this." He plucked it out of my hand and put it back in place. "You should only concern yourself with this one," and he tapped it again in its sheath.

"But what if I miss? What if I lose it?"

"You can't lose the quarrels. They return. Here." He patted the little slot that held it.

"Free chances, then."

His hand was suddenly on mine over the crossbow. The pressure was solid. "You will not get that many chances. Tonight the moon is almost full. You may not get a better chance."

"W-what do you mean? Now?"

"Yes. We must hunt. If we do not catch it, it *will* kill again." He tugged me to my feet but I held back at the foot of the bed.

"How come it isn't the friendly little sucker you read about in those books? How come it just doesn't"—I waved vaguely—"just create those nocturnal emissions and be done with it?"

He sighed. "Because the people who write these books don't know what they are talking about. They get their information second- and third-hand. You can't translate a Sumerian scroll literally. And your medieval sources cannot be relied upon at all. Most of the writers were monks. They didn't have the least idea what was happening."

He grabbed my arm and dragged me toward the doorway. "Wait! I don't know what I'm doing!"

"That's why I'm going with you." He pulled and I stumbled after, nearly losing my grip on the crossbow.

"I don't understand. Why can't *you* just do this? Why do you need me?"

He didn't stop even when we got to the stairs. I lurched down the steps, his hand gripping my arm like a steel band. "Because *you* are the Chosen Host. The book chose you."

"Stupid Booke." I pulled up short when we got to the front door. "Let me get my coat at least."

He grunted his answer and reluctantly released me.

I pulled my arm into my jacket. "What about my purse? Won't I need my car keys?"

"We aren't taking your conveyance." He heaved an impatient sigh. "Will you hurry up!"

"Suddenly we're in a hurry," I muttered. When I'd buttoned up my coat, he pulled the door open and yanked me after him. "Do you have to drag me around like a caveman?"

He released me and stepped back, rolling his shoulders indignantly. "I am doing no such thing."

I shook out my arm. "That's better." The cold night air hit me and I immediately longed for the dying embers of my fireplace. "Lead on."

The moon had crested the nearby hills and cast silvery light over the road. The trees splayed a cross-hatching of shadows over the dried grass of the verges. Erasmus crossed the street without looking, but it didn't matter. The village was quiet. There were no cars along the road. I could see golden rectangles of light from distant houses, their windows covered with flimsy curtains. Blue light, too, flickered on their shades as people settled in for the night in front of their televisions. But those were only distant comforts. It wasn't until the night lay heavy over us that I noticed how lonely my little shop was all by itself at the end of the road. There wasn't another building within fifty yards of me.

Erasmus moved quickly and I had to trot to keep up. He leapt up the grassy verge and plunged into the woods, moving as if he could see perfectly well in the dark. He probably could. "I should have brought a flashlight," I muttered as I tripped for the third time over a root I couldn't see. And I had forgotten my stupid phone. The moon cast a lot of light, but it did no good under the canopy, even when most of the trees had cast off their leaves. The empty branches shivered overhead, moved by the soft breeze. They clattered like old bones and made a maze on the ground that effectively camouflaged all the traps for my feet.

I tripped again and stopped, nursing my sore foot. "Erasmus!" I hissed. "Will you slow down!"

He stopped. All I saw was a dark shade blocking the path of moonlight. Just the edge of his hair was lit, glowing a little. He was looking back at me but I couldn't see his eyes.

"How do you expect to hunt when you make all that noise?" he said.

"I can't see anything."

"Are you telling me your eyes haven't adjusted yet? I was led to believe that humans could see very well in the moonlight."

As I rubbed my toe through my shoe, I glanced about. I did start to see better now that my pupils had dilated enough. The details of the forest came to life under the muted light. Enough to make out the stumps and rocks that tripped me up.

"Fine," I muttered and caught up to him. When I looked up at his face I could see the details. The moonlight edged along his patrician nose and his lips. Lips I had kissed only a few minutes ago. Maybe I stared at them a little too long because when I lifted my gaze to his eyes they were glittering, scrutinizing. "Where are we going exactly?" My voice seemed to ride on a cloud of breath between us. His usual stiff posture relaxed and he leaned a little toward me. I thought he was going to kiss me again, and I was ashamed to say that I would have let him. I turned my face away to avoid it, pretending instead that I was looking around.

"We are hunting a succubus," he said quietly.

"Yeah, I got that. But where?"

He loosed a sigh, breath pluming around his face. "I forgot. You are human. You can't smell it."

I wrinkled my nose. "What does it smell like?"

He smirked. "Sex. And death."

"Charming." I adjusted the crossbow at my hip. "So…does that mean that the succubus is having sex with the victims first?"

"Not necessarily. But the scent usually attracts males of your kind. That allows her to get close to them."

"What does it look like? The pictures in the book weren't very helpful."

"It looks like a woman…and not like a woman."

"That's not very helpful either. Any more words of advice?"

"Stay close."

He turned and stomped into the woods again, though his tread was muffled. I couldn't hear one twig he broke, or any leaves crunching beneath him. "Hey," I stage-whispered. "How are you doing that?"

"Doing what?" he hissed over his shoulder.

I came up right behind him. "Not making any noise as you walk."

"I try to behave as if I weren't a limping herd of elephants."

I muttered something that I hoped he didn't catch…or maybe I hoped he did. He didn't acknowledge it in any case, and he still hadn't told me where we were going. It seemed we were wandering aimlessly. And as I looked back at the tangle of brush and low-hanging boughs to the path we had traveled, I couldn't actually *see* a path. And it struck me with a hot jolt to my chest that if Erasmus left me now, I'd have no idea how to get back out of the woods.

The scarier scenes of *The Blair Witch Project* loomed in my mind.

Over his shoulder, Erasmus said, "It is best to capture the creature in a glade in the moonlight."

"You're kidding me."

He frowned. "I don't 'kid.'"

Come to think of it, I didn't believe he did.

I stuck close, listening to the comforting sound of crickets as we moved through the scratching branches and dark columns of trees, and suddenly came upon a clearing. Dew clung to the expanse of dried grass and glittered in the moonlight like thousands of tiny diamonds. The moon was higher now and its remarkable light painted only one side of the rough bark of the alders and maples. The trees seemed to shy away from the fully lit clearing, veering back into the shadows of the woods around us. *Stay out of the shadows*, I remembered Jolene's possessed voice saying. *What has begun cannot now be stopped.* I should tell him about that. I should…

"And now we wait…" His voice trailed off and he held a finger to his lips.

The crickets stopped.

I held my breath. My eyes were wide, searching the clearing. I licked my dry lips and clutched the crossbow hard. It had armed itself with the correct quarrel again. Good ole chthonic crossbow.

Erasmus hadn't budged. The only movement I saw was his hair lifting with a breeze. It was a stupid careless moment reminiscing about my fingers in that hair, how soft it had felt, because I wasn't prepared when a shadow swept down over me, knocking me off my feet and whooshing the breath out of me with a harsh thud.

CHAPTER THIRTEEN

I smelled it this time. There was something trailing over my face, like lace or silk, and it smelled like turned earth and decay. I was on my back in the wet leaf duff while shadows swirled above me. I caught a glimpse of a white arm gleaming in the moonlight before it disappeared into the shadows again. Remarkably, I still had the crossbow in my hand, but I wasn't about to fire, in case I hit Erasmus.

I turned, struggling onto my hands and knees. Something slammed into my head and pain exploded in a shower of stars. I flopped down on my stomach. The edges of my sight were darkening. No way was I going to let myself get knocked out and at the mercy of a succubus. I shook my head—and stopped when that made it worse. I just lay still, letting the darkness slip away and the light come back to my sight. I stumbled to my feet with the butt of the crossbow in my shoulder. Something was happening in the center of the glade but I couldn't quite tell what I was looking at. Swirling shadow with flashes of pale skin and hair, which flew outward like flowing seaweed. It, too, was pale and captured the moonlight. But there was also darkness, and they intertwined like some strange bolero. A tornado of leaves surrounded them and the grass was mashed and muddied beneath it.

Them. I realized that Erasmus was wrestling with the creature.

"Kylie!" he yelled.

"Erasmus! I'm here!"

"Shoot!"

"I...I can't see it. I don't want to shoot you."

"Dammit, woman, I said shoot!"

I squinted at the whirling mass of leaves, dust, shadow, and light. "But—" I had to trust him, didn't I? I lifted the crossbow up to my shoulder, closed my eyes, and fired. It kicked back a little and I blinked as the quarrel shot forward with a twang of the string.

There was a shriek, a howl that I had heard before, and the churning mass roared and whipped, leaves flying like a giant blender. I raised a hand to my face to defend against the scratching leaves as they flung at me. Something shot outward and the leaves froze in the air for a long second before they simply fell to the ground, like cut puppet strings. The meadow was suddenly silent again, and it took another few moments for the first tentative crickets to begin their song once more.

A dark lump remained in the center of where the cyclone had been and I stepped closer, aiming the crossbow, now armed again. The closer I got, the tighter my hold of the weapon became, until I stood right over it. But when the moon passed beyond a cloud and cast its light, I could see that it was Erasmus.

"Oh my God!" I dropped the crossbow and fell to my knees. "Dammit, you said you'd be all right!" He was lying on his side. I ran my hands over him. "Erasmus! Don't be dead. Please don't be dead."

A groan. My heart jumped. I gently turned him, looking for the quarrel, expecting to see it in his chest. But nothing was there.

I glanced at the crossbow and all quarrels were back in their sheaths.

"Erasmus." I pushed his hair out of his face. He opened his eyes and blinked, looking a bit dazed. I caressed his cheek, feeling how cold the skin was. His eyes focused on mine and he seemed to realize his position. He shot unsteadily to his feet and dusted himself off.

"It got away," he said.

"Did I graze it?"

"No. You grazed *me*."

"Erasmus!" I grabbed his shoulder to turn him and he winced.

"The shoulder," he said and gently removed my hands.

"I'm sorry."

"Not your fault. I told you to shoot."

The adrenaline high I had been running on was leaving me, making my limbs feel heavy. "Do we follow it?" I asked, dreading the answer.

But Erasmus shook his head, rubbing his sore shoulder. "No. It's spooked. In hiding. The good news is it might not kill tonight after all."

"Well…that's…something."

Without another word, he turned away and headed back the way we had come. At least, I thought it was the way we had come.

I picked up the crossbow and followed him. With the weapon tight to my chest, I clutched my arms. I was cold.

We trudged back through the woods and I was never so relieved to see asphalt. We reached my shop and I unlocked the door. I didn't need to ask. He came through as I held it open for him. Once I switched on the lights, I saw the dark patch on his coat.

"Are you *bleeding*?"

He stared at the patch curiously, dipped his finger in it, and brought it to his lips and tasted. I swallowed down the tang of bile.

He raised surprised eyes. "That appears to be correct."

"You're such an idiot. Get that coat off and let me look at it."

His hand clutched protectively at the collar of his duster. "Why?"

"So I can fix you up."

"What do you mean?"

"What do you mean what do I mean? You're hurt. I'm going to bandage you. You don't want to get an infection." His face was still perplexed as I grabbed for the collar. "Come on. Get it off. It does come off, doesn't it?"

He pushed my hands away and unbuttoned the coat. Carefully, he peeled it over his good shoulder and then even more carefully over the hurt one.

"Let me help—"

"I can do it!" He winced, shutting his eyes tight as the coat slipped to the floor. The patch of dark was even bigger on his black long-sleeved shirt, which was torn where the quarrel hit. The fabric was strange, like silk but it wasn't shiny at all.

"The shirt, too," I said.

He looked at me as if I had suggested he do a striptease on the city hall steps. And then my mind went there. I blinked, getting rid of the image as best I could. "I can't very well bandage you *over* your shirt."

He sighed again and reached for the first button, undoing them mechanically. I was worried about his arm, sure, but I realized I was also staring in anticipation. He parted the shirt, revealing a well-toned abdomen with a little dark hair on his chest. But as he pulled it back, I also noticed a strange tattoo reaching from his chest down his torso. I knew I was staring, but I couldn't tear my eyes away.

He grunted when he dropped the shirt. Naked from the waist up, he wasn't what I expected. Not like any demon I'd ever imagined. More like an underwear model.

"The wound is up here," he said.

"Sorry," I muttered, turning my attention to the blood-streaked graze on his shoulder. At first it seemed like the quarrel had cut a good chunk off of his skin along the shoulder, but it wasn't as deep as I first thought. There was a lot of blood, or what I took for blood. In the light, his blood wasn't quite as red as I expected. It was darker. Red, but almost black.

I maneuvered him to a chair and urged him to sit. "What about the poison?"

He shook his head. "It's only making me a bit woozy, nothing more."

"Let me get my first aid kit."

I ran to the kitchen to fetch the little white box hanging on the wall. I pulled it free and set it beside the sink. Grabbing a towel from the drawer, I wet it under the faucet, squeezing out the excess water.

Erasmus was sitting stiff and straight in the chair when I returned. I set down the first aid box and knelt beside him. "This might sting," I warned, laying a gentle hand on his arm to steady myself, and then I bathed around the wound with the wet towel. He didn't wince. I cleaned it up and lay the towel aside, and then I opened the box and rummaged for a bandage. There were antiseptic wipes in little packages, and I picked one up and looked from it to his wound. With his physiology, would it do more harm than good? I opted for leaving it aside, deciding on a large sticky bandage alone.

I tore open the package and laid the gauzy part over the wound, smoothing the adhesive over his warm skin. My hands might have wandered unnecessarily over his arm, but I left him alone when I was done, sitting back to look at my handiwork. "Is that all right?" I hadn't noticed he was staring at me until I had finished. He was looking at me strangely and used his other hand to tentatively poke at the foreign object now stuck to his arm.

"Thank you," he said in a roughened voice.

"You're welcome." I gathered the detritus and took it all to the kitchen again, setting the box and towel down on the counter. When I returned he was still examining the bandage. I didn't mind at all watching the muscles flex under his skin. I stood in the doorway a long time, it seemed, and I felt my face warm when he looked up, catching me in the act.

"No human has ever helped me before."

I folded my arms and leaned against the doorjamb. "It couldn't be your sparkling personality getting in the way, could it?"

A ghost of smile passed over his face but he turned away and grabbed his shirt. "Certainly not."

I busied myself fiddling with knick-knacks on shelves while he dressed. When I glanced over my shoulder, even his duster was back in place. He said, "I'll leave you now."

"Oh." I followed him to the door. It was late. I didn't have to look at the clock to know that. "You don't want any coffee or something? Wine?"

He straightened his collar, flipping it up before he reached for the door handle. He stopped and angled his head. "It's late."

"I know." My hand reached the door and slid up the molding. Clumsily I leaned against it. "But it wouldn't take long…"

He grasped my hand from the door and he was suddenly holding both of them. "Kylie," he said gruffly. "What do you expect from me?"

"Expect? I don't really expect anything. Well, I expect you to help me with this Booke thing. That's all I meant." I was babbling and closed my mouth before I truly embarrassed myself. But I couldn't stop the trembling he could surely feel. His hands were warm enclosing mine, as warm as his amulet, resting heavy and hot against my chest.

He smiled again. It changed his face to something brighter, less world-weary. "I will help you with the book. But nothing more."

I tossed my hair back with what I hoped was nonchalance. "I don't know what you mean."

He let my hands go, and his smile faded. "No, of course not." He pulled open the door and hesitated in the doorway. "Stay safe," he said without turning around. And then he plunged into the night and vanished.

"Neat trick," I muttered and closed the door. I slammed the bolt in place.

• • •

I woke far too early the next morning. I had had a hard time getting to sleep and when I finally did, I dreamed of pale arms and long weedy hair chasing me into the shadows. I felt pretty rough and even a hot shower didn't vanquish all the cobwebs. But the routine of making coffee and pricing and sorting tea helped. Though the monotony gave me time to dwell on last night, going over it too many times, thinking of how it felt to kiss Erasmus and how I felt in his arms. I shook my head.

The phone rang and got me out of my funk. It was Marge from Moody Bog Market.

"Thanks for taking me under your wing yesterday. It was good to meet the villagers." Though as I said "villagers," I instantly formed a picture in my head of Ruth Russell and John Fairgood with torches and pitchforks, leading the others to a tar-and-feathering.

"It was my pleasure. I think you bring a breath of fresh air to this place. But that was yesterday. Since I'm the new manager, Bob Hitchins—may he rest in peace, the poor man—had a note to call you about some kind of deal with baked goods, selling them at your shop?"

I explained what I wanted and we agreed on a price and a delivery schedule. She talked me into ordering the apple pecan loaf as well. I felt guilty about Bob, because I knew what happened to him and I felt a little responsible. As Erasmus was fond of telling me, *I* had opened the Booke and released the succubus.

I hung up, a little poorer but looking forward to fresh baked goods on opening day. However, it did remind me that I hadn't yet heard from Ruth Russell about her Knitting Society.

I got out my phone and checked. Sure enough, there *was* a terse email from her.

> *Our Knitting Society meets at 2 o'clock. 559 Mill Pond Road. Don't be late.*

Was this an invitation or a slap on the wrist? I tucked the phone away just as the bell over the door tinkled. I poked my head out of the kitchen to spy Sheriff Ed picking up a delicate saucer, turning it this way and that. His large fingers overwhelmed it and his face seemed to say, "Why would anyone want this?"

"Hey," I said, and giggled when he jumped.

He set the cup down and tipped his hat. "Hey, yourself." He glanced around. "It's looking good. Are you open yet?"

"Friday's the grand opening. But you're welcome to come in. I have coffee. And a little apple pecan loaf."

His eyes brightened. "If it's not too much trouble."

"Not at all." I fetched the loaf from the pantry. "It's better heated. I can just pop it in the microwave."

"That would be fine, thanks." He took off his hat and shrugged out of his heavy jacket, draping it on the back of the chair.

"So, what brings you here, Sheriff?" I cut a generous slice from the loaf and placed it on a plate, licking my fingers. I slid the plate into the microwave and switched it on. Then I poured the strong Ethiopian Harar into a mug. "Cream? Sugar?"

"Cream and sugar, please. I know I'm not supposed to but old habits die hard."

I placed the sugar bowl in front of him and set the mug on the table. The microwave dinged; I pulled out the plate and laid a fork beside the warmed slice.

I sat opposite him and watched as he scooped three sugars into his mug and picked up his fork. "Aren't you going to have any?"

"I just ate." *Two* slices, but he didn't need to know that.

He drank his brew and mmmmed over the mug. "That's good coffee. You know your beans and teas, I guess."

"You could say that."

He chewed a forkful of apple pecan loaf and grinned. "Moody Bog Market. Finest bakery this side of the Mississippi."

I picked at a ravel of my sweater sleeve. "So…you were saying? You dropped by because…?"

He swallowed and set down his mug. He looked a bit sheepish. "Well, you said to drop by and I hoped…it wasn't just talk."

It was my turn to smile. Sheriff Ed was handsome, broad-shouldered, and tall. I didn't yet know the quirks of his personality, but he seemed the opposite in just about every respect to my former boyfriend, the One-Who-Shall-Not-Be-Named.

While I was admiring Sheriff Ed's dimple as he chewed, I felt a twinge of guilt. It was just last night that I had kissed Erasmus and harbored some mighty intricate fantasies about the man. Demon. He wasn't a man, not really. But this one was. A human man. And Erasmus had closed the door on anything that was poised to develop. And here was another opening up. It reminded me how lonely I had been the last two months.

I brushed my hair back over my ear. “No, it wasn’t just talk.” I smiled. I was a little rusty at this but I knew it would come back to me. Like riding a bicycle.

• • •

He cleaned his plate and turned down a second slice, but said yes to more coffee. I watched with widened eyes as he scooped more sugar in and drank that down, too. We talked for about half an hour, about the village and some of the personalities in it. He shook his head when I asked about the Wiccans. “Doc and his Wicca.” His tone was cynical.

I sat stiff-backed. “You disapprove?”

He stirred his coffee absently. “Not…in theory. I just…it’s silly, is all.”

“Some people don’t think it’s silly,” I said a little too primly. “Even Reverend Howard gave it his blessing.”

Ed snorted. “Love thy neighbor,” he muttered. “Look, don’t get the wrong impression. I respect Doc. He’s got a good head on his shoulders. And the others are nice enough. But I think that there are just some things people should not mess with. Things they don’t fully understand.”

“The same could be said for *all* religions.”

His gentle smile was back. “That’s certainly true.”

“Besides, they don’t do any harm.”

Ed’s eyes darkened behind his coffee cup. “I suppose,” he muttered. “You’re not getting into that stuff, are you?”

I didn’t meet his gaze. “Well… I mean I think they’re interesting people and they seem to like to use my place. I think they’ll be good for business.”

“I see.” He set down his mug and checked his watch. Rising, his chair scraped back.

Uh oh. I hoped I didn’t scare him off. Perhaps he saw the

worried look on my face and smiled to allay my fears. "As long as that's all it is. Not every day should be Halloween. No offense to Doc's Wiccans." He wiped his lips on the napkin and set it down. "Look, I've got to go. I don't want to, but I've got to." Lifting his jacket from the chair he punched an arm into his sleeve.

"I'm glad you dropped by."

He smiled and stuck his Smokey Bear hat on his head. "Me, too. Ms. Strange, I was wondering if I could take you to supper some time. Maybe tomorrow night?"

"It might be a bit tight time-wise. I've got to be ready to open Friday." He blinked, hesitant. "But I am getting help today. From those Wiccans you so disparage."

"Now wait a minute—"

I laughed at the worried look on his face. "I know. You like Doc and his friends."

"I did tell you that."

"Okay, okay. I give."

He rocked on his heels. "So? Tomorrow night?"

I grinned. "Yes, I suppose that would be fine. But you are going to have to start calling me, Kylie, Sheriff."

"Then you're going to have to start calling me Ed."

"Okay. Ed."

I walked him to the door. He smiled down at me. "Tomorrow night, then. Pick you up around seven?"

"Sure."

He shook his head. "Okay." I closed the door after him and watched that spring in his step as he got into his black and white Interceptor.

A real person. Not some vanishing demon. You couldn't build a life with a demon, after all, now could you? Erasmus had ended it before it had begun, and I was fine with that. Really fine with it.

• • •

At 1:15, I rushed around Moody Bog looking for knitting needles and an instruction book. At 1:30, I tried to knit something, anything, but it looked more like a refugee from a washing machine disaster. At 1:45, I cut the label out of one of my favorite old sweaters and stuffed it into my coat pocket, and with keys in hand, locked the shop door.

I found Mill Pond Road without much trouble and parked along the grassy edge of one of the older neighborhood streets. There was, in fact, a mill, a stream, and a pond on Mill Pond Road. Gotta love those literal founders. The Russells lived in a house that was made to look as old as mine, but considerably larger. There were a lot of expensive cars parked in front of the manicured lawn that stretched up a rise to the house, and I hurried along the street and up the flagstone pathway. There was a decorative medallion on the porch right before the front door in in a mosaic of tiny glass tiles. No expense was spared for the Russells.

Even in my nice slacks and dark sweater, I felt a bit underdressed. Was this a Knitting Society or Knitting Cotillion? Ladies about Ruth's age were in dresses and smart business suits, with plenty of bling. I smiled as a maid in a uniform opened the door and allowed me in. She was taking my coat before I remembered and grabbed the mangled sweater from the pocket. I stepped down into a lavish living room, with two large sofas facing each other in front of an enormous fireplace. The house was decorated in a harvest theme, with plenty of pumpkins, gourds, Indian corn, fall leaves, and enough raffia to make Martha Stewart envious.

The women were in klatches with teacups and saucers in their hands, when many of them turned to look at me. Maybe they thought the help had come to join the party.

Ruth was suddenly there beside me. "Oh, you came."

"Your house is amazing."

Her stiff posture loosened a little and her pursed mouth even tried a smile. "Thank you. Won't you sit down? Stella will bring you some tea. I hope it's adequate to your preference."

"I like all kinds of tea...as you might imagine."

"Yes," she said noncommittally. "We'll be starting in a minute." And then she whisked away.

A woman in a maid's uniform—Stella, I presumed—offered me a cup and saucer, and I took it with a spoon of sugar and a splash of milk. And then I found a spot on a loveseat next to a silk-scarfed woman who looked me over speculatively. "You're new," she said.

"Not that new," I said with a smile. I sipped my tea, a standard black leaf of no particular distinction. "But I did just move to Moody Bog."

By the look on her face, I could tell she didn't get the joke. "I'm Kylie Strange. I'm opening Strange Herbs & Teas this Friday. The tea shop on Lyndon Road."

"Oh, I see. That's…delightful." Before I could ask her name and what she did about town, she had already turned away to chat with a woman in a wingback chair to her left.

I sipped and looked around. The bluebloods of Maine, I supposed. How rude of me to be so common.

After another few minutes, someone rang a little bell and the ladies, like trained dogs, all turned their attention to Ruth, who set the bell on the wide mantel. "Thank you all for coming today. I'm sure we're all anxious to get started and talk about our latest projects. But first I'd like to present our guest." She turned her eyes toward me and gestured. "Kylie Strange. She's just moved to Moody Bog."

Everyone looked my way. I slowly rose and gave everyone a wave. "Hi, everyone. Thanks for having me today. It's so marvelous to meet you all. As Ruth said, I've just moved to your charming village. I'm opening my herb and tea shop at the end of the week and I hope you can all come to the grand opening." I saw the sparkle of jewelry, and heard the soft click of a spoon on a saucer, but nothing else, not even a smile. "Sooo…let's…get to knitting!" I punched a fist in the air and sank back to my seat.

Another long moment passed with the stares of strangers raking over me, before Ruth called on the ladies to share their latest. The room burst into animated discussion, with half-finished sweaters and scarves coming out of nowhere.

I stared down at my fakery and tucked it away in the seam between the couch and the cushion. Everyone was busy and no one seemed interested in talking to me. So I decided to get to what I came here for—snooping.

I made my way casually across the living room, making a point to ooh and ah at the examples of purling prowess. When I made it to the hallway without being stopped, I perched in the doorway for a few moments, making sure no one was looking at me, and headed down the corridor. I could always plead that I was looking for the bathroom.

I expected there to be a library and I found it almost immediately. Closing the double doors, I looked around. "Family history," I muttered, eyes scanning the book spines. And there it was. "Howland Family" boldly printed on the side of a thick archive box.

I dragged it down, placing it on a wide carved desk. Opening it, I thumbed through the papers. Down deeper were the parchmenty ones, and I went directly to them. They were difficult to read, handwritten in that ornate script, but there was a Prosper Howland, a Humility Howland, Grace, John, Ethan, Isaac, Jasper, Peter, Francis, Elizabeth—finally! Constance Howland.

I pulled out that sheaf and studied it. Mundane information, like the year she was born, brothers and sisters—and there were many—but nothing pertinent to my situation. I dug deeper into the archive box and pulled out a torn parchment. I squinted at the spiky writing, and as I read, I realized that this was in Constance's own hand. She had written it hurriedly, it seemed, and some of the ink was smudged with splotches of drops. I took it to the lamp and began to read:

> *—my nature. But I fear it was more than that. For having read certain entries of letters from my ancestors, I began to see that I was not the only one. There were others leading*

> *farther back than I ever knew, back to England, back to the sands of Egypt itself, I reckon. It is the Curse, then, of my ancestors, just as the Dark Man said—*

And that was all. I turned it over. Nothing. I blew out a frustrated breath and put the scrap back. Was Constance hinting at a family business of Chosen Hosts? Digging deeper I found a folded paper. As I unfolded I realized it was a lot larger than I originally thought. Wall map sized. A detailed genealogy.

Howlands as far back as the eye could see. I was about to fold it back up when another surname caught my eye. Married to the Howlands sometime around Constance Howland's era was the name…Strange.

"What the…?"

My finger started following. Holy cats! They branched off but there was a distinct line of Howlands and an equally distinct line of Stranges.

My head snapped up when the door opened.

Ruth clutched her hands before her. "What are you doing?"

My gaze cast unwillingly toward the open archive box and the scattered pages. I winced. "Oh…well…I was looking for the bathroom and when I passed the library I just had to take a peek. I love libraries and this one is fantastic." There was no way I could block the evidence of my snooping. She saw it immediately and stomped over, glaring at the open box.

"What is the meaning of this?"

I couldn't think of one plausible excuse and came as close to the truth as I dared. "I saw the name 'Howland' on that and just thought I'd take a quick look. I understand a Howland used to live in the house I now own."

With trembling fingers, she scooped up the papers, plucking out the folded genealogy still in my hand, and carefully shuffled them back into place. Her hand closed the box and she took up the whole thing and slid it into the empty space on the library shelf. Slowly she pivoted and faced me.

"You and Karl Waters," she sneered. "I knew you had something to do with him."

"What? No! I—"

"He managed to get his hands on a lot of the Howland papers when my father died before I could stop him. He had no right. And now you're trying to steal the rest!"

"You've got it wrong. It's not what it looks like."

"I think you should leave now."

I swallowed, feeling like the biggest thief, though I hadn't stolen anything. "Look, Mrs. Russell, I didn't mean any harm. I'm just trying to find out more about Constance Howland—"

"I said that you should leave. Do you want me to make a scene?"

"No. No, let's not do that." Feeling like a whipped puppy, I moved toward the door. She was still trembling with anger. "I'm really sorry. But I only wanted to find out more about Constance Howland. I *need* to."

"Get out."

Her voice was low and clipped. I figured I'd better go before she started yelling.

I slipped out of the doorway and when I got to the living room and all the chattering ladies, I found Stella standing nearby. "Can I get my coat? I've got to leave."

She helped me put it on and then handed something to me. "I believe you dropped this."

It was my fake knitted sweater that I had left stuffed into the sofa. "Oh, uh, thanks." I plunged it into my coat pocket. When movement down the hallway caught the corner of my eye, I turned my head.

Ruth was staring at me, eyes narrowed. Crap. This was going to get to the rest of the Chamber of Commerce and then I'd never get to join.

And worse. That note from Constance Howland. It seemed that she knew more than at first appeared. What was that she was saying? Something about the "Curse of her ancestors." She had to mean the Booke.

And just how close were the Howlands to the Stranges? I gave a tiny wave toward Ruth. "Later…*cuz*."

• • •

I had to let it go. I knew Jolene was arriving at four today and I hurried back, trying to get there before she did. When she arrived, I looked her over in her heather gray hoodie, still worried about her run-in with the evil vortex.

She sighed at my prolonged scrutiny. "I'm fine!"

"Just checking. Can you blame me? It's not like I ever experienced someone getting possessed before."

She shook her head with all the disdain a teen was capable of. When she set her bag down and slipped off her coat, I was on edge. "Look, Jolene, can you do me a favor?"

"Sure." She hung her coat on the hall tree and straightened her dark wool skirt.

I rubbed my clammy palms down the jeans I had slipped back into upon returning from the Knitting Society. "I need to know more about the life of Constance Howland. I tried to glean what I could from some papers at Ruth Russell's house."

"She let your look at her archives?"

I registered her astonishment. "Not exactly. She sort of caught me doing a little unauthorized investigating and, uh, threw me out."

She clapped her hands to her mouth, but it was more to stifle a laugh than to express incredulity. "Oh my God."

"Yeah." My face was burning.

"Did you find out anything?"

"Actually, yes. I found something in Constance's own hand. She seemed to think she was destined for this, that she was only the most recent in a long line of Booke caretakers."

"Wow." Jolene gnawed on her thumb. "Well, if Ruth Russell

has these papers, there might be copies in some library. Even if it's in the county seat. I'll look around."

"If it's true what Constance Howland said," I said quietly, afraid of demon ears listening, "I want to know if anyone knew what *really* happened to her."

"Mr. Waters's papers seemed pretty complete."

"But just in case someone else has more. I'd like to know."

She nodded.

"Oh. And one more thing. It looks like the Howlands were pretty closely tied to another family. Surname…Strange."

Her mouth dropped open. "Whoa."

"Yeah. I'm pretty sure she wouldn't be pleased to know we're related. *If* we are. I'd like to get ahold of some genealogy to find out."

"There are plenty of sites online. I'll look. Wouldn't that be cool, though? I mean, you'd be rich!"

"I'm a little more concerned with the family business." I cocked my head toward the Booke to make my meaning clear.

She nodded solemnly. "But besides the familial connection, it's kind of neat to think that you might have been coming home when you moved to Moody Bog."

I stiffened. Was that what had happened? I didn't just randomly choose that ad on Craigslist but was somehow compelled to come here? That wasn't a cool thought at all!

Jolene, without a care in the world, turned to look around the room. "You got a lot done since yesterday." She moved about the shop, peering at the shelves and cubbies. "I've been reading up on herbs and their properties so I can be a competent salesperson."

I shook off my anxiety. Shop to run, remember, Kylie? "Oh?" I said. "Should I quiz you, then?"

"Fire away."

I opened a cubby and pulled out the dried herb. "Know what this is?"

She held it and sniffed. She made a face. "St. John's wort, also known as goatweed, or chase-devil. It's supposed to be good for depression."

"Very good."

She twirled the stem in her hand. "Chase-devil. Might come in handy. If you know what I mean."

I plucked if from her hand and stuffed it back in the cubby. "I know what you mean," I said.

Jolene proved to be a good worker, and I made a point of telling her how well she was doing.

"Thanks. I don't have a lot of friends so it's good to be doing something useful. And earning money at it."

"How did you get started with Wicca, Jolene?"

She was working on a display of teapots and pre-packaged tea as she spoke. "I'd heard about it from Seraphina. She shops at my dad's nursery all the time. She started talking about it and I thought, why not?"

"And your folks are okay with it?"

"It's better than some of the stuff I could be doing. And they trust Doc to look after me."

I smiled, dusting around the knick-knacks on the mantel. "And there's something else, too. You like Nick, don't you?"

Her cheeks instantly reddened. "No! Why would you say that?" She ducked her head further into her hoodie.

"I just saw you looking at him. He's kind of cute."

She stopped and clutched the pricing gun to her chest. "He is, isn't he?" She sighed theatrically. "But he's gay. I get it. I can check him off the list. Not that there was a list or anything." She sighed. "Does it ever get easier?"

I patted her shoulder. "Nope. Never."

She lazily slapped a sticker on the box of tea with the gun. "That's what I thought."

We worked for several more hours until Seraphina arrived, and before I knew it, my shop was actually ready for business a full two days early.

"Wow, you guys. I really appreciate this."

"No problem," said Jolene. "Shouldn't I be filling out papers, or would you prefer to keep this under the table?"

I shook my head at her. "No, I'd better give you papers. After all, the sheriff is bound to be here pretty often."

"And why is that?" asked Seraphina with a glint in her eye.

"Well…" Now it was my turn to blush. "He sort of asked me out and if all goes well…"

Seraphina squealed in delight. "Oh, he is a hunk, isn't he? I'm so jealous. I've tried to catch his eye for years and you swan into town and nab him first thing."

"Beginner's luck?"

Jolene wrinkled her nose. "No offense, but he seems kind of old."

I rested my arms akimbo. "How old do you think *I* am?"

"Uh…" She pushed up her glasses. "As old as you need to be…Boss."

I laughed.

It wasn't long after that when Nick showed up bringing the promised Chinese food in greasy bags. It smelled heavenly. We spread it out on the table and I brought out dishes and pulled out the chopsticks in their paper wrappers with the mustard and packages of soy sauce.

The later it got, the more I thought about Erasmus. I thought at least one of the Wiccans should know what had happened between us. Jolene was too young, Seraphina had too lascivious a leer in her eye, and Nick seemed as if he might be too grossed out by it. I needed an impartial voice, someone who could give me solid advice, and so I decided to tell Doc.

When Doc arrived and we had settled everywhere we could, balancing plates of lo mein and egg foo young on our laps, I told everyone about the succubus hunt.

They were all stone quiet as I told my tale, eyes rounded and attention rapt. Doc asked a question or two. Of course I left out the bit about Erasmus kissing me. I could fill him in about that later in a moment alone.

"The succubus," I explained, "is just as dangerous as we were told. Erasmus was wrestling with it and I don't think he was winning. He made me fire at the thing…and I missed. I grazed Erasmus."

"Was he hurt?" asked Doc.

"Yeah, a little. I cleaned off the blood and bandaged him up."

He straightened. "Cleaned off the blood with what?"

"Just a towel."

"You don't still have that towel, do you?"

"Uh…yeah. It's in the laundry room."

"I'd like to see it, if I may."

I shrugged. "Sure." The others stayed behind, a little creeped out, I think, about looking at a demon blood-soaked towel. Doc, being Doc, was interested. I took him to the laundry room and showed him the towel, still sitting where I had tossed it on the washing machine.

He picked it up and looked at it in the light. The towel was stiff but the blood dried black, not brown. I grimaced, staring at it. "Not too pretty, is it?"

"No," he said distractedly. "Not pretty." He gripped it tight in his hand. "Can I keep this? I'd like to further analyze it. It's possible I can come up with a real chemical demon deterrent."

"Sure. I guess."

I found a plastic grocery bag to put it in and he wadded it up and stuffed it into his jacket pocket.

When we returned to the group, I told them about Constance Howland's note and the Strange family connection. Doc was thoughtful but quiet, and then we began strategizing. Would it be possible to lay a trap for the succubus? "I mean," I said, "why look for her when we can make her come to us?" Jolene got out her tablet and set to work researching. They were in mid-discussion when I signaled Doc for a quiet moment in the kitchen.

"Tea?" I asked. "Coffee?"

"Tea, if you please." He followed me in and sat at my kitchen table.

"What about that scryer? Do you think that could be used to find the succubus, or do you think it's too dangerous to use?"

"It's not dangerous...ordinarily. I think we *should* try to use it. It's what it's for, after all."

"I don't feel comfortable with Jolene using it."

He nodded. "We'll discuss it when the tea is ready." He watched me prepare it for a moment before he said quietly, "Looks to me as if you've been trying to catch my attention all evening."

I paused over the tin of China Yunnan, my scoop full of the rich herby leaves. "Well...yeah." I worked on autopilot, preparing the teapot, filling the infuser, and watching the kettle. "Last night...um. Last night, something else happened." I was facing the counter. I didn't want to look him in the eye. I had a feeling I knew what he was going to say. "Something between Erasmus and me."

I heard the chair scrape back and felt the reassuring presence of Doc behind me. "Kylie," he said softly. "Are you saying what I think you're saying?"

I spun around to face him. "Nothing happened! I mean...we kissed. But that was it."

His lips were parted and his gray eyes searched mine. "I don't think I have to tell you what kind of fire you're playing with."

"I know!" I moved around the room aimlessly, pinging from counter to counter. "And nothing *will* happen. He put the brakes on. He said...he said..."

Hands on my arms finally stopped me. "Kylie. He's right."

"I know."

Doc paused a moment before letting me go. He leaned back against the tiled counter. "I don't pretend to really know about you; who you are and what your life was like before. We haven't known each other long enough for that. But I do know something about self-destructive behavior. As a country doctor, people have confided all sorts of things in me, and I've had to keep up on psychology and all that. Your coming here to Maine, uprooting yourself. It must have been something mighty big to make you do that. Something that you keep hidden. But *you* know and *I* know that we can't really run from the things that cause us pain. We confront them and then come to terms with them."

I gestured, trying to get the words out. "I wasn't really… running…"

"Whatever it is, you seem to be doing a fine job of building something new here. But we are creatures of habit. We fall into our old ways very easily. And if part of that was choosing a partner who wasn't exactly the best for us…"

I held up my hand. "You don't have to say it. He's a bad choice. The worst choice. I mean…a demon? My ex-boyfriend was a real winner. If I wasn't so sure he was human I might put him in the demon category." I saw the concern on his face and shook my head. "He wasn't abusive. And I guess he wasn't as bad as I paint him. But he did get to me in lots of ways. And then my mom passed away." I breathed. "So I decided all new scenery was the ticket. I just wanted out of there. I don't know if it means I was running away. I fell in love with this place the first time I saw it. I felt more like I was running *to* something. Know what I mean?"

He nodded. A kind smile—his doctor smile, no doubt—gentled his face.

"I think I can be happy here in Moody Bog. And…" I picked up a tea towel and absently wrung it in my hands. "I was attracted to Erasmus. He's pretty good-looking. And that accent. But…I know he's all wrong. And he was nice enough to end it before it began. But I just thought you should know. I wondered why *he* was attracted to me but… He's been trapped in that Booke for so long that maybe anyone with a pulse would do." I twisted the towel the other way. "As it happens, I'm having dinner with Sheriff Ed. That, too, is a different choice for me."

He jerked his head back in surprise. "By Godfrey! I'll be darned. Right. I wish you all the best."

"He seems like a nice guy."

"He is. I've known him for a number of years. He's a genuine person."

"That's what I need," I muttered, turning back to the whistling kettle. "A genuine *person*."

CHAPTER FOURTEEN

"Kylie! Ky-lie!" My grandfather's voice. I turned and there he was, waving at me from his vine-covered porch. I could almost smell the gooseberry pie cooling in the kitchen. My six-year-old self lifted freckled cheeks to the sunshine. To my left was a view far below of the vast Atlantic shimmering in the sunlight. To my right, a dense forest full of trails to discover and fallen trees to climb.

I glanced toward my grandfather again and he was still waving, but he looked farther away than he had before.

Suddenly my mother's voice came from over my shoulder. "You go in and help your grandfather. Summer's almost over and we'll have to go home."

"But I don't want to go home."

"You have to," said my mother sternly. I tried to see her over my shoulder, but no matter which way I turned, she wasn't visible.

"We can't stay in Maine in the fall. Grandpa said it's too dangerous."

"Why?" I asked. "I want to stay." When I looked back at my grandfather, his face had suddenly saddened. Clouds had gathered and darkened the yard and he was even farther away than before.

"Grandpa!" I called, but he was shaking his head and retreating into the old clapboard house.

I awoke, eyes wide.

Memories flooded my mind. My grandfather. We had spent summers with my grandfather…in *Maine*. I remembered now. But where in Maine? I scrubbed at my face. I couldn't believe I never remembered that before. I remembered that yard, the view of the ocean where the sun rose instead of set, the dark forest that sheltered, the gusts of wind, the lazy days in a quiet place. A place I had inexplicably forgotten.

Where in Maine? There was no one left alive to ask. But I had my mother's things in storage. Maybe there was a photo album. Maybe I could find out. Maybe the Stranges *had* come from Maine. Why had I forgotten? And then there was that mention of the Stranges in Ruth Russell's family tree. Coincidence? Two branches of Stranges in Maine? Was that even possible? Another trip to the library to look in their archives was in my future.

I lay back in the bed. A chill washed over me as those memories played in my head. Always the summer. Never the fall. What was so dangerous about the fall? Was that just the dream, or was it a real memory?

I tried to sleep, rolling over and over, looking for that elusive comfortable spot. Finally I sat up and turned on the light on my nightstand. Pulling the blankets and quilt with me I propped up my legs and hugged my knees, laying my cheek on them.

The dream was fading and the memories with them. I definitely needed those photo albums. But even as I wondered about those happy long-ago days with my mother and grandfather, my man troubles slid to the fore, pushing the old memories aside. Men! It was no good moping over men. Especially one whose address was situated in warmer climes. "A demon is not a suitable partner," I said aloud. My voice sounded lonely at this hour, out of place with the darkness at the edge of the halo of light from the lamp. Now more than ever I wished my mom was here. I could tell her about Erasmus and she would say something silly like, "Follow your heart."

I could just make out the dark shapes of the stacks of library books on my corner desk. Sighing, I whipped off the blankets and I ran across the floor on bare feet. I was wearing a thin cami and short sleep pants, both much too skimpy for the deep cold of the room. But I managed to snag the books and run back to bed with them. I jumped under the comforter and secured it over my chest, propping up the pillows behind me before I spread the books around my legs. I hefted one I had not looked at earlier and cracked it open. "Succubus, succubus..." I muttered, looking down the table of contents. I opened the book to the proper page and read. *Ancient Sumer, blah blah; attacks men in their sleep, yadda yadda; can suck the life force out of men and kill them, etcetera, etcetera.* Same ole, same ole.

I lowered the book to my lap and lay back against the pillow. These books all said the same thing, and not one of them had a suggestion for getting rid of the creatures.

The Booke lay on the desk, too, without the others for companionship. I gathered the library books, set them in a pile on my nightstand, and couldn't help but glare at that big old Booke of the Hidden, sitting patiently on its own.

With a world-weary sigh, I threw the covers back again and ran across the cold plank floor. Grabbing the monster Booke, I ran back to bed and hopped in. Under the covers once more I hefted the tome and laid it out on my legs. Its gold-leafed letters taunted, glinting in the light of my bedside lamp.

"Booke of the Hidden," I read aloud. "What else are you hiding? And why couldn't you have *stayed* hidden?"

My fingers touched the gold leafing, ran over the engraving of the letters in the leather. Hidden secrets. Hidden desires. Hidden dangers. I bet Mistress Howland felt trapped like this. Weighed down by the responsibility. How I wish I knew for sure. My cheeks warmed again at the thought of being caught by Ruth Russell, Constance Howland's many times great grandniece. And *my* cousin as well, it seemed.

Had it all, ultimately, proved too much for old Constance? How much would *I* feel at the end of all this? Maybe the Powers That Be didn't want to destroy it, but I sure did. Maybe I could find a way. With the help of my Wiccans. I wanted to make sure there were no more Chosen Hosts to get trapped by circumstances or get tossed over cliffs or question their morality late into the night.

And that vortex voice that haunted my waking hours kept

playing in my head, too. It had called it a game. "*The game is not for the weak of heart.*" And "*what has begun cannot now be stopped.*" What game was it? And did Erasmus know the rules?

Sliding down the Booke's cover, my fingers lighted on the cold metal clasp. I lifted it with a soft click and opened it. The leaves of parchment lay before me, blank as a desert. There was a pen on my nightstand and I took it up. The Booke lay open on my legs and my hands smoothed over the buff parchment. Nothing marred it. No line, no indentation, no ink smudge. It was as if nothing had ever been written on it.

I put the tip of my pen to the top left-hand corner of flat vellum and closed my eyes. Taking a deep breath, I let my hand go, allowing no thoughts to influence me, no outside intrusions. All of my senses were attuned to the Booke, and I absorbed it like leaves took in sunshine. When I opened my eyes, I began my first sentence:

> *A succubus has escaped the pages of this Booke and it is my sacred duty to subdue and capture the beast in any way I can.*

I lifted the pen point from the page and simply stared at the letters in my own hand, scratched onto its even surface with heavy black ink. My heart swelled at this moment of triumph...but only for an instant. As I watched, this ink, too, began to sink into the plane of parchment and disappear. It was as if I had never touched it. No indentations from my pen remained. And I had been so sure, *so* sure it was going to stay!

I set the pen aside and stretched my palms over the pages before me. "What is it you want? Why me?"

No answer, of course. With a grunt of disappointment, I closed the cover. Because it was too big for my nightstand, I leaned over the side of the bed and set it on the floor.

Outside, the wind was kicking up, rattling leaves and twigs. A scratching noise started softly, but was getting louder. A tree branch. I threw off the covers a third time, tiptoed over the cold wooden floor, and drew back the curtains. The moon was getting ready to set over the distant hills and there wasn't much light left. But I could still make out the crackling foliage in my back garden, the silver-toned half-fence encircling the yard. A large oak tree near the house swayed from the wind, but its branches weren't close enough to touch the clapboard wall. So what was making that noise?

I looked down again into the yard. An old glider swing, an arbor with dead morning glory vines on it, a pile of firewood and more to be split. And something else. Something in the middle of the yard I didn't recognize. I couldn't quite make it out, and I was trying to figure out if it was some wayward bit of laundry blown off of a neighbor's line...when the *something* uncoiled. At first, I couldn't believe what I was seeing. It was as if something was being inflated like a balloon right in the middle of my backyard. It slowly rose, unfolding. And as it grew I started to make out first a torso, then shoulders, and then head. My mouth opened with a gasp and I pressed my hand against the cold windowpane to steady myself.

The blob unfurled into the shape of a person. A willowy figure with long stringy hair whipping about with the wind. And there was the shadow of horns on its head. No—*her* head, because it was a distinctly female shape. She wore a light fabric that fluttered about her. At first, I thought it was also a long skirt, but realized with some horror that it was a tail! It did not move with the vagaries of the wind as her ragged dress seemed to, but it whipped slowly back and forth like an agitated cat's tail.

She turned her head and lifted her chin, searching, and found me. I could not see her face but with the merest glint from the disappearing moon I thought I saw fangs. And I did see eyes. Red, glowing eyes, staring right at me. She walked toward the house in a strange gait, as if unused to using her two limbs.

I couldn't move or scream, though I longed to do both. She reached the wall, still looking up at me, and ran her nails down the sides of the clapboards, and I could *feel* the sounds of those scratches vibrating through my bones.

And then she climbed. She dug her nails, her talons, into the wood and pulled herself up. Her mouth gaped open, I could see it now. Her long tongue thrashed over her protruding fangs, flicking them, leaving them shiny and glistening. The hard scrabble of her talons against the clapboards shocked me into taking a step back.

What was I going to do? I was in complete panic mode. I couldn't even run. And where would I go?

The skittering behind me made me jump and turn. The crossbow had armed itself and it rattled on the chair, itching to come to me. Breathless, I raised my shaking hand. That was enough, and it soared across the room and slapped into my grip. Its solidity gave me strength, calmed me down. "Okay, bitch," said my quaking voice. "Let's take care of this now."

I threw open the casement, put the crossbow into my shoulder, and aimed out the window.

Nothing. She was no longer there.

"What the—?"

A dark shape flew up and slammed me backward. My head hit the floor hard. Something rolled into the room and my crossbow... *my crossbow!* It had been knocked out of my hand, and it was gone. Where the hell was it?

The dark thing ricocheted around the room. The lamp arced overhead, crashed against the wall, and the light went out. I scrambled across the floor, feeling with my fingers in the dark for the crossbow. I lifted my hand for it, but I was knocked aside.

A slash at my shoulder. Bright pain, like a hundred knives. I rolled, trying to get out of the thing's way, trying to find safety. I was smothered with the smell of damp leaves and the sickly scent of death. I crawled away across the floor but something had grasped my ankle. I kicked wildly at it but it was far stronger. I was flipped over and then a ghastly weight took my breath away. It was on top of me, glaring down at me. Fangs, red eyes, breath full of decay. I gasped, inhaling to scream but all my breath suddenly reversed and was going the other way, sucking into her.

I choked, tried to push her, kick her. Her taloned hands held my wrists and pressed them into the floor. I fought like an animal, wriggling, arching, kicking, but there was no breath. I couldn't let it win. I had come so far, not just in miles but in every other way, too. I wanted this new life. It couldn't be cut short.

Her stinking breath was too close to me, but suddenly she made a gurgling sound and drew back. Those weird red eyes were staring at my chest. She pushed her way off of me, grinding my shoulder blades into the floor.

Relief and oxygen flooded my lungs. Something had spooked her and I wanted to know what it was. I felt around on my chest. In my struggle, the amulet had worked its way loose from my cami. That had to have been it. I sat up on my elbows. She was still in the corner of my room, breathing hard, crouched as if to pounce, lit by the last vestiges of moonlight.

I edged my hand out, hoping the crossbow would get the message and appear in my hand. A scraping sound along the floor, and I felt the cool metal and the smooth wood once again under my fingers. Without moving from the floor, I slapped it quickly to my shoulder and fired.

She jumped. Straight up to the ceiling. I heard the quarrel smack hard into the wall where she had been. Now what?

Another shadow zoomed past, soaring up to the ceiling, and slammed against the creature. They tumbled, dark and light, making no sound but the swish of fabric and the slap of muscle colliding with the hard wall and floor. With one bounce she was out the window and Erasmus Dark paused on the sill, crouched unnaturally like a frog, coat trailing behind him like a long tail. He didn't look human in that instance. He was all animal, on his haunches, ready to pounce.

Panting, I stayed put on the floor, propped up on my elbows. The crossbow lay across my lap, bow unstrung and quarrel back in its slot. I looked up sharply and spied the hole in the wall it had left behind.

"I almost had it," I wheezed.

He snapped his head toward me. He leapt from the window,

took one step, knelt and scooped me up in his arms. The crossbow clattered to the floor. When he kissed me this time, I was all in. I clenched my arms around his neck, warming my mouth on his. He urged my mouth open with a heated tongue and my head fell back, surrendering.

He kissed me for a long time, angling his head, and I loosened my hold on his neck to grab at his coat, gripping the lapels.

When he finally drew back, his eyes dropped to mine. "She hurt you," he breathed.

I had almost forgotten the sting of my shoulder. He gently pushed me back to look at it. "Not deep," he muttered, fingers grazing it. I hissed at the tenderness of the flesh. He dropped his hand away. "It will be slow to heal, but in time it will."

"She attacked me. I thought they wouldn't attack a woman."

He gusted a long sigh, still holding me like some prince in a fairy tale—a very dark tale. "You are the Chosen Host. She knows that. She knows if you write her into the book she will be imprisoned."

"The Booke! I should write in the Booke!" I popped up from the floor out of his arms to leap over the bed, but his hand encircling my wrist held me back.

"Not until you subdue her. Writing into the book seals her capture."

His arm was stretched out and my body was elongated in my need to get to the Booke. All of a sudden I sagged. The loss of energy, the futility struck me all at once.

He slowly drew me in until I fit against him, warm and firm. It was comfort at first, but his enveloping presence became more. I knew this was a bad idea, and as I looked into his eyes, the flicker of uncertainty was there, too. But he didn't loosen his hold.

"I wanted you once before, but held myself back," he said huskily. "If you don't want my attention now, say so." Very slowly, the hand that was holding my wrist slid up my arm, sending tingles over my skin.

I shook my hair back out of my face and looked him square in the eye. "It wasn't me who pulled away before."

He made a sound of triumph, and his hands reached for my face and held it. He just looked at me, eyes scanning over my face, my hair, my lips, until they stayed on my mouth and pulled me in. With quickening breath, he bent closer and his tongue tip flicked up over my top lip, tasting me like an animal might, before he covered my whole mouth in a deepening kiss.

I didn't think I'd ever been kissed quite like that before. With power and tenderness and absolute need. My arms went around him, feeling the muscles move under his jacket.

Quickly he drew back, shoved the straps of my cami down my shoulders, and attacked my neck, leaving hot damp kisses on my skin. I arched into him and pushed at his ever-present coat, trying to shove it off *his* shoulders.

Releasing me, he stepped back while I swayed dazedly, a little bereft. He had been warm against me. Very warm. But he'd only stepped back to whip off his coat and cast it to the floor. He tore open his shirt, spraying buttons across the room.

I could do nothing but stare and pant. I remembered that hard chest from when I fixed his wound. I noticed vaguely that his shoulder was now free of its bandage and even a scar. When he came at me again, it was to tear open *my* shirt. "Favorite sleep shirt," I muttered but couldn't seem to muster the urge to care.

His warm hands were on me, touching, kneading, eyes intense as he stared down at my naked chest and at what his hands were doing. Had he ever done this before? With a human woman? Again, didn't care. He bent his head to mouth me with his lips, stroking with his tongue.

"You are so…so…" He never finished, so I didn't know what I was. He murmured something against my flesh. I grabbed a handful of his hair and lifted his face.

"So are you."

"I must warn you," he purred, hand dragging over my ribs, my hip. "This may be dangerous."

The old horror movie *Rosemary's Baby* flitted through my head. "You can't…um…impregnate me, can you?"

He looked affronted. "Of course not. We are a different species."

That didn't exactly make me feel better.

His expression softened. His hand cupped my cheek, thumb moving over my lips. "That shouldn't deter you. I won't…hurt you." He pressed a soft kiss to my mouth as if to prove it. "But I never said it won't be rough." And then his thumb returned, dipping into my parted lips to touch my teeth. I nipped him and his eyes widened in delight.

He moved in and took the skin of my neck between his teeth and gently bit. Hot breath blasted over my throat as he nuzzled, sucked.

My head lolled back, eyes closed. Suddenly I was being lifted and carried. I felt the comforter beneath my back and the bed dip as he crawled up after me.

Are we really doing this? the practical side of me wondered. I told it to shut up.

Erasmus had lied. He wasn't rough. He took his time. His hands and mouth moved carefully, tenderly. It had been too long, feeling the touch of another, and longer since feeling the gentle touch of someone who seemed to care. Lying back on the bed, I heard more rustling of clothing and I raised my head, not willing to miss it. He'd divested himself of his trousers and underwear, if he wore any.

"Damn!" I rasped.

His brow rose in question, even as his dark eyes grew darker with blown pupils.

I'd never slept with someone who looked like…like… "Wow," I breathed. Demon or not, he certainly looked like a man, and a fine specimen if ever there was one. Firm defined muscles, strong thighs, and, uh, impressive attributes.

The smile he offered me was utterly feral. Fingers gripped my sleep pants and drew them off in one swift move, leaving me naked. And before I could squeak about it he was lying atop me, sliding his muscled frame over mine with unabashed hunger.

His lips found my neck again, and trailed up to my earlobe, gnawing and flicking his tongue at it.

My hands roamed over his back, his flanks. He was all hard muscle without an ounce of fat. I reached over and grabbed handfuls of his firm buttocks and squeezed. I was rewarded with a grunt in my ear. I was really glad he didn't have bat wings or a tail.

His hardness slid against me and I opened my legs, wrapping them around his waist just in case he had any doubts about my willingness.

He didn't, and with a rumbling growl, he suddenly plunged into me. I guess he wasn't one for foreplay, but at the moment, it didn't really matter to me either. He writhed above me, moving his deliciously hot skin over mine and filling me. I could almost forget who and what he was.

I moved with him, clutching his hips tightly with my thighs. He ran his hands up and down my calves in appreciation, and I grabbed his face to bring it down to kiss me again. His mouth devoured mine. His tongue swept wildly until I stopped it with my lips and sucked on it. He groaned, his hips snapping forward. I couldn't stop touching him. I ran my nails up his chest, leaving red marks over his pecs, scoring near his tattoo. But when I touched the strangely marked flesh he grabbed my hands and pulled them up over my head, holding both wrists with one hand against the bed. He looked down at me as he breathed in great heaving gusts. His skin began to literally smolder.

"Erasmus," I gasped. "Don't…set the bed…on fire."

He quirked a smile and the smoke wisped away, but his eyes seemed to darken, and he lowered his face to my breasts, taking them each in turn roughly into his mouth.

"You…you're really…good at this."

He smiled, baring his teeth in something more predatory than genial. He thrust harder. "And you…are more…than a surprise to me. You're…so animated. I thought…the only emotion you possessed…was anger."

"I'm not angry…*oh*…right now."

"No," he said, moving with assurance. "Let's keep it that way."

"Keep doing that and it's a sure thing."

"What?" he said, lowering his hand between us and moving it. "You mean…this?"

I threw my head back, seeing an explosion of white bliss. He continued making little circles and hard strokes. With a trembling tension in his thighs he suddenly leaned into me and gasped his release.

And that's when the pillow above my head burst into flame.

"Whoa!" I screamed, and shot prematurely out from under him and off the bed, slapping at my smoking hair.

The fire snuffed out immediately all by itself, or from his own brand of magic, but I'd definitely fallen off of my cloud.

He was lying on his front, leaning on an elbow. "Sorry," he drawled. "I can't always control that."

I had a good view of his gorgeous rounded backside. I'd almost forgive him anything for that. But my pillow was toast. Literally. The pillowcase was blackened and the toxic fumes from the pillow's stuffing lingered.

It took that long for his words to sink in.

"Do you…do this a lot?"

Erasmus turned over and stretched. Over his head, he grasped the burnt pillow and tossed it across the room. Droopy-eyed, he looked at me. "No. I only come here every hundred years or so."

"Oh. So…with human, um, women?"

"Well, certainly not cattle."

"That makes me feel so much better."

He gazed at me for a long moment before his lazy expression turned to a frown and he sat up suddenly. Staring at me, then at the pillow, his face grew darker. "Beelze's tail," he murmured. He scrubbed at his hair and launched himself from the bed. "I shouldn't have done that."

"I can replace the pillow."

"Not *that*! This! Us. It was incredibly stupid and shortsighted of me. I tried to resist." He looked up sharply and narrowed his eyes. "Did you use a charm?"

"No! Why would I need to do that?"

"All the same. It was a mistake. You should have stopped me." He said nothing more and began gathering his clothes.

I should have… My jaw hung open in shock. What the hell? "Isn't it a little late for regrets?" I folded my arms over my chest, feeling suddenly a bit vulnerable standing there naked with the window wide open. I hurried to the casement and pulled it closed. I couldn't help but run my eyes over the yard. No mysterious lumps out there. Just night and wind and silence.

I watched him dress for a moment before barking out a little snarkily, "Not exactly what the Powers That Be prefer, eh? Humans and demons don't mix? Gonna write you up, give you a demerit?"

He snapped his gaze at me. Far too much alarm was visible in his eyes. Crap! What might a demon demerit be like?

"D-do they have to find out?" I said more quietly. "I mean, they aren't *watching* us, are they?" A chill rippled down my neck. That was just what I needed: voyeur gods.

He rubbed his palms into his eyes. "I'm…sorry."

"But…" I wasn't going to plead with him. I had more pride than that. I found a quilt draped over my desk chair and wrapped myself in it. "So that's it?"

"Yes." There was an uncertain tone to his voice. He was dressed in his trousers again, at a loss for what to do. I couldn't help him. I was a little lost myself. "I'm…"

"If you say you're sorry one more time…" I said, teeth clenched.

"I'm…hmm."

"That's great. That's just great. Good discipline there. At least it's only every *hundred* years or so. Not like every day with a different human in every county."

He wore an unreasonably hurt expression. "I wasn't exactly on my own here. I recall a certain willingness on your part."

"Because I thought it meant something to you!"

"Meant something to *me*?" He looked away. "Don't be absurd!"

I wiped harshly at the sting in my eyes. "Fine. It's over, then. You've chalked up another for this epoch. Now you can wait another hundred years for your next willing victim."

He made an impatient sigh. "Kylie…"

"No, you're right. This was a really stupid thing to do. Too bad we couldn't come to our senses about ten minutes earlier."

He brooded, arms folded taut over his chest. I felt like throwing something at him, but the lamp was already broken. What had I expected? He was a demon. At least I had known that upfront. *I* was the stupid one.

"I'll…return tomorrow," he said.

"I have a date tomorrow night."

I could hear his teeth grinding. "You still plan to go through with that?"

I glared. "*You're* the one leaving."

I'd been a world-class idiot for not thinking it through, and I was usually better at that. But here I was, rushing in. A demon of all people! Especially when there was a decent man waiting for me tomorrow. A real flesh-and-blood man. What the hell was I doing messing with another *species*? I sure knew how to pick them.

As the silence drew on I grew angrier. *Fight for me, you jerk!* He wanted me but now he was running scared. And of course, he wouldn't even tell me why.

He muttered under his breath and yanked on his jacket. His shirt hung wide open. After all, the buttons were scattered all over the floor. "I'll be back in the morning, then," he grumbled.

"Not too early. I'm sleeping in."

He nodded. "Fine."

"Erasmus." I waited for his eyes to settle on mine. They were their usual darkness, unreadable, glistening. "Um…thanks. For saving me. Again."

"It seems to be my lot in life."

I nodded. "I'll get her next time. I didn't know she'd attack me. Now I know better."

"Yes," he grunted. "I suppose you do." He swept away, stomping heavily down the stairs, until I couldn't hear his footfalls anymore.

I flopped on the bed. My head hit the remaining pillow and I stared at the ceiling, cringing at the claw marks and boot scuffs among the rafters, thinking about my demon lover and the man I was going to date tomorrow. Like I was going to get any sleep now.

• • •

In the morning, I cleaned up the broken remains of the lamp, making a mental note to pick up another at Moody Bog Hardware, and looked at my scratched shoulder in the bathroom mirror. Four angry red lines raked across my fading tan. I pressed tentative fingers to it and hissed at the raw pain. I dabbed it with a cotton ball and antiseptic. What kind of infections could I get from the Netherworld? Erasmus had said I'd be all right…and then I thought of him and his damned kisses…and everything else.

He was too good at that, which made me wonder where he got his experience. A little incubus work on the side, maybe?

Was I really in the mood to go through with this date? What would I say to Ed? "Sorry, I'm having a good time with another species at the moment, but I'll give you a call when something opens up."

A hot shower was needed, and after drying off and slipping on a warm sweater and my favorite skinny jeans, I set up the French press, pushing down the plunger until the coffee was dark.

With hot mug in hand, I ventured to the back garden. In the daylight, it didn't look as scary. The glider swing needed a little oil and some sanding, but I decided I liked it and would work on it soon, as well as the climbing tea roses that could use a lot of pruning.

But then I looked at my wall.

I inhaled a sharp, cold breath. Up the aged-dark clapboards on the side of my house were long deep scratches from very familiar claws. She had lured me to the window with the sound of scratching. She had climbed up my wall to attack me. It gave me a chill to look at them, to give truth to my nightmares.

"Are you all right?"

"Dammit!" I spilled coffee on myself as I jumped in surprise. I wiped at my pants and turned an accusatory glare on Erasmus. "Do you *have* to do that?"

The corner of his mouth ticked into a smirk. "I don't *have* to, no. But I always enjoy the result."

"Oh, nice." The hot coffee dampening my jeans cooled quickly in the cold air. I decided that the best course of action was not to mention last night.

"Look, about last night," I said, completely ignoring my own best advice.

He glowered at the wall, not looking at me. "It was a mistake. There is nothing else to say." Except that it looked as if he wanted to say more.

"Yeah, sure," I muttered. I tried to assuage the lump in my throat with hot coffee. I took a breath and gestured with my mug toward the scratches. "Is this usual succubus behavior?"

He nudged me aside and strode forward, raising his hand to run a finger down the roughened edge of an abrasion. "Not usual, no. But as I said, she is aware of you, of what you are. She knows you can stop her."

"I thought I was protected. I thought the Wiccans had done a spell or something."

"So did I. The magic they did should have worked. May I examine their pentagram?"

"Yes, of course." I walked across the crunchy lawn with Erasmus following. I led him through the kitchen area and into the shop, pointing to the fireplace. "It's under the rug. I covered it."

"And that would be the problem. You may not hide the pentagram. In effect, you were creating the reverse result." He stooped and grabbed the rug, flipping it to the side. The chalk line was still clearly visible, as was the brownish stain from my blood. I rubbed the scab on my finger in sympathy.

"I screwed up?"

He nodded. "The magic was negated when you covered the pentagram."

"So we have to do the ritual again? My poor finger."

He arched a brow. "It is unlikely to help a second time. Once you call upon the gods for help and then turn away that help, you cannot expect accommodation."

"Um…gods, huh? So just because I didn't want a pentagram in my shop I pissed them off?"

"If you want to put it that way." He dusted his hands and rose. Looking around, he wrinkled his nose. "That infernal tea!" He sneezed and wiped at his nose with disgust.

I handed him a tissue. "It being a tea shop, it's hard to avoid."

He glared at the tissue, holding it with thumb and forefinger. "What am I supposed to do with this?"

"Wipe your nose." I retreated to the kitchen for more much-needed coffee, and to wet a towel to scrub the coffee stain from my jeans. I realized that I actually had a free day, since all was ready and the grand opening wasn't until tomorrow. "Erasmus?" He had slunk in after me, picking up various things from the counter and examining them before putting them back down again. "Is it possible to hunt a succubus during the day? Does she have a lair somewhere?"

He was busy studying my electric juicer and ended up tipping out the juicing part. It tumbled across the counter and clattered into the sink. He raised his brows and gingerly returned the machine to its place. "An interesting suggestion. It is not known where she might have a lair. But I imagine any cave or abandoned building, as long as it was sufficiently dark, would do."

"A cave? I'll have to ask around. I need to make a trip to the hardware store anyway. Maybe the locals would know."

"Excellent. I will accompany you."

"You will?" I sipped and warmed my hand on the mug. Erasmus looked uncomfortable in the light of day. I supposed he was more of a night person.

"Of course. It occurs to me that I know little about your world in its current era."

"Okay." At least he was being civilized about it. I could work with that. I finished my coffee, rinsed the mug in the sink, and donned my coat. With keys in hand I motioned him out the door. "I know you aren't used to it, but we mere mortals use doors and such to get from here to there."

"I use doors," he said smugly, like a pilot might brag that he flies a helicopter.

"Look at you," I muttered. "With your door expertise." I headed down Main Street, crunching fallen leaves under my boots. Hard to believe that under all that New England fresh air and fall color lurked a deadly creature. With each stride my shoulder ached, and I was pissed off royally by the succubus just now.

Erasmus's long strides caught up to mine. I was happily taking in the village; the market, the square with its old oaks and bell tower, the barber, the old church from yesterday, gift shops, clothing shops, and even an art gallery. We passed a man standing in his yard, leaning on his rake beside a small burning pile of leaves, and I inhaled some of the woodsy smoke. I waved and he waved back.

"So what do you think of our quaint little village?" I asked Erasmus.

He snorted and pointed to the village green. "Did you know that used to have a pillory?"

"No. When?"

"Early seventeen hundreds. It was used quite a bit. Women like you would be put there to humiliate them for gossiping. It was very amusing."

"Oh ha, ha. It would be to *you*."

He smiled, thrusting his hands into his coat pockets. "I assure you it was."

The hardware store was at the other end of Main Street, right next to the new and used bookstore. I climbed the steps and pushed open the door. It was stifling inside and I was soon unbuttoning my jacket and flapping it.

"Be with you in a minute!" said a voice from behind a shelf full of plumbing fittings and galvanized pipe.

"Wow, it's warm in here."

"Yeah, that jeezly furnace doesn't understand the new thermostat I installed." The face that belonged to the voice popped up from behind the shelves, and a middle-aged man with a graying goatee smiled at me.

"Perhaps you were ignorant in its proper installation," said Erasmus unhelpfully.

The man's smile faded but I stepped in front of the demon and offered an apologetic smile. "Hi. I'm Kylie Strange and I'm opening up the Strange Herbs & Teas down at the other end of town." I fished around in my pocket for a business card and handed one to him.

He looked it over. "Oh! I heard about you. Sorry I missed you at the get-together the other day. Had to leave early. When you openin'?"

"Tomorrow. Come on down for some free coffee and tea. There'll be free scones and apple pecan loaf as well."

"From Moody Market? I'll be in, then. Anything I can help you with? I'm Barry Johnson, by the way." He offered his greasy hand to shake but I demurred. "Oops," he said, reddening. "Sorry 'bout that. Hazard of the business."

"Well, I hope you have some lamps. I broke mine yesterday."

"Lamps are down on aisle eleven. Just thataway." He gestured.

We wandered down the aisles, and I slapped Erasmus's hands a few times as he picked up breakable items to examine.

We got to the lamps and there were many serviceable types. Nothing too exotic, but then again, the furnishings in the house were all fairly standard early colonial. I chose something that looked like a hurricane lamp only electrified and took it to the front cash register.

"I hate electric light," muttered Erasmus.

"I know you do. But it's *my* house, isn't it?"

Barry wiped his hands down his dirty overalls and ducked under the counter to get behind the register. "Is that going to do it for you, Ms. Strange?"

"Kylie. Um…you don't happen to have any pillows, do you?"

"A few. Aisle two."

I left the lamp and hurried down the aisle, picking a reasonably firm pillow. I brought it up front and set it alongside the lamp. Erasmus and Barry were staring at one another.

I all but waved my hand in front of them. "This will do, I think."

Barry snapped out of it and rang it up. "That will be $51.45."

I handed him my debit card and perused the colorful kitchen gewgaws hanging on the wall behind him. "Say, Barry, you don't know of any caves hereabouts, do you?"

"Caves? Plan on doing some spelunking?" He laughed at his own joke and I tried to smile. Erasmus frowned. Barry coughed to hide his silenced laughter. "Do you mean the old Indian caves up Falcon's Point? They got those drawings in there. Petroglyphs or something. Old Indian paintings. County is trying to make it a preservation spot. That was Karl Waters's bailiwick, but now, of course…" He shook his head. "Savage shame what happened to him. And curious, too. I heard the rumors, but…" He handed my debit card back and was suddenly looking below my chin. "That's a mighty unusual necklace you got there," he said, reaching for the amulet.

Erasmus's hand darted forward and grabbed him by the wrist. "Don't touch it!"

Barry froze, eyes round as he stared at Erasmus.

"Erasmus!" He let the man go. "I apologize for my friend here. He's just visiting me. From California."

"He don't sound like he comes from California," said Barry, rubbing his wrist.

"*Northern* California," I assured, took my lamp and pillow, and made a hasty exit.

We got a few paces down the street before I rounded on him. "Do you have to act like a complete lunatic when other people are around?"

"He was going to touch my amulet. He must not."

"Really?" My hand went to it automatically. "What would happen if he did?"

He raised his chin, shaking back his long hair. "I would have to kill him."

"Oh, is that all. Nice of you to tell me that ahead of time. How come you aren't killing me?"

"The day isn't over yet."

I snorted a laugh, though, come to think of it, it wasn't very funny. "Hey, Erasmus, the succubus saw it, too, and it scared her off."

A car whizzed past and his eyes followed it, full of curiosity. I found my gaze following him and I metaphorically kicked myself. "Yes, she would recognize it as a demon's amulet," he said absently, still looking behind him at the retreating car.

"And? She seemed scared of it. Can that help us in some way?"

"Yes. Always keep it around your neck. It might provide a modicum of protection."

We walked back to my shop. This cave excursion was going to require the car.

I opened the shop without a word, deposited my purchases on the counter, and gathered a few things: the crossbow, a flashlight, and a map of the area. Scouring the contents of the map, I found Falcon's Point and I saw that the caves were mentioned. Erasmus followed me silently around the shop, picking up the flashlight and turning it on and off, before I hefted the crossbow and map and headed out the door again.

I locked up and loaded the stuff into the back seat, taking the flashlight out of his hand and motioning for him to get into the passenger side.

I took the highway and drove up the winding road. Because the foliage was still in all its splendor, there were a few leaf peepers on the road as well, driving a bit slowly for my taste as they hung their cameras out the window to take in the fall colors.

I was able to snake past one particularly slow BMW and punched it going up the hill.

"Must you?" rasped my companion. When I glanced at him he was looking a bit green.

"I want to get this over with."

"By getting us killed? Brilliant strategy."

"Such a whiner," I said, shaking my head. "When's the next turn?"

"How should I know?"

"Look at the map."

With a world-weary sigh, he snatched up the map and glared at it. "I don't see what you want?"

"It's upside down, genius."

He raised his brows and slowly turned it. "Ah. So I see. You are on this blue line?"

"Yes."

"Then you will need to turn on something called Falcon's Point Road...oddly enough."

"Ever so helpful," I sing-songed. Fortunately, a sign up ahead proudly proclaimed Falcon's Point and its cave and I made the turn at the painted arrow.

"Now just up the hill," said Erasmus, pleased with himself as he folded the map into its precise rectangle.

I wasn't able to enjoy the view, even when the trees opened and imparted a breathtaking vista of undulating fall color and distant blue hills. I followed the road until it narrowed and finally became a dirt road. I threw the switch that put the Jeep into four-wheel drive and bounced over the washboarding until it opened to a wide expanse that served more or less as a parking lot. A sign indicated that we were at a trailhead.

Only one other car was parked there—a silver Acura with

a bike rack strapped to the back. The bikes were missing which might have meant the tourists were biking on the trails.

I couldn't worry about them. I wasn't going to hide the crossbow. I needed it at the ready, and tourists be damned. I slammed the car door and grabbed the crossbow and flashlight from the back seat. Stuffing my keys and cell phone in my jacket pocket, I hid my purse under the blanket in the trunk and closed it up.

With the crossbow on my shoulder, I looked up the trail. "Coming?"

He was beside me instantly. I wished I could learn that trick. "Of course," he rumbled.

"Let's go." I marched forward, following the sign, feeling an eerie sense of déjà vu for poor Constance Howland. It made me ask, "So you've been here before?"

His gaze slid toward mine for only a moment. "Yes."

"You never said. If you did chase her off the cliff."

"As it happens, no, I did not."

The cold weight that had borne down on me lifted. "Well, that's…good."

I thought he might say more, but he just turned and looked straight up the trail, with something of an angry expression.

"Why are you mad now?"

"This lack of faith. Even as I've tried to help you. You do not trust me."

"I do. But only so far. Can you blame me?" And then it occurred to me. "Did you and Constance Howland…?" I didn't want to think about it, even though she was long dead, almost three hundred years ago.

He bared his teeth. "NO! Stop asking ridiculous questions."

"It's not ridiculous," I mumbled.

He grunted and tossed his duster open, kicking the long tail of it out of the way of his stride. "Look," he said grudgingly, "I don't know why…I was…attracted to you. This…never happens."

"But you said you do this with human women…"

"Sometimes. Not often. I…I don't generally like…humans."

"So why me? Why do I rate special treatment?"

His eyes raked over me hungrily. "I don't know," he said quietly, before he hurtled away from me up the road.

"I'm going to kill that succubus," I snarled, "and write about it in that damned Booke and then this can all be over. And you can go back to whatever place you came from and we can forget this ever happened. Okay?"

His cold, angry expression dissipated. He looked back as if he wanted to say something but held himself in check. Instead, he continued on the trail with sure strides.

I was getting a bit winded as the trail steepened. I kept looking around us for any signs of the succubus, but I saw nothing except birds, squirrels, and the occasional wary deer way off in the undergrowth.

It would have been a pleasant hike under other circumstances.

Erasmus wasn't winded at all. I wondered again about his physiology. I recalled, with a blush, having seen and felt quite a bit of it last night. How human-like was he, really? "How's your shoulder?" I managed to ask with a roughened voice.

He reached for it involuntarily before he let his hand fall away. "It's fine. Healed." He snapped his head toward me. "And yours?"

"Still hurts a little." I rolled the shoulder. "I guess it will heal."

"Likely."

"So what's with the tattoo?" I blurted.

"I don't know what you mean," he said in that voice I was coming to learn meant "keep off."

I frowned. "You have a tattoo, a marking on your..." I made a vague gesture toward him. "Your body. What does it mean?"

He shook his head. "Nothing important."

I'll just bet. It was a strange marking, like nothing I'd ever seen before. I'd have to ask Jolene later.

The farther we walked the more I wished I had brought some water. The air was dry and dusty from the trail and though the weather was cold I was working up a bit of a sweat. Erasmus didn't seem to sweat or get winded. "Is it that you just *look* like a human or is that your real…um…body?"

"It's as real as it needs to be."

"Now that. See that right there. That is *not* a straight answer. Wholly unsatisfying."

He smirked. "Is it?"

I couldn't help but smile back. "You're doing that on purpose. It's a joke. Erasmus Dark, demon of the Netherworlds, is joking with me."

The smirk deepened. But he didn't look at me and said nothing more.

We hiked farther. My phone rang and I quickly grabbed it. Without thinking or looking at the number, I put it to my ear. "Hello?"

"Kylie, I just want to talk to you."

I stopped and glared into the middle distance. "Jeff, why can't you just leave me alone? I'm four thousand miles away."

"That's killing me, babe. That you're so far. And we were together for so long."

"It was only two years, Jeff. It just *seemed* like an eternity."

"Kylie, this is seriously messed up that you thought you had to escape across the whole country to run away. You didn't have to—"

"I *didn't run away*!"

"Fine. If it makes you feel better to think of it like that—"

"It *was* like that. You cheated on me both as a business partner and a lover."

"Kylie!"

"I'm hanging up. Don't call me again. I'm blocking you." I clicked it off before he said one more word. I looked at the phone in my hand a long while before I slipped it back into my pocket. When I raised my head, Erasmus was looking at me.

"Who was that?" he said in a deadly voice.

I took a deep breath. "Just someone I used to know."

"Another of your paramours."

"Well…yes. But not anymore. Definitely not anymore."

"You dislike him."

I moved on, shielding my eyes from the bleak sunshine through the trees and looked up at the rocky outcropping ahead. "You could say that."

"I could…help you."

I stopped again. "What…what do you mean by that?"

"I could stop him from ever bothering you again." Smoke puffed up from his jacket.

"Whoa. No, you don't have to do that."

"But it would be my pleasure." His bared teeth suddenly looked sharp.

"Would you stop that! You're going to start a forest fire. I don't need that kind of help. Just…leave it."

"But—"

"Leave it!"

He pouted. There was no other word for it.

"Look, it's a kind offer, but humans these days don't go in for revenge. Or shouldn't. *I* won't. I just want to leave him to his life and let me work on mine. That okay with you?"

He shrugged, rolling his eyes. "As you wish."

I shook my head and we continued on before coming to a steep bend. The ground dropped away.

"Falcon's Point," said Erasmus.

"So you do remember it."

"As I said."

I walked to the edge and looked down. The rocky ledge was only just that and cut straight down with no sloping, no hand holds. If you went over that, you'd go all the way. I wondered about poor Constance Howland. How long did it take to fall down it? Had she done it to herself? Were her bones still down there? Likely her remains were dragged away by some animals centuries ago. It still gave me a shiver and I stepped back from the edge, running into the solid body of my demon companion. He grabbed my arms to steady me. But for a fleeting moment, I felt the rush of fear that he might be preparing to push me over.

"Wouldn't do to fall now," he rasped in my ear.

Contrary to my better judgment, I leaned back, resting against his warm frame. His breath hitched and his hands tightened on me, his lips against my hair.

"That's a long way down," I said softly.

"Very long," he said, just as quietly.

"I'm certainly not ready to die."

"You have much to do before that happens."

I turned in his arms, and he let me go. His intense gaze scoured mine.

"You're such a romantic, you silver-tongued devil." My voice was a little shaky and I managed to step incrementally away from him.

He tried to smile. "Not *the* Devil. Just a demon."

I smiled back and gestured toward the sign that indicated another trail to the caves. "Shouldn't we keep going?"

He made a slight bow and stepped aside for me. "Be my guest."

I hefted the crossbow to my hip, then girded myself and headed upward.

We climbed for a long time. A cold breeze rustled the leaves, seeming to tell me to shush, to keep quiet. I walked more carefully, softly. I watched where I stepped and pricked up my ears for anything that might mean danger.

And then I saw it. A dark gash in the hillside, like a groaning mouth in the rock. The forest service had erected some signs about the cave and its petroglyphs but I had no interest in them. My attention lay fully with that dark cavern.

I felt Erasmus come up beside me. "Use all caution," he murmured.

Like I didn't know that! I brought the crossbow to my shoulder. The string was already taut and the quarrel was in place. The silver-tipped one, with the poison.

"Do you have the flashlight?" I whispered.

"I don't need it."

"But *I* do. Please. Turn it on."

"Very well." It clicked and a beam of light strafed across the mouth of the cave. And then touched on something shiny right outside of it. I hadn't noticed it in the forest shadows but there, leaning against the rock face, was a mountain bike.

"Crap," I said. "Someone went into the cave."

Erasmus regarded it mildly. "What will you do?"

"Go in. We have to. The bicyclist doesn't know what he's getting into." I tightened my grip on the crossbow and walked in. Immediately the air felt colder, wetter. It smelled of damp stone. The floor was powdery and kicked up as I walked. My heart was hammering and my breath came quicker. I surveyed the cave at the end of the flashlight beam and down the bead of my crossbow, not daring to neglect the ceiling. I remembered how the succubus scrambled up my own ceiling like a spider.

I walked carefully. This time, the element of surprise seemed important. Last time I gave her too much warning, and the ache in my shoulder attested to the wisdom of that.

I cast a worried glance at Erasmus. How far into the cave should we go? It was already giving me big-time creeps. It didn't take many steps for the gloom to surround us. I looked back and saw the entrance, a white strip on a black background. It was farther away than I thought. Another few steps around the corner and we'd be plunged into darkness.

We walked farther and the cave curved, narrowed, before the entrance was lost. Lit by the flashlight's beam, the walls were rugged plains of rock with dry stalactites dipping toward us from the ceiling like fangs.

Erasmus suddenly switched off the light.

I gasped. "Why'd you do that?"

"Listen," he said, close to my ear.

I did. Snuffling and a dragging sound. Something was definitely in there with us. "Can you smell it?" I said as quietly as I could. I wanted to grab his arm, to know he was there. The blackness was complete. I literally could not see a thing. But I kept the crossbow at the ready anyway, uselessly straining my eyes wide, listening to Erasmus and anything else that might be nearby.

"Yes," he breathed.

I didn't dare ask more. I shuffled in the dirt, sliding my foot forward, trying to avoid any rocky outcroppings. The last thing I needed was to trip. I shallowed my breathing and listened with all my might. And then my nose came into play. Yes. I could smell it, too, though probably not as strongly as Erasmus could. The smell of damp earth and that sickly sweet scent of decay.

Erasmus was at my ear again, his breath tickling my hair. "When I tell you to, you must fire."

I nodded. I figured he could see me even if I couldn't see him.

"Ready. Lift the crossbow another few inches. There now. Fire!"

I clamped down hard on the trigger. The string twanged, the bolt shot forward with a whoosh, but I heard a swish of fabric, and the quarrel clanged against rock several yards away.

"Dammit!" I cried.

The light nearly blinded me when Erasmus switched it on. No sign of her.

But on the ground was the biker. I swallowed my scream. I think he had seen better days than today.

CHAPTER FIFTEEN

So that was what Karl Waters had looked like. The bicyclist was shriveled. His bike pants and long-sleeved shirt looked far too large for him, like someone had dressed a mummy in a much bigger man's clothes. Gray skin and sunken cheeks, eye sockets, and neck. I could see his bones as if his skin were just papier-mâché draped over his skeleton.

"Holy shit," I gasped. I couldn't stop staring, but I knew I had to. There was still a succubus on the loose.

"It's gone," said Erasmus, aiming his flashlight down the long passage of the cave, where it forked and perhaps forked many more times.

"Can't we follow it?" I asked half-heartedly. I really didn't want to go after it into the dark. That seemed like a suicide mission.

"That's not wise," he said. I was relieved to hear it. "But you were close. You almost hit it. We shall have to try again."

"Won't it expect us now? Go somewhere else?"

Erasmus bent to pick something up, studying it. I didn't want to know what it was. He tossed it away and sighed. "Possibly. We'll try again tomorrow."

"Tomorrow will be too late. It will kill again."

"Perhaps. But it has killed today, so it may not kill again tonight."

"I can't take that chance!"

"What choice do you have? You will never find it in there and you cannot follow it at night."

Was it my imagination, or was there a greenish glow down one fork of the cave? "What's that?" I pointed.

He looked and his brow furrowed. "Let *me* go."

"No. I'm going with you."

"Stubborn, foolish woman."

"Yeah, yeah. I've heard it all before." I readied the crossbow and marched toward the cavern. He was right beside me. The cavern was dead quiet.

The floor was damp or dusty, but when it got irregular and rocky, it became smooth and slippery. I would have lost my footing several times if it hadn't been for Erasmus's steadying hand.

I looked down the bead of the crossbow, turning it this way and that, but mostly ahead. That was where the eerie light was, after all. It reflected off the stalactites and stalagmites, gleaming like a *Phantom of the Opera* set. We turned at an outcropping of flowing stone columns and saw the source. I tightened my hand on the crossbow.

A vortex. A swirling mass of light and shapes, shadow and sparks, hanging in the air as if a doorway opened to another room that didn't exist—not on this plane, anyway.

"That's it!" I gasped. "That's that evil hole. What's it doing here?"

Erasmus said nothing. When I glanced his way, his cheeks gleamed green and the swirling light danced in his eyes. He walked closer. I darted forward to grab his sleeve but he shook his head. He motioned for me to stay behind but it was tough allowing him to go. Would it possess him as it possessed Jolene?

He walked steadily forward. The vortex had made no sound before, but now shushing noises like waves against the shore began issuing forth. The sounds changed, twisted, becoming more like voices, and then I was *certain* they were voices. One voice rising above the rest. It spoke a language I had never heard, that probably few mortals had. The tones were twisted, guttural, with sibilants going on longer than they should. And when they stopped talking, Erasmus answered in the same language. It sounded almost backwards, as if the articulation would be impossible to pronounce. I shivered. As I watched him, it made me realize how different he really was from me, how alien. It was important not to forget that.

The answer from the vortex came back swiftly, harshly. Erasmus answered in rapid-fire succession and I had the feeling a shouting match had ensued. A burst of power exploded from the vortex and we both fell back. A scream tore from my throat as I landed hard on my backside. From the ground, my instincts took over, and I aimed the crossbow into the heart of it and fired.

A howl of rage soared up to the ceiling, rattled around the stalactites, and then fell away in dying echoes. The quarrel was spit from the vortex and fell to the cave's floor. It was blackened and smoldering. And then the vortex suddenly receded, growing smaller until it became the way it looked at the museum, like a ragged tear in the air, glowing green.

When I could breathe again. I sat up. I didn't notice how long Erasmus had been offering me his hand, but I finally took it and he pulled me to my feet. I scuttled to where the quarrel lay and picked it up. It was twisted and burnt. Oddly, I felt that the crossbow would resent me for it, but I stuffed it in the waiting holster anyway.

"Are you all right?" said Erasmus.

"Yeah. Just…yeah."

He took my arm and hauled me back the way we had come. We stumbled around the corner and leaned against the wall. "You were talking to them. It," I said. "What did it say?"

"The vortex is not an 'it.' It is merely a gateway. Those within the gateway, however, were not pleased by its being open. They object to having congress with your world."

"And did you tell them the feeling's mutual?"

"In so many words. They felt insulted."

"Hence the explosive belch."

"Yes."

"So if they don't like it why don't they just close up shop and go home?"

"Because there is this book…"

"Oh." Again, my fault, or so he would have me think. "So how did this vortex get here from the museum?"

He studied me with his piercing gaze. "That's what troubles me. This gateway is connected with the book. This sort of gateway doesn't travel as a rule. Which makes me suspect that the one in the museum is a *second* gateway."

"Another one? That's all we need."

"That is indisputably a very bad thing."

"Oh crap. If *you* think it's bad…"

"We must see this other opening."

"I saw it last night. We went over there."

He rounded on me. "You went over there? Alone?"

"No. The Wiccans were with me."

"The Wiccans! Beelze's tail!"

"The point is it seemed dormant, like a crack. Sort of like this one looks now. But then Jolene had this scrying stick, this crystal, and she pointed it at it, and instead of the nice white glow it went all red and wicked and then it possessed her."

His glare was piercing. "It possessed her?" His voice was low, monotone…and angry.

"Um…yeah. And it said something about this being a game. And then it said to stay out of the shadows and that 'the game is not for the weak of heart. What has begun cannot now be stopped.' What does that mean? And why did the scrying stick glow really bright when she aimed it at me?"

He grabbed my shoulders and glared full power right in my face. "Why didn't you tell me all this before?"

"There was the shop and the pentagram and all sorts of other… things." The latter made me drop my gaze. Those "other things" were a distraction indeed, a fact even *he* couldn't deny.

He released one arm, but kept a tight grip of the other and led me back the way we'd come. The fellow did like to manhandle.

"It follows the book," he said. "Always the book. There has only ever been *one*. One gateway."

"Shoot. Well, we'll have to go look at it. Again. We think it was the Ordo. That they summoned it or conjured it or whatever. They do have a demon helping them."

"I have not forgotten," he bit out.

"But what about that other stuff? What it said about a game and the scrying stick being bright when aimed at me?"

He pondered. "I imagine that the book is merely a game to the Powers That Be. And…all must be complete before it is done. It cannot be stopped before it is complete."

"You mean when we capture the succubus?"

"Yes."

"But why did it glow…?"

"I don't know. These are your Wiccans' toys. These are not Netherworld objects."

We arrived back to where the biker lay, shriveled and dusty. I swallowed. "Then we've still got to plan how to catch the damned succubus to get this over with."

"Aren't you forgetting something?" said Erasmus.

"What?"

The sneer was back, all teeth, gritting. "Your little *date*."

"Holy cats!" Ed Bradbury. I had to call the sheriff. And how would I explain my being here this time?

No help for it. I dug the phone out of my jacket pocket and dialed 9-1-1.

• • •

The rock was pretty uncomfortable, but it was better than sitting on the ground. I told Erasmus to beat it, but he was having none of it. I knew it was because Sheriff Ed was on his way, and for some twisted reason he enjoyed taunting him.

At least the vortex had dwindled and didn't seem to give off any light. I didn't want any deputies to go wandering around and get sucked in.

I rose on the approach of the stamp of many feet. There was a ranger with them, and what looked like a couple of paramedics, one of them with an old-fashioned wooden stretcher leaning over his shoulder.

Ed hurried up the trail when he spied me. He wore his full-on policeman's face, all square-jawed and uncompromising. The Smokey Bear hat shadowed his eyes, but they were burning with intensity.

"Kylie," he said, stopping before me. He flicked his eyes at Erasmus and the demon postured right back at him. "Mr. Dark."

"Constable," he replied with mock civility.

Ed ignored him and turned to me. "What's going on?"

"Like I said to the 9-1-1 dispatcher. It was the same thing that happened to Karl Waters. At least I think so."

He glanced toward the abandoned bicycle. "George," he said over his shoulder. The young mustached deputy trotted forward. "Dust it." The deputy moved quickly.

"Did you touch it?" Ed asked me.

"No. Neither of us did. No reason to."

He motioned for the paramedics and the other deputy to go on through into the cave. "Why were you here, Kylie?"

"Just checking out the local sights. I'm new here."

"And him?" He lifted the brim of his hat toward Erasmus.

"He's visiting. He wanted to see the petroglyphs."

He glared at Erasmus. "Big on old stuff, huh?"

Erasmus raised his brows. "You have no idea."

"Ed." I stepped between them and their pissing match. "What happened to him? *Is* this what happened to Karl Waters?"

"And Bob Hitchins. What I really want to know is…" He turned to me, voice low. "What do all of these have to do with you?"

"Me? I didn't do anything!"

"But they all have some connection to you."

"What do you mean? I don't even know this guy."

"And yet it was you who found him."

"All innocently, I assure you."

He stuffed his hands in his jacket pockets and frowned. I wondered if it might be a good idea to tell him the truth, get his help.

But all I had to do was glance at Erasmus to realize what a stupid idea that would be.

I squeaked in surprise when Ed grabbed my arm and took me aside. "Look, if there is anything you know, anything you're holding back, I'd like you to tell me now, no harm done."

I gave him my sincerest expression. "No, there's nothing. Really. I'd tell you if I did, believe me." I felt bad about the lie, and even worse when Erasmus snorted softly behind me.

Ed nodded, chewed on his lip, and then released me. "You two can go now."

I tapped Erasmus on the arm, motioning for us to depart. Walking backwards I waved to Ed. "See you tonight?" By the stern look to his face, I wasn't certain we were still on.

Ed seemed to snap out of his cop reverie and nodded. "Yeah! Of course I'll be there."

But my sense of fair play was getting the better of me. I walked up to him, leaving Erasmus behind. "Um…look. Are you sure? I mean, if you suspect me of something it might be a conflict of interest. I wouldn't want you getting into trouble on my account."

"Kylie." He cocked his head at me. "You are not a suspect. I certainly couldn't fraternize with you if you were."

"Oh. Good." In one sense I was relieved. I couldn't help but sneak a glance back at Erasmus. "I wonder…I wonder if we shouldn't wait till all of this blows over."

He took a deep breath. "Are you backing out of the date?"

"No! I mean…if you still think it's a good idea."

He took my shoulders in a strong grip and looked at me steadily. "I'd very much like to take you out tonight. It's just supper. We'll talk, see where it goes."

He had very nice eyes. They weren't dark and unfathomable like Erasmus's. They were human eyes, full of warmth and light. I nodded.

"Okay," he said. "See you tonight."

I hurried away with my head down, not wishing to catch the

eye of his suspicious deputy. Once on the trail I breathed again and Erasmus was suddenly at my elbow.

"Charming," he said dully. "Good to see that a little murder won't come between lovebirds."

"What's it to you? At least we're the same species."

"Is that what's bothering you?"

"What's bothering me is you! We made a mistake. No need to rub my nose in it."

He glared, saying nothing.

"I'm human, he's human," I went on, heedless. "You're a demon. It's supposed to be humans with humans. Right?"

He laughed. "You think this upsets me? You're mad. Go on. Go on a date with him. Go fraternize with other humans, with a thousand! I have no interest in a human as anything other than a curiosity. And you were certainly an interesting specimen."

I jerked to a halt with every intention of giving him the smack of a lifetime. But on looking at him, I held back. He was breathing harshly, eyes slightly wild. His lip curled in a snarl, revealing a canine tooth. I let go of the tension in my shoulders and brushed past him as I headed back down the trail. "Whatever helps you sleep at night," I muttered.

"I don't sleep, as it happens. Demons do not sleep. It's part of that being *another species* thing."

"You're the one who said it!"

"That's right! Don't you forget it. I am a Demon of the Netherworlds. And I don't need humans!"

"I *know* you don't—" He pushed me aside and marched on ahead with a great stomping gait. What the hell was *his* problem? I sighed and followed.

We hiked back down the trail in silence until we finally reached the car.

I unlocked the door and he paused. "I have no wish to continue in this hellish conveyance."

"Are you sure?" I asked, but was actually happier he decided to depart. A sullen demon was not my idea of good company.

He pulled his coat brusquely over his chest. "Quite sure. I'll investigate the museum. Off with you, then," and he made a rudely dismissive gesture.

"A graduate of the demon school of dickheadery," I muttered, putting the car in gear.

• • •

I pulled up in front of my shop and looked at my watch. Almost four. I hadn't realized how late it was. Jolene was scheduled to arrive shortly.

I grabbed the crossbow and headed inside. When I walked in I was immediately greeted by the enticing smells from the herbs and tea leaves. Smelled like home. I could forget the Booke's drag on my life for at least a little while.

Setting down the crossbow in the back room, I thought of making myself a pot of tea to calm me down. I had a lot to process. I pulled down a canister of Linden Flower and scooped it into my infuser. I tried to clear my mind as the water boiled, and when I poured it in and the tea blossomed, I inhaled it and instantly felt better.

Letting it steep, I wandered into the main room, thoughts whirling, trying to calm, when I felt a strange sensation of not being alone. When I looked up, I startled at the sudden appearance of a woman, clad all in leather, standing in the middle of my floor.

CHAPTER SIXTEEN

I hadn't heard the bell above my door ring. And I was also pretty sure I had locked it. Then I looked her over. Definitely another in a long line of unusual Moody Bog inhabitants. Why hadn't I noticed these characters when I was checking out the neighborhood? She was in a black leather cat suit, for wont of a better description, the kind Black Widow wore, high-heeled boots and all. Her long dark hair was streaked with green tresses, matching the green of her eyes. She looked at me steadily.

"I'm sorry. But I'm not open yet."

That didn't stop her from walking toward me. She stopped a little too closely into my personal space and I took a step back. "Kylie Strange," she said, a sort of purr of an English accent.

"Um…yes."

With a cock of her head, she frowned. "There doesn't appear to be anything particularly special about you."

I frowned right back. "Okaaay."

She sized me up, deliberately taking her time, counting every freckle, I imagined. "You don't seem to be much of a threat."

I didn't like her attitude, and too many odd things were happening in this town for my liking. I crossed my arms over my chest. "Okay, who are you?"

A sharky smile. "You haven't guessed? Not too intelligent either."

It was the grin that did it. She had that same sharp smile, and the illusion of more teeth in her mouth than necessary. My arms unfolded and dropped to my sides. "You're a demon," I whispered.

Only a raised brow for my efforts. "Not that dense, then." She walked a slow circuit around me. My eyes flicked toward the archway of the back room, where my crossbow lay. Maybe she didn't know it was there. Maybe I could…

"Don't think I haven't noticed the crossbow." Okay, so much for that. "I'm curious as to whom you…ah!" She darted a hand forward, and before I could protect myself she had grabbed the amulet in her hand. She glared at it and tossed it back, striking me in the chest. I rubbed my sternum.

"Erasmus Dark. I should have known!"

I snapped my head toward where the crossbow was, and it flew through the archway right into my hand, loaded and ready to fire. I looked at the chosen bolt curiously before bringing it swiftly up to my shoulder and aiming. "I think you need to tell me who you are."

She tightened her shoulders but her expression didn't change. "You know *what* I am. Isn't that enough?"

"A name." I remembered Doc whispering to me that to know their name was to have power over them.

She smirked. "Wouldn't you like to know."

I dredged up my encounter with the bikers. "Shabiri," I tried.

The effect was instant.

She snapped her head and glared at me with hate-filled eyes. There was a green glow to them before they settled down again. "Those pathetic fools! Those idiots!"

"Not nice to talk about your bosom buddies that way."

"They're not my…" She tossed her head back. "Maybe you aren't as stupid as I thought."

"Yeah, thanks… *Shabiri*," I added for good measure.

She winced slightly.

"That won't harm me, you know." She tilted her head toward the crossbow.

I adjusted my grip tighter. "And I know demons lie."

Her smirk fell. "Listen to you. Fresh and innocent. Yes, that is appealing. So naïve. So eager to please. The book chose well, as it always does. But as for Erasmus Dark...You don't have the power over him you think you do."

The urge to touch my amulet was strong, but I didn't want to relinquish my hold of the crossbow.

She smirked again, seeming to sense what I was feeling. To prove it, she nodded toward my amulet. "That will only help you for so long. You see, I've known him for centuries. Known him well." My stomach flipped. She smiled languidly, gazing at me from under her lashes. "There is so little you understand. It's amusing to watch."

Unconsciously, while listening to her, I had been lowering the crossbow by increments. I lifted it and took careful aim again. "I know you don't like *this*."

She was scared. I could see it in her eyes. But she stood her ground. I didn't know if I could really shoot her anyway, unless she attacked. And at this range, I didn't know if I could react in time.

"It's the book, you know," she went on. "It's *all* about the book."

"And what do *you* know of it?"

"Oh ho! Well now. The book is ancient. Like me. There is so much to tell. It's so tantalizing."

"Then why don't you just take it? Take it off my hands."

"I think you know I can't do that, no more than Erasmus Dark can. The book is *your* burden now. But you can make this easier on yourself. You should hunt, day and night. Get it over with as quickly as possible. It's such a sad end."

I couldn't help but think of poor Constance Howland. Was that the destiny of all us? *What has begun cannot now be stopped.* I adjusted my grip on the weapon. "At least I'll go out fighting."

She threw her head back and laughed, and it wasn't any tinkling pleasant sound either. "Such a little fool. So trusting."

Was it bravado or something more? I didn't like the swagger on her any more than I did on Erasmus. I faced her squarely. Enough with her bullshit. "What is it you're helping the Ordo to do? Why do they want this crossbow?"

She sneered again. "Those bumbling fools. They obviously talk too much." She sighed. "They have greed in their hearts. Surely you must have gathered that with your human senses. They, too, do not understand what they are dealing with."

"So why help them?"

"Why? They summoned me. And they were surprised and so pleased when I came."

"And they got the drop on you and took your amulet."

Her eyes narrowed and glowed again. She said nothing to that. I felt a keen sense of satisfaction at shutting her up for at least a moment. Were all demons this arrogant?

"Kylie Strange," she said, speaking carefully, eyes still piercing. "So mortal. So doomed."

"Yeah, yeah. Broken record. Is that all you got?"

"Let me at least offer you a little piece of advice."

"Like I'm going to listen to you."

She leaned in anyway, her reptilian smile still pulling at her facial muscles. "There is one thing you must never, ever do."

And suddenly she was beside me, her arm tight around my neck as she hissed into my ear. I stood stock-still. That crossbow had been useless against her after all, if she could move like that.

I felt her face tickle the hair covering my ear. "You must never, ever give your heart to a demon. Oh I can see it in your eyes, my dear. He is seductive, I'll give you that. But it only makes the game that much more delicious." When she drew away, she licked her lips with a long serpent's tongue. I gasped and staggered back.

"G-game?"

"Surely you knew," she said, pushing down the crossbow that had frozen my arms in position. "It's all just a game."

"You mean…the Powers That Be." The vortex voice had said it, too. It *was* a game. But if it was a game, then that meant at least two players, and someone had to win and someone had to lose. If I understood the game better, I could come out the winner.

"Just what *is* the game and how is it played?"

She shook her head. "Now, now. You think I have to answer

you? Just because you know my name means nothing. You do not hold the amulet. I don't think dear Doug will give it up that willingly."

"Shabiri," I said. She recoiled slightly. "What is the game?"

She licked her lips again. "Erasmus Dark has told you much. But obviously not enough. Take heed, Kylie Strange. At the moment, you *might* have the upper hand. But it won't always be that way. And just when you least expect it, the serpent always strikes!"

A clap of thunder made me jump. I glanced quickly over my shoulder toward the window, looking for rain and clouds, but there were none. When I turned back, she was gone.

• • •

By the time I recovered, my tea was steeped to death. I poured it out into the sink, contemplating making another pot. I sure needed to relax. I nearly dropped the canister when the knock sounded on my door.

I rushed to the front room and saw the shape of Jolene through the wavy glass. I pulled it open and she looked up, squinting at me through her glasses.

"Hey, Jolene," I said, closing the door behind her.

"You look like you've seen a ghost." She paused, a look of glee forming on her face. "Did you?"

"No, that is the one thing this place seems to lack: a ghost." I ran my hand over my face. What must I have looked like?

Nervously, I slipped behind the counter for something to distract me and opened my laptop to check emails. I had sent press releases to every local business and women's group I could think of, and if the email response was any indication I was looking at a spectacular grand opening tomorrow. If there was a tomorrow.

Jolene sidled up to the counter and leaned on it, glancing at the centuries-old graffiti carved into it. "So why did you have that look?"

"Um…" Where to begin? First things first. "Jolene, can you look something up for me?"

She perked up. "Sure!"

I grabbed a notepad and a pen and sketched, as best I could, the tattoo on Erasmus's chest. It was all arrows, curlicues, and dots. I turned the pad to face her. "What do you think?"

"It's not easy looking up symbols. Where'd you see this?"

"Um…it's on, uh, Mr. Dark's chest."

She toyed with the corner of the notepad before looking up at me sidelong. "And…how did you see that?"

I busied myself behind the counter. "His shirt was open," I said quickly. "When I was fixing him after I shot him with the crossbow. I thought it might be important. And what about that amulet? That appears to be pretty important, too."

"Still checking," she said, tearing off the paper and stuffing it into her backpack. "It has something to do with power, though. The fact that it's silver is very significant, one of the important metals in demonology. But Mr. Dark was able to wear it and it didn't hurt him. Must be spelled in some way…" She cocked her head, staring at it.

"Is it dangerous for *me* to have? Because it sure scared the heck out of our friendly neighborhood succubus."

"When did it do that?"

"Last night. She paid me a call."

Jolene's eyes widened.

"I should probably call Doc. I have a lot of things to report."

"Kylie," he said when he answered my call. "What's happened?"

"Well, a few things." I related the story of the succubus the night before as Jolene stood there, mouth open. Then I told him about the bicyclist and vortex number two.

I could hear his concern even over the phone. "This is getting very bad."

"And that's not all." I looked at Jolene as I said it. "I was just paid a call by…another demon. Her name is Shabiri. And she knows all about Erasmus Dark and the Booke."

Jolene threw her hand over her mouth.

"Did…did she hurt you?" said Doc.

"No. No, but she threatened me. Well, more like warned me. Everyone is warning me but no one is helping!"

"I'm helping!" piped Jolene.

I smiled at her. "I know you are."

"What did she say exactly?" asked Doc.

"Well, pretty much what the vortex voice said—that this was a game and we didn't have all the answers. But you were right. When I called her by her name, she didn't like it. And Doug the biker has her amulet and has control over her, too. She wouldn't tell me why they wanted the crossbow."

He hmmed on the phone for a moment. "I think, under the circumstances, we should try to summon that succubus, trap her in the meadow. Get this over with."

"I do, too, but I've got a date. With Ed Bradbury, remember?"

"Perhaps you should break that date."

"No!" I hadn't meant to sound so desperate but I needed that distraction from Erasmus. I sputtered an explanation to Doc. "It just wouldn't be right. And he's already suspicious of Erasmus. I don't want to blow the one good thing to come out of this because of these damned demons and that stupid Booke."

"Well, we *could* start without you."

"No you don't. Not without me and my crossbow."

"It's getting mighty sticky."

"You're telling me." Shabiri scared the bejesus out of me. "I could make it an early night," I suggested. "We could meet after I get back."

"You sure you want to do that? Might make things a bit… well, *rushed* for you."

Despite everything, I smiled. It had been a long time since a parental figure cared about me. "What kind of girl do you take me for?"

He sputtered, backpedaling. "I-I didn't mean anything disparaging."

"I know. It's just…I don't want to lose this opportunity. Either of them."

"I'm sorry our protection charm didn't work…"

"It did. I ruined it by covering it with a rug."

Jolene made a scoffing noise. She seemed to understand exactly what I had done. And so did Doc.

"We should have told you."

"Not your fault. But I do have the amulet, and that seemed to ward her off. A little bit."

"Jolene with you?"

"Yeah, she's right here. Did you want to talk to her?"

"Please."

I waved the phone at her as she inspected my braided rug and the smeared chalk line underneath it. "Doc wants to talk to you."

She skipped back over and took the phone, nodding as she listened to his muffled voice. "Okay," she said. "Okay. Okay, yeah, I got it." She handed it back.

"So…?"

"Jolene will fill you in," said Doc. "Be careful. See you later tonight." And he hung up.

I turned to her as she rifled through her backpack. "What did he tell you to do?"

"I'm going to try a few warding charms. See if that won't help you."

"All by yourself?" I hugged my arms, staring at the stuff she was taking from the backpack. Did she always carry her junior Wiccan kit around with her?

She set up a candle and a stick. *Wand*, Seraphina's voice corrected in my head. "I'm going to need a few herbs, if that's all right?"

"To save my hide? No problem."

She retrieved one of the woven baskets I had stacked by the door for my shoppers and joined me around the counter. She scoured the little cubbies and moved methodically, pulling out drawers and plucking the dried plant pieces from the first one.

"Agrimony," she said, laying the twisted plant into the basket. She moved on to the "liverwort" drawer and pulled out the herb, something that looked like flattened moss, taking only a portion of one and placing it beside the other in the basket. She turned to the counter and grabbed a small set of bamboo tongs and opened the drawer marked "Nettle," withdrawing the spiky leaf and laying it, too, in the basket.

"We have Devil's Shoestring, don't we?"

"*Viburnum alnifolium*? Right here." I pulled open the drawer. I'd forgotten its quainter moniker. But the name now made me feel ill at ease, like something dragging over my neck. I rubbed my sore shoulder unconsciously and glared at the root she tweezed from the drawer. It suddenly looked more sinister, like a fleshless bone. I shivered.

"And wood rose," she said. "That oughtta do it."

"Do what, exactly?" I asked.

She smiled and thrust the basket's handle into the crook of her arm. "We're gonna make a potion!"

CHAPTER SEVENTEEN

"I don't have a cauldron lying around, you know," I told her, only half-kidding.

"That's okay. We'll just use whatever you have. It should belong to you, anyway. Have you got a Dutch oven, maybe? Iron's best."

I did, as it happened. I dug it out from the back of the pantry and set it on the stove on its three legs. I stepped out of the way to let her do her thing, but I hovered, anxious and curious.

"I'll need a few other things. Some distilled water, kosher salt, and an egg, preferably one with a blood spot on the yolk."

I winced. What was with Wiccans and blood? "I don't know that I have one of those."

She shrugged. "That's okay. Those really become hard to find unless you have your own chickens." She laid the ingredients out on the counter, using the tongs to lay the nettle aside, away from the others.

"So what kind of potion is this?"

"It's for protection."

"Wait." I looked over the ingredients. "I don't have to drink this, do I?"

"No! That would be dangerous."

"Yeah, I know!"

"But you do have to smear it on the windows and doorways."

"I do?"

"Uh huh. Since you nullified the Craft protection we did—" she looked over her shoulder at me disparagingly "—this will have to do."

"This will keep the succubus at bay?"

"Yup."

"What about Shabiri? Will this keep her out, too?"

"It should. I'll add a little more salt. Demons can't cross over the salt."

"Salt? As simple as that?"

"Well, you can't just pour table salt on the floor and expect great results, but in a pinch…as it were."

She turned on the fire to high so that the flames just licked the bottom of the pot, and then she asked for a knife. I took one from the knife block on the counter and slid the cutting board toward her.

"Here you go. Will there be chanting?"

She set about to carefully chop each herb in turn. "I sense a certain amount of skepticism in your tone."

"Sorry. Even with all the stuff I've seen I still find it tough to believe that a mixture of herbs and a few chanted words will have any effect on the universe."

"You mean like manipulating a few atoms and saying 'fire in the hole'? That seemed to have an effect on the planet back in 1945."

"This is not the same thing as an atomic bomb."

"Isn't it? I've been doing research on it…surprise, surprise." She grinned as she dropped the chopped herbs into the pot. She added a few dollops of distilled water from the plastic jug I gave her and sprinkled in a pinch of salt. "And what we do in our Wiccan practices seems to affect the nature of the world around us. In small ways, of course, but still. So it isn't so much hocus pocus, but just a little bit of Newtonian physics. A little bigger than on a quantum scale."

"I think you lost me."

"What I mean is, what I'm doing will matter. Not just the actions and the ingredients, but also because our will has a lot to do with it. Our intentions."

"How can that—"

"Even moving from this position to that position—" she gestured with the wooden spoon from her to me "—makes small changes in the temperature, the position of molecules, and the air displacement in the room. Imagine what it's doing to the different planes of existence."

I was still a skeptic, but at least she seemed to know what she was talking about.

After adding all the herbs, she cracked the egg on the edge of the pot. She separated it, then tossed the yolk into the pot and threw the rest of the eggshells into the sink. Then she stirred, and I felt that uneasy feeling again. Here was my little Wiccan stirring her cauldron, and now she was beginning to chant. I didn't understand the words, didn't know what language it was in, but I felt that chill again. As I watched, the room darkened slightly, or was it just that the stuff in the cauldron was glowing?

I stepped closer, even though I had meant to step back. Peering in, the stuff *did* look like it was glowing, faintly, like iridescent paint.

"Is it supposed to do that?" I whispered.

"Shush!" she admonished, and continued stirring and chanting.

Finally, she tapped the spoon on the side of the pot and set it down beside the stove. She turned off the fire and looked into the pot. "Looks good," she said.

I leaned over her shoulder and looked in. The glow was gone. And all it looked like was a goopy mess to me. Didn't smell too good, either.

"My grand opening is tomorrow. Is this going to stink up the place? And how am I going to let anyone in here when there's goop smeared all over my window sills and doorways?"

"You can wash it off tomorrow. But at least you can rest easy tonight."

"Tonight I hope to get rid of that bitch in the meadow. So now what do we do?"

"We let it cool. Which gives us time to get the shop ready."

"There's not much left to do. And I have to knock off early, 'cause I have a date."

"With Sheriff Bradbury. So I heard. He's cute, isn't he?"

"Um, cute? I don't know about that. He's handsome, yes." I grabbed a rag and a spray bottle of lemon cleaner. She followed me back into the shop. "Let's clean this place till it sparkles."

• • •

The shop was as clean as it was ever going to get. I glanced back at the former hole in the wall that had once housed the Booke for a few centuries, but Doc had done a stellar plastering job, and with new paint on it and a display of porcelain teapots in front of it, no one but me would know the difference.

I looked around, pleased with my new enterprise. "I think this is going to work."

Jolene smiled, pushing back a loose strand of hair and tucking it under her knit hat. "Yeah. Looks like a great little business."

In a burst of camaraderie, I hooked my arm around her shoulders and sighed. "Yeah." But then I caught the time on the clock on the mantel. "Holy cats, is that the time! I've got to get ready. What am I going to wear?"

"I can help you pick out something."

Her face was hopeful. Looking at her drab clothing and ever-present knit hat, I had the feeling she seldom got the chance to do something girly. "Okay, come on up. But I warn you; there aren't a whole lot of choices."

She followed me up the stairs and when I got to the bedroom I opened wide the wardrobe doors. No one had ever gotten around to updating the room and putting in a closet. But then again, I wasn't exactly a fashion plate, preferring my jeans and sweaters.

Jolene stepped forward and started pushing hangers around. "Wow, you aren't kidding."

Now I felt a little stupid. Maybe I should have shopped earlier at The Ragged Hem, Moody Bog's answer to J. C. Penney. But vortexes and succubi didn't leave me with a lot of free time.

"I should probably wear a dress, shouldn't I?" Had it really been that long since I'd had a date? I had forgotten so much. I looked down at my worn jeans and baggy sweatshirt. Maybe I'd gotten a little sloppy in my bachelorette-hood.

"Definitely," said Jolene, continuing to rummage. "Sheriff Ed's kind of an old-fashioned guy. He strikes me as the hold-the-door-open sort."

"Really? I don't think anyone's ever done that for me."

"Me neither."

I smiled. "You've got time. It will happen."

Sighing, she fingered one of my softer sweaters. "I guess. It just feels like it never *will* happen."

"Not if you spend your time moping over Nick."

She squinted at me over her shoulder. "I should find someone my own age…and orientation? Is that what you mean?"

"Don't worry so much. You're pretty young to settle for the first boy who comes along. And having a few relationships is good. They teach you things. Like what kind of guy is entirely wrong for you."

Maybe I'd said that with a little too much heat. And by the look on her face, I guessed I was right. "What I mean is," I said, softening my approach, "is that it's good to go out with a variety of guys. It helps you to get to know yourself as well as them. Keep it light, you know." And because I felt a little responsible for a vulnerable teenager, I quickly added, "And definitely no sex until *you're* ready. And then always use protection."

She rolled her eyes, as expected, but I saw a tinge of blush to her cheek. "How old were you when you first…you know."

"Oh." Was I having this conversation with an essential stranger? A *teenage* stranger? "Well…I was a little older than you. But I'd done my research. To avoid…*things*." Yeah, way to be a grown-up, Kylie. Smooth.

She giggled. "Yeah, I know how to avoid *things*, too." Then she frowned. "There's just no one interested in finding out."

"Don't be in such a hurry," I muttered, hearing my mother's voice in that. "I bet there's someone at school."

"There is one guy…but he's such a nerd. No one really likes him."

"Who cares about everyone else? What do *you* feel?"

"I don't know. I mean, I know *I'm* a nerd, but he's a nerd in a different way. And kind of weird. But I guess he's kind of nice, too."

"Just keep it light. It doesn't have to be a great romance. And maybe you'll make a friend."

"You think I should ask *him* out?"

"Why not? Last time I looked, this is the twenty-first century." I grabbed a hanger and pulled out the dress I had been thinking of. It was a black long-sleeved number. A nice slinky one that came to just above my knees, with a neckline that wasn't too low but not too high either. "What do you think of this?"

"Conservative, yet says minx as well."

"'Minx'? I guess I could use a little minx tonight."

• • •

After helping me pick out appropriate bling to go with my slinky dress, Jolene did me the favor of smearing the protective goop on my window and doorframes. It smelled a bit odd but not too off-putting, and after rinsing out the "cauldron," she finally left me to my fate with a shouted, "Good luck tonight!"

I still had some time till Ed showed up, so I decided to spend it on research, or at least as much of it as I could find on succubi, demon amulets, and trying to find something resembling that tattoo on Erasmus's chest. His very nice, well-defined chest.

I shook my head. "Not now, Kylie." I was about to go on a date with someone else.

I sat at my laptop and tried to look up tattoos. I saw quite a variety of tattoo imagery done in places on the body I never wanted to imagine someone sticking a needle. I looked up demon marks and anything else I thought of to Google, but nothing came close. Clearly, I was not as skilled at this as was Jolene.

Another glance at my clock and I jumped up from the desk. I ran to the bathroom, freshened my make-up, dabbed a bit of long unused perfume at my pulse points, and stood at the top of the stairs just as someone knocked on the shop door.

Tucking the amulet into the neckline of my dress, I clomped down the steps, trying not to twist my ankle in those heels, and hurried to the front door. Pausing, I took a moment to brush my shoulder-length hair back, took a breath, and opened it.

Ed Bradbury looked good in his uniform, but he also looked good in a suit jacket over a dark sweater. Without his Smokey Bear hat he seemed a little lost as to what to fidget with, but he brushed his hand down his sweater instead and gave me a sheepish smile. "Hi," he said.

"Hi. Would you like to come in or should we—"

"Why don't we just go? Our reservation is for seven."

"Then we'd better go."

He escorted me to his SUV and opened the passenger side door for me. I squirmed girlishly inside; it had been a long time since a man treated me so politely. "Thank you," I told him as I slid into the seat and belted myself in.

I grabbed surreptitious glances at him as we drove. He had a nice profile, the kind one might see on a Marine recruiting poster from World War I; square-jawed, nice nose, take-no-prisoners eyes. And then he turned toward me, catching me staring. My cheeks reddened with embarrassment but his gaze was warm and he smiled. Definitely a nice smile.

We were headed toward the far end of town to a little restaurant I had wanted to check out when things got a little calmer. It was a converted house made into a chic café, with candlelight and white tablecloths. Sheriff Ed had good taste.

We went in together and were seated promptly in a cozy corner, with a few "Hi, Sheriffs" along the way. I took in the twinkly lights sprinkled among the branches of the potted trees, the sparkling tableware, the gentle buzz of conversation and clinking glasses, and felt a little easing of the tension I'd been wearing around my shoulders. I smiled at him across the table. "Well, here we are."

A dimple creased one cheek. "Here we are."

I suddenly remembered our earlier meeting today and leaned forward, keeping my voice confidential. "I hope everything went okay after I left the caves. You know. With the bicyclist." I hoped no one encountered the vortex. I supposed since he hadn't cancelled our date no one had.

A frown stole his smile and I was instantly sorry I said anything. He took his time unrolling his linen napkin and laying it in his lap. "It's fine. And I really can't discuss it."

"Sorry. Sorry. It's just…well."

"I know." He brightened. "Surely we can come up with other conversation."

"I hope so!"

Since this was my first time in the café, Ed described the tastier dishes and I settled on some of the local fish. The wine arrived soon after, and once I had a little alcohol in my system I was feeling even more relaxed.

"So are you a genuine Mainer?" I asked, twirling the stem of my wineglass.

"Ay-uh." He winked. He had that slight accent like Doc's that I found appealing, leaving off the sound of his r's. "Which means I'm many generations a Mainer. Just being born here hardly counts."

"I've heard that."

"And are you a native Californian?"

"Born and bred. But we don't have those rules. If you've got one foot in California we consider you a fellow native."

"So why pick up and leave? Things are pretty different here."

I set my glass down and ran a finger over the rim. "Sometimes, you just have to make a change. And the time was right. So here I am, a fish out of water, I guess. And you're right. It might take me a while to get used to things. The weather, for the most part. It gets pretty cold here, doesn't it?"

"Except for a few weeks in the summer." He smiled. That sparked a memory again of Grandpa's house. A memory I definitely needed to explore. Later.

The waiter came with our salads and set the plates down before us.

The sheriff cut his greens, gazing only at his plate. "I heard a rumor today. About you and the Knitting Society?"

My fork paused midway between plate and my mouth. "Uh… what did you hear?"

He chewed, then dabbed his lips with the napkin before replacing it in his lap. "Oh, just that you didn't stay very long, and Ruth Russell has some sort of vendetta against you."

"Vendetta?"

"Maybe that's too strong a word. But you definitely got on her bad side." He finally looked up at me, quirking a brow. "Care to elaborate?"

I took a bite of greens that had been on my hovering fork and chewed purposefully. I swallowed, grabbed my wine glass, and took a hearty gulp. Amused, Ed watched my every move. "I have nothing to say. She just doesn't like me."

"To tell you the truth, I didn't think she was your kind of crowd."

"I was just trying to get to know the village folk better. And to learn a bit about Moody Bog's history. Is that so bad a thing?"

"No, not at all. She's definitely the person to talk to about the founders. Though she can be pretty protective about her own family's part in it. A more reliable source was Karl Waters, but…"

We both chewed quietly for a time, thinking our own thoughts. It wasn't good to be maudlin on a date, so I quickly shook it off and leaned in. "Why don't you tell me about Ed Bradbury?"

He shrugged, giving me a bit of that "awe shucks" sort of mannerism that I found oddly appealing. "Not much to tell, really. Born in Moody Bog. Small family. Mom and Pop retired. Got a degree in law enforcement. Did a brief early stint in Bangor and returned here and eventually worked my way up to sheriff. I'll likely stay here until I retire and probably even after that. I'm a Moody Bog boy."

"Wow. Must be kind of—" I wanted to say "weird" but at the last minute, switched it to "*—comforting*, plotting your life out like that."

"I'm just the kind of guy who likes to know what I'm going to be doing in ten, twenty years. What about you?"

"Me? I'm happy when I figure out what I'm going to do that afternoon."

His gaze took in all of me and a small smile curved his shapely lips. "You're a bit of a free spirit, then. To tell you the truth, that kind of lifestyle scares the heck out of me."

"It hasn't done too much for me lately," I muttered. His brows questioned, and I said more articulately, "I like to be able to roll with the punches. Open myself to new possibilities. It might seem crazy to some to strike out across the country to start a new life, but I guess it's sort of the old pioneer spirit. And I wouldn't have met you."

"True enough."

He took a quick drink and finished his glass. He reached for the bottle in its ice bucket and offered some to me before he poured himself more. "So…this Mr. Dark," he began casually, or what I'm sure he believed was casual. "You say he's an old friend?"

Thoughts of Erasmus Dark easily filled my mind and I didn't want them to, especially with this rather handsome and polite man sitting across from me. "Do you really want to talk about him?"

He watched me steadily for a moment. I could tell he wanted to ask more. Perhaps it was the policeman in him. Or perhaps just the man. A tiny bit of me was hoping it was the latter. He suddenly smiled again and shook his head. "Come to think of it, no. Why don't you tell me all about this tea business instead and then about exotic sunny Southern California?"

We talked, and when dinner arrived, we continued our conversation. I almost forgot he was a cop and I was a succubus stalker.

By the time dessert and coffees were served, I excused myself to go to the ladies room. I had a smile on my face as I wended my way lazily between the tables. Pleasantly buzzed with wine and good company, I could admit that I really liked Ed and he seemed to like me. I could almost forget my indiscretion of the night before and I was beginning to regret my little self-imposed curfew, but I reminded myself that these things shouldn't be rushed. *Take the advice you gave to Jolene. What's the hurry?* If I hadn't rushed so much, last night never would have happened…

That made me frown as I strolled through the arch to the restrooms. Before I had a chance to push open the door, someone grabbed my wrist. I sucked in a breath to shout when another hand clamped over my mouth. "Don't scream," he hissed in my ear and dragged me through the exit.

The parking lot was cold and I was instantly snapped awake. Jerking out of his arms, I rounded on Mr. Dark. "What the *hell*! What are you doing?"

"I was…merely curious." He stepped back, brushed his long jacket aside, and examined his nails, like he accosted women all the time and it was no big deal. "I wondered…what does one do on a date? Mortal rituals are strange to me."

"Are you out of your *mind*? You don't just kidnap a person from their date. Their date with a *cop*!"

His accent was at its poshest when he tilted his chin up in irritation. "I beg your pardon, but I did no such thing. At no time have I held you against your will."

"You grabbed me and dragged me—" I held up my hands, stopping my own tirade. "Never mind. Just…go away." I rubbed my arms, trying to warm them, and headed back to the door.

"May I remind you that we have an appointment in the meadow tonight?"

"I know! Later, for God's sake." I grabbed the door handle but it was locked. An emergency exit. Great. Stomping through the parking lot I headed for the front entrance.

"Won't you catch your death? Here, put this on." He started to take off his duster but I gestured angrily at him.

"Keep your damned jacket." I whirled to face him, grabbing the amulet and holding it up to his face. "And if you know what's good for you, you'll beat it!"

He immediately froze. "Are you threatening me?"

I stalked closer with the amulet still held forward. I was pleased when he took a step back. "Yes!"

He seemed to shrink. "I just thought you'd want to know about the museum. But if you aren't interested..."

I pivoted. "What did you find out?"

His smug satisfaction irritated me. "Something very interesting. It *is* a second gateway."

"The bikers."

"Quite. A ritual was performed and the gateway was opened. Such a gateway is difficult to open. It requires skill, determination...and a death."

"Death? You mean a sacrifice?"

"Not necessarily. No doubt it was done at that location because of the very recent death of your museum curator. But as I said, this is highly sophisticated magic borne of great ability. I was not aware that such abilities of Craft were available to those of this area. I am very much afraid that by opening the book, you have unwittingly allowed those of mediocre skill a significant rise in said expertise."

"Wait. So...the Wiccans. They said that they've never been able to do the things they're now doing."

"Precisely. Where before they might have been able to perform mere rudimentary charms and spells, now they have absorbed capabilities far beyond that of a skilled mage."

"Skilled mage." I remembered that glowing scrying stick. Was the Booke making a mage out of me?

"Those biker guys didn't strike me as particularly skilled. Are you saying they were able to summon Shabiri because I opened the Booke?"

His breath hitched. "You mustn't use her name."

"She knows yours well enough."

"Wait. You…met her?"

"Yeah. She came to the shop earlier today. What a bitch, if you pardon my French."

"You spoke with her?" He grabbed my arm a little too hard.

"Hey!"

"You must not speak with her!"

I shook his hand off. "Believe me, I didn't want to. But she did confirm something about a game and it was great to know how eager and naïve I was."

"Beelze's tail!" He muttered to himself. I wasn't sure if it was English or some of that strange backwards vortex speak. Finally, he turned to me. "If she comes again, summon me."

"Summon you?"

"Call my name. I will come to you."

That burned something low in my gut. Maybe lower. I turned away. "All right. You can go now."

"But I haven't told you the worst of it, about the vortex. I believe that a second succubus was released. Correction. *Incubus*. One who stalks *women*."

"Well, crap. Now I've got *two* after me?"

"Yes. And while one is bent on your destruction, the other is supremely equipped to achieve it."

I dropped my head into my hand. "This is a nightmare."

"If only it were."

"Look," I said, "thanks for telling me, but it really could have waited. It would have been nice to have one night…well…then this kidnapping me…" I blew out a frustrated breath. "Just go, Erasmus, okay?"

"Very well. It's clear my information isn't welcomed." Steam or smoke began billowing from his coat. "How much longer will you be with that oaf?"

"He's not an oaf, and I'll be done when I'm good and ready to be done. And stop…smoldering!" He looked down at himself, and with an exaggerated huff, the smoke dissipated.

An older couple was making their way across the parking lot. They gave us a wide berth and looked on with deep frowns. I nodded politely to them and bit my lip, waiting for them to pass before I laid into Erasmus again. "Now go home!"

"*Your* home or—"

"I don't care!" I glanced at the couple again as they paused by their car to watch us. "Just go!" I hissed and turned on my heel. My teeth were chattering by the time I made it to the front door, and then I had to march all the way through the restaurant again because I really had to *go* by now. I passed our table and Ed looked up perplexed. "Made a wrong turn," I said with a sheepish smile.

By the time I made it back to our table from the ladies room, Erasmus was sitting at the extra chair and Ed looked less than pleased. I stood over him, my hands at my hips. Where's a chthonic crossbow when you needed one? "What are you doing here?"

"I went home but I can't get in."

I wanted very much to wrap my hands around his neck, but it isn't good form committing murder with the police right in front of you. "Why don't you use your *key*?" Code for his appearing-anywhere-he-wanted-to act.

"My *key* doesn't work. Something seems to be preventing me from getting inside."

The goop! Apparently, Jolene's potion worked too well.

"Oh! I forgot. Um…I added an extra *lock*, what with all the stuff going on around here."

"So I surmised. What am I supposed to do while I wait for this *date* to be over?"

He made an emphasis on the word "date" that made Ed flinch.

"Well, you can't wait here."

Erasmus got to his feet and the chair screeched back. Diners at the other tables were beginning to stare. "Right. I'll just go then. I suppose I could wait outside the shop."

Ed got to his feet. "You're just going to wait outside her shop all night in this cold?"

"I don't seem to have any other choice."

Ed looked at me pleadingly. "Can't you just give him the new key?"

"It's not a key. It's…a special alarm service." Exasperated, I glared at Erasmus, which seemed to have no effect at all. "Why don't you just go to Doc's?"

Erasmus rolled his eyes and gave a world-weary sigh. "If there is no alternative."

"There isn't," I said, sitting. I gestured for Ed to do the same. "So why don't you go. Go *now*, Erasmus."

He lifted a disdainful brow but adjusted his lapels and nodded curtly to me. He turned, his duster spinning out around him, and stalked to the exit. By now, everyone was staring at us.

I took a large gulp of my wine. It didn't help.

Ed stirred his coffee for a very long time before he quietly asked, "So…*how* long is he staying with you?"

• • •

We chatted brokenly after that. The mood was effectively ruined. There was a certain demon I wanted to slay. Plus, I was distracted now by the possibility of two succubi after me.

We got into Ed's car and drove back to my place without any words exchanged. When he pulled up in front and killed the engine, we both sat in the quiet of the car. I turned to him. "Look, Ed. Despite the last half hour, I really had a good time tonight. And I promise that my annoying houseguest won't be here much longer. What I'm saying is, I'd really like to see you again." With a big sigh, I added, "But I will totally understand if it's too much trouble."

With his hands still on the steering wheel, he looked straight ahead through the windshield. "He's a wicked pain in the neck, Kylie, I won't lie to you. But…" He turned to me then. "I don't think one irritating houseguest is going to make much difference to me." He unbuckled his seat belt and I did the same, thinking we were getting out of the car. But it only freed him to reach over the center console to take my arms and haul me toward him. His mouth was on mine in a kiss so sudden I didn't have time to prepare myself. It started off sweet, but as I laid a gentle hand on his chest, not to push him away, but to gather his sweater to keep him close, he deepened it.

There was nothing demanding about it. Just a leisurely kiss as if he had known me a long time. His whole controlled power thing immediately flooded me with want in a way that had been absent from boyfriends of days past. And it was different than what I had had with Erasmus the night before. With the demon, it was urgent and unfettered. It had left me no time to think. Yet with Ed my pulse quickened and I opened to him.

We kissed for a while, until breathless, I canted back. We pressed our foreheads together and he chuckled. "All right?" he said.

I giggled back. "Yeah, all right."

He drew back and opened his door and I did the same. He walked me to the front door, holding my hand. "Tomorrow's your big day, then? Good luck on that. I'll try to come by and see how it's going."

"That would be nice. Police the big crowds," I said, grinning.

"When can I see you again?"

And he hadn't lied, either. That was a novelty. I stood and smiled at him for a moment or two, simply amazed that, indeed, there were real men out there who could be relied upon to tell you the truth. With no strings attached, no magical Booke mucking it up and bringing dangerous creatures into my life.

I opened my mouth to answer when, over his shoulder, I saw two glaring red eyes.

"Duck!"

Everything seemed to happen in slow motion. Ed started to turn but the succubus was coming up fast and slammed into him. I dashed out of the way, but Ed fell hard, smacking his head against the doorpost. Dropping to one knee, I looked up just as the door flew open and the crossbow slapped into my hand. But by the time I swung around to aim it, she was gone.

I looked around for Ed, but the poor man was lying on the ground, out cold.

CHAPTER EIGHTEEN

Doc arrived in record time. I had called him first thing and asked him if I shouldn't call 9-1-1, but he told me to wait. He was less than five minutes away.

Ed roused on his own, and Doc had him propped up against the doorpost with a blanket tucked around him. Doc was shining a small flashlight in and out of his eyes.

"Looks okay to me," he was saying.

Ed stared at him perplexed, obeying Doc's instructions hazily until he turned to me. "What happened?"

"It was an owl!" I blurted. "It just came out of nowhere! And then you…you slipped. Hitting your head."

"I don't remember an owl," he muttered.

"Well…what *did* you see?"

He shook his head carefully, rubbing his temple. "Uh…nothing. You hollered 'duck!' I turned, and then blackout."

I was relieved. First that he was going to be all right, and second that he hadn't seen the succubus.

"I've called Deputy Miller to pick you up, Ed," said Doc.

"I'm fine," he argued, rising. He winced when he stood unsteadily on his feet and rubbed his head. "I'm sorry about all this, Kylie."

"It's not your fault. I'm sorry about…you know."

He waved it off. "Couldn't be helped."

Doc was handing him a cold pack from his doctor's bag. "You've got a sizeable bump on the head, Ed. Better keep this on it. And call me if you feel nauseated. I'd be happier if someone stayed with you tonight, keep an eye on things."

He flicked a hopeful glance at me and I was ready to volunteer when the deputy drove up, his car's headlights sweeping over us. He got out, wearing work boots, jeans, and a heavy plaid jacket with a fleece collar.

"What's up, Sheriff? Doc called me and—Jeezum! That's a honkin' big bump you got there."

"Thanks, George," he grunted.

"No kidding, Sheriff. How'd it happen?"

"An owl. I was attacked by a freaking owl."

"Are you kidding me? No way!"

"Deputy," said Doc. "I wonder if you could take Ed home and maybe stay with him tonight. He's had a slight concussion, but I'd be happier if someone stayed by him, just to make sure it doesn't get worse."

"Ah sure, Doc. No problem." He took Ed's arm and eased him toward the car.

"I'm fine," Ed grumbled, but I noticed he leaned heavily on Deputy George. The deputy helped him into the passenger side of his Interceptor but Ed wouldn't let him close the door just yet. He motioned to me and I trotted over and leaned over into the warmth of the car interior. Deputy George frowned at me as if I was the root of Ed's ruination. I couldn't argue with him.

Ed took my hand. "Kylie, I had a good time tonight. I'm sorry this spoiled things."

"It didn't. I mean, it would have been nice to continue what we started in the car, but that can wait."

"You're sweet. I'll make it up to you. And I still plan to come by to see how your grand opening goes."

"Only if you're up to it." I squeezed his hand, leaned in, and gave him a chaste kiss on the cheek.

He smiled. "Okay. I'll talk to you soon."

I stepped away and the deputy slammed the door a little too close to my face. I glared, remembering the chums he had at the

Chamber Get-Together, Ruth Russell among them. He ran around to the other side and got in behind the wheel.

I felt terrible, but I suppose it could have been worse. The succubus hadn't gotten him, but she was getting bolder. It was time to take her down.

I waved as they drove away. And then I felt that presence suddenly at my elbow. I whirled. "You just had to interfere, didn't you?"

Erasmus Dark stood unruffled beside me. A ghost of a smile was on his lips. "I have no idea what you're talking about. I came to impart some very important information to you."

"Well I'll have you know it didn't ruin anything. We're going out again. So there!"

"Mr. Dark," said Doc, coming up between us, though he stayed a healthy distance from the demon. "Are you aware that the succubus attacked Sheriff Bradbury?"

Erasmus glared at him and sniffed the air. "No. I did not know that."

"Too busy bothering people," I muttered, but he ignored me.

More headlights flashed across us as a car pulled up beside Ed's. With the engine off Seraphina stepped out, wearing khaki pants and a fashionable leather jacket. Nick climbed out of the passenger seat and thumbed toward Ed's car, looking around. "What's the sheriff doing here?"

"It's a long story," I said. "Let's go inside."

I opened the door and everyone followed me in. All except for Erasmus.

"Ahem!" he said. I turned. When I saw him eyeing the goop around the doorjamb I felt a certain satisfaction with giving him a little wave and closing the door on his infuriated face.

I picked up the crossbow I had stashed by the door and ran my hand over it. It had returned the quarrel to its place, as I knew it would. But then I examined it more closely. I plucked the burned quarrel out of its slot, but it was no longer burned. It had repaired itself.

Seraphina was putting her phone away. "Jolene will be over in a few minutes. Her dad is going to drop her off."

Everyone settled in around the fireplace and I told them about the attack.

Nick raised his hand. "Why is the, um, demon guy outside?"

"Because Jolene made a protective potion and it's keeping him out."

"Oh. I just wondered. He sure looks mad out there."

I turned toward the window and watched as an irate Erasmus stomped back and forth, throwing his hands up and moving his mouth in a muffled tirade.

Good. Let him suffer.

"He was being a jackass tonight."

"How did your date go?" asked Seraphina with a purr.

I rolled my eyes, set the crossbow behind me on the counter, and joined them by the fire. I told them, not about the date but about the vortex and the attack on Ed. "Listen, that isn't the worst of it. Erasmus went to check on our friendly neighborhood vortex at the museum and he said it was actually a *second* one. And someone summoned it, caused it to open."

"The melted wax," Nick breathed.

"Yeah. Our Ordo friends."

"Whoa," said Nick. "I've never heard of them being able to do stuff like that!"

"Like the stuff you guys can do?"

We all turned and looked at the Booke.

"You don't think…" said Nick.

"I do think. I mean, think about it. Were any of you able to do anything remotely this sophisticated *before* I opened the Booke?"

Seraphina played with her rings. "It's true," she said softly. "The book is giving us more power."

"That's pretty much what Erasmus said. But I don't like the power it's giving the Ordo. Not only did they get themselves a demon to do their bidding, but they opened that vortex and apparently they summoned an incubus."

"That's very bad," said Seraphina, turning her bracelets around and around on her wrist.

"Yeah, it's bad. So do we change our plan? Maybe laying a trap for a succubus isn't such a hot idea when an incubus is also in the picture."

The door opened and Jolene flew in. She stared back at Erasmus for a moment while he sent an ice-melting glare at her. "What's with him?"

"He can't come in," I said, "because of the potion."

"Seriously? Cool!" She shut the door on him and I got a tingle of pleasure as his shout of outrage was cut off.

She settled on a chair, putting her Hello Kitty bag beside her. "What did I miss?"

• • •

I changed and trotted downstairs. Everyone had on their jackets, and they all turned as I reached the bottom step. "Are we ready to roll?" I asked, sweeping the crossbow up in my hand.

"I guess," said Nick.

I patted him on the back. "Don't worry, Nick. We'll get her. And you guys can go back to doing whatever it is you do on a Thursday night."

The others exchanged significant looks but no one said anything.

"What?"

Seraphina took me by the arm. "Shall we?"

I shrugged and went with her, opening the door to Erasmus's sour face. "It's about time!"

I gave him a smug smile. "Oh, were you waiting for us?"

He sputtered and mouthed some strange curses I'd never heard before in that garbled language.

We marched across the street, heading into the woods. The plan was to trap the succubus in the meadow with Nick as bait. I just needed a nice clear shot at her.

I scoured the dark, swinging my crossbow from the hip like a video game heroine. I was anxious, but now my body was thrumming with excitement. Maybe it was the chase. Maybe it was because this would all be over soon. I could feel the crossbow's excitement as well. Whatever it was, I felt I was ready this time.

"The crossbow is quite attuned to you." I sensed Erasmus beside me even before he spoke. "It trusts you."

"I know. I trust it. That's more than I can say for you."

I saw him winding up to deny it, but all at once he stopped in mid-sputter. He frowned instead. "About this evening. I… apologize."

"You *should* be sorry," I hissed. "That was very rude of you."

"I know. Appalling behavior for a minion of the Netherworld." I saw the gleam of his smile out of the corner of my eye.

"Well, next time curb the urge, okay? I've got my own life to live. When we're done here tonight, I don't expect to see you again."

He looked at me strangely. He seemed about to say something when we made it past the trees and entered into the meadow.

We gathered in a little circle. "Got any creature-summoning charms?" I asked my Wiccans.

They looked at one another. "It's never come up before," said Jolene. "But Doc has the scryer."

Doc fumbled at his coat pocket and wrestled it out. Erasmus leaned over and looked at it, muttering to himself, but didn't seem to want to touch it.

"Never mind. Nick," I said, turning to him. "You're on."

"I don't suppose anyone's changed their mind about this?" He checked our faces in the moonlight. "No? I didn't think so." Defeated, he trudged into the center of the meadow, looking back at us over his shoulder. His face was white and stark. He was scared and, catching his eye, so was I. "What if it's the incubus that shows up?" he called out.

He had a point. "Seraphina, Jolene—you two be on the alert for the succubus and Doc and Erasmus will keep an eye out for the incubus."

I knew I'd had my chance to get the succubus two times in the last twenty-four hours and I'd screwed up both times. What made me think I could do it this time?

I have to, that's all. This has to be over! I didn't want to be the butt of any Netherworld god's games. And I sure as hell didn't want to end up like Constance Howland.

My fingers opened and closed over the weapon resting on my thighs as I crouched in the undergrowth. We were all as quiet as we could be. Even Nick was barely breathing, though I could detect the clouds of breath puffing over his head.

Erasmus made no sound at all.

And then the moonlight that had flooded the meadow before suddenly darkened, as if a cloud had passed over it. When I looked up, I realized fat ghostly clouds had lumbered in and covered the face of the moon, shadowing the expanse of meadow around us. I looked toward Erasmus and he looked back at me. "The moon," I mouthed.

He nodded. I wondered if it would affect things. If the succubus would only come out in the moonlight, then maybe it wouldn't show.

And then the crickets stopped.

I held my breath. My eyes darted across the meadow. I saw a faint glow and realized it was the scryer in Doc's hands. Crap. This was it. My keen ears picked it up, the rustling in the distance. I squinted. It looked at first like branches rising out of the undergrowth but then I recognized them as antlers. It looked like a big buck, but it seemed odd that it would come toward the meadow where Nick was obviously sitting, clapping his hands on his arms to keep warm.

When the antlers kept rising, I realized they weren't antlers, but twisted horns on the top of something like the shape of a man.

Incubus! I raised my crossbow but it hadn't loaded itself. What the…?

The apparition strode toward me, ignoring Nick. I stood. The jig was up, anyway. If the incubus attacked, I hoped that Erasmus would have my back.

For an incubus, it sure walked like a man. As he drew closer the details of his face became more distinct. He looked like a goat and was wearing leather from head to foot.

And he laughed, an almost familiar sound. *Wait a sec...* It *was* familiar because the goat guy was—

"Kylie Strange," said the voice of Doug the biker. It was then I noticed he was flanked by his other biker buddies. The goat head was a sort of hat worn on top of his shaggy hair and trailed down on either side of his face, resting on his shoulders. The weird goat eyes with their sideways pupils must have been made of glass, but their eerie glitter was no less creepy. The twisted horns on its head reached up at least another foot and a half, making his already tall frame that much taller.

I tucked the crossbow into my hip. "Last time I looked, this wasn't Hansen Mills." I glanced behind me to share my little joke with Erasmus Dark, but the damned demon had gone AWOL again. I was alone.

Just me and my chthonic crossbow. Which I noticed *had* loaded itself with an entirely different quarrel this time.

His eyes darted covetously toward the weapon in my hand. "No. We usually stay on our side of the hill, but for some reason the signs pointed to our being in this meadow at this time. Got any idea why?"

"Nope. Not a clue."

"And yet, here you are."

"I was here first."

He chuckled. His Ordo flunkies didn't have keen goat hats like him, but they had painted their faces with funny squiggles in black paint. At least...I hoped it was black paint.

"Did Shabiri send you?"

Doug shook his head. The horns swayed a little. "She said she was none too pleased that we'd let that slip." The Ordo shuffled uncomfortably behind him. "And she said she also paid you a little call."

"Just a friendly welcome-to-the-neighborhood thing. She didn't tell me why she wanted this crossbow. How about you?"

He shook his head with a smile. "Nothing doing. But I had hoped to run into you again, Kylie. You are one sexy bitch."

I hitched the crossbow higher. "I'm sure you say that to all the girls with crossbows. Right, Charise?"

The redhead lunged but skinhead Dean Fitch held her back. "You got a mouth on you," he growled.

"Hey!" said Nick, rising out of the meadow like the Great Pumpkin. "That's a lady you're talking to."

"Who the fuck are you?"

"We're her friends," said Doc, levering himself from the underbrush. "Now keep your language civil, Dean Fitch. Remember, I know your folks."

The skinhead shuffled back, lowering his head.

"Fred Boone," said Doug in a loud voice. "Don't get excited. We're only here for our own ritual. As are you."

Slowly, the Wiccans came out of the bushes and met at the edge of the meadow. I tried to study the new quarrel covertly. But I also tried to keep an eye on the Ordo since I had no Netherworld backup.

Doc Boone folded his arms and stood face to face with Goat Head Boy. He was considerably shorter than Doug and if the biker had wanted to, he could have flicked his finger and knocked Doc over. I hoped he wouldn't. "Doug," he said, "I don't want to have to make a fuss here, but we were doing something mighty important. It's best if you and your club move on."

"Club?" cried Charise. "It's not a club, old man. It's a coven."

"It doesn't cost extra to be polite, Charise," I said.

"Hey, bitch. Fuck you!"

"Ladies," said Doc. He shook his head and then looked at me. I had to agree. The trap was effectively sprung and we'd get no succubus activity tonight. Unless…

"Doc, let's go. I have an idea."

"What's your hurry, Kylie?" said Doug.

I had been a scared mouse before. After all, I had been their kidnap victim surrounded by all their biker buddies. There had been nowhere to turn. But not now. Not with *my* coven, I guessed, and my trusty crossbow that seemed to endow me with random acrobatic abilities. "Well, you've got your ritual and we've got ours. This meadow isn't big enough for the both of us."

"Then why don't you stay with us, let this little coven be on their way."

"Sorry. They kind of need me."

Doug changed tack. He relaxed his posture, tried for suave, as suave as someone could be with a goat head hat. "Listen, about that crossbow. Sorry we tried to, um…"

"Forcibly take it?"

"Yeah. Actually, we'd be happy to buy it from you."

"Sorry, it's not for sale. We need to go." I backed away. Nick was beside me.

"Hey look," said Dean, pointing at Nick. "It's the faggot."

"Didn't recognize you there, barista," Doug said, showing his teeth. "I see you took second best."

"It was a good choice after all, as it turns out." I was proud of Nick for standing up for himself. He raised his chin. "I like being on the side of good."

"Spoken like a queer," Bob said, shaking his head.

"Do you think your little junior coven corners the market on magic?" said Doug. "We have our own, and it's growing in strength. Maybe you felt it, too."

"Let's just all say good-bye—" I began.

Bob clenched his fists. "Are we going to take this?"

No one said anything more and I thought that was our cue to leave. I turned, keeping one eye over my shoulder on the Ordo, with Doug's inquisitive-looking goat head looking on, and Bob and Dean flanking a twitchy Charise.

The Ordo didn't look like they might follow us. They just

stood there staring. But then Doug smiled a feral grin. He said nothing, but made a quick motion with both hands.

Knife blades flashed in the moonlight. Before I could react, Charise and Fitch lunged at me.

"*SUFFLAMINO!*" cried Doc.

Instinctually, I raised the loaded crossbow, but they suddenly froze. A golden light showered down on the Ordo and they remained motionless. I thought at first that they were just surprised that Doc had yelled that nonsense word at them, but I soon saw that they couldn't actually seem to move.

"Doc!" I swung around. "What was that?"

He seemed just as surprised as I was. "By Godfrey! I can't believe that actually worked."

Nick gave Doc a high five. "Doc, dude! Seriously dope!"

Doc snapped out of it with a grim expression. "We'd better go. I don't know how long this will hold them. Heck, I still can't believe it worked!"

"Wow." I didn't stand around wondering. Keeping my eye on the Ordo, I walked backward a long time. They were still frozen, knives raised, faces grimacing, in a grisly tableau. Doug's goat head became a silhouette against the vague silver light in the meadow and the crickets began to chirp again.

The chthonic crossbow had disarmed itself when I wasn't looking. I wished I knew what *it* knew.

Once we were safely away someone switched on a flashlight and we started jogging. "That scotches our plans for this evening," Doc said breathlessly. His beer belly didn't look like it got much running.

I stared at him. "You're really a warlock."

He nodded sheepishly. "I've been called worse in my day."

I looked around at the coven. Sure, they had done their pentagram, and Jolene's potion *had* kept Erasmus away, though I scarcely believed it. But this! This was really something. And useful.

"You guys can do lots of that kind of stuff?"

"Only lately, like you said," said Doc. "I thought it might slow them down a bit, but by Godfrey, that worked!"

"I hope they'll be all right," said Seraphina, looking back.

"They know what they're doing," I muttered. "Or think they do. By the way, where the hell has Erasmus Dark escaped to? Bastard left me alone back there."

"My apologies," he said without emotion as he appeared jogging beside me.

"Don't *do* that!" I said, hand over my racing heart.

Jolene giggled. "I think it's kind of cool."

"It's not. And where were you? You left in an awful hurry."

"Did I? I thought I heard something and went to investigate."

Right. Demon equates to liar. I really had to remember that.

Seraphina didn't seem to care about our exchange and plowed on through. "The Ordo have never attacked us before. Why were they going after you, Kylie?"

"Because of the crossbow. When they kidnapped me the other day, they took the crossbow, but it wouldn't work for them. I figured that they realized they'd need *me* to go with it."

She shook her head. "Too much disturbance in the planes. I don't like leaving this undone. That succubus might kill tonight. And what about that incubus?"

I nodded and slowed to a walk. Everyone slowed beside me. "I don't think we should leave it undone. Maybe we should go to the caves. Split up when we get there."

"No way," said Nick, who looked even paler in the moonlight. "Every time they split up in a horror movie bad things happen."

"This isn't a…hmm," I said, taking stock. Maybe it *was* like a horror movie. "I still think we should go to the caves."

Doc sighed. "What does Mr. Dark think we should do?"

Everyone stopped and turned to him. He looked back at the coven mildly. "I think you should take your little witches' brooms and go home."

"Now wait a minute!" Seraphina stalked up to him. He reared back, eyes wide with alarm. "You've been almost no help this entire time. You left Kylie alone back there when those goons faced off with her, and every time we ask a direct question you answer us with some prevarication. You want to close the book? So do we. Now start answering some questions."

Nick crossed his arms over his chest. "Yeah, what she said."

Jolene clasped the shoulder strap of her canvas witch kit with a whitening hand. "You have to, Mr. Dark. Kylie has the amulet. You *have* to do what she tells you."

"Within reason," he said, teeth clenched.

It seemed wrong that they were ganging up on him, but then again, maybe because he looked like a man we were treating him like one. And maybe *that* was wrong. I felt it most keenly, especially when his glance darted toward me with a plea in his eyes.

"Guys," I said. "Listen…Erasmus." I felt so tired suddenly. My shop was opening for the first time tomorrow, but what was that to life and death?

Erasmus watched me steadily, especially since I used his name. "We need to finish this. Should we go to the caves? And if we do, will you be there to help? I really need you."

His eyes were shadowed but he lifted his head incrementally, and I looked into those eyes. As usual, the irises were dark, almost as dark as his pupils. But something more was there. It was so quick I barely registered it. But it was there. A longing. Was that for me? Or…something else? I shivered, looking away.

He cast his eyes downward, kicking at the turf. "Very well. But dangers await along that trail. It might be in hiding outside the cave. And then there is the other."

"The incubus," I said.

"Yes."

"But you'll be there to help, right?"

"I said I would."

I breathed deep of the damp night, smelling moss and duff on the breeze. "Then I guess we're going to the caves."

CHAPTER NINETEEN

"There's only room for four others in my Jeep."

Everyone turned to Erasmus. "I have no wish to ride in that hellish conveyance. I shall meet you at the trailhead."

"Okay. Be careful."

He looked at me oddly before he stepped backwards into the swirling breeze and blended into the night.

"Wicked," said Jolene.

"I have to admit," Nick said, "That was pretty awesome."

"Nick," said Doc as we got into the car. Nick, ever the gentleman, took the middle back seat. "I suppose you weren't kidding about your earlier aspirations to join the Ordo."

"Oh...uh...Well, at one time, I thought it would be cool to be an Ordo member," Nick said. "You know, motorcycles, leather jacket. But that was before I really knew what they did. I mean, I didn't want to worship Baphomet and didn't think they *really* did that. But now I'm not so sure."

I started her-up. Turning my head to back out, I asked, "Just who or what is Baphomet?"

Jolene cleared her throat, interrupting what Nick was getting ready to say. "Baphomet signifies the duality of male and female, Heaven and Hell. At least in a sort of representational sense. It's the 'sabbatic goat' or the ritual sacrifice, but at the same time it stands in for, well, Satan."

I turned onto the highway. My headlights swept the forest, capturing small reflective eyes from nocturnal animals before settling into two beams on the black ribbon of road ahead. "So the Ordo are really a bunch of Satan worshippers?"

"Well, demon worshippers," said Nick. "I mean like really heavy-duty demon worshippers. It's not just lip service or some logo they found cool. The word is they really do it. I think we saw evidence of that tonight."

"We didn't really see anything," said Seraphina. "Just that man's goat headgear. They didn't have an animal to sacrifice, thank goodness."

"Not an *animal*, no," I said.

"But what was it they were *going* to do?" asked Jolene. "What do they want with you, Kylie, and do you really think they opened the portal at the museum? They don't seem very…"

"Smart?" Nick interjected.

"Well, no," she answered. "They do seem to be a few bristles short of a broom."

"But motivation can make up for whatever it is they might be lacking in the brain department," he said.

She cocked her head. "Motivation?"

"It's like Kylie said. Riches and power and stuff."

"And they want the crossbow and me to go with it," I sighed. "They summoned the demon first, and it was just dumb luck it was the same time I opened the Booke. No doubt she helped them open a vortex. Jolene, did you find anything out about Shabiri?"

"The name is from Jewish mythology. She strikes people blind, apparently. At least in the myth. But I get the feeling she has more powers than that, like Mr. Dark."

"It doesn't say how to get rid of her, does it?"

I saw her shake her head in the rearview mirror. "I've looked up a lot of demonology books, but none are very informative on that. But there are other books out there. I just might have to take a trip to the university."

"That's not going to help us tonight. Okay. We know that the Ordo opened the vortex. But I wonder why Erasmus got shy around them suddenly." I steered around the curves, uncharacteristically slowing down for the benefit of my passengers. "What are they doing? Do they have powers like you, Doc?"

Doc tapped his finger thoughtfully on the center console. "I don't have any particular powers, Kylie. It's the gods and goddesses of Nature that endow me with abilities. As well as the spirits."

Boy, it was weird hearing him say that.

"It's complicated," he went on, "but they might have those abilities, too. But *their* powers are coming from…*elsewhere*," he said meaningfully. "And with the presence of the book…well. I think it's likely it serves as an amplifier of sorts. We must be wary from now on. Kylie's shop will need protecting full time and I think we should do our Craft for each of our own houses, too. The winds have changed. They want the crossbow for some purpose, Doug and his gang, and they're stirring up forces no one should be messing with."

Reality was slamming me pretty hard. Demons, demon worshippers, witchcraft.

"They opened that portal with the help of a demon," Doc went on. "But it seems mighty plain to me that they wanted to summon an incubus."

I couldn't get my head around it. "But why an incubus in particular?"

"Well," he said, taking his time. "To take care of *you*, I expect."

"*Kill* me?"

"As you said, if they can't get you to cooperate with that crossbow, chances are, if you're out of the way, they can get it to work for them."

We all fell silent. As I thought about it, several emotions ran through my chest. Fear was certainly foremost. That these people would summon this creature to dispatch me seemed terrifying and surreal. But then anger took over. How dare they? They didn't even know me!

"Could that really be it?" I wondered aloud. "They never even heard of me before."

"Ay-yuh," agreed Doc. "But as you said, they were…told."

"Shabiri. And she knows all about Erasmus."

"At least he sort of seems to like you," said Jolene. "You could play on that."

"That's not a good idea," I muttered.

Seraphina waved her hand as she spoke. "Just as long as you don't become intimate with him. He seems a little smitten with you. That could be very dangerous."

I gripped the steering wheel and chewed on my lip. I could tell Doc was looking at me. When I flicked my glance at him he wore a worried expression. Hadn't Shabiri warned me about that, too? Or was she just messing with me?

"I never should have torn into that wall." My eyes stung. I knew it wasn't really my fault but it did all come down to me. All I wanted to do was open a shop in this nice little town that had no crime…until *I* showed up.

We drove on in silence, everyone within their own thoughts. If I could take back the last thirty-six hours…But my mind lighted on my brief night with Erasmus. How he looked above me. How he felt. How he kissed and looked at me as if he couldn't breathe without me, and my touch was something new in the universe. Maybe it was. Had he lied about being with other human women? I couldn't tell. And wasn't that the problem? All I knew was that I ached thinking about him, about that evening that could never happen again.

But then there was Sheriff Ed. He was sweet and kind without the whiff of demons or the occult around him. He was just the sort of man one's mother would hope you'd find.

But there was just one small problem. I couldn't get Erasmus Dark out of my mind.

I was so preoccupied I almost missed the turn. I veered off the highway and up the long stretch of road that led to the caves. It was all so different at night. We came at last to the gravel parking lot, and when my headlights swung around and lit up a lone figure, we all screamed until we realized it was Erasmus.

I killed the engine and switched off the headlights. The

woods fell into darkness. The moon was still up but it was hidden behind the hills and everything had a ghostly pallor from dim reflected moonlight.

I hurried up to him, thoughts of *that* night still fresh in my wandering mind. "Did you see anything?"

"No," he said quietly. "This is a very dangerous prospect. A daytime visitation is one thing. But night is *her* time."

"I know. But what can we do? It has to be done."

The breeze rustled his hair over his face, but he never moved the strands. I wanted to tuck it behind his ear, to touch him in some way. He seemed to sense my feelings because he leaned toward me. "I won't leave," he assured.

"Why did you leave before?" I blurted. "In the meadow. It was kind of dicey. They know they can't use the crossbow themselves and so I had the feeling they would just as soon take me *with* the crossbow. And they tried."

His eyes narrowed and I thought I detected a rumbling growl. "They will not take you," he rasped. "I will see to that."

"What about Shabiri?"

"I'll…take care of her."

Doc cleared his throat. I stepped away. I didn't know how long we were staring at each other but it must have been long enough for Doc to figure things out. He frowned at Erasmus and had a stern look for me. "We'd best get going."

I hefted the crossbow over my shoulder and set out. It had not yet armed itself, but I kept snatching glances at it in the reflected light of Nick's flashlight.

The trail seemed longer at night. Shadows twisted along the trail and trees bent toward us, their branches like long-taloned fingers. A few crickets sang, but the forest was mostly quiet.

Erasmus was beside me. Ahead were Doc and Seraphina and behind were Nick and Jolene. Everyone had paired up, afraid of both incubus and succubus.

I leaned toward Erasmus, inhaling his scent, something

between wet granite and pine forest. "Did you know Doc could perform magic?"

"I shouldn't be surprised."

"No, really. He stopped the Ordo guys from attacking me. Yelled some magic word and they all stopped dead."

"Hmm."

"Is that all you can say? 'Hmm'? It's magic! Maybe they can do more to stop this creature. Maybe we can use them in some way. If they're stronger because of the Booke…"

"That might become useful in some sense, but because the succubus has already had a taste of you, their efforts will be wasted."

"A taste of me?" My hand went to my throat. "You mean… when she sucked at my breath?"

"Yes. You are…irresistible."

"So are you," I whispered.

He looked at me sharply.

"Sorry. I know we aren't supposed to…you know. And I really like Ed."

"Then it is wiser to stick with your own kind."

"My own *species*. Yeah, I know." Quieter, I said, "Then why did you do it in the first place if it's such a bad idea?"

He sighed. "There's no time for this."

"Right. Sorry. Hunting succubi."

I turned away from him. What made this guy so desirable? Couldn't be the fact that he seemed to be panting for me, could it? Or was that my overactive imagination? I snuck a look back and he was still staring at me in that smoldering way of his. *Nope, not my imagination.*

"If you two would stop drooling at each other," said Nick sarcastically, "maybe we can get out of here at a reasonable time tonight."

Oh crap! Was it that obvious?

Doc and Seraphina were looking at us over their shoulders with scolding expressions.

I guess it was.

I pulled the crossbow forward and held it in both hands. Time to concentrate. It hadn't loaded yet, but I was still wary.

We walked on. Doc's flashlight lit the path and shimmered in the pines and oaks around us. The breeze kicked up dead leaves, scattering them and they rolled along the duff-covered forest floor, crackling as they went. Every rustle, every shake of a tree bough made me dart my eyes. But when the breeze flowed again, I touched on the whiff of something dead, that sickly sweet scent.

It took too long for my mind to click in. I should have been ready.

Jolene screamed and there was a tussle behind me.

I turned, crossbow armed and ready. My throat constricted by what I saw.

Jolene was on the ground, struggling while a large shape crouched over her. It was in rags, or so it seemed. But there was a whipping tail above, like a rat, and long-fingered hands clutching Jolene's shoulders. Her scream had stopped abruptly, as if someone had flicked off the volume. She was staring up into the face of it. Her mouth was still open and I could tell that she was struggling to breathe.

Nick pounded on its back and shoved at it. "Get off of her!"

I had a clear shot. Until Jolene kicked hard and they tumbled. I raised the crossbow, but Erasmus's strong hand closed over it, pulling it down. "You might hit her. And it *will* kill her."

Just then the thing's head snapped up and looked at me.

It wasn't like the succubus. The creature's eyes were hollows in its face and its horns were smaller. But I could see the fangs stretching past its bottom lip, the long tongue swiping over them. It almost smiled, or appeared to. Before it leapt.

Heavy crushing weight, pushing me down into the duff. The crossbow was in my side, wedged by my hand, which was partially buried beneath me. I couldn't scream. My breath was being sucked away. I felt dry, papery. Thirsty. So thirsty.

I inched my hand around. I knew the butt of my crossbow was close, digging into my side. Which meant that the business end was aiming right at the incubus's chest. But without air, thinking was becoming tough. If I closed my eyes maybe I could concentrate.

I shut out the sight of that open maw, those hollowed eyes. My chest was constricting and I felt light-headed. I could just give up and it would all be over. But my spirit wouldn't let me. My hand kept moving, wriggling its way free, until I could feel the smooth metal of the butt's carvings. Inching along, pulling, twisting. My finger slid until it was solidly lodged on the trigger. I opened my eyes and fired.

The incubus threw back its head and wailed, the sound echoing through the rolling countryside. Surprised birds scattered from the branches above us and took flight, leaving a cascade of falling leaves and feathers. A bright light encompassed the incubus, and it seemed to be bubbling away, like melting film in a hot projector. Parts were disappearing and the weight on top of me was getting lighter and lighter as more and more of him disintegrated. Finally, it burst into a shower of sparks that lit the forest all around us in a brilliant flash. And then it just wasn't there anymore.

I took a loud breath, and then another. The crossbow and all the quarrels were back in place.

There was a pause before everyone converged. But it was Erasmus who gathered me in his arms and brought me to my feet. I let myself melt in his embrace for a moment. Surely he would have kissed me if the others hadn't been there. Doc tore me away from him and grabbed my shoulders. "Kylie, are you all right?"

"I'm…I'm fine. How is Jolene?"

Nick was holding her and she seemed fine. More than fine from the mooning look she was giving him.

I turned to Erasmus. "The Booke! I've got to write it in the Booke!"

"No. This was not summoned from the book but from another place. It had the stench of Baphomet about it."

Could a demon blaspheme? I got in close and said quietly, "Are you allowed to say that kind of stuff? I mean, I thought Baphomet was one of the Big Guys, a head honcho."

His sneer turned to incredulity. "Where do you get this from? Baphomet is not Satan. He's merely a poor substitute."

"Minor league, eh?"

"As you say. And so this creature belonged to him and will go back to him. The succubus, on the other hand…"

The crossbow remained unarmed, so we had a few minutes of peace.

"Does that mean that the vortex, portal, whatever, is now closed?"

"No. But it must be closed soon, or something else might emerge."

I studied his features in the darkness. His eyes tracked over my face. "Erasmus, can you transport me the way you transport yourself?"

"I…I don't know. I never tried it."

"Try it now. From here to there."

Doc stepped closer. "Kylie, I don't think that's a good idea!"

Erasmus and I locked glances.

"Do it," I told him.

He grabbed my arm and the night grew dark as pitch around us, like I had been stuffed into a sack. My body was suddenly cold, freezing, but when I opened my eyes I was across the trail. I breathed again. "Okay, weird."

"Kylie!" Doc was yelling at me from where I had disappeared. "Kylie, that was very dangerous!"

"What about any of this is safe? Look, this is what I want you to do. Take the Jeep." I fished the keys from my pocket and handed them to him. "Go to the museum and close up that portal. I have to hunt for this succubus. Erasmus will take me back home when I'm done."

"Kylie…"

"Doc is right," said Seraphina. Her face seemed pinched and she suddenly looked older. "Don't do this alone."

"I think I have to. And someone needs to close that portal. I can't."

Nick was rubbing the back of his neck. "What if *we* can't?"

"We will," said Jolene, raising her face. "I'll find a way. Or Doc will. Besides, we have powers now!"

"What about the portal in the cave?" asked Nick.

Erasmus strafed him with a glare. "It is from the book. It cannot be closed by unorthodox means. Only the cessation of the book's powers can close it."

We all stood around staring at one another for a moment before I gestured shooing motions. "Go! I'll be fine."

They still hesitated. Until as one, they hurried back down the trail. I watched them go, hoping they'd be all right, too. I hoped the Ordo were delayed enough that they wouldn't think to go to the museum.

Resolved, I headed up the trail when Erasmus grabbed my wrist. "What?" I tried to say, but his lips were on mine, stopping anything further. His other hand cradled my head, my hair cascading around his fingers. The kiss, which had begun with purpose, softened. With lips warm and firm, his tongue snaked in and found mine. My breathing had turned light and quick, and my free hand came up and clutched at his jacket. I returned the kiss for a moment more before I reluctantly pushed him back. "You said this was a mistake."

"It is," he whispered to my lips before he leaned in and kissed me again.

I tore my face away. "No. You're right. And this certainly isn't the time." I stepped away from him and he let me go. The hand that had held my wrist fell to his side.

He made a rumbling sound, clearly annoyed.

I lifted the crossbow. Not armed. "We have to get to the caves."

"And if it's not there?"

"We wait."

"Not wise."

"Then what do you suggest?"

"We don't wait." He smiled a predatory grin. "We hunt."

• • •

We crested the trail and I saw the cave dimly ahead. I hadn't thought to ask Doc to leave me a flashlight, but I figured at this point it wouldn't matter. I was feeling just a wee bit fatalistic. I was treading in places and with elements I neither had any business dealing with nor knew *how* to deal with. But Erasmus was beside me, and my crossbow...well, *his* crossbow...was in my hand. I felt like this was it, the last stand. It was either her or me. Maybe the Booke would win this time. Maybe it would succeed in letting out the baddie. Heck, there was probably another Chosen Host waiting in the wings somewhere. But whatever. I was going to give it my best tonight.

Erasmus stopped about thirty feet from the mouth of the cave.

"What's wrong?" I whispered.

He shook his head and put a finger to his lips. I looked around, staring hard into the undergrowth, trying to see, hear, or smell whatever had alerted him.

When he moved, I moved. I thought we'd be going into the cave, but he was veering away from it and plunging into the woods. The moon wasn't much help in lighting the way so I stumbled after him, doing the best I could to keep up.

He flung his arm out and I collided with it. We both sunk to a knee, crouching among the dead fern and tall grasses. There. On the wind. I smelled it. Something dead.

Erasmus turned deliberately to me and I watched his face. He motioned with a hand, two fingers pointing to his eyes and then outward toward the woods. He was to be my eyes. Okay. I could do that.

He got up from his crouch and moved into the forest, keeping himself low. I did the same, always keeping the crossbow ready, though it still had not armed itself.

He stopped and pointed far ahead. I couldn't see anything under the layers of shadows. Except—yes, there was movement ahead. The crossbow knew exactly who it was. The poison-tipped bolt was now at the ready.

Erasmus seemed to be asking me if I had a clear shot at it. I wasn't sure, because as soon as I took a bead and closed my other eye, I lost the creature in the tangle of shadows and foliage. I tried it with both eyes open and still lost it. I shook my head.

He pressed his hand to my shoulder and motioned for me to follow. We were going to get closer.

I could barely breathe; I was that scared. Or excited. Or both. This was a new experience for me—life or death. I didn't actually know if I'd survive the evening. And there were quite a few things I was regretting never having done yet. Though one…I stole a glance at my demon companion. I didn't regret sleeping with him. But I did regret not having the chance to do it again.

I wanted to tell him…what? That though it might have been a mistake I wouldn't take it back for anything? I wanted him to know that before I died.

But there was no time. The succubus was on the move and didn't seem to have detected us yet. I kept her in my sights and moved as stealthily as I could. We were obviously downwind of her because I could smell her, but she didn't seem to be able to smell me. My confidence rose and I stalked forward…and promptly cracked a twig.

Red eyes instantly glared at me and she suddenly shot straight up into the trees.

"Shit!" I pointed the crossbow upward, aiming for tree after tree, but by the breaking of branches and pine needles showering all around us I could tell she was hopping from one to the other. And getting closer.

"Kylie!" said Erasmus. "Run!"

I didn't stop to think. I turned tail and ran. But not fast enough.

She landed on me hard and her claws dug into my shoulder blade again. A scream tore from my throat and cascaded up and down the mountainside.

Instinctually, I rolled over and over, trying to dislodge her. Erasmus must have come to the rescue because she was suddenly gone. Well, at least not attached to my back any longer. She crouched in the distance between the trees, red eyes flashing, tail whipping the air.

"Now, Kylie! Shoot her now!"

I pulled the crossbow up to aim but my shoulder stabbed with pain and I dropped it. With a grunt, she pounced off again.

Erasmus was by my side in an instant. "Kylie, what's wrong?"

"My shoulder. Hurts like a son-of-a-bitch."

He tore off my coat and pushed up my sweatshirt and t-shirt. His fingers touched my naked back, probing. "Seems she knew just where to strike you. She reopened the wound she inflicted before and dug in deeper. Can you go on?"

"I…I don't know whether I can shoot this thing. I can't lift it higher than my waist."

"Beelze's tail!" He stalked back and forth while I gingerly pulled my jacket back on.

I offered him the crossbow. "Can't you do it?"

"No. I am not the Chosen Host. It would do no good."

I let it drop. I felt like a failure. Just when I had her…

"Don't despair," he said. "There will be other opportunities."

"No! You don't get it. I want this over with. I can't keep going on like this. It has to be over!" I slapped my hand into the dead leaves around me and sprayed them up into the air with my sweeping arm. "Dammit!" Hot tears burned at my eyes and spilled over, wetting my face. I let them fall, didn't even wipe them away.

Erasmus stopped pacing and crouched beside me.

"I had plans, you know," I went on, my voice shaky with tears. "I was going to have my nice little shop in this nice little town. Everything was finally going to go my way. And then this!" I laughed bitterly. "And you. You come into my life and screw it up. Sheriff Ed is a nice guy, and I deserve a nice guy after the idiot I've been dating for two years. I mean Sheriff Ed is good-looking. He's got a decent job. He's a gentleman. But what do I do? I throw it all away on a one-night stand with *you*."

He sat back on his haunches and took a deep breath. "You haven't thrown anything away. He is still there, waiting for you."

"I'll have to tell him. It isn't fair to him."

"You don't have to tell him anything. How absurdly stupid of you! Whom will that assuage? Only you. Selfish, foolish mortals. He's best not knowing."

"Why are you defending him? You don't even like him."

"*You* seem to. And he is better for you…than me."

His dark eyes glittered in the scant light. He was looking at me sadly. I leaned over, took his cheek in my hand, and kissed him. There wasn't any pretense of his holding back. His arms slid around me instantly and held me tight, angling his head to kiss me deeper. I opened to him, teasing my tongue along his. I nipped at his lips before he dropped his head and licked at my neck.

"Erasmus…" I sighed.

"We shouldn't be doing this…" His voice was low and husky.

"No, we shouldn't." I dug my fingers in his unruly hair and dragged his face upward, taking his earlobe between my lips and nibbling, licking the shell of his ear.

He had a rather silly look on his face when I pulled back. But soon his expression grew serious. He held me at arm's length. I winced at the ache to my shoulder blades. "No. I won't let you do this."

"A selfless demon," I said. "Who would have thought?"

He sneered. "Yes. Who would have thought."

As much as I wanted to continue, I admired his fortitude.

"Help me up." He offered me a hand and I rose, trying to roll my hurt shoulder but crying out, breathing through my teeth. "Crap, that hurts."

"You should have that doctor of yours look at it."

"Yeah. After. After you take me to the museum. I need to see if they need help."

"You should go home."

"I can't. I failed here but if they need my help I have to give it."

"Stubborn, foolish female," he mumbled.

"Take me."

He glared at me until his eyes dropped to the amulet around my neck. He grabbed my hand, and the world darkened and chilled around me.

• • •

We reappeared without a sound, not in front of the museum as I thought we would, but somewhere behind it. "That's still weird," I muttered, shaking it off.

Then I heard the sounds. Unearthly noises issuing from the depths of the building. "We've got to go in!"

I headed for the back door, but Erasmus grabbed the back of my coat. "Not that way. This way." He took my hand and the dark and cold encompassed me again before I was instantly standing behind the Wiccans, and they were chanting like mad while the vortex in front of them swirled and howled.

Surrounding the vortex on the floor was a circle of salt. Beside the Ordo's black candle stubs the Wiccans had placed their own white candles that flickered with each turn of the vortex's central spiral. I noticed the willow wand and some bundles of herbs and what looked like a pyramid of soil also within the circle of salt.

"Is it working?" I yelled.

Jolene, who was reading off of her tablet, whipped around. The others did, too.

She shook her head. "It needs something to complete the circle," she cried above the din. "But I don't know what."

I thought of the protection pentagram they first performed at my house. "It wants blood," I shouted. I looked at Doc. He seemed to be working it out, and then referred to an old book in his hand. Jolene swiped through her tablet. "You might be right," she said.

"It wants mine," I told her.

"That's insane!" Nick yelled.

Seraphina shook her head. "That's not a good idea, Kylie."

I shrugged, wincing at the effort. "I know. But I gotta do it all the same. If the Ordo conjured this to get rid of me, it makes sense that my blood is what's needed."

I turned to Erasmus, and close to his ear asked, "Should we take it from the succubus wound?"

His eyes widened, but he nodded. "Yes. That would be best."

"Okay, everyone. Um, Nick, Doc, could you please turn around?"

"Why?" asked Doc.

"Because that damned succubus wounded me before it got away and Erasmus agrees that the blood from my wound would work best. And I…uh…have to take off my shirt."

"No!" said Nick. "No way. Don't believe him."

Jolene frantically searched on her tablet.

"Jolene?" asked Seraphina. "Is it safe for Kylie?"

She looked stricken. "I don't know. I can't find out anything."

"Look, we don't have any more time. Just turn around, you guys."

Reluctantly, Nick and Doc turned. Seraphina helped me off with my jacket and then each shirt. But she stopped when she looked over my shoulder. "You turn around, too."

She was talking to Erasmus. He snorted. "I've seen it all already."

I glared at him and he raised a smug brow. Way to let the cat out of the bag.

Seraphina scowled and continued to lift the shirts. She gasped when she saw the gash on my shoulder blade. "Oh my God! You have to have Doc look at that right after this."

"If there is an 'after this,'" I said.

She motioned to Jolene. "Get a cloth. A clean one."

Jolene dug in her bag. "Hurry up," I said between clenched teeth. Not only was the room cold, but the vortex seemed to take a fancy to me and was reaching out with misty tentacles. I wasn't excited about getting snatched into it.

Jolene got a white cloth and brought it over.

"Dab the wound," Seraphina said as calm as any nurse. "And then take it to the circle."

Jolene gently dabbed, even as I jerked away from her touch.

"Sorry!" she said. She dabbed until I couldn't stand it and then ran to the circle of salt, reached over, and tossed in the cloth. "Now, chant!" she cried.

I righted my clothes as the others began to chant loudly. It was not Latin and not that strange guttural thing Erasmus had used to argue with the other vortex. I had the feeling it was just as old, though. It grew louder and more intense and this time, it looked like the vortex was paying attention. It seemed to pulse, the swirling slowing down.

"Pick up the salt!" said Seraphina. The Wiccans stooped and each took up a handful of the salt around the circle and on the count of three, hurled it toward the vortex. Something within it screamed, the candles blew out, and there was a loud thunderclap.

It sucked in on itself and for a moment my eardrums felt the pressure. We were all drawn forward. The vortex pulled inward until it was one bright dot, and then that suddenly winked out of existence with a loud pop. I felt like a string was cut and I wobbled back on my heels.

Silence fell all around us.

My ears felt normal pressure again. "Was that it?"

Erasmus moved forward, steering clear of the salt. "Yes. That was it. It is closed. I must say…well done."

Nick gave a muted laugh. "We did it. We really did it."

Seraphina took him into a hug. "We did!"

"By Godfrey!" said Doc.

Jolene shook her head. "That was awesome."

I agreed. But something was wrong. It was all getting dark again, as if Erasmus were transporting me somewhere. Except the only place I was going was the floor.

CHAPTER TWENTY

When I woke again I was in my bed and Doc was bending over me. "There she is," he said cheerfully. "Better?"

For a fleeting moment, I thought it might all have been a dream. But my shoulder felt packed with bandages and though there was no pain I could still feel a deep ache somewhere in the distance. "Yeah," I said, my throat scratchy and dry. "Could I have a drink of water?"

"Of course." He had one ready and offered it. I took the glass and drank it all. "That's better. I used an old-fashioned poultice. I must say, you have a wonderful inventory of herbs. I hope you don't mind that I took some."

"Not at all." I could actually move it. It felt numb but good. "Dare I ask what you used?"

"A little of this, a little of that…and some Novocain. No use in going overboard."

I chuckled and relaxed. "We closed the portal?"

"All closed. But as far as the succubus…"

I shook my head, angry and frustrated all over again. "I didn't get her. She got me first and when I tried to shoot—"

He laid a gentle hand on my arm. "Calm down, Kylie. It's all right."

"It's not all right! I've still got this creature hanging over my head." I looked up in the rafters just to make sure she wasn't literally doing that. "And my grand opening is tomorrow."

"We're staying here tonight to make sure you're all right."

As soon as he said it I could hear movement downstairs, furniture being slid across the floor and pots and pans rattling.

"Really? You'd do that?"

"Of course. You're the Chosen Host. We can't let anything happen to you. And besides, I want to see this business a success!"

I smiled.

He grabbed my desk chair and brought it over. Sitting, he put his hands on his thighs. "Now. There seems to be something we need to discuss. I think you know we can be honest with one another, especially after all that we've been through lately."

I nodded. "Yes. Absolutely."

"Then you won't get your hackles up when I get a little personal. Kylie?" He looked me in the eye more like a father to a daughter than a doctor to a patient. "Did you sleep with that demon?"

Direct and to the point. I gulped. "Uh…yes."

He slapped his thigh and swore. "Young lady, I do not know what to say to you."

"I know, I know. It was monumentally stupid."

"You got that right."

I knew I was furiously blushing. "It was sort of the moment. I mean, he has this…sex appeal…"

"And it didn't occur to you that this might be his demon's wiles working on you to get you in his power?"

I searched my thoughts. "No, it's not like that."

"It's exactly like that. We have a little more experience with this than you have. Well, at least in theory." He settled himself on the seat. "I want you to make a promise to me. I want you to promise you won't have any more relations with that creature."

Doc was right. Even Erasmus agreed with him, though he couldn't seem to keep his hands off of me either. But what if all this sex appeal *was* to get me to do what he wanted? Maybe it was the same thing that drove Constance Howland off the cliff. He had said he hadn't pushed her, but maybe he didn't have to.

My heart ached. I didn't know what I felt, but it was mixed up in a little betrayal. Just like Jeff all over again.

I wiped a loose tear away and nodded. "Okay. I promise."

He patted my hand and rose. "Good girl. Remember, you're dating Ed Bradbury, who happens to be a friend of mine."

"I feel bad enough about that. You're not going to tell him, are you?"

"No. No reason to. As long as you keep your promise."

I nodded.

"Good. At the moment, that demon can't come into the shop because of Jolene's potion and I recommend keeping it that way. Until all this is over anyway."

I nodded again. "You're right. Okay."

He smiled and rose. "I think you need to get some sleep. You've got a big day tomorrow. We'll be downstairs if you need us."

He switched off the light and headed for the door. "Goodnight, Kylie." He went through the doorway, and closed the door but not all the way. A strip of reflected light on the stairwell gave the room a warm glow. I listened to the low murmur of their talking downstairs, and though I knew I should be trying to sleep, my mind was aflutter with everything.

Everything.

• • •

I hadn't slept but for a few moments here and there. My shoulder ached but not like the stabbing pains of earlier. As day filtered in through the window I smelled coffee wafting up from downstairs and though feeling a bit weak, I sat up and swung my legs over the side of the bed.

A creak at the stair and Seraphina's face peered in through the door. "Mind if I come in?"

"Sure. I could use the help. I'm still a little wobbly."

She came in and closed the door. "Long night, huh?"

"Do I look that bad?"

"I've seen you look perkier. Maybe a little breakfast will help."

"There's so much to do. I've got deliveries coming from Moody Bog Market."

"They already arrived. Jolene is slicing and putting apple pecan loaf on plates. I hope you don't mind."

"Mind?" I slowly rose and she was there with a supporting arm. "I'm very grateful to all of you."

She waved her hand in dismissal. "We're friends now. As Nick would say, 'that's how the coven rolls!'"

I laughed as I walked slowly to the bathroom. "Yeah, okay."

"One thing, though."

I held onto the doorjamb and turned back to her.

"About Mr. Dark."

My cheeks warmed again and my gaze fell away from her. "No need for a scolding. I already got that from Doc. I've sworn off demons, okay?"

"That's good. I want you to know you can talk to me if you need to. I've had my share of…troubled relationships, too."

I offered her a grateful smile. "Thanks. I appreciate it. Is, um, Erasmus still around? He promised to…"

She sighed with an irritated sound. "Yes. He's outside, patrolling, for want of a better word. He can't get in."

"So I heard. Okay then. I'm going to take a shower."

"Do you want me to stand by? In case you have a fall?"

"No, I'm all right. But I could use some coffee when I get out."

"Coffee with cream coming up!" she said, and hurried out of the room.

• • •

I felt more human after my shower. I tried to avoid getting the bandage wet but was sadly unsuccessful. In the steamy bathroom, I managed to pull it off and had a look. I was aghast before I realized that part of that mess was Doc's poultice and not some other horrible reaction. I still couldn't raise my arm more than a few inches.

The knock on the bathroom door came just in time. "I could use some help getting a new bandage on this, Seraphina."

She set the coffee down on the bathroom counter and helped with the gauze and tape. "There now," she said. "Get dressed and you'll be ready to face the day."

I certainly hoped so.

She left me and I went to my wardrobe to get a shimmery t-shirt and black skinny jeans. I put on a little make-up to take away some of the pallor from a rough night. Some beaded necklaces and a bracelet slid over my wrist and I felt ready.

I couldn't help but glance at the Booke. It radiated a sense of waiting, of impatience. I felt compelled to approach it and sat at the desk chair. My hands glided over the leather cover, traveling again as they always seemed to, over the engraved words—Booke of the Hidden—and then the lock. I fingered it for a moment and then snapped it open. I laid the cover aside and turned the blank parchment pages, one over the other.

Soon, I felt more than heard the word. *Soon.*

• • •

Once I got downstairs, I gasped. My Wiccans, my coven, had done a splendid job, no doubt following Jolene's directions. The selected teas were steeping in the urns around the room, the twinkly lights were hung, cascades of flowers (probably from Seraphina) were perched artfully here and there, and the whole place smelled of apple pecan loaf, spices, herbs, and brewed tea. It was just the way I'd pictured it all those months ago when the notion had set in.

"You guys," I said breathlessly, looking around. "It's perfect!"

Nick greeted me at the stairs. "We hoped you'd like it. Jolene is quite the taskmaster. I think she deserves a raise."

"I second that motion!" shouted Jolene from the kitchen.

I stepped into my shop. *My* shop! "Wow. This is going to be great."

Nick grabbed his jacket. "I'm going to run home for a shower and then I'll be right back. Don't open without me."

He pulled open the front door and nearly ran into Erasmus. The demon pushed him roughly out of the way and peered in at me.

"Hey, demon boy," said Nick as he trotted away. "Watch it!"

Erasmus stared at me through the doorway and I stared back, but it was Doc who stepped forward and closed the door. He looked at me meaningfully and I gave him a quick nod. *None of that now, Kylie. I have a shop to run.*

• • •

Nick returned after forty-five minutes. His hair was still wet but he bustled about the shop, taking my orders. I could see cars beginning to park out front and people milling. I was suddenly giddy.

"Okay," I said to Jolene, who was closest to the door. "Open her up!"

She unlocked the deadbolt and the surface bolts at the top of the doors. When she pulled it open, the bell tinkled.

Red faces from the cold peered in, and patrons in bundled coats arrived, oohing and ahhing at what was on offer.

The first person through the door was a rather round-bellied man in a dark green suit. He was clean-shaven, but his sideburns came down to his jawline in gray muttonchops. The hairline on his wide forehead receded until there was little more than a center tuft. He barreled in and came right up to me. "Well, young lady," he said in a booming voice. "Do I have the pleasure of addressing Kylie Strange, of Strange Herbs & Teas?"

I took the plump hand and shook it. "Why yes, you do."

"I am Hezekiah Thompson, council manager of the fair village of Moody Bog. If we were a town, I'd be what you call a mayor."

"Well…your honor…it's a pleasure to meet you."

He fairly glowed. "Not being an actual mayor, 'Mr. Thompson' will do. Or how about Hezekiah?"

"Hezekiah," I said with a smile.

"I was sorry to miss the Chamber to-do earlier this week. Folks said you made quite an impression."

I kept my neutral smile in place. I was sure Ruth Russell was doing her best to add to my reputation.

Manager Thompson glimpsed the Wiccans chatting amongst themselves near the front counter, and his wide grin faded. "Uh… new businesses are important to the fiscal health of any municipality and none so important as in a small one. Small in size but not in stature!"

"Of course. I was happy to meet my fellow business owners."

He still had an eye on the Wiccans. Doc looked up, caught him staring, and winked at him. Thompson blustered and tried to focus on our conversation. Leaning in toward me, he said in a quiet voice, which seemed like a strain to him, "It's such a nice little shop. I hope you don't plan on getting too cozy with…the wrong element."

Hackles up, my smile frozen, I tilted my head. "And just what is it you consider the wrong element?"

"Well, the tea is splendid. Really splendid. But the herbs. You know, those would attract the wrong kind of business."

"I guess I'm still a little fuzzy on that."

Reverend Howard surprised me by poking his head over Thompson's shoulders. "He means your Wiccan friends."

Thompson was flustered. "Now Howard, I didn't say that."

"But that's what you meant, you old coot."

"Now gentlemen." They both stopped squaring off and turned toward me. "Today is my grand opening. And the scones and apple pecan loaf won't eat themselves. And today only, they're free, so if I were you, I'd take advantage of that."

They looked at each other, took a surreptitious whiff of the pastry-scented air, nodded, and strode off in separate directions.

I caught Doc's eye, and he gave me a triumphal nod.

After that, I chatted and served tea, explaining the many varieties. Some ladies from a garden club wanted to learn about the herbs and their healing properties and I slipped behind the counter to pull out the cubbies, showing them twig and leaf, letting them smell their aromas, and handing out little cards I had printed out on what to do with them. I told them I would be happy to come to their club and give a lecture.

I had just rung up a set of tea towels when Jolene skipped up, dragging with her a couple in their mid-forties. The woman was in jeans and a patchwork sweater, and her brown hair was caught up in barrettes on either side of her head. Her husband wore black, cuffed jeans and a white button-down under an argyle vest.

"Kylie," said Jolene with a proud smile, "this is my Mom and Dad, Jan and Kevin Ayrs."

I shook both their hands. "You've got a great daughter there, and a good worker."

They beamed. Kevin released my hand and rested it on Jolene's knit hat-covered head. "Our Jolene is a very enterprising young lady. Never showed much of an interest in working at our nursery, but I guess a prophet in your own country and all that."

"Dad!" she complained, rolling her eyes.

"I guess she's a bit tired of it. Though here you are, pumpkin, still working with plants. Only these are dead and dried. Go figure."

"Sounds like a perfect transition," I said.

Jan sidled up and asked softly and a bit sheepishly, "So...uh... are you a Wiccan, too? They're such *nice* people."

"I'm not converted yet, but you never know."

"It's nice of you to let them use your shop. Gives Doc a break."

"No one's getting any younger," said Kevin, elbowing her.

I straightened a teapot on a shelf, being careful of my painful reach. "I really love having them here. You're right. They are nice people."

We exchanged a few more pleasantries before the conversation lagged and they waved their good-byes, mingling with the others. I mingled as well, moving around the shop and greeting people, answering questions, and demonstrating wares. Teapots were purchased, saucer sets, bags of tea, and some of the antique doilies I had picked up in Oklahoma when I had driven across the country.

Business seemed brisk. My shoulder ached a bit, and Doc was suddenly there with some tea. "Chamomile with a smidge of white willow bark. For the pain." I took it gratefully and then called in an order for lunch from the local sandwich shop.

We had a lull, and when the sandwiches arrived I fed my coven. A fed Wiccan is a happy Wiccan.

We all chatted while devouring our sandwiches (I didn't realize how ravenous I had become) as if we hadn't escaped death or closed a Netherworld portal just the night before.

I'd have been lying if I said I hadn't been stealing glances out the window at the sour-looking Erasmus Dark. Sometimes he paced by the front door. Sometimes, I saw him lurking in the shadows of the backyard. I felt a little bad that he was relegated to the outside, but it seemed better that way.

But when the Wiccans weren't looking, I wrapped a sandwich and snuck out the back. I found him by the glider swing, pushing it absently back and forth with his hand.

"Hi," I said, startling him. Great. What kind of watchdog was he when a mere mortal could sneak up on him? I lifted my parcel. "I thought you might be hungry."

He eyed it suspiciously. "And whatever made you think that?"

Come to think of it, I hadn't ever seen him eat. "Well…you were just out here…alone. Do you…eat?"

"Not food, no."

My neck hairs stood up. "Do I want to know?"

"I sincerely doubt that." He thrust his hands in his pockets and sniffed the wind.

I glanced over my shoulder. "Any sign of the succubus?"

"No. It worries me."

"Really? Why? Maybe she's just laying low."

He shook his head, eyes hooded. "She should be especially keyed up after last night. She's spilled more of your blood." His eyes softened and he looked me over. "You seem well. Are you… all right?"

"Yes. Doc fixed me up."

"Good."

We seemed to have run out of conversation. "Well, the sandwich is here if you want it."

"I said I don't eat food." He showed a canine tooth…or were there more? It seemed like his mouth was full of them, but in a flash the image was gone.

I picked up the wrapped sandwich from where I left it on the glider. "All right, all right. No need to get your pitchfork in a twist."

He scowled. "I don't have a pitchfork."

"It's only an expression."

He snorted and tossed his head. "You seem to have many customers today. I congratulate you."

"Oh. Thanks."

He nodded, shifting from one foot to the other. "I suppose there is much commerce in *tea*."

My lips quirked in a smile. "As much as you despise it, others seem to like it."

"Good for them." Suddenly his mannerisms screamed of impatience. "Off with you, then. Stay inside where it is safer." With a sneer he added, "Your *constable* is here."

I whipped my head toward the kitchen window and saw Sheriff Ed and his reluctant deputy wandering around. Without a backward glance, I rushed inside, letting the backdoor slam shut, and grabbed Ed's arm from behind.

He turned to me with wide eyes and suddenly smiled on recognizing me. "You look all right," I said, meaning his bump on the head, but actually he looked more than all right. The ache I had for Erasmus Dark seemed to dim under Ed's gentle gaze.

He touched his head gingerly. "Yeah, I'm okay. Feel like a damned fool, but I'm okay."

I couldn't very well share my trauma from the night before so

I smiled like an idiot instead. I rocked on my heels and noticed the sandwich still in my hand. "Sandwich? Here's an extra. And Deputy? George, is it? Can I get you anything? Sandwich, scone, coffee?"

Deputy George seemed surprised to be addressed and his usual scowl fell away. I don't know what made him so sour against me but it was still there in his eyes. "Sure, Miss Strange, I'll take a sandwich if it's not too much trouble."

"None at all."

I took Ed aside once they both had sandwiches. "I'm sorry about last night, too."

"Not your fault. Weird about that owl."

"Yeah. Weird."

"But I was thinking. I get off at seven tonight. How about I take you out to celebrate your grand opening success?"

I grinned, feeling a bit of the heaviness lift. But I still didn't know what to do about the succubus. I couldn't take the chance that it might attack Ed because he was with me. Or worse, if he wasn't. Kind of hard to explain why I was taking a crossbow on a date.

"That sounds like a great idea. But I might be pretty wiped by the end of the day. And I owe the coven for sticking with me."

His smile faded. "You sure got close to Doc and his cohorts mighty quick."

I laughed to hide my nervousness. "Well, coven…herbs. It's a natural."

"I guess. I suppose they're harmless enough." I didn't like the frown shadowing his eyes. Or the fact that this was the second time he'd said that.

"How about you drop by later for some champagne? Get to know the coven a little."

The frown smoothed away and he nodded. "All right. Fair enough." He checked to see no one was looking before he bent down to kiss my cheek. "I'll see you later then."

It felt like the warmth of his lips left a permanent brand on my face. I refrained from touching it but I couldn't stop my smile. "Okay," I gushed.

He left the kitchen just as Jolene entered. She gave me a knowing look.

I ignored her and joined the main shop again, answering questions and happily manning the cash register.

• • •

When I counted up the day's tally around six o'clock I shook my head in wonder. "I feel like I should share this with you guys."

Nick's eyes widened at the prospect but Doc waved him off. "It was our pleasure, Kylie. I hope it goes just as well this weekend."

"It's still leaf peeper season," said Seraphina. "Bound to be lots of tourists from off the highway. You're really in a prime location."

"Let's hope." I glanced at the sunset, red streaked with gold stretching along the horizon. The silhouettes of trees blocked some of the colors and the street was cast in shrouds of shadows with the merest hint of gold gilding the facades of the shops along Lyndon Road. I'd seen no sign of anything out there, not that I'd been paying attention. The only movement was Erasmus moving among the shadows.

Nick followed my gaze outside. "It's been quiet."

"Yes," said Seraphina. "Too quiet."

"I hope you don't mind," I said, putting the last of the money in the safe under my counter. "But I invited Sheriff Ed to come over for a little champagne."

They all looked at me.

"Uh…I'm dating him, remember?"

"*And* Mr. Dark?" asked Jolene, clearly impressed.

"No! I'm not dating Erasmus."

"Just sleeping with him?" she said.

Heh, kids today.

"*No*," I said firmly. "That's over. I have to concentrate on more human prospects." I absolutely refused to look out the window.

"Do you think that's wise?" asked Doc. "You don't want Ed to get mixed up in all this."

"I don't want him to disappear either," I said to the counter I was wiping down. "And I feel bad about yesterday."

Doc opened his mouth to speak when the lights suddenly went out. We all froze for a moment in the shadows.

"Dang old buildings," said Doc. "It's like that all over this village."

But I was the first one to hear the gravel outside. Several pairs of feet crunching over my parking lot. "I don't think it was an accident," I whispered.

Someone tried the door. I didn't remember the succubus being that polite.

"Ky-lie!" It was Doug. Shadows passed over the windows as the Ordo made their way around, trapping us.

"Come on, girl, open up. You and your little witches have been very naughty."

Where was my crossbow? On a hunch, I held my hand out, and sure enough, something came whistling out of the air and smacking into my hand.

"No way!" gasped Nick.

It was armed again with that strange nondescript quarrel.

"Doug!" I called out, motioning for the others to go upstairs. "We're closed for the night. I'm sure you don't want to cause any trouble."

"Oh, baby!" he laughed. "I sure as hell do."

"The crossbow won't work for you. And I won't help you with it."

"I think we've found a way around that little problem. So it's time to come out and hand it over."

The door rattled hard again.

"I'm just going to break this door if you don't open it."

I heard glass breaking behind me in the kitchen. They were already getting in that way. Where the hell was Erasmus?

I lifted the crossbow to my shoulder. I tried, but the pain left by the succubus made it impossible. Now what?

The front door shattered.

I bolted upstairs. When I got to my bedroom the Wiccans were in full chant mode, sitting on the floor in a circle of salt with a candle in the middle. As much as I liked them, I couldn't help but feel a conjured Uzi would be better about now.

The crashing below from the front door and the back didn't sound good. All my work, all my stuff!

"Guys!" I pleaded to the Wiccans. "Whatever it is you're doing, do it fast!"

Someone stomping up the stairs.

I turned. Doug stood in my doorway. The candlelight lit his toothy grin. "Looky here."

Behind him were the Three Stooges—Bob Willis, Dean Fitch, and Charise. They were in their leathers, as always, knives in their holsters tied to their right legs.

The Wiccans stayed as they were, sitting and chanting. Why didn't Doc do that freezing thing again?

Doug stepped into the room with Bob right beside him. He glanced over at the Wiccans. "Seriously? Willis, take care of them."

Bob hesitated only a moment before shouldering him aside and striding forward. He reared back, aiming a kick right at Doc's head.

"Doc!" I cried, lunging forward. But it was too late. His foot hit…and passed through.

"What the hell?" we said at the same time.

He passed his hand through Doc and then Nick and Seraphina. Their images didn't waver but he never touched solid flesh either. It was like a film or a hologram only looking completely solid.

"Neat trick," said Jolene from behind Bob. She swung the fireplace poker.

He hit the floor with a bellow of pain. The chanting circle blinked once and then disappeared. Darkness fell around us followed by the sound of struggling. I didn't have time to marvel at their magic. The Wiccans were too busy getting medieval on the Ordo.

"Baphomet this!" I shouted, and with all my might, I swung the crossbow up and smacked Doug in the face.

He made a grunting noise and fell, and I ducked and managed to push past Charise, who Seraphina was dousing with hot water. I didn't know if she conjured it or had a bucket, but I was motioning for my posse to head back downstairs.

At the bottom of the steps I stopped dead. That smell. Death. The succubus was here.

I fell into a crouch…and Nick and Jolene tumbled over me onto the floor.

"Stay down," I hissed. "The succubus is somewhere in the room!"

Doc and Seraphina stopped behind them. "We have to leave!" said Doc, out of breath.

"She's here," I said.

He gasped. "Oh Lord."

I moved forward. "All right. You guys head for the door." We could all see the exit as a rectangle of twilight because stupid Doug had smashed my nice glass door *and* destroyed the lovely goop-protected wards at the same time. "Hurry up before they sort themselves out."

"What about you?" said Nick.

"I'll be fine," I lied. "Just go!"

Cursing and rumbling down the stairs, the Ordo were coming up from the rear. "GO!" I told them.

The Wiccans took off arm in arm. Something swooped low over Doc and Seraphina and I heard her scream, but they made it out, followed by Nick and Jolene. I breathed easier, even though the Ordo were bearing down on me.

I scrambled into the room in the darkness, hoping the shadows would shield me. I held the crossbow tight to my hip. "Doug!" I yelled, and the tromping down the steps ceased. He argued with the others in the dark until they were still.

"You have to leave. I'm not kidding. There's a succubus in here."

"Oh, sure there is," he said, voice a little nasal. I supposed I'd broken his nose...if there was any justice in the world. "Maybe it's an incubus. I heard they don't take well to little girls like you."

"I already killed your incubus and we closed your little black arts portal."

I kept moving so they couldn't tell where I was.

"So you say," said Doug uncertainly.

"I did. With my little crossbow. So get the hell out. I'm warning you."

"To me!" he said. I supposed he meant his minions. Now *they* started to chant. I didn't like the sound of it. It was a low growling noise rather than the harmonious sound of the Wiccans.

"Stop that!" I yelled. "This is a black magic-free zone!"

But, of course, they didn't listen. Until one of them stopped abruptly. I heard choking noises, and then Charise screamed. There was a mad scramble for the door. But they couldn't seem to get around the dark shape bending over one of them.

"Shoot it, Kylie!" came a shout in the doorway. I looked and there was the outline of a man in a duster coat.

I tried to lift the crossbow to my shoulder but I couldn't.

The succubus turned from the man in her grasp, and the body slid to the floor. Red eyes fastened on me.

I saw the shape of her stalking forward, long fangs glistening in the fading twilight.

Erasmus pounded hard on the doorframe, impotent with rage. If the succubus could come in, why couldn't he?

"Draw it outside," said Erasmus. "Make it come out. To me."

I edged toward his voice, never taking my eyes from her.

"Almost there," I heard over my shoulder. "Come on, Kylie."

My shoes encountered broken glass and shattered teapots. I passed over the threshold and then Erasmus grabbed my elbow and I fell backward with him onto the flagstone porch. The succubus swooped and missed, passing over me with the stench of dead things.

The Ordo moved, too. They were helping their victim—it looked like Bob Willis—toward the door. Though Fitch was also limping from the blow Jolene gave him.

The creature hadn't left. She was homing in on the men, diving for poor Willis again. He held up his arms and screamed like a girl.

But it swerved away from him. That wasn't her intended target, after all. It was me.

She rose up again, horns and teeth sharp as nails.

"*You* must do it, Kylie," said Erasmus from the side. "I can't help you in this." His voice was thin and distant, as if he was fading away. I took a chance and looked toward him; he did look somewhat transparent. What was going on?

A female figure appeared out of the twilight, stalking toward him. She tossed back her long hair and gnashed her sharp teeth. "Erasmus Dark," said Shabiri. No one wore a cat suit like she did.

Erasmus spun and fell into a crouch. "You! Damn you!"

"Too late," she said with a laugh.

"Stay away, Shabiri. I'm warning you. Do not get mixed up in this!"

"But I so enjoy mixing in your affairs, Erasmus. Remember the last one?"

"Too well. That's why I'm warning you."

She sauntered forward, leading with her hips. "And somehow I am not afraid."

Erasmus growled, an unnerving sound and Shabiri fell into a crouch, facing off with him. Suddenly, he rushed her, and it was as if they were covered with roiling smoke and sparks. They spun and the smoke billowed around them, shielding them from view except for an arm, a leg, a scowling face sometimes visible, sometimes lost in the smoke.

Doug stared at them in their fighting embrace, and smiled through the blood running down his bearded chin. "I call on

Baphomet," he said in a low voice. "I call upon my Lord Baphomet to deal with you!"

The earth rumbled and anyone who was standing was tossed to the ground. But it didn't seem to affect the succubus. She was still coming toward me, talons at the ready. My shoulder suddenly ached and the backs of my knees felt weak, too.

I tried to raise the crossbow again, but couldn't.

She was almost on me. I did the only thing I could think to do. "Come on chthonic crossbow!" With a scream of pain I brought it as high as I could and shot from the hip.

The quarrel left the crossbow in the truest straight line I had ever seen and plunged into her, disappearing completely. She stopped and threw back her head, releasing an unearthly scream. And just like the incubus, she began to fragment like burning film. Light shot out of her from all angles. But unlike the incubus, she would not disintegrate completely. She just hung there, screaming, light shooting out in glowing rays. And the sounds. Great howling noises came not just from her open mouth but from all around her, from the places opened up in her.

"Erasmus, what's happening?"

He shoved off his demon nemesis long enough to yell over his shoulder, "You must write in the book!"

"The Booke!"

I turned to run into the shop but there it was, hovering right in front of me. The cover had unclasped and it was open to the first blank page, the quill lying across it.

I grabbed it and knelt in front of it, holding both sides of the cover. Ink. I needed ink.

Shabiri had disappeared from Erasmus's grip and appeared suddenly beside me. "Give up, little mortal. You can't hope to survive this!"

"Shut up, Shabiri!" I spat.

I tried to leave the Booke but my hands were glued to it. "I need ink," I yelled to anyone who would listen. I caught Jolene's eye, and she was ready to run back into the shop.

"No," said Erasmus, rushing Shabiri again. He grabbed her arms.

"Let the human figure it out, Erasmus," Shabiri growled. "What's the fun in it if it's too easy?"

He head-butted her and she fell back, dazed. "Not ink," he said to me. "Blood. Your blood."

"What? No one told me that!"

The creature was still suspended in a light storm, and everyone was rocking with the earth's tremors. Shabiri had recovered and dashed toward Erasmus again, but he glared at her with glowing red eyes. She stopped and laughed, her own eyes glowing bright green. She began to fade from view, her laughter fading with her, like a Cheshire cat, and she was suddenly gone. For good, I hoped.

I clutched the quill and looked at my hands. Blood. I had to cut myself. "How do I…?" I looked pleadingly at Erasmus.

But he seemed to be disappearing in small increments. He was definitely transparent now. What was happening? But even as faint as he was, he stepped forward and took my left hand. He looked at me for permission and I nodded solemnly. He pointed his finger at the fleshy part of my palm and suddenly his fingernail grew into a claw. I tried to pull back in horror, but just like Doc had done during the Wiccan ritual, Erasmus held my wrist tight. His claw dipped and pierced. I hissed at the pain and as soon as he withdrew his hand, the blood spilled over my palm, forming a little pool of red in my hand. I dipped the quill in and then put it to paper.

I killed the succubus, I wrote. The words suddenly flowed freely, and I wrote and dipped and wrote. *A disgusting creature that takes the lives of men by sucking out their essence, leaving the stench of death in its wake. It is an old creature and must be hunted down in the moonlight or within the dark caves it calls home…*

I wrote about our hunts, both unsuccessful and this final confrontation. And the more I wrote, the more holes appeared in the screaming creature. The light shooting out of it became dimmer and dimmer. Soon the sounds grew faint and with a deep groan in the universe, she winked out with a flash and a boom that crashed over us in a shockwave. The Booke yanked from my hands and fell to the ground. The cover slammed shut and the lock closed with an audible click.

I sat back on my feet, arms wide. My left hand was dripping blood and my right with still clutching the quill as if my life depended on it.

I did it. It was over.

Except it wasn't. Something tall and dark was rising from the ground, from the tiny puddle of my blood that had flowed to the center of the driveway.

But I killed it. It's dead.

It wasn't the succubus. This had the head of a goat and the torso of a man.

Baphomet?

It didn't stop rising until it pulled the last cloven-hoofed foot from the puddle and stepped forward. It turned its sideways-pupiled eyes at me and slowly bowed.

No, no, don't thank me, I wanted to yell, but I was frankly terrified.

It ignored me and stalked toward Erasmus. That must have been why he had made himself scarce around the Ordo. They had powers. Powers that could stop him.

He was fading fast, still on his feet but just barely. He stood stoically as it approached. Why hadn't he run? Was it for me he stayed, to protect me?

I looked down at the crossbow on the hard gravel beside me. It had armed itself. I dropped the quill and opened my hand, and felt the solid form of it slap into my palm. I raised it up from the hip and aimed.

"Hey, Baphomet!" It stopped and turned its great horned head at me. "Eat crossbow!" And I fired.

The Ordo members screamed.

The Wiccans screamed.

I screamed because everyone else was screaming.

Baphomet looked down at the arrow embedded in his

human-looking chest. He kept looking at it until he raised a human arm. He closed his fingers around it and yanked it free. Black ooze came with it and slithered down his hairy chest. He didn't look affected. But he did look pissed, and he changed direction toward me.

Shit.

I crawled backward. I glanced at the crossbow, but as if it was saying, "I got nothing," it had not re-armed itself. Double shit.

The green light was small at first. It came from the hole in Baphomet's chest. It was faint and then it brightened so much I raised my hand to shield against it. The hole widened and the green light got even brighter. It was the same light from the vortex, or so I thought.

Baphomet looked down at his chest again, and this time he raised his head and bellowed. The rest of him seemed to be sucked into the hole, and in a bright flash, he too, was gone.

A pause…before a deep boom under the earth erupted and we all fell over again.

Silence.

Two lights flashed over us and we all screamed again, before we realized they were headlights.

The car skidded over the gravel and before the gears were lurched into park, the door flung open and someone charged out.

"Freeze!" cried Sheriff Ed. "What the *hell* is going on here?" He stepped forward and I felt his shadow over me. "Kylie?" He must have seen the blood. I was holding my hand tight to my hip, trying to stop the bleeding. "Are you all right?"

"I'm fine. Fine."

Seraphina was at my side, followed by Doc. He shook out a clean handkerchief from his pocket and pressed it to my palm.

Ed shined a flashlight at the Ordo, who looked as miserable as we did. Doug had a bloody and swollen nose. Charise was soaking wet and shivering. Fitch was using his good leg to stand on and Willis looked a little thinner and a little older from his run in with a succubus.

Ed lowered the flashlight slightly. "Doug," he said in a deadly voice. I imagined the run-ins he'd probably had with this group before. That is, until Doug replied, "Bro. 'Sup? How's the cop biz?"

"If you bothered to talk to Mom and Pop every now and then you'd know."

"Wait a minute." I pushed Doc and Seraphina aside. If Ed wore a beard they'd almost be twins. "You mean Doug is your *brother*?"

"Yeah. Much as I hate to admit it." Ed aimed the flashlight at the shop front. "Jesus, what have you done?"

"It was just a little misunderstanding," said Doug, his hands open.

"I'm taking all of you in."

"Wait," I said. I looked them over. They looked pretty pathetic. A little more messed up than we were. "I'm…I'm not pressing charges."

Nick leapt forward. "What? Of course you are."

"That's his brother," I said.

"Yeah, I know. We all knew that."

"And no one bothered to tell me?"

"We thought you knew."

Ed still had his flashlight and his gun trained on Doug and his buddies. "Are you pressing charges, Kylie? Looks like assault, malicious mischief, breaking and entering…"

"He's your brother."

"He's been in jail before."

"Ed. Just…let it go."

His jaw worked. He was grinding his teeth. "You can't just let it go."

"If *I* can, anyone can." I turned to Doug. "You'll leave us alone now, right?"

"Of course," he said smoothly. So that was why I felt the need to trust him. He sounded like his brother.

Ed hadn't lowered his weapon. "You can't believe him, Kylie."

"I'm going to try. I do this for you, Doug, you stay away from me. And…mine." I gestured toward the Wiccans and the crossbow.

Doug smiled. There was blood on his teeth. "I promise. Scout's honor."

"You were never a scout," growled Ed.

"Then demon's honor."

Ed hissed out a swear under his breath. "Up to you, Kylie."

I wanted to give Doug a break. I really thought we could work out our differences. Make him see we were playing on the same team. Maybe with different tools, but the same team.

"Let him go," I said gruffly.

"Okay. So you aren't pressing charges," he said. "But I'm taking them in anyway to talk about Karl Waters. And Bob Hitchins. And Joseph Mayes, the cyclist. Get on the ground."

Doug, with hands still raised, took a step forward. "Bro—"

"I said get on the ground!"

Doug hesitated, glanced at his stooges, and slowly got down on his knees and then fully onto the ground.

"Doc," Ed said tensely. "Get your phone and call 9-1-1 for backup."

Ed never moved from his gun-aiming stance as the Ordo got to the ground, and then we all waited for Deputy George to arrive.

• • •

Once backup had come, Ed talked quietly and sometimes not so quietly to Doug for another half hour as he sat, handcuffed, in the back of the sheriff's SUV. They gestured and argued. Doug acted like a spoiled kid brother, which was what I supposed he was.

In the meantime, Nick got the lights back on—the Ordo had only thrown the main circuit—and the others started cleaning up while Doc ministered to my hand. He wanted to give me stitches but I couldn't stand the thought of them. He bandaged me tight instead and told me to be careful.

Later, after the sheriffs finally drove the Ordo away, Ed called Barry Johnson on his cell and asked him to open his hardware store. Barry was kind enough to bring some plywood, and he and Nick made a temporary fix to the front door and the back window.

I didn't know how long the sheriffs would be able to hold the Ordo. They hadn't killed those men. No *person* had.

The shattered glass from my door and window was swept and the ruined inventory tallied. All in all, I probably broke even.

Ed sat with me on the glider swing in the backyard and took my good hand in his. He didn't even know about the shoulder. I hadn't told him about a lot of things. "Maybe I should stay here with you tonight."

"No. I'll be fine." And yet, I was thinking of Erasmus. Where was he? Was he all right? Now that the Booke was closed, maybe he wouldn't be back. I tried to think of that as a good thing.

"Are you sure? I could camp out on the sofa."

I looked up at him and, with my bandaged hand, cupped his cheek. "When you spend the night here, it will be in the bedroom...with me."

"Oh." He sputtered and I think he actually blushed, though it was hard to tell in the moonlight. "Well...uh...okay, then."

"But not tonight. I'm beat. Literally."

"Kylie, I told you we should have charged them."

"I believe in second chances."

"It's not exactly his *second* chance."

"How did two brothers become so different?"

He rubbed his hand over his chin. "The scary thing is we aren't that different. But he got involved in this Baphomet crap and he's never been the same. Someday I'll tell you about it."

"I'd like to hear it."

"Look." He lifted me from the glider and escorted me to the backdoor. "Why don't you get some sleep? I'm taking the night shift and I plan to patrol this street. Sleep with your cell phone."

"Not as romantic, but..."

He looked at me grimly and I tried a smile.

"It'll be okay," I said, only half-believing it.

We went inside, where the coven was busy putting everything right again.

I walked him to the plywood-covered door. "Thanks for everything," I said.

"You take care of yourself, Kylie Strange. I want this shop to be a success. I don't want you scared off and moving away."

"Believe me, it takes an awful lot to scare me off."

"Good." He leaned over, and this time it wasn't a kiss on the cheek, but on my lips. He lingered there, even though he didn't press for more than his mouth on mine. His fingers trailed through my hair and moved softly along my jaw before he let me go. My skin tingled where he touched.

He waved and left. When the door closed—the broken bell tinkling pathetically—I turned to my posse. "Well, that was certainly a day and a half."

"Indeed it was," said Doc.

"Did I just kill Baphomet?"

"No, not likely. I think you just sent him back to where he belonged. You'll have to be careful. I don't think he liked that very much."

"But it's all over. We're done." I stared at the Booke sitting on the desk, its tarnished lock sealed for good.

"Well, funny thing about that, Kylie," said Doc. "Though it's true the succubus is gone, I don't think it's true that it's all over."

My elation drained away, replaced by a sinking feeling. I didn't want to ask, but I had to know. "What do you mean?"

"Well, Jolene and I have been doing some digging. I went up to the library in Portland a few days ago and looked at some archives. And the book does seem to have a history in New England."

"Yes. And?"

"And…it never seems to be just one creature that escapes the book. I'm afraid there is a crowd of creatures." The other Wiccans had gathered and looked sorrowfully over Doc's shoulder. They knew. They knew all this time but didn't tell me. "The Chosen Host has a lot to do to dispatch them before she's done," Doc went on. "So I'm afraid, Kylie, and I'm very sorry…but this was only the beginning."

I slid all the way to the floor. Only the beginning? How was I ever going to survive this?

I felt the walls closing in. The Booke. Demons. Gods. And there was still that pentagram I saw in the church janitor's closet. Or at least, I *think* I saw it. Was it another helpful Wiccan…or another enemy?

"Something else," said Jolene crouching beside me. "I did some checking on your ancestry with the info you gave me. I can't seem to find any information on the Stranges, not in California or, well, anywhere. Maybe they had a different name at one time?"

I shook my head. "No. Always Strange. My father and his father. And I guess…*his* father." That was weird. If they had ever told me stories about our family tree, I couldn't remember a thing about it now. My heart raced. And I didn't know why.

"So I don't know how you could be related to Ruth Russell, though her archives are hard to come by," Jolene went on. "I think we need to do some additional research at the local library. They might have something." She hesitated. "And there's something else."

"Something else? Isn't that enough?"

She and Doc exchanged glances. "Well…you know that tattoo you wanted me to look up? The one on Mr. Dark? I found that, too, in the online demonology archive. I had a hard time with the translations, but finally sorted it out. Either it means 'follower' or…"

She bit her lip.

"Well?" I urged. "What?"

"It doesn't matter if he's gone, I guess."

"I don't think he's gone," said Nick. "Not for good, anyway. If the book isn't done then neither is he."

"But he was fading," I said.

Seraphina edged forward. "That's true. But I think that had more to do with Baphomet. I don't think it's a good idea if they're present together on the same plane. I think it's a very bad idea, in fact."

So maybe he was fine. I felt only slightly lighter at that news. But what did that mean for Shabiri? Would she be back, too? I turned to Jolene. "Go on. What else might that tattoo mean?"

She licked her chapped lips and studied me. "It might mean 'follower' or…it also might mean…'assassin.'"

I thought long and hard about it. "Follower" could mean the Booke and all that went with it. I grabbed for the amulet that still hung around my neck. It warmed my hand as it always did. I found comfort in it, even though it had that awful demon face.

Yeah, it could also mean he had to follow me, because of that amulet…or even the crossbow. But that other meaning…

I knew I had no business worrying or caring, but I still did. I still cared. And I still wanted to know.

Where the heck was Erasmus Dark?

EPILOGUE

The Lake of Fire rippled with molten waves, glowing bright when a cooled crust of rock slipped below a swell and disappeared. Smoke feathered upward and the orange sky was hazy with the smell of sulfur and death.

Erasmus Dark walked in long strides over the hills and down deep into the valleys of black rock, his duster swishing over his legs. He looked straight ahead, neither veering his glance toward the shimmering lake, nor toward the volcano above the ridge, spewing its glowing rocks and liquid fire down its treacherous sides. He tried to clear his mind. He knew they would try to listen to his thoughts and it was vitally important that they not be able to hear them.

The trail descended through a canyon so steep and dark that even the light from the molten lake barely penetrated. The sheer canyon walls were black obsidian, their vitreous edges sharp.

Still he descended, until he reached a land bridge made of rough black marble. Below that, a river of dark listless sludge meandered. He never knew where it went exactly, but he had no wish to find out.

The land bridge ended at a cavernous arch, and he passed under it into darkness. Torches set in recesses in the rough-hewn rock gave off feeble light compared with the surroundings, but their flicker was of some comfort. *Yes*, he thought viciously. He seemed to need comfort now.

The woman. What had compelled him? She had sworn it was not a charm or spell and he believed her, mostly because he knew she was not competent enough to have crafted them herself. Why was he drawn to her then? Why was he so completely enthralled to his own detriment?

He crushed these thoughts like a shoe could extinguish an ember and walked up to the altar of black stone, stone so old no one remembered where it came from or who had made it. It was older than the gods, so it was said. Stone so black it gave no reflection.

He stopped and waited. Time was nothing here. He could have waited a thousand years, and would scarce have known it. But he had the feeling he would not wait long this time.

A small green flame erupted from the altar and hovered, growing little bigger than a candle flame. And then the chorus of voices began. It arose from all around him, shimmering the steamy air with its discordance. It grew louder and soon the different voices joined until it became one echoing voice, yet still sounding like many. They spoke slowly, precisely.

"Erasmus Dark," said the chorus in a harsh whisper.

He bowed. "My lords."

"The Gateway that should have been closed now yawns wide. The book—"

"I know, my lords."

"It has awakened you, has it not, Erasmus Dark?"

"Yes."

"The Chosen Host emerges. Has she been made known to you?"

"Yes, my lords."

Tendrils of thought curled about him, teasing his senses, probing his mind that he had carefully prepared as a blank slate. It pushed. He gently nudged it back. If they truly wanted to penetrate his thoughts, there was nothing he could do to stop it.

"Well? What have you done to secure the book?"

"One creature has been contained. A succubus. I am keeping watch for more."

It sounded like laughter, the susurrating sound. It lingered and rolled over the syllables of "succubus." They were clearly amused at the choice.

"Contained?" The chorus was surprised. "Such a dangerous creature. But not so much to females."

"Another clutch released an incubus. That, too, she subdued." He made certain there was no pride in that statement.

"Incubus." The syllables of that word were lovingly caressed. There was a pause. And then: "We wonder, Erasmus Dark, why you simply do not accomplish your task."

"My lords—"

"It is your nature, your destiny, to seal the book. Or is it that you enjoy the sport of delicious deception?"

"Y-yes, my lords. For if I am to be locked behind the prison of the book once more, then I will taste my freedom for as long as I can."

Laughter. Shimmering sounds like rocks sliding over rocks into a molten pool. A long silence followed.

He took a breath. "And…there is a complication."

The tendrils reached for him again, but did not push harder than before. They seemed to want him to say it, not force it from his mind.

"Shabiri. She…"

A loud rush of wind…or was it a roar…swept up, ruffling his long hair. He endured it stoically.

"Ah…" said the chorus of voices. "The Shabiri. But you will not allow it to complicate matters."

"No, my lords. But…she is aligned with…with Baphomet…"

The roar swept up again, swirling around him in displeased gusts.

"It is a minor complication," he said as smoothly as he could. "I shall deal with her as I have done before."

"Yes. See that you do." There was a hushed sound, like distant laughter. And then: "So be it. You may go."

He almost sighed with relief. But even as he turned, the chorus called him back.

"Erasmus Dark," said the chorus, stringing out his name so that it almost sounded like many more syllables. "Do not delay too long. If the Chosen Host escapes, if she somehow frees herself, you will suffer the everlasting torment of your failure. We hope that this is very clear...Erasmus Dark."

He took a deep breath and bowed. "I have not failed in four thousand years, my lords. I shall not fail this time."

The shimmering sound rose to a crescendo and then cascaded down all around him like sparks, dead once they touched the ground.

END

AUTHOR'S AFTERWORD

Would you believe the plot and general idea for this series came to me in a dream? I'm not kidding. It was one of those serendipitous things. I dreamed of the Booke (which was amusingly called "The Big Book of the Occult" in my dream), Kylie, the demon, and the monsters beaten with a crossbow. The whole Magilla. When I awoke I lay there for while absorbing it. It was so entertaining, I immediately told my husband who was just getting up for work. He told me, "Write it down!"

So I went off to my office to write down as much of it as I could remember. Then I fleshed it out a little more, trying to make sense of dreamscape logic, and had a half a page of a loose synopsis. Before he left for work I read that to him. He said, "Write the book!"

So I did. Even more fleshed out with a planned-out universe and everything. "Booke of the Occult" became "Booke of the Hidden," the demon got a name, and so did everyone else (although Doc was always Doc). It's strange what the sleeping imagination can dream up. I'm glad it did and made it past the memory sensors. It's a fun series to write. I usually write medieval mysteries, which are heavy with research and dense with prose. To shake things up a bit with a fantasy/horror book is a good stretch of the writing legs, and getting me back to my roots when I was immersed with reading fantasy and science fiction in my teens and twenties.

There will be six books in this series. I hope you will enjoy following Kylie and the gang through them as she works to make right what she unwittingly made wrong, and through the trials of her indecision where men and demons are concerned. The next book in the series is DEADLY RISING, where something is luring young women to their doom in the swampy marshes outside the village. Kylie must figure out a way to stop this new fiend without following its siren song herself, except she's preoccupied with thoughts of another demon—Erasmus Dark. The Ordo are up to their old tricks, and a new danger only stirs up more questions about the hidden secrets just below the surface of Moody Bog.

See more about me and the series at
BOOKEoftheHIDDEN.com.

Los Angeles native and award-winning author JERI WESTERSON writes the critically acclaimed Crispin Guest Medieval Mysteries, historical novels, paranormal novels, and LGBT mysteries. To date, her medieval mysteries have garnered twelve industry award nominations, from the Agatha to the Shamus. *Kirkus Review* said of her latest Crispin Guest Medieval Mystery *A Maiden Weeping*, "Once again Guest's past misdeeds actually help him in the present in a case that includes plenty of red herrings and an interesting look at medieval jurisprudence." Jeri is former president of the SoCal chapter of Mystery Writers of America and frequently guest lectures on medieval history at local colleges and museums. She lives in Southern California with her home-brewing husband, a complacent tortoise, and 40,000 bees.

CPSIA information can be obtained
at www.ICGtesting.com
Printed in the USA
BVOW08s0707261017
498600BV00002B/2/P

9 781635 760507